MW01015953

MOONLIT DAYS and NIGHTS

Rock on, Neil

David Toole

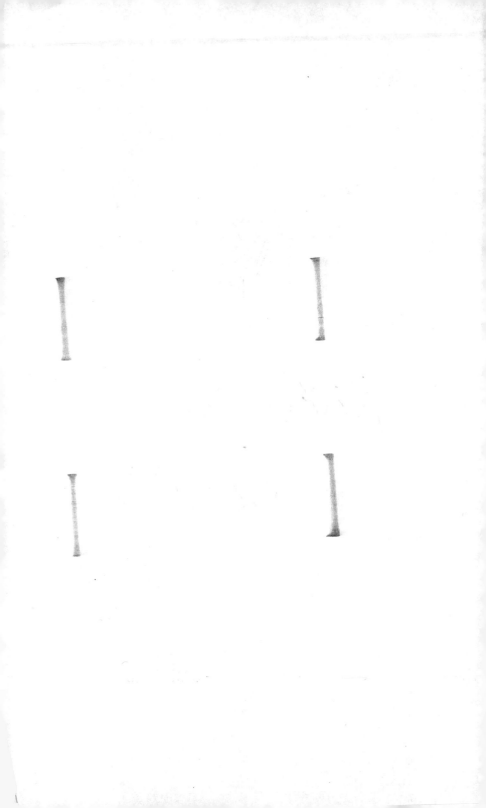

MOONLIT DAYS *and* NIGHTS

Being the Thrilling Adventure of
Reginald Ravencroft and Belvedere La Griffin:
Two Self Creationists and
Notable Canadian Poets of Cloth

by

D.H. Toole

CORMORANT BOOKS

Copyright © D.H. Toole, 1995

I wish to thank my literary agent, Doreen Potter, and Jan Geddes of Cormorant Books for their support, and Peter Bresnen for his inspired illustrations. Most especially, I wish to thank Mr. Mavor Moore for his belief in my talent.

Illustrations © Peter Bresnen, 1995

The publisher wishes to acknowlege the financial assistance of the Canada Council, the Ontario Arts Council, and the Department of Heritage through the Ontario Publishing Centre.

Cover design is by Artcetera Graphics in Dunvegan, Ontario.

Author photograph by K. Ward.

Edited by Gena K. Gorrell.

Published by Cormorant Books Inc.,
RR 1, Dunvegan, Ontario, Canada, K0C 1J0.

Printed and bound in Canada.

No part of this publication may be reproduced, stored in a retrieval system or transmitted, except for purposes of review, without the prior written permission of the publisher or, in case of photocopying or other reprographic copying, a licence from CANCOPY (Canadian Copyright Licensing Agency), 6 Adelaide Street East, Suite 900, Toronto, Ontario, M5C 1H6.

CANADIAN CATALOGUING IN PUBLICATION DATA
Toole, D.H. (David H.), 1952-
    Moonlit days and nights : being the thrilling adventure of Reginald Ravencroft and Belvedere La Griffin, two self creationists and notable Canadian poets of cloth
ISBN 0-920953-85-9
    I. Title.
PS8589.0659M65 1995   C813'.54   C95-900181-6
PR9199.3.T612M65 1995

For my darling Karen

CHAPTER I

MOONLIT AWAKENING

I awoke with a start. The candle on my bedside table had guttered and the amber light of a full September moon created a wonderfully romantic effect as it spilled across my bed and illuminated the room. I was still wearing my spectacles and Professor Dudley Ward's *The Art of Talk: Large and Small* lay open across my chest. I lay still, listening to the ticking of the clock in the downstairs hall, and soon I heard the familiar whirring sound it made just before the hour chimed. The chimes sounded twice. It was past midnight and therefore September 2nd, 189— had at long last arrived. I was now eighteen years of age and this was the day Fate had decreed to be the date of my death and glorious rebirth.

My bedroom looked familiar yet different to me in the moonlight, as if I were seeing it again on a return visit home after a long absence. My genuine alligator bags sat quietly waiting for me by the door and my travelling costume hung on the back of the wicker chair. The ladder leading to the trap door of my Church of Self Creation looked odd standing straight up in the middle of the room and the moonlight hitting the ladder rungs threw slanted shadows across the spines of my books and magazines that rose up to the ceiling on shelves against the wall.

I rolled over on my side and through my window I could see the moonlit fields stretching up to the oak tree on the crest of the hill. The scene looked remarkably like my Uncle Jasper's Chandler lithograph hanging downstairs in the parlour above the settee except that in the lithograph there were cattle sleeping under the tree as opposed to my dead parents. The picket fence surrounding their graves shimmered white in the moonlight and above it one stout tree limb stood out in particular. As I stared at the limb I could see my body in silhouette slowly twisting at the end of a rope attached to the limb. I watched myself turning in the gentle breeze and I thought how lucky I was to be in my warm bed instead of in the cold, dank earth with my mother and father.

My parents died during a typhoid epidemic when I was nine years old. Father was Doctor Ambrose Tweed, the physician in the village of Balls Falls, Ontario, and a man of great kindness and courage. It was while tending the stricken ones that he contracted the dreaded disease. Mother's name was Annie Tweed and she in turn fell ill while nursing my father. It was from my mother that I inherited my height of six feet two inches and my slightness of build. She was an exceptionally pretty woman but there was always a look of worry in her eyes and, as it turned out, quite rightly so. Father died on a Saturday morning and mother died on the following Tuesday evening. I was left at rather a loose end and, as there were no other candidates for the job, the provincial authorities decided that I should go to live with my two bachelor uncles on their farm outside Balls Falls.

Harold and Jasper Tweed, my father's older brothers, were both in their sixties when I came to live with them. They were very pleasant to me and showed no sign whatsoever of being annoyed by my arrival, but nonetheless I missed my parents dreadfully and felt very much alone and insignificant. In time my despondency deepened to such a point that I firmly believed I had no chance of ever finding happiness in this life, and thus set about plotting my own demise. After careful study, I decided upon hanging as being the best manner in which to dispatch myself, and I had gone so far as to select an appropriate length and strength of rope and the aforementioned tree limb when I chanced upon an article in *The Strand Magazine* that was to save my life.

The article was entitled "La Divine Sarah Bernhardt—Sorceress of the Stage" and in it I read the true story of a young French girl who, by dint of outrageous courage and perseverance, transformed herself from an impoverished, illegitimate waif into a woman commonly accepted to be not only the greatest actress of all time, but the Eighth Wonder of the World. I read how, from the moment she could walk upright, little Sarah Bernhardt declared herself to be in a constant state of war with Doubt—be it the doubt of others or that most insidious and stealthful foe: self-doubt. She was a full-fledged warrior in need of a battle-cry to rouse and sustain her spirit and so she created the cry *"Quand Même!"*, which, roughly translated, means "Against All Odds." This battle-cry acted as both a shield and a bludgeon—meaning that she used it both to deflect blows and to smite her enemies. Conformity, Banality, Doubt—all such threats to her destiny fell before her piercing cry. *"Quand Même!"* was emblazoned on everything she possessed—embroidered on her linens, engraved on her wine goblets, etched on her stained-glass windows—everywhere possible. She rose to staggering heights of achievement and adoration, and was equally famous for her eccentricities—the most notorious being a silk-lined coffin in which she delighted to sleep. This goddess, this sorceress, was living proof that faith in one's abilities, faith in one's destiny, was all-powerful. She showed me through her example that I did not have to remain Willoughby Tweed of Balls Falls, Ontario, if it no longer amused me to do so. I could be anyone and do anything if only I could hold on to my faith in my ability to create a new and glorious identity. And so from that day forward I scoffed at the notion of hanging myself and devoted my entire being to Self Creation. Indeed, following La Divine Sarah's lead (I do not deny it) I too created a battle-cry. *"Fidem Servo"*—I Keep Faith—became my cry, and has remained the motto adorning my family crest to this very day.

Of course the question that immediately presented itself was who precisely did I wish to become? Who, realistically speaking, had I any hope of being? At first, as might be expected, I thought I should follow in my revered father's footsteps and become a physician. He had given his life in the service of the sick and the idea of carrying on this noble Tweed tradition greatly appealed to my romantic nature. Upon further reflection, however, I realized that the idea of standing about in rooms stinking of carbolic acid and putrescent flesh could never hold any real charm for me. A career of soldiering was appealing—especially when I envisioned myself in a nobby officer's uniform swirling beautiful young ladies around the floor at an unending succession of glittering military balls—but then I recalled that, unless one comes from money, one is usually required to undergo a great deal of physical discomfort and possibly even pain on the field of battle in order to reach high rank, and I did not see either condition as being in any way a part of my programme.

I continued to ponder this question of my vocation until around the time of my eleventh birthday, when I began to suspect that the answer lay somewhere in the fact that really I had no desire to toil at any job whatsoever. Then one day while I was studying the latest issue of *Saturday Night Magazine* the answer was delivered unto me in the form of the poet and playwright Mr. Oscar Wilde. In his article, Mr. Wilde stated quite definitely that the art of living is the only truly Fine Art, and that if one wanted to know how to truly live, one should read the philosophy of a Mr. Walter Pater. I did so as quickly as Eaton's mail-order department and Her Majesty's mails could oblige. Mr. Pater told me this:

> Not the fruit of experience, but experience itself is the end. . . . To burn always with this hard, gem-like flame, to maintain this ecstasy, is success in life. . . . While all melts under our feet, we may well catch at any exquisite passion or any contribution of knowledge that seems by a lifted horizon to set the spirit free for a moment, or any stirring of the senses, strange dyes, strange colours, and curious odours, or work of the artist's hands, or the face of one's friend. What we have to do is to be forever curiously testing new opinions and courting new impressions.

I immediately committed that passage to memory, and continued my investigation by reading everything written by the great philosophers of the day. I learned from Mr. Wilde that "One should either be a work of art, or wear a work of art," while in his "Discours sur le Style" Georges-Louis Leclerc de Buffon informed me that *"Le style est l'homme même"*—style is the man himself. And thusly my reading continued, until gradually it became stunningly clear what role I was meant to play on the Stage of Life. I was destined, quite obviously, to be a Gentleman.

Now, I know what you are thinking: you are thinking that my goal—the transformation of my hairy-heeled bumpkin self into a Sophisticated Gentleman of Means—was quite impossible. But let me point out to you that when La Divine Sarah instructed us— her loyal subjects—to transform ourselves, she did not simply mean that we should make the most of our abilities. No, she meant that we should effect our self-transformation on an alchemical level rather than on a mere chemical level. I mean to say: one has a lump of brass and makes the most of it on the chemical level by shaping it into, for example, a brass goblet. But on the alchemical level one transforms that lump of brass into a golden chalice. It is a type of magic trick one performs on oneself.

Naturally I was aware of the fact that a considerable amount of money is required to lead a life of refinement and leisure, but unfortunately such a sum was not in my possession. My father, being a country doctor, was more often than not paid for his services in the currency of poultry and vegetables, and was therefore far from wealthy when he died. However, with the sale of our house and the furnishings therein, a sum of six hundred odd dollars was raised. I received one hundred of those dollars immediately and was told that the remaining five hundred was to be held in trust for me until my eighteenth birthday. During the intervening years I spent most of my one hundred dollars on books and magazines, and my remaining five hundred dollars was hardly sufficient to fund a life-long devotion to sensual gratification, but I reckoned it to be enough to start me on the only reasonable course of action open to me. Namely, to make a brilliant marriage to a woman whose beauty of person and kindness of heart were exceeded only by her enormous wealth. To find such a bride I would simply have to infiltrate high society and pass myself off as the sort of chap to whom a rich papa would wish to see his daughter betrothed. That is to say, I would have to appear to be from an even wealthier background than my intended. I reckoned that my inheritance would enable me to live in a fine hotel for between four and six months in the style to which I wished to become accustomed, and therefore that was how long I had to find my wondrous bride.

From the moment of my revelation, I dedicated my entire

being to the pursuit of knowledge that would transform me from an ignorant rustic into a gentleman of the world. It was tremendously exciting. I felt just like a general sitting down to plot out a campaign of war. First I chose Toronto as the site of my invasion, and then I turned my attention to the development of an appropriate identity for myself. I briefly considered becoming an English lord—Lord Alexander, second Earl of Dorwich instantly came to mind—but that would necessitate the maintaining of a consistent English accent and, besides, it would be far too easy for someone to investigate my pedigree or lack thereof. Eventually, after a great deal of thought, I decided upon becoming a wealthy young American from New York City, newly removed to Toronto for purposes of a highly secretive commercial venture.

Next began the search for a name that both possessed an aristocratic connotation and, at the same time, mirrored my true inner being. Over time I composed a list of some forty choices, but the perfect appellation eluded me until late one winter night when I was rereading my Walter Pater and his admonition "To burn always with this hard, gem-like flame" caused the veil of indecision to be lifted from my eyes. I put it to myself: since my life is dedicated to being a flame, why not call myself one? "Flame" would be my given name and, as for my Christian name, why not take the name of an Oscar Wilde character? Thus—"Cecil Flame". Why not indeed?

With my new identity settled and my course of deception neatly plotted out, I settled into life with my uncles on the farm and began my years of self-tutelage in the ways of high society and gentlemanly behaviour. Of course I was expected to help out with farm chores before and after school but, by the time I began living there, the number of livestock had dwindled considerably from when my father was growing up, and by and large Uncle Jasper ran the farm single-handed while Uncle Harold worked at the Balls Falls Mill as both manager and book-keeper. In addition to running the farm, Uncle Jasper also filled the role of mother, in that he did all the sewing and baking and made all the meals. He was a prodigious reader of romantic novels—especially those by Charles Dickens and the Brontë sisters, which he read over and over again. In the summer Uncle Jasper roamed the windswept Yorkshire moors on the front porch while in winter he prowled the streets of London in front of the cook-stove. He was highly emotional and many times I returned home from school to find him hunched over the kitchen table sobbing without apology as he repeated the plaintive words "Nell, oh, Little Nell." Each brother defined the other by contrast, for Uncle Harold was anything but sentimental. Practicality was his lord and master, and while Uncle Jasper was in the grips of tragedy and intrigue in his rocking chair of an evening, Uncle Harold would be in his straight-backed kitchen chair poring over sums of one origin or another—quite often exhorting his brother to "stop all that damned weeping for pity's sake!" Of course, while the brothers were reading downstairs, I was reading upstairs. Reading, and memorizing.

My research was as far-reaching as it was never-ending. I read countless novels to learn how a gentleman converses and strikes attitudes, and when I was not learning through the world of literature, I was reading instructional tomes on the art and science of gentlemanly adornment and deportment. Professor Dibben's *Ball-Room Dancing without a Master* for example—"embracing the whole theory and practice of the Terpsichorean Art which gives the individual that graceful demeanour and easy deportment so essential to a correct appearance in cultured society", and Focoud's *Food and Wines Français*—"exposing for the inspection of the novice all that must needs be known on the subject"—were meat and drink to me. As for the doings of high society—the specific people and their ways—there were countless organs of journalism available for my edification. *The New York Times*, despite the fact that it was two weeks old by the time it reached me in Balls Falls, taught me everything I might need to know about New York City society figures and the fine shops and restaurants they frequented. As for Toronto's elite, I had only to study Lady Gay's Society Column in *Saturday Night* and the theatre reviews in *The Toronto Star* and *The Globe* to learn about the people and events that would eventually constitute my world. The latest ball at the Royal Canadian Yacht Club and the symphonic concert at Massey Music Hall were mine to enjoy in print. The tantalizing details of the charity tea held at the Palm House Pavilion were laid open to me, while over at the Grand Opera House yet another theatrical triumph was being enjoyed. You may rest assured that no one, not even my uncles, had the slightest inkling as to what I was up to. During the day I attended school like a normal Balls Falls youth. My grades were adequate but only slightly above average for I had little incentive to apply myself to the common curriculum. I mean to say, why would I choose to memorize the names of African rivers when I could be committing the *Gentleman's Guide to Fine*

Vintages to memory or, if mentally fatigued, practising the artistic manipulations of my walking stick? Needless to say, I did not encourage friendships with my school-mates, for I had little time and still less inclination.

My years of self-tutelage passed more or less uneventfully, but that is not to say that I never stumbled or fell during this period. Many times, despite my motto of *Fidem Servo*, I lost faith in my pilgrimage to knowledge and identity. Indeed upon more than one occasion I became convinced that "Cecil Flame" was but a ridiculous figment of my infantile imagination. It was during these bouts of despair that I came to see that, just as in all other religions, I too needed a physical symbol of the deity around which my faith revolved. I started out by stitching *Fidem Servo* on my pillowcase so that every night my head might lie upon my motto. Later I carved my battle-cry into the oak headboard of my bed so that it might watch over me during the night. Then one glorious day I came across a coloured portrait of La Divine Sarah in a special supplement of *The Toronto Star*. It showed her reclining on the fur-draped divan in her famous Turkish bedchamber, wearing a trouser-suit made of silk. I immediately framed it and hung it on the wall opposite my bed so that her beautiful face was the first sight to greet my eyes every morning upon my awakening and the last thing I saw every night before extinguishing my candle. In time I fell into the habit of kneeling in prayer before her portrait and asking that she might grant me the strength to sustain my faith in my destiny. It was while in this supplicatory posture that I realized the time was nigh to have a quantity of Cecil's personal cards printed up. This I arranged forthwith—once again taking full advantage of Eaton's excellent mail-order department—and within a matter of weeks I had the inestimable joy of seeing my future name in print.

CECIL FLAME

NEW YORK CITY

FIDEM SERVO

My cards were superb specimens, for I abjured mere lithography for the genuine gold-stamped variety and chose gents' thick vellum paper so as to achieve a smart snap when presenting it to persons. They were in perfect taste, decidedly elegant without being ostentatious—just as one would want for what is, after all, the title page of one's book of self-creation. And I must say that, although I have travelled under many aliases over the intervening forty odd years and had many corresponding personal cards printed, Cecil's card remains to this day my most revered.

When I received my new name in published form I sought a way to display one of these fine cards to best advantage in my bedroom, but given the diminutive size of a calling card it proved to be something of a challenge. Then one day after school, while rooting around in the box-room across the hall from my bedroom, what should I find but a huge stuffed raven with outstretched wings. Mere minutes later that raven was sitting atop a plant pedestal in my bedroom with the card of Cecil Flame proudly, nay triumphantly, clenched in his beak. In time I knotted a white silk scarf about his long neck and at his feet, or rather talons, I sprinkled the ashes of one of my earlier cards. (These "Willoughby Tweed, Esq." cards were merely cards I made myself years earlier for inclusion with my letters of inquiry, mail orders and the like.) Then, as a finishing touch, I constructed a large paper moon with my *Fidem Servo* battle-cry printed around its perimeter and tacked it on the wall above the raven. Thus the raven, bearing the symbol of my new identity, was rising up phoenix-like out of the ashes of my former identity and reaching for the moon. I remained utterly delighted with my symbolic creation for some considerable time thereafter, and I felt greatly encouraged every time I looked at it, but I had forgotten how circuitous one's Path of Destiny so often is. Strangely, my reminder occurred as Uncle Jasper and I were doing the dinner dishes one night. I recall it vividly. I was drying a tea-cup and picturing my raven in my mind's eye—thinking what an extraordinarily handsome and powerful bird he was—when I suddenly thought: Raven! My name should be Raven. Flame is far too literal a name and while, yes, it is wonderfully romantic, it does not convey the same sense of dash and go as Raven does. Then I thought, no, not Raven, Raven*croft*. My name shall be Ravencroft and that is all there is to that. As for my Christian name, I thought Cecil Ravencroft worked very well but I decided to hold off until I had a chance to consult the *Big Book of Names* at school. When I did so on the following day the perfect name fairly leapt off the page. Reginald. It had to be Reginald—firstly due to its meaning as derived from the Old English—powerful, mighty—and secondly owing to the delightfully melodious alliteration it produced. Thus: Reginald Ravencroft. Later, as I walked home from school, I decided to add Ambrose as my middle name in tribute to my father. Before nightfall I had composed my request to Eaton's mail-order department for my new cards, and within the month my raven proudly clutched in his beak the card of one Reginald A. Ravencroft, Esq.

REGINALD A. RAVENCROFT, ESQ.

NEW YORK CITY

FIDEM SERVO

Time passed and my self-education progressed well but, despite being armed with my fine new name, little by little I began to lose faith in my destiny. After all, how could I, Willoughby Tweed from Balls Falls, Ontario, expect to convince the rich and the rare of Toronto that I belonged among them? What special ability did I possess which others did not? In my dark hours of doubt and despair I turned once again to La Divine Sarah, and for six successive nights I knelt before her portrait begging her to tell me what to do. Finally, on the seventh night, after praying in vain to her yet again, I fell into a fitful sleep and La Divine answered me in the form of a dream-vision. In my dream I was sleeping in my bed when suddenly I felt myself rising up in the air, into the dim interior of a church not unlike the Balls Falls Presbyterian church which my uncles and I attended. In the distance I could see the red glow of the sanctuary lamp suspended from the vaulted ceiling, and below this lamp lay an open coffin surrounded by white candles. I was frightened by the thought of what might be lying in the coffin but a force began drawing me down the aisle towards it. I began shaking uncontrollably for, as my feet inched me ever closer to the coffin, I grew more and more convinced that when I looked inside I would find the putrefied remains of my sainted mother. Still I could not resist the force and finally I drew alongside the hideous box and peered over the edge. It was La Divine Sarah who lay within—beautiful, radiant, glorious Sarah, not my putrefied mother. She was sleeping but, as I gazed down upon her shimmering face, her eyes fluttered open and she spoke. "Fly, Raven, fly!" she said and I suddenly found myself sitting bolt upright in bed—my faith fully restored, and knowing precisely what I must do. If I could create just such a church, with just such a coffin, I would be able to go there whenever I felt my faith beginning to flag, and by praying in that cloistered environment, I would always find the strength to carry on my quest. And so I did create a church and coffin just like in my dream-vision, and I called it my Church of Self Creation. For the next two years I knelt in prayer before La Divine Sarah's coffin and not once did I leave its presence without a renewed sense of purpose.

Not once, that is, until precisely twelve days before my eighteenth birthday, when, faced with my imminent departure, I awoke that morning with a numbing feeling of futility and dread. As I contemplated saying good-bye to my uncles and assuming the identity of Reginald Ravencroft my nerve failed me utterly, and I knew in my heart that I was a fool. All of my studying and committing to memory, my travelling costume, my personal cards in the raven's beak, yes, and even my Church of Self Creation—I saw everything now as being utterly stupid and useless, for I quite simply did not have the nerve to play out the charade. I spent the better part of the morning vomiting in my room—so much so that I filled the water pitcher to near overflowing with the vile excretion. Finally in a fit of desperation I fled to the barn, saddled Cathy, and rode off wildly down the road with no thought as to where we might be headed. Up and down the concession roads we thundered until finally I found myself—wearing nothing but a wool nightshirt and a pair of work trousers—trotting down the main street of Balls Falls atop Cathy. Then, for no discernible reason, I dismounted and hitched her to the post in front of Johnson's Dry Goods store. Johnson's was the store that for so many years had been for me a magic depot where I picked up all my wonderful books and newspapers and parcels. Now its simple country-store façade—formerly a thrilling sight—was just a sneer, a cruel reminder of what a tin-horn goober I really was. I stood on the porch staring dumbly in the window at the lanterns and bolts of cloth displayed therein. Nothing had any meaning to me any more. Then suddenly my eyes focused on the headline of *The Globe* newspaper and the huge glorious print swam before me as in a vision.

FRENCH ACTRESS SARAH BERNHARDT
TO PERFORM IN TORONTO

The wondrous words struck me like a length of oak. In the

next instant I was inside the store, fighting to control my raging emotions so that I might comprehend the text before me.

> Mr. O.B. Sheppard, manager of the Grand Opera House of Toronto, announced today that the world-famous Parisian actress Sarah Bernhardt has extended her American theatrical tour to include the city of Toronto. She and her company will perform Racine's *Phèdre* at the Grand Opera House on Saturday, the 3rd day of September. Audience reactions in the United States have run the gamut from frenzied adoration to profound outrage. Curtain calls of unprecedented number and fervour have been coupled with protests by religious groups at times violent. Diatribes against Mlle. Bernhardt have appeared in prominent organs of the press such as *The Methodist Magazine* and considerable protest is expected here in the "City of Churches" as Toronto is so often called.
>
> Mlle. Bernhardt will be in Toronto for one performance only and a large turnout is expected. Tickets will be available to the public commencing at 1:00 p.m. on the day of the performance. Immediately following her Toronto engagement the famed thespian will be returning to France.

I stood in Johnson's Dry Goods store struggling to contain my astonishment and joy, when suddenly a grotesque fear stole across my brain like a huge black rat. My stomach fell out from under me and, had I not already spent the better part of the day vomiting, I do not doubt I would have retched yet again. Was it even remotely possible that I would be too late to obtain a ticket to her performance? I fought to hold my panic in check while I reviewed my itinerary. *Tickets are to be offered to the public at 1:00 p.m. My train is due to arrive at 2:00 p.m. The earliest I can be at the Grand Opera House ticket window will be 2:15 or even 2:30. What if the tickets are all gone and I, her most ardent supplicant in all the world, am shut out?*

But then, just as quickly as it had arrived, my hideous fear melted away like ice in a flame. I knew in the depths of my very soul that rather than being a mere coincidence, La Divine Sarah's impending arrival was an extraordinary omen sent to me by my Fate Goddess. It was quite natural that I had suffered a crisis of faith but look here—on the very day when my nerve failed me, I learned of La Divine's impending performance! Furthermore, the confluence of events: my eighteenth birthday, my transformation into the dashing Reginald Ravencroft, and, almost simultaneously, my witnessing a performance by the incredible goddess who had made my self-transformation possible in the first place—it was incontrovertible proof that I was on My Path. I was doing precisely what She intended me to do and therefore, since I was acting exactly in tandem with my Destiny, I had nothing whatsoever to fear. There simply was no possibility that She would be so cruel as to raise me up to the moon only to dash me down to the ground. I knew it as I knew my own name.

I remember walking out onto Johnson's porch, clutching the glorious *Globe* organ and standing stock still in dumb wonder at the magic of my life. Within hours of my rebirth I was to be baptized in the light of inspiration by the high priestess herself! Then, as if that were not enough, yet another momentous thought exploded fully formed in my mind. Would she too be stopping at The Queen's Hotel? Although not assured, it was highly probable. Opinion was divided as to which hotel was the finest in Toronto—The Queen's or The Rossin House. The Queen's had the pedigree but The Rossin was known to possess slightly more marble. Still, there was at least a fifty per cent chance that La Divine Sarah and Reginald Ravencroft would sleep under the same roof! Of my ride back home I remember little save that, by the time we turned in at our gate, I had composed in my mind my Eaton's order for the set of evening clothes I would require for the theatre.

That spiffing set of evening clothes was now neatly encased in my brand-new, genuine alligator Gladstone bag sitting on the floor in a pool of moonlight. I heard the hall clock chime three a.m. Sleep was clearly out of the question. I decided that the most productive way to employ myself until morning was to review Doctor Sigmund Garland's *The Manners That Win* and I therefore proceeded to place a fresh candle in the brass candlestick on my bedside table, and turned to the final chapter—the good doctor's dissertation on bathing, entitled "Never Too Clean".

The importance of frequent bathing cannot be over-emphasized. The prophet Mohammed made frequent ablutions a religious duty; and in that he was right. The rank and fetid odours which exhale from a foul skin can hardly be neutralized by the sweetest of devotion. . . .

CHAPTER II

I PERFORM A MAGIC TRICK ON MYSELF

W hen I awoke, the magical moonlight had been replaced by
glorious sunlight. Incredibly enough, I had drifted off to sleep
once again. A quick consultation of my timepiece revealed the hour
to be ten minutes past nine o'clock, which meant I really had to get
a move on if I was to complete all my tasks before catching the train.
First on my list was the deconsecration of my Church of Self Creation,
so I quickly mounted the ladder to the trap door in my bedroom
ceiling and entered my place of worship. The dark old beams soared
upwards to form a vaulted roof and four pointed Gothic windows—
one set into each dormer—provided a soft golden glow in the
chamber, for I had painted the panes to simulate stained-glass
windows with the aforementioned card-bearing raven flying up to
the moon. La Divine Sarah's open coffin lay on the floor in the centre
of the room, surrounded by six tall brass candlesticks, while a brass

sanctuary lamp with a red globe hung suspended a few feet above it. This chamber, empty except for these few sacred bits, was of course the dream-vision brought to life that La Divine Sarah sent to me.

I knelt beside the coffin and as I surveyed its sacred contents I felt once again that quieting, secret intimacy with La Divine Sarah. I had lined the interior with raccoon fur to represent the fact that La Divine, being hopelessly addicted to fur, was constantly swathed in it even in the humid heat of a Paris summer. Then I had artfully arranged throughout the furry bottom symbolic objects to represent her body and her life. To wit:

> Twenty eight white almonds representing her teeth, which were said to be of astonishing whiteness despite the fact that she was known to be constantly munching chocolate bon-bons.

> A string of white pearls symbolizing her favourite necklace, which, although at first glance it appeared to be a string of pearls, was in reality a rope of petrified human eyeballs given to her by Peruvian Indians.

> Five miniature crowns representing the crowned heads of Europe and a silver crucifix to represent the Pope of Rome— all of whom she was known to have seduced in her youth.

> Three miniature dolls symbolizing the illegitimate children she had conceived, with the Emperor Louis Napoleon, the Tsar of Russia, and a condemned murderer.

> A small clay bust fashioned by myself of Darwin, her monkey (known on six continents for his filthy habits), to symbolize the menagerie of beasts with which she surrounded herself at all times.

> And finally, at the head of the coffin, a clump of tangled grass dyed red to represent the mass of riotous red hair which crowned her divine head.

I closed my eyes and, as the feeling of calm pervaded my being, I repeated for the last time the vow I had recited every night for all those years. "Divine Sarah this I do vow to you: I vow to array myself as aesthetically as possible and thereby become a clothes-wearing man of note. I vow to become a man in the embrace of the finest *fille de joie* in the most exclusive sporting house of which Toronto can boast and, by dint of exhaustive tutelage therein, become a lover of astounding accomplishments. I vow to find, and make my wife, a woman of immense beauty, kindness, and wealth. I vow to dine at the finest table life can offer me and to guard my life from monotony by the daring of my whims. I vow, in short, to burn always with a hard, gem-like flame. All this I do swear in your name. Amen." I rose from my knees, drew the red sanctuary lamp to my lips, and with a puff of air the sacred lamp was for ever extinguished and my Church of Self Creation deconsecrated.

With that act of deconsecration I abruptly ceased being a man of mere words and became one of action. It was time to burn the coffin and its contents. Fortunately Uncle Harold was off at the mill and Uncle Jasper was out in the fields, so I did not need to fear pointed inquiry into the nature of the coffin or why I was burning it behind the barn. The old wooden planks caught fire almost instantly and the acrid smell of burning fur filled the air. I had prepared a ceremonial recitation to be read aloud but as the flames gathered strength I realized that words would be superfluous. Her coffin was now simply an old wooden box that I did not need any more, and in lieu of my recitation I simply waited at attention until it was reduced to smouldering ashes and then scattered them with a stick.

I had bathed the previous night so a rapid wash of face and a quick pomading of hair was all I required before I was able to begin the most important stage of my toilette—the waxing of my prized Imperial moustache. I had begun growing my Imperial in my sixteenth year and for the past two years I had worked doggedly to promote its growth and perfect its design. I was forever hoeing and weeding it and I prided myself that the effect could not justifiably be termed common garden. Indeed it was my belief that, with its perfectly upturned points, my Imperial combined the aura of the genuine dandy of yesteryear with the rectitude and aplomb of the modern military warrior. I felt, in short, that it reflected my personality admirably.

I had also packed all my bags the night before, save for my genuine alligator club bag which I would be keeping by my side at all times throughout the journey. Into this I now stowed all items too precious to entrust to the care of the baggage handlers, such as Father's fine sterling-silver toiletry tackle and those items of his jewellery which I would not be wearing on my person. I also added some items which I felt I might require on the train, such as my diary in case I should feel the need to capture a particular moment on paper for posterity, and my small red leather folio with my lists of Oscar Wilde's aphorisms and the other quotable quotes I was constantly memorizing so as to salt my conversation when out and about in society.

Next I had the immense pleasure of donning my highly fashionable cinnamon-coloured walking suit—Eaton's finest, and completely up to the mark in every way—followed by my two most precious possessions in all the world—Father's watch and signet ring. The ring bore his initials and the gold hunting-case of his watch was engraved with two cupped hands symbolizing the healing hands of his noble profession. The watch had been given to him as a token of heart-felt gratitude by the mayor of Balls Falls, Jim Barnes, after Father saved his son Jacob's life. Attached to the watch by a stout gold chain was a fob in the form of a six-pointed gold star with a compass in the centre, that he might never find himself lost in a dreadful winter storm while embarked on an errand of mercy and healing. I slipped the ring on the baby finger of my right hand, dropped the watch into my right waistcoat pocket, and then swagged the gold chain and fob across my abdomen. It pleased me greatly that I had taken care never ever to wear either article until that moment.

With the outfitting of my person, I was now ready to say good-bye to my parents, so I made my way across the pasture and up the slow rise to the oak tree at the crest of the hill. I knelt in prayer.

"Dearest Mother and Father, I do most humbly beseech you, hear my prayer. Go with me now as I embark upon my adventure. Grant me the courage to plunge headlong into the glorious existence waiting to embrace me and give me the courage to quaff the purple cup of life to the very dregs. Father, I salute you. Mother, I embrace you. *Fidem Servo*. Amen."

Without further ado I returned to my bedroom to collect my bags. I had already decided not to hide the contents of my room away in anonymous trunks but rather to leave the room exactly as it was—books, raven, and all. All, that is, except La Divine Sarah's portrait. Its inclusion had been a source of long and heated debate in my mind, for the idea of presenting myself at the reception desk of the noble Queen's Hotel totting a paper parcel filled me with horror. But, in the end, I decided once and for all that I wanted Her with me, and that Reginald Ambrose Ravencroft, Esq., would not concern himself with the opinions of jumped-up little hotel clerks.

When I finally made my way to the front porch I found that Uncle Jasper had Cathy and Heathcliff harnessed to the wagon as per arrangements, and I had merely to place my luggage in the back alongside the wooden boxes of butter he was taking into Balls Falls to sell. Our journey into town was uneventful save for the memories awakened in me as we passed the township schoolhouse and I remembered all the attacks upon my character, and in some cases upon my person, I had been forced to endure in that schoolyard. When I first began attending the school I was instantly christened "Four-eyes" in reference to my spectacles. Then, several years later, when I gave myself a monocle on my thirteenth birthday, I made the colossal blunder of wearing it to class. It was a very nobby piece of facial furniture but its debut was greeted not with the awe and admiration I anticipated but rather with hoots of laughter and cries of derision. Its eventual theft and destruction brought the episode to a tawdry conclusion but I consoled myself with the thought that, given my tormentors' total ignorance of things sartorial, one could hardly expect better from them. My penance, however, did not end with the destruction of my monocle, for from that day onward I was no longer known as "Four-eyes" but rather as "One-eye", which I must say I found rather pathetic. I mean to say, had they the intelligence required to make leaps of logic they would have called me "Three-eyes", and, further, if one was determined to emphasize the one-eyed aspect one would want to use the much more imaginative jibe "Cyclops". Nonetheless the reception of my monocle taught me a very valuable lesson: peculiarity breeds contempt; and I resolved to act with greater discretion in future. I also, incidentally, acquired another monocle, to be worn only within the confines of my bedroom, but unfortunately the attendant eye strain and headaches rendered its employment untenable. I did, however, have the satisfaction of denying my schoolmates the pleasure of receiving one of my hand-written Willoughby Tweed personal cards.

Uncle Jasper and I passed our journey into town in silence and, with the exception of the occasional sniffle, he managed to hold the inevitable tears at bay. Both my uncles were under the mistaken impression that I was moving to Toronto in order to find work as a tailor's apprentice. I deemed it a kindness to foster this untruth because if they knew that my life was dedicated to the pursuit of wealth and pleasure and feats of derring-do, they would worry about me and undoubtedly create something of a fuss. In addition, my little falsehood helped them to understand my preoccupation with sartorial splendour. Even Uncle Harold admitted that one could hardly expect to find employment with a tailor if one was dressed in a pair of old farm coveralls. They also believed me when I told them that I would be stopping at The Arlington Hotel upon arrival in Toronto. It was a plain but clean hotel much frequented by farmers who were forced to spend the night in Toronto after delivering their produce. In their minds, my intention was to remain at The Arlington for only as long as it took me to locate an inexpensive but respectable boarding house in which to reside permanently. Uncle Harold could not have coped with the knowledge that I would be putting up indefinitely in the finest suite at the best hotel in the Dominion of Canada. As far as correspondence between us went, it seemed perfectly logical that since my precise whereabouts would be uncertain for a time, they should write me via general delivery Toronto.

Upon arrival in town Uncle Jasper let me off at Lawyer Hog's office while he continued on to deliver his butter. He was then to check my bags at the railway station down the street, where we would rendezvous after my interview with the lawyer. Lawyer Hog's office— pronounced "Hoog" or so he claimed—was located on the lower floor of a white frame house next to Hallowell's Apothecary. His establishment consisted of a vestibule, a reception area wherein resided his clerk, and an inner office containing Lawyer Hog himself. I deposited my overcoat, hat, and stick on the oak hall tree in the vestibule and presented myself to Lawyer Hog's clerk, Mr. Browne. To my dismay I was informed by Mr. Browne that Mr. Hog was busy with a client at that moment; he asked would I mind taking a seat. I had little choice but to do so.

Shortly thereafter a most handsome woman of about thirty years emerged from the inner office and took up a seat opposite me. She was wearing a stunning green satin gown and possessed a most luxuriant quantity of chestnut coloured hair—drawn up in a bun, naturally, but I could easily imagine it falling about her naked alabaster shoulders. In fact, as she sat knitting and gazing demurely out the window, I slipped into a reverie of a highly erotic nature in which she suddenly threw her knitting to the floor and wheeled on me.

"I believe you to be staring at me most lecherously sir!" she cried.

"No, no, not at all ma'am," I stammered. "I was merely admiring your fine gown. Satin, is it not?"

"You were imagining my nakedness. You want me dreadfully, don't you?" she persisted.

"No," I protested. "I really—"

"Silence!" she commanded as she abruptly rose to her feet. "You want me, sir, and you shall have me here and now."

I stared wild-eyed as she deftly slipped her gown down over her shoulders, wiggled it down the length of her body onto the floor, and stepped away from its crumpled folds. She stood proudly across the room daring me to gaze upon her steaming flesh—naked save for her corset and hose. Then she began slowly walking over to me, her creamy love apples fairly exploding from the top of her corset, her thighs giggling voluptuously. I was completely mesmerized by so erotic a sight and I became aware that my limb had long since grown rigid with inflamed passion. She halted directly in front of me, and with one violent motion, she burst her two glorious orbs out of her corset.

"Won't you let me guide you through love's labyrinth?" she purred.

"Yes," I answered, "if it should please—"

"If you would be good enough to follow me, Mr. Tweed," Mr. Browne intoned.

At the sound of Mr. Browne's voice I bolted to my feet, only to discover that my rigid pego was causing my trousers to distend rather like the centre pole in a circus tent. Walking was clearly out of the question so I abruptly sat down, bent over, and commenced untying and tying my shoelaces, while complaining bitterly about the shoddy construction of laces sold at Johnson's Dry Goods store. Fortunately I was not long in resuming my former physique and I allowed myself to be escorted into the inner office.

Lawyer Hog and I exchanged civilities and, proffering my gold cigarette case, I said, "Won't you take a Turkish Beauty?" But he declined my offer and as I fired up a Beauty he got right to the nub of the matter, as I knew he would do.

"Now then, Willoughby. Do you really think it prudent to take possession of your entire inheritance in cash money given that you are about to embark on a train journey? I feel it is incumbent—"

"Yes thank you, Mr. Hog," I said, interrupting his paternalistic and, I may say, condescending bombast. "I do fully comprehend your reasoning, however I have my own agenda, and as it is now my money and mine alone I suggest we say no more about it. I have a train to catch so I am somewhat pressed for time. I assume you have my cash at hand as I requested."

"Now you see here, young man, do you fully understand the danger in which you are voluntarily placing yourself? Your action is not merely precipitous but—"

"Yes, quite, sir!" I said with a deal of heat as I sprang to my feet. "Mr. Hog, I am neither a callow youth nor a country rube and frankly I resent being addressed as such. I suggest we now draw our interview to a hasty conclusion. My money, sir, is precisely . . . where?"

Mr. Hog sighed and withdrew an alarmingly slim brown envelope from underneath his desk blotter. "Please be so good as to count the money here in my presence and sign this receipt," he said with resignation.

"With great pleasure, sir," I said and proceeded to extract two hundred-dollar bills, five fifty-dollar bills, three ten-dollar bills, and twenty-nine one-dollar bills, for a grand total of five hundred and nine dollars. I endeavoured to remain nonchalant in the presence of currency of such high denomination for in truth I had never seen a hundred-dollar bill before, or likewise a fifty—or, though I blush to admit it, a ten-dollar bill. Of course I saw at once what the sly Hog was up to: he was deliberately saddling me with bills of astronomical denomination to force me into going to a bank to cash them—hoping I would succumb to the temptation to play safe by depositing the money. Of course, what Lawyer Hog did not realize was that Reginald Ravencroft abjured "playing safe", in life, in love, and in matters of finance.

"Excellent" I said with a languid wave of my kid-gloved paw, everything seems in perfect order."

I slipped the envelope into the inside pocket of my walking-suit coat and felt the safety pin I would later use to affix the envelope to the lining of my coat pocket. Lawyer Hog extracted a receipt form for me to sign; I accepted a proffered pen, and smiled inwardly as it occurred to me that I was about to sign the name Willoughby Tweed for the last time in my life. I did so. Lawyer Hog rose from his chair and offered his hand. "Good luck to you, Mr. Tweed, I fear you will need it," he said, now all stiff and frosty.

"Thank you, Lawyer Hog, and the same to you," I said with a grin, never suspecting how soon I would regret my arrogance and blush at my naivety.

When I arrived at the railway station platform I was surprised to find Uncle Harold sitting on the bench beside Uncle Jasper, in that I had said good-bye to Uncle Harold the night before and had not expected to see him again before leaving. As for our good-byes, I will not recount them verbatim. Suffice it to say that our parting was even more emotional than I had feared it might be. My worst fears were realized when each of them in his turn embraced me and gave me a birthday present wrapped in gold paper. I fully expected Uncle Jasper to carry on, and indeed would have been dreadfully hurt had he not wept openly as he embraced me and made me swear to write them often, but I was very nearly emotionally undone myself when Uncle Harold too became rather damp as he placed a dollar into my hand with orders to cable them immediately upon my safe ensconcement in The Arlington Hotel. Fortunately they insisted that they could not wait for the train to arrive, nor did they want me to open my gifts in their presence. Uncle Harold had work waiting for him back at the mill and Uncle Jasper was sobbing so uncontrollably as to render dialogue impossible. And so I promised to write them often and to take care of myself and watch out for confidence tricksters and be sure to put my money in a large bank with a solid safe the moment I arrived in Toronto, and so on. I stood and watched old Harold Tweed leading his brother away and I tried in vain to fight back the sobs. "I'm sorry," I said through my tears. "I'm very sorry." But there was nothing I could do to ease their pain, for my Destiny had decreed that I must leave them. I felt dreadfully wicked and guilty for deceiving them but I reminded myself that it was in their best interest not to know the true nature of my mission. And besides, as Oscar Wilde told me, "The aim of the liar is simply to charm, to delight, to give pleasure. He is the very basis of civilized society."

I turned away and, leaving my possessions on the bench, I wandered down the platform attempting to compose myself. I fished Father's Waltham timepiece out of my waistcoat pocket. It was 11:51 precisely. Assuming that the twelve o'clock was on time, Willoughby Tweed had exactly nine minutes to live. I paced up the platform and glanced back at the handful of people scattered at the far end. No one suspects, I thought to myself, they're all blind! The long black shaft of Father's malacca walking stick glittered in the noon-day sunlight. Its weight was beautifully balanced and I let it twirl languidly through my fingers one by one. How exquisite it felt against my fine kid gloves. A consultation of my timepiece was not encouraging, for although it was 11:57, I had yet to hear the twelve o'clock's whistle, and that meant she had not even crossed the township line. The Canadian Pacific train to Toronto was going to be late and the tickets to La Divine Sarah's performance were due to go on sale in one hour's time.

"This is quite all right, Willoughby old son," I remarked aloud to myself. "La Divine will watch over you."

I debated how I might employ my time to best advantage and briefly considered retrieving my red leather folio in my club bag so as to review the Oscarisms therein, but I discarded this notion as impractical due to my state of nerves. It all seemed so incredible! I mean to say, it is not uncommon for people to see in retrospect where their lives have taken profoundly important turns for either good or ill, but there was I, fully aware of the importance of the moment as I lived it! I looked down the long platform and I asked myself: what if it was thronged with people? What if Mrs. Johnson from Johnson's Dry Goods store was standing just down the way? She would probably be wearing her black bombazine dress, with her gloriously ample bosom covered with a quantity of amber beads. In this bright sunshine she would undoubtedly have her brown silk parasol up to shield her creamy complexion. How would I appear to her? I imagined Inspector Lestrade, fresh from an interview with Mr. Sherlock Holmes, questioning Mrs. Johnson about me. He would be stout, in his middle years, wearing a brown sack suit, sporting a long straggly soup-strainer moustache, and would have both his pencil and notebook at the ready.

"Er uh tell me now uh, Mrs. Johnson," he would say and pause to lick the point of his pencil, "when you were standing on the platform waiting for the train, did you happen to notice a tall, thin young man of about eighteen years uh, wearing wire spectacles and sporting a handsome Imperial moustache? He was very fashionably turned out, really the epitome of fashion."

"Well now let me think a moment, Inspector," she would say, momentarily frightened at the suggestion that she might have been standing near someone of interest to the police. "Oh for heavens sake, you must mean young Willoughby Tweed. Of course I noticed him, what woman could fail to notice the most nattily dressed young man in Balls Falls? Do you realize his eyes possess a magnificent azure blue quality not unlike the Mediterranean Sea?"

"Uh no I was not aware of that fact mawm."

"Oh yes, inspector, you cannot miss them. I trust no ill has befallen him."

"Well now that is precisely what we do not know, mawm, for the plain fact of the matter is that he seems to have disappeared—vanished off the face of the earth as you might say."

"Oh good gracious, what if he is lying hurt and alone somewhere, dreadfully in need of comforting?"

"Er . . . yes. Now then, would you say that he was acting in any way peculiar? Er that is to say—"

Then for some strange reason my reverie suddenly changed, and I imagined the same polite interrogation scene but with both Mrs. Johnson and Inspector Lestrade stark naked. I winced at the sight of the inspector's big hairy belly hanging down—a large ball of guts suspended in a hairy skin sling. His shrunken member was just barely capable of poking its little one-eyed head out from between the folds of fat, and his two bandy little legs were all hairy and knobby. . . . Then suddenly the scene shifted yet again and Mrs. Johnson was no longer standing naked in front of the police inspector but rather reclining seductively on a feed bag in the back room of her store, where all the supplies were kept—still naked as a jay bird.

"Will you allow me to guide you through love's labyrinth, Willoughby Tweed?" she inquired.

"Yes, of course, if it should please you Mrs. Johnson."

"We shall begin by you shamelessly gazing upon my nakedness without reserve," she said.

I did as directed—gaping unashamedly at the curves of her alabaster anatomy. Her succulent orbs rendered me breathless and the sight of that area of Mrs. Johnson's person dedicated to Venus quite literally made me feel light-headed. Undoubtedly my expression grew damnably coarse but I was powerless to conceal my unbridled lust. She reached out and commenced stroking that most private area of my trousers. "Come, Willoughby, and lie here with me the while," she said. I fell upon the feed bag in a frenzy of desire and planted my lips full upon hers. She neither struggled nor hesitated to meet my salacious advances. We both began to pant in expectation of love's seraphic act. A sensation of abandonment o'ertook me and, hardly knowing what I was doing, with the twist of a button I fetched out my stiff yard for her inspection. Nothing loath, Mrs. Johnson took my privates in her tiny hand and commenced fondling them in a wanton manner. Then she became even more lewd and whispered an indecency in my ear which, I freely confess, made my cheeks burn scarlet.

By conservative estimation I would say that I leapt fully a foot in the air at the deafening hoot from the locomotive's whistle as she came thundering down the track in front of the shaking platform. The train squealed to a stop and instantly the door nearest me swung open. A smartly dressed conductor jumped down and placed his little footstool on the platform.

"Good afternoon, sir," said the noble minion with a formal salute. "Please watch your step." He scuttled off down the platform to tend to the other passengers.

I ran back to the bench, scooped up my belongings, and returned to the bottom of the steps leading to the open carriage door. I paused, took a long slow breath, and then sprang aboard my train to Destiny. At the top of the steps I turned to face the Balls Falls railway station for one last time and squared my shoulders.

"Willoughby Tweed!" I cried out to the empty platform. "Destiny calls me, La Divine Sarah awaits me. I salute you and I bid you—farewell!"

And with that I touched the gold knob of my malacca stick to the brim of my fine bowler hat in silent adieu, spun smartly on my heels, and strode manfully into the carriage to begin my grand adventure. Willoughby Tweed was dead but Reginald Ravencroft was alive and burning with a hard, gem-like flame!

CHAPTER III

MY GRAND ADVENTURE BEGINS

The instant I took my seat the mighty train whistle shrieked, the carriage jerked, and I was on my way to my glorious new life in Toronto. Moments later we were in open countryside and Balls Falls, Ontario, was lost in the distance. After the conductor came by and took my ticket I turned my attention to the birthday presents on my lap. Uncle Harold's turned out to be a weighty treatise entitled *Tricks on Travellers* by Detective Campbell of the Toronto Police Department. The flyleaf was inscribed: "To Willoughby Tweed on his 18th birthday, September 2, 189—, from his Uncle Harold Tweed." I opened it at random and was presented with a list of some twenty dire warnings. I noticed that Uncle Harold had taken the trouble to underline several which I will now offer for your edification.

If you are lost in the street beware of accosting anyone but a policeman. Him you will know by his uniform—blue coat, black helmet, and brass buttons.

Beware of giving street beggars, organ grinders, and their ilk more than a penny.

Beware of saloons with "Pretty Waiter Girls". They are among the most dangerous in the city.

Beware of exposing your watch, pocket-book, or jewellery in the streets, lecture-rooms, theatres, or in streetcars. You should suspect anyone, man or woman, well or ill-dressed, who crowds or presses against you; the contents of your pocket are in danger. Ladies, keep your pocket-books in the bosom of your dress.

Beware of leaving any considerable sum of money or any valuables in your trunk, or of carrying them on your person. There is a safe in every hotel where you can deposit such things without charge. (This last warning was extra-heavily underscored in red pencil.)

Tucked in between the pages of the book was a note. It ran:

Willoughby
I am assured by Constable Pike that this is a book no rural traveller can afford to leave unread. Indeed I would have given it to you earlier that you might already be forewarned and therefore forearmed, but its arrival was delayed until yesterday due to some oaf's error in Eaton's mail-order department. Please heed it well for the clever frauds and humbugs used by wily men and women to entrap the innocent are laid open for you to inspect. Also find enclosed a five-dollar bill to be used should some emergency present itself to you. Hide it well. Good-bye and good luck to you. Write us.

Uncle Harold

I withdrew the five-dollar bill and discovered that he had taken the precaution of writing across the face of it, in his tight regimental hand: "For Emergency Only!" and I placed it in my new genuine seal-skin pocket-book with calf lining.

Uncle Jasper's present, also a book, proved to be a copy of Robert Louis Stevenson's *Treasure Island* handsomely bound in gilt-edged chamois leather. How appropriate, I thought to myself, to give me this particular book as I begin my journey, for it is a Treasure Island of sorts to which I am bound. Its flyleaf was inscribed: "Happy Birthday Willoughby from your Uncle Jasper. You have enriched our lives," and within its pages I discovered a handkerchief of fine Irish linen with my initials crocheted upon it. Given his propensity for weeping, the handkerchief spoke volumes, and I was not surprised to discover the absence of a note. It was a pity I would be unable to use the handkerchief, but that was quite impossible given that the initials W.T. were no longer appropriate.

I felt the train slowing and we pulled alongside the platform in Crooked Creek. For some reason there seemed to be quite a crowd of persons getting aboard and the sparsely populated carriage quickly began to fill up. I was soon joined by a pleasant-looking elderly woman carrying a great many parcels who volunteered without preamble that her name was Mrs. Clara Miller. I immediately saw this as an excellent opportunity to present one of my spiffing new cards.

"Charmed, Mrs. Miller," I said as I touched the brim of my bowler respectfully. "Reginald Ravencroft—my card." I deftly extracted one of said cards from my genuine Moroccan leather card case and presented it to the good woman with a resounding snap. To my horror however I snapped with rather too much gusto and succeeded in launching my card across the carriage. It darted through the air like a startled sparrow and took up residence on the brim of a gentleman's homburg hat directly across the aisle.

"Whoops a daisy!" cried Mrs. Miller.

Miraculously, the gentleman on whose hat my card now resided remained unaware of his new adornment. Since Mrs. Miller and the gentleman were seated directly across the aisle from each other, she took it upon herself to retrieve the errant missile. She accomplished this with good humour but, judging by the scowl on his face, the fellow appeared to be quite put out—as if we had conspired to play a juvenile prank upon him. I assumed Mrs. Miller would simply keep my card and read it but no, to my added chagrin, she passed it back to me.

"There now, dear, don't be embarrassed. I have no doubt you will get the hang of it in time. Try it again, won't you. I'll go first. Good afternoon young man. My name is Mrs. Clara Miller," she said in a jaunty stage voice.

I stared at her in disbelief but she stared back at me with a look of such cheery innocence that I had no choice but to proceed as she directed, despite my intense awkwardness.

"Charmed Mrs. Miller." I said as my cheeks flushed scarlet and I touched the brim of my bowler respectfully. "Reginald Ravencroft—my card." I opened my card case, extracted a fresh specimen, and presented it to her without mishap. (For the record, however, I did not attempt another "snap presentation" but rather executed the "sedate presentation", which involves an elegant sweeping motion of the wrist but no snapping of the fingers.)

"Thank you very much, young man, and incidentally, very nicely done. I am afraid you will think me rude, but I have no card to give you in return. Mr. Miller thinks them an unnecessary extravagance."

I assured her that it was of no consequence and watched as she examined my card with interest. "You're from New York City!" she cried in wonderment. "Whatever brings you way out here?"

I had not anticipated being quizzed on my identity quite so soon in my new life but nonetheless I rallied. "I am journeying to Toronto and thence to New York City having just spent the past two weeks visiting my cousin Willoughby Tweed at The Abbey Grange just outside of Balls Falls."

"I see. And will you be stopping with friends during your stay in Toronto, Mr. Ravencroft?"

Oh the thrill of finally hearing myself addressed as Mr. Ravencroft! "No," I responded, "I have reserved the Red Parlour Suite at The Queen's Hotel."

"Oh my, that does sound grand—how very exciting for you."

"Yes, but that is not all, Mrs. Miller. While in Toronto I shall have the great honour of attending La Divine Sarah Bernhardt's performance of *Phèdre* at the Grand Opera House. She is widely held to be the Eighth Wonder of the World, you know. In fact I credit La Divine Sarah with having saved my very life," I blurted out.

"Gracious!" exclaimed Mrs. Miller. "As important as all that. Fancy!"

I had it in my mind to list some of La Divine's achievements but just then she leapt up and started collecting her parcels.

"Goodness me, here we are in Bethany already," she said

"Good-bye young man, I hope you enjoy your theatrical."

I bade Mrs. Clara Miller good-bye and watched her bustle across the platform and into the Bethany station. Of course I was shocked by her reference to La Divine's impending performance as a mere "theatrical", and my cheeks were undoubtedly still flushed with embarrassment at my disastrous "snap presentation", but nonetheless I was encouraged by my encounter with the kindly old lady. It proved what I knew in my heart all along—that people will believe you are who you say you are, especially if you have the appropriate personal card to present. Also her reaction to my American citizenship showed me that my reasoning had been correct when I decided upon adopting an American identity. You see, I reasoned that the typical Canadian could be counted upon to view a wealthy American with something approaching awe and that this would be especially true in Toronto society. Whether the individual felt envy or disdain—the two usual attitudes held towards Americans by Canadians—it would be important to the Torontonian that the American be shown the very best of everything Toronto society possessed—including its daughters.

What with all my chatting, I had not had the opportunity to assess properly the clothes of my fellow passengers, but as I took the opportunity to do so it was all too apparent that, with the rather glaring exception of myself, the travellers of the male sex made up an extraordinarily unimaginative if not downright dowdy group. Sombre greys and stove-pipe hats with great heavy boots—I despaired. My outfit, on the other hand, was anything but sombre. When I first sat down to plan my travelling costume I flirted with the notion of sporting the latest cut in Inverness cape and deerstalker hat á la Mr. Sherlock Holmes, but when I received Eaton's new catalogue I spontaneously chose their new double-breasted walking suit constructed out of Mahoney's finest Irish Blarney serge in classic cinnamon colour. To complement the cinnamon hue I selected a shirt of mossy green, and set off the shirt in turn with the addition of a forest-green Windsor neck-tie held in place by Father's ruby stick-pin. As for my feet, they were elegantly shod in a pair of Balmoral Oxfords made of genuine Australian kangaroo leather over which I sported a nobby pair of fawn linen spats. What with the addition of a herringbone overcoat in Nottingham green, a fine black English bowler, and a pair of double-clasp fawn kid gloves which matched my spats to perfection, well, what can one say? Très neat, très nobby. Really my wardrobe felt more like a trousseau than mere finery. I was cast in the role of the dashing young groom off on my honeymoon—my golden bride's name being Adventure. I would enter Toronto, not with her hanging on my arm as do ordinary men's brides, but with her burning in my heart, firing my soul and setting my eyes alight!

The train stopped briefly in Nestleton and Manchester and I thought to myself how very glad I was that I had successfully resisted the temptation to mount a reconnaissance expedition to Toronto, for this being my first trip to the metropolis made it all the more wondrous. Of course that did not mean that I was by any means ignorant of Toronto topography—far from it. My study of Toronto guidebooks had been exhaustive and had included the use of a large "bird's eye" photograph of Toronto which I received free of charge from the Campbell Soup Company upon sending in five of their soup labels. The photograph was taken from a hot-air balloon and with the aid of my guidebooks and Goad's Atlas of Toronto I was able to identify and mark the roof-tops of all the important buildings in the photograph. Indeed I would venture to say that, given the depth of my research, few native Torontonians could match my detailed knowledge of street nomenclature and buildings of note.

Just then a most comely-looking young woman of perhaps twenty-five years walked past me and filled my eager nostrils with an intoxicating *eau de parfum* scent. I could not help but wonder if by chance she too would be stopping at The Queen's Hotel. Indeed, I thought to myself, what a coincidence it would be if we were to meet each other in the hallway outside my suite.

"Excuse me, miss," I would say, "but am I right in thinking that we shared a railway carriage on the C.P.R. train to Toronto?"

"Why yes, of course I remember you, you're the man with the fine Imperial moustache. My name is Gwendolen Robertson. Might I have the pleasure of knowing your name, sir?"

"I am Reginald Ravencroft—*enchanté*. My card. Are you staying in one of the suites on this floor?"

"Oh goodness me, no, I just have a pokey little room on a lower floor."

"Well, this is the door to my Red Parlour Suite. It is quite famous, you know. No less a personage than Sir John A. Macdonald, the founder of our great Dominion, always reserved this suite when he was stopping in Toronto. And not only that, Mr. Oscar Wilde stayed in it during his lecture stop here in Toronto in 1882. I wonder, would you care to see inside?"

"I should love to Mr. Ravencroft, but would it be quite safe? What if I am suddenly. . . ."

"What if you are suddenly overwhelmed by the desire to guide me through love's labyrinth?"

"Well yes, that is what I was thinking."

"Fear not Miss Gwendolen Robertson, for I would love nothing better than—"

"Next stop Myrtle. Myrtle next," the conductor intoned.

The train stopped and I fought to calm my mind as I was joined by a tall, rather cadaverous-looking man in his middle years. He was dressed in a tight-fitting black frock coat and black stove-pipe hat and my nose told me that he was a liberal user of rose-scented toilet-water. Upon sitting down beside me he presented both his card and his compliments.

"Charles Mortimer, at your service, sir," he said with a deal of solemnity.

I accepted his card and presented him with one of my own— once again abjuring the "snap presentation" in favour of the "sedate"—and upon examination of his card was not overly surprised to learn that Mr. Charles Mortimer was a mortician. I fought back a smile as I imagined a music hall ditty entitled "Mortimer the Mortician". For his part Mr. Mortimer fell to studying my card with great interest. However, a look of annoyance soon appeared upon his face.

"Oh, I perceive that you are an American, Mr. Ravencroft."

"Yes, from New York City."

"Do you, by any chance, have any relations in the area?"

"Yes I do, Mr. Mortimer. May I ask why you are interested?" I asked, knowing full well the answer to my question.

"Forgive me, sir, if I appear a trifle too direct, but my time is limited. Your relations in the area, would any of them be of advanced years?"

I thought of Uncle Jasper and Uncle Harold and found the undertaker's brazen solicitation highly offensive.

"My relations in this area, sir, are advanced in years but thankfully none is in danger of dying at this time, if that is what you are wondering," I responded bluntly.

Mortimer evidently sensed my annoyance and immediately became most servile. "Allow me to apologize for pressing the matter,

Mr. Ravencroft. But may I just tell you that at our firm—Mortimer's Undertakers of Markham—we are thoroughly posted in all the most approved methods for the care and preservation of the dead. Indeed we are the first firm in Ontario to dispense with the use of ice for that of chemicals in the embalming process. But I hasten to add that we have never lost sight of the importance of having all work done on thoroughly sanitary principles. We can also justly boast of the finest funeral equipage in this part of the country. I must now bid you good afternoon, but may I entreat you to keep my card in your possession against the sad but inevitable day when you shall have need of funereal services. Good day to you, sir, and please remember to keep my card. Thank you for your attention, Mr. Ravencroft."

With that the impertinent Charles Mortimer sprang up from his seat and sought the vacant seat next to a man down the aisle. I watched him and sure enough, out came his card, along with his patter. I continued looking on for some minutes and witnessed him repeat his performance with several more passengers. Clearly the man was working the entire train. Suddenly I suspected that there might be more to Mr. Mortimer than met the eye, and I shot my hand inside my coat, praying that my money was still in residence. It was. But I had to wonder, had the fact that my money was safety-pinned to my coat lining saved me from being robbed? I could prove nothing, of course, but I was badly shaken and, despite the fact that security still remained anathema to me, I resolved to be more alert in future. Indeed, spurred on by my encounter with the cadaverous undertaker, I took up *Tricks on Travellers* once again and began an intense study of that most edifying work.

It was some time later that I was greatly surprised—not to say alarmed—to hear the conductor crying a warning of our pending arrival in Toronto! Clearly it was time for a spruce-up of my person and so I made the journey to the gents' at the end of the carriage and, with the aid of my handy pocket tin of Sergeant-Major Patsy Donovan's Excellent Moustache Wax, I set about refurbishing my Imperial. I had only just begun, however, when I felt the train beginning to slow.

"Egad, man!" I cried aloud. "You must witness the entrance!" Without a second's hesitation I dashed out into the open area between the cars and leaned out by one arm that I might see ahead up the tracks. Great God in heaven, will I ever forget that sight? There in the distance soared the famous towers of the mighty Union Station, and by squinting my eyelids together I could make out the face of the four-sided clock in the central tower. It was twenty minutes past two o'clock, which meant that after a late start our train had lost time and I would be later than anticipated in arriving at the ticket office of the Grand Opera House. Moments later we entered the massive covered train shed with its arched iron girders supporting the glass roof. Lordy, the acres of glass and iron-work involved! I saw six or seven trains standing idle but there was easily room for a dozen more. How, I could not help but wonder, could the builder be confident that the roof would not come crashing down some day as the mighty locomotives thundered in beneath it? Suddenly I gasped. Some five or six tracks over, a festive arrangement of red, white, and blue satin banners hung suspended from the arched girders, while beneath it stood a large crowd of persons and a brass band obviously awaiting the arrival of a special train. Was it even remotely possible? As our train squealed to a halt I stared in dumb disbelief as a train adorned with flags lumbered past us and up to the waiting crowd. It was the Sarah Bernhardt Special!

I ran back to my seat at full speed and collected my belongings, but when I turned to go to the exit door I saw that a long line of disembarking passengers had formed. If I did not take immediate action I would lose vital minutes standing in line! Out the door at the far end of the carriage I charged and, clasping my club satchel, La Divine's portrait, and my walking stick to my bosom, I leapt out for the platform. Unfortunately I gave my ankle a nasty twist in the process but I was not to be deterred by mere pain. I forced myself to leap off the platform onto the open tracks and limped over the series of rails as rapidly as the stabbing pain in my ankle would allow—all the while berating myself without mercy. "Typical Tweed!" I shouted. "Preening in the gents' while La Divine Sarah casts her magic spell on everyone but you! Idiot! Imbecile!" Finally I scrambled up on the appropriate platform and joined the happy crowd just as the brass band struck up "Ta-ra-ra Boom-de-ay". Then the carriage door opened and amid tumultuous cries of "Bravo!", "Hurrah!", and my own " *Vive* Sarah Bernhardt!", to my complete astonishment, Ned Hanlan, the champion oarsman, came bounding down the steps and up onto the dais. Cries of "Welcome Home Ned!" and "Atta boy Ned!" filled the air. I was of course astonished, to say nothing of embarrassed. I had all too obviously joined the wrong welcoming crowd and my hearty cries of *"Vive* Sarah

Bernhardt!" made me look the fool. At the downstroke of the band-master's baton, the music came to an abrupt conclusion and Ned addressed the crowd. "My fellow Torontonians, thank you so much for your rousing—" But no sooner had the celebrated athlete begun to speak than his voice was drowned out by the wild hooting of a fast-approaching train. Everyone turned in unison to see what the hoopla was all about and I was no exception. My blood fairly froze in my veins as I saw that the approaching locomotive was flying La Divine's famous *"Quand Même"* flags from poles mounted on the sides. In the next instant we heard the striking up of a large but unseen brass band. "Look! It's Sarah!" I bellowed at the crowd. The crowd stared back at me in stupefaction. "Sarah Bernhardt—the actress!" I shouted. Then her train suddenly switched to an alternate line and disappeared from view. It was obviously going to stop alongside the outside wall of the shed and I realized that the band and welcoming crowd must be located around the corner beyond my view! Once again I gathered up my belongings and made off in search of La Divine. My ankle, now throbbing, was as naught to me as I streaked across the tracks and around the end of the shed to the other side. I looked back once and to my astonishment not one soul was running with me. They had all turned back to face Ned Hanlan, who, it appeared, had resumed his speech. "Egad!" I cried out in disbelief. "They're giving La Divine the go-by!" I rounded the shed limping at the top of my speed and saw that the group of "Sar-adorers" numbered a good two hundred persons. I prayed that I had not missed any of the ceremony and when I finally took up my position on the edge of the crowd I saw to my inestimable relief that no one had as yet appeared from within La Divine's Palace Car. Fortunately, my greater than average height offered me a fighting chance against the many ostrich feathers and various other millinery adornments of an ornithological nature so often guilty of obscuring one's view. I could see the two members of the official reception committee on a dais and at first glance I had no idea who they might be, but then I recognized their august faces from the photographs that often accompanied Lady Gay's Society Column in *Saturday Night*. The large, handsome woman wearing a huge hat liberally festooned with peacock feathers I knew to be the renowned Toronto actress Mrs. Morrison, while the tall gentleman was Mr. O.B. Sheppard—manager of the Grand Opera House. Standing next to the platform were many artistically dressed persons whom I took to be local stars of the theatre in attendance to welcome the brightest star ever to grace the theatrical heavens. Also prominent around the platform was a cluster of men who, judging by their scruffy appearance and poised pencils, I took to be reporters from the Toronto newspapers. Suddenly the carriage door opened and the band abruptly ceased playing. Out stepped a man no one who had ever perused a *Theatre World Magazine* could fail to recognize as the "Bismark of Managers"—Mr. Edward Jarrett. Without a word he stepped down onto the dais and turned to face the door. He held up his hands for silence and the crowd, all two hundred souls, fell silent. And then she appeared. All those assembled let out a collective "Ah" as a living miracle of delicacy appeared before us at the top of the steps. The hush persisted for a moment and then with one voice the crowd erupted. "*Vive* Sarah Bernhardt! *Vive!* Welcome!" I lent my voice to the effort. "Yes! Yes, Divine One! Welcome! Welcome! A thousand times welcome!" I cried. At an unseen signal the band struck up "La Marseillaise" and we all fell silent. While her country's anthem played La Divine stood solemnly at attention with her right hand resting gently upon her breast and her gaze looking off skyward into the distance over our heads. I stood transfixed, staring up at her in astonishment. Despite the heat of the Indian summer we were enjoying, La Divine was wrapped in a voluminous chinchilla cloak with its high fur collar up-turned and her two beguiling eyes, framed by her crown of riotous red hair and the folds of fur, peering out at the assembly. Such exquisite frailty—she could not have been more than five feet in height—she bore closer resemblance to an exotic little animal than a human being. This magical doll-like creature was the woman who had seduced all the crowned heads of Europe, including the Pope. This was the woman who had saved me from the gallows. When "La Marseillaise" came to a thundering close I was the first to renew the cheer. "*Vive* Sarah Bernhardt!" I cried. "Hail to thee, La Divine!" My cries were picked up and echoed by the crowd. But she had only to raise one of her tiny gloved hands to silence us once again. Mr. Jarrett held out his hand to her, she accepted it, and stepped lightly down the steps and onto the dais.

Mr. Sheppard was the first to step forward. He bowed solemnly.

"Madame Bernhardt, may I have the honour of being the first to welcome you to Toronto and to say how deeply honoured we are by your presence."

La Divine bowed her head slightly in acknowledgement and whispered her thanks. Next Mrs. Morrison stepped forward, curtsied to her Queen, and presented her with a huge bouquet of red roses. When she stepped back and no one else approached La Divine, I braced myself for I knew the magic moment was at hand. La Divine Sarah Bernhardt looked out over the heads of her worshippers.

"Good people of Toronto," she said with a voice of disarming power—given her petite frame, "I am deeply touched by ze warmth of your welcome. I can only pray zat my company and I will leeve up to your expectations tomorrow night when we 'ave ze privilege of performing ze immortal Racine's *Phèdre* for you."

She paused and looked at Mr. Jarrett who instantly took command of the stage.

"Ladies and gentlemen, Madame Bernhardt regrets that she must leave very shortly in order to prepare for tomorrow night's performance at the Grand Opera House, but if you gentlemen of the press desire it, she will answer a few of your questions now."

The gentlemen of the press needed no further encouragement.

"Madame Bernhardt, can you tell us if you brought your coffin with you to Canada?"

"Yes of course," purred La Divine. "I am never without it. It makes for me the rejuvenation."

"Madame Bernhardt, is it true that people were shielding themselves with crucifixes as your carriage drove through the city streets in Washington?"

"Zat ees very possible. I attract all ze lunatics of ze world."

"Did you bring your cheetah with you on this trip, Madame Bernhardt?"

"Alas no, I had to content myself only with Bizibouzou my parrot, and leetle Cross-ci Cross-ça my chameleon. It has been zo lonely for me."

"What do you think of Canadian art?"

"From what I have seen, ze Canadians are still ze Iroquois Indians when it comes to ze arts, but do not despair for you are young and you will learn."

"Madame Bernhardt, how did you feel when the Catholic Bishop of Chicago threatened to excommunicate all Catholics who attended your performance?"

Here Mr. Jarrett stepped forward as if on cue.

"I am glad you asked that question," he said. "I have here a copy of a letter which I sent to His Holiness and which I will now read to you.

> Your Holiness,
> I had intended to spend four hundred and fifty dollars on advertising Madame Bernhardt's appearance in your city but since you have done half the advertising for me, please accept two hundred and twenty-five dollars for the poor of Chicago.
>
> Sincerely,
> Alfred Jarrett

I can promise you folks that I made darn sure my letter was published in the *Chicago Tribune* the following day. So when you ask me how I respond to such hysteria I say, rage on, philistines, and see you in the theatre!"

Amid wild cheers Alfred Jarrett whisked La Divine down off the dais and disappeared with her through a doorway guarded by helmeted police constables. And so, just as suddenly as she had appeared, like a jaguar in the jungle night, La Divine was gone and I was left standing immobile, stunned by the magic of the apparition I had just seen. But not for long, for suddenly I snapped awake and whipped out my timepiece, only to discover that I was now over one hour behind schedule. I set out at full speed in search of the street exit and thence the Grand Opera House—my face a study in panic.

CHAPTER IV

MY FATEFUL BAPTISM

I raced down a flight of stone steps and found myself amidst a crush of travellers in the vast marble chamber of Union Station. I was powerless in such a raging sea of persons so I had no option but to trust that the current would carry me out to the street. Thankfully this did prove to be the case and, although the throng was no less dense outside the building, I quickly spied the gleaming black bodies and bright yellow wheels of the hansom cabs lined up in front of the station awaiting their fares. In spite of my panic I remembered from my research that one was not to engage the nearest cab but rather to go to the head of the cab rank. I did so forthwith and barked out "Grand Opera House, cabby—double quick!" and was rewarded with a "Right you are, sir!" as I climbed aboard. There then ensued an infuriating pause. There was nothing preventing him from at least attempting to pull out into the flow of traffic and yet the oaf of a driver sat there motionless. A full minute passed in mute idleness before I suddenly realized that the good man was awaiting my signal that I was nicely settled in my seat and wished to begin my journey, and I gave two sharp raps on the communicating trap door above me with my stick and we were off. As it happened, my impatience was to be sorely tried during my inaugural hansom cab ride, for we had no sooner begun our journey than we came to a full stop. Front Street was clogged with every manner of two- and four-wheeled conveyance imaginable. Cabs, drays, wagons, and divers private equipages were jammed in solidly and, much to my surprise, dozens of bicycles darted hither and thither as well. I debated leaping out of the cab and sprinting the short distance to the Grand Opera House but I was fearful that in my desperate state of mind I might get lost despite my encyclopedic knowledge of Toronto topography. Having now seen La Divine, my determination to witness her performance was doubled in strength, if that was possible. There simply *had* to be a ticket remaining for me to purchase! The minutes ticked by and we sat while my ears were assaulted by the din of shouting drivers and protesting horses. Finally, just as I reversed my decision to leg it and reached for the door handle, we began creeping along Front Street. At Bay a policeman stationed in the middle of the intersection was attempting with some success to maintain a steady flow of traffic. Once through this bottleneck our pace quickened and we soon turned into Adelaide Street. I scanned the street and spotted the soaring mansard tower of the Grand Opera House, glorious with its royal coat of arms and Union Jack. A consultation of my timepiece revealed the time to be forty-three minutes past three o'clock—over one hour later than anticipated. I bowed my head and quietly prayed, "La Divine Sarah be with me now I beseech thee." The cab drew to the curb in front of the magnificent theatre and I gazed up at the huge playbill festooned with red, white, and blue bunting.

SARAH BERNHARDT IN RACINE'S PHEDRE
ONE PERFORMANCE ONLY
8:00 P.M. SATURDAY

Strangely, there was neither milling crowd nor line-up in front of the theatre. My heart began beating treble time as I stepped down from the hansom cab and said, "Please wait," to the cabby. I then turned, faced the entrance, and without pause strode resolutely through the arched portal into the theatre. A sign indicated the direction of the ticket booth. As I walked down the long empty corridor to the main foyer, I became aware of a ringing sound in my ears growing ever louder with each step. Finally I found myself standing stock still in front of a mahogany ticket booth. I stared in horror at the brass plaque affixed to the window bars. The two most hateful words in the English language stared back at me, so cold, so impersonal, so final: SOLD OUT. I sank to my knees without warning and promptly vomited on the marble floor, three times in rapid succession. Scalding tears coursed down my cheeks as I stammered out, "You fool, Willoughby! You're too late!" I heard someone making strange, animal-like moaning sounds and realized that I was the author of the pitiful moans. It seemed there was no one but me in the theatre. No one to whom I could explain my hideous predicament. And what good would it have done me if there had been a theatre official at hand? Doubtless he would think I was just an ordinary person who had arrived too late to purchase a ticket to the play, and in consequence befouled the magnificent foyer with a huge pool of vomit. After a time I instinctively began taking large breaths, and as my vision slowly began to clear I saw my fine new bowler hat lying in the spreading puddle of vomit. I cleaned my spectacles and managed to get to my feet, but my legs were so wobbly I surely would have fallen had I not grabbed hold of a large marble urn supporting a palm tree. La Divine Sarah's face swam before me. I had just assumed that my Fate Goddess would watch over me but I had been tragically naïve. Now I would be the one standing alone outside the theatre while everyone else was inside basking in the glow of her genius. I shook my head violently from side to side. It was too devastating an image for me to accept. My lungs heaved convulsively and with the flood of air that filled them a feeling of iron-hard resolve took hold of me. "I *will* be in the audience tomorrow night—come what may!" I shouted. "La Divine, I shall return!" And with that I staggered down the long corridor and back out onto Adelaide Street—abandoning my hat to its ignoble fate.

I instructed the cabby to convey me to The Queen's Hotel and sat staring at La Divine's portrait wrapped in wrinkled brown paper. To me it was now naught but a gibe and a taunt. I sat back in my seat and tried frantically to formulate a plan. I have five hundred dollars in my pocket, I told myself, and I will give it all if necessary to acquire a ticket. Of course that will mean dire poverty, an end to all my grandiose plans and therefore suicide, but I will do it. I will also acquire a revolver and, if I cannot bring myself to dash all my dreams, doubtless the business end of a six-shooter will secure me a seat. I will go to *any length* to acquire a ticket! Larceny, assault, murder—no infamy is beyond bounds. It is this simple: I will acquire a ticket or forfeit my life in the attempt. Then I thought, perhaps all I need do is force someone at gun-point to hand over his ticket. "Mention this event to a living soul," I could say, "and I shall surely find you and shoot you dead. Now simply go home and console yourself with the fact that you have not been injured here tonight." Then as the man walked away I would hear him mutter to himself: "Oh well, I suppose I'll just do as the young gentleman says, best forget about it, not worth dying over." But what if he called my bluff? Was I capable of shooting a human being? Perhaps I could just wound the person, or possibly tell him to turn around and cosh him over the head when his back was turned. What if, whether by shooting or by coshing, I accidentally killed an innocent man? Could I live with myself? Perhaps I could force some person with two tickets to give me one of them and we could sit together at gun-point— that way I would not have to hurt anyone and I might even make a successful escape. No one knew my face in Toronto, and with the family funds at my disposal—but what if he were to cry out in the theatre: "Help! Help me! I'm being held at gun-point! He's got a revolver!" They would stop the performance and hunt me like a animal throughout the theatre. And what of my virginity? Whether I lost all my money or was imprisoned or killed in a gun duel with the police, the end result would be the same: I would go to my grave having never been guided through love's labyrinth. I was sweating profusely and I felt my nausea returning. "I am overwrought," I remarked aloud to myself. "I am decidedly overwrought. Surely there must be a middle ground between not seeing La Divine Sarah and destroying my entire life. I must be overwrought, this cannot be right." The word "overwrought" suddenly brought to mind a snippet of advertising copy I had often read in my magazines, for a brain tonic which boasted two full ounces of cocaine in one pint of Bordeaux wine.

Vin Marinani—the wine of life for the overwrought hostess.

Take a small dose before receiving guests or going out to

dinner to prepare for the rigours of the evening ahead and to stimulate the appetite.

It was reputed to be without parallel as an elixir and certainly it was unique as far as endorsements went, for no fewer than three popes, sixteen heads of state, and eight thousand physicians were known to recommend it, to say nothing of Jules Verne, Emile Zola, and Thomas Edison. John Philip Sousa recommended it especially for brain workers and even the noble Sherlock Holmes swore by the efficacy of cocaine, despite what Doctor Watson might say on the subject. The more I thought on it, the more clear it became that "the wine of life" was just what the doctor ordered to refresh my brain and counteract my morbid imaginings. As luck would have it, just as I resolved to take refreshment at the earliest opportunity, what should catch my attention but the familiar red and green glass globes signifying an apothecary shop. Better still, upon investigation I discovered we were opposite Bingham's Drug and Soda Oasis—the famous drug emporium and soda fountain so often pictured in my magazines.

Moments later I found myself standing before the polished walnut counter in Bingham's dispensing department with a pint of Vin Marinani in my hand, and without further ado I tore out the cork and took a sizeable draught of the elixir. I waited a moment and then experienced an aftertaste so extraordinary that I was compelled to investigate it once again with gusto. In a trice the bottle was empty and I realized that I was not only feeling considerably better, I was feeling better and better as the seconds ticked by. The three popes, sixteen heads of state, and eight thousand physicians were absolutely right! Vin Marinani was most definitely a topping brain tonic. In fact I had never felt better in all my life. Even the throbbing pain in my ankle had magically disappeared. The elixir's effect was marvellous! My powers of resolve and optimism fairly flooded my poor, overwrought brain. Good grief, I thought to myself, what's all this twaddle about failure? In the blink of an eye I whipped out one of my personal cards and presented it to an imaginary person with a snap that could have been heard out on the street. *"Fidem Servo* Reginald Ravencroft," I said aloud to myself, *"Fidem Servo."* I would get a ticket to see La Divine Sarah, all right, and not just any ticket but the finest in the house! I felt as if a dirty brown veil of pessimism and confusion had been lifted and it was clearly time I celebrated with the finest concoction Bingham's could give me.

I passed through the etched glass doors into the Palm Garden Oasis and found myself amidst a veritable jungle of potted palms in huge brass jardinières, and hanging ferns of a brilliant green hue—all endlessly reproduced in mirrored wall panels. The soda fountain itself possessed a grandeur the like of which I have not seen equalled to this day. Thirty or more stools stood before this marble shrine to digestive delights, while gas lamps with leaded glass shades coloured in pinks and greens adorned the counter surface—no doubt so as to suggest the iced concoctions awaiting the adventuresome patron. Behind the counter was a maze of brass spigots and valves which reminded me of the elaborate controls of a train locomotive. Certainly, I felt confident, it required little short of an engineering degree to successfully manipulate this monster devoted to the staggering of both the imagination and the digestive organization. Everything about the room invited the weary shopper to rest and ingest and it was with great anticipation that I occupied a stool and placed my order for a Buster Brown Sundae with the soda jerker.

As I sat delighting in my sundae I discovered that, with my brain wonderfully refreshed by the Vin Marinani, I could see my quest for a theatre ticket in an entirely new light. I would definitely arm myself forthwith, and it was still imperative that I patronize Toronto's finest joy palace that evening, just to be on the safe side, but surely the odds were good that I would be able to purchase a ticket at a reasonable price. That is to say, for a hefty sum, undoubtedly, but not my entire fortune. The more I thought about it, the more convinced I became that I had over-reacted and that if I simply remained calm and did not go running around pointing a revolver at hapless theatre-goers I was sure to be in the audience the following night. It was clear to me that the best thing I could do was to get over to The Queen's without further delay and get myself and my luggage ensconced therein. And thus, having finished my Buster Brown Sundae and a subsequent Claret Float, I took my leave of Bingham's Oasis a much wiser and more confident man.

As I stepped out onto the sidewalk I noticed for the first time that standing directly across the street was the huge Toronto Daily Star building. How well did I know the configuration of its roof-top in my "bird's-eye view" map of Toronto. I thought back to the hundreds of *Stars* from which I had gleaned so much information—to say nothing of the portrait of La Divine I held under my arm. Now here I was looking at the very building whence they all began their journey to me in Balls Falls. I was deeply moved at the thought of it, I confess it freely. But I was determined to resist the temptation to stand in the street gaping up at the soaring roof lines like some artless rustic, and so I broke with my reverie and levelled my eyes. The volume of traffic, both vehicular and pedestrian, on Yonge Street was overwhelming and, as on Front Street, there was a veritable army of bicycles passing by. I had read that over eighteen thousand of the species existed in Toronto but at the time I had not fully grasped the implications of that number. Iron steeds jockeyed by wheel-men in natty costumes and wheel-women in the most modish of cycling garbs seemed to be everywhere. Indeed I was quite certain I saw one bicyclette sporting the latest in bloomer cycling-costume, and from a rearmost vantage point it was a most interesting spectacle, I must say. I was tempted to walk down Yonge Street the better to soak up the bustle and go of the city but I knew that inaction could not be a part of my programme. I therefore hailed a passing hansom cab and before long I espied the Queen's famous golden cupola. What a majestic sight! As we passed the east garden with its chevalier lawns and huge ornamental fountain, I saw a dozen or more guests playing croquet while other persons strolled the carefully tended gravel walks. My cab drew to the curb and the hotel's liveried doorman—resplendent in red cape and black silk topper—escorted me through the massive doorway into the sumptuous world of The Queen's Hotel. Here was truly an island of luxury and privilege befitting the highest class of person. The foyer was panelled in deep red mahogany and a massive staircase fully eight feet wide swept majestically up to a second-floor gallery. Perched in this gallery, a string quartet played soothing airs while, high above them, a crowning dome of multicoloured glass acted as one enormous jewel, casting a rainbow of coloured light throughout the grand hall and over all persons there assembled. Plush oriental carpets silenced footfalls and, scattered amidst the palms and marble columns, elegantly attired guests seated on ottomans and in wing-back chairs were taking tea. This was clearly a hotel for those serious about their comfort, a place of elegance and refinement as opposed to mere showy grandeur. I was, in short, home at last. I squared my shoulders and strode up to the long marble reception counter to present both my card and my compliments.

"Good afternoon. I am Reginald Ravencroft of New York City. My card. You are holding the Red Parlour Suite in readiness for me."

"Yes indeed, Mr. Ravencroft, we most certainly are," responded the short, bespectacled man behind the counter. "Your cousin, Mr. Tweed, has left us in no doubt as to your requirements. I trust you had a pleasant journey from New York, sir?"

"My trip was tedious, thank you, but mercifully it is very nearly at an end."

"Quite so. Will you please honour us by signing the register, Mr. Ravencroft?"

"Of course."

He turned a most handsome register to face me and handed me a fine gold-mounted fountain pen which I instantly recognized as being the latest model in Waterman's "Ideal" line, advertised so regularly in all the finer magazines. As I entered my signature in the noble Queen's tome I saw that I was in a conspicuously small minority of guests stopping without a personal maid or valet in tow, for the words "and servant" appeared after nearly every guest's signature. I also noted that midway down the page a rather singular guest had registered—one William Shakespeare and lady, Stratford upon Avon. For some reason I found it comforting to know that there was a wicked wag lurking among the respectable class within. The clerk thanked me for signing the register and then inquired as to whether my valet would be seeing to my bags.

"Alas no," I said, my mind revolving. "Owing to my man's rather untimely contraction of typhoid fever I have been forced to travel unattended, and for the time being I fear I shall simply have to struggle on alone. Here are my luggage checks."

"Very good, sir, we shall fetch your bags without delay," he said as he handed the brass checks to one of two smartly garbed young lads wearing red fez hats who had silently appeared from I know not where. To the other lad he said: "Mr. Ravencroft is in the Red Parlour Suite."

Suddenly a thought occurred. "Excuse me, can you tell me if Madame Sarah Bernhardt is honouring your hotel with her presence?"

"Oh yes, Mr. Ravencroft. I am delighted to say that Madame Bernhardt is stopping with us. She is occupying the Green Suite directly above your suite, as a matter of fact."

"Capital! I bear greetings to extend to her from Mr. Oscar Wilde, the playwright."

The youth scooped up my alligator club bag and La Divine's portrait and led the way towards the "elevator". Naturally I had read the notice in *The Globe* of the installation of this contraption a year or more earlier. It was described as being a steam-powered perpendicular railway intersecting each storey and consisting essentially of a rising room designed to convey skyward the upward-bound and earthward the descending without excessive labour to mortal muscle. Upon entering the ornate metal cage I was greeted by a middle-aged man in a natty plum-coloured outfit whom I took to be the machine operator. He immediately pointed out to me that the plush-covered bench therein was provided that I might repose during transit, and having deposited me safely on the third floor he assured me that his "elevator" was available for use at all hours of the day or night.

The upper hallways of the Queen's formed a luxurious maze of turns and levels, with rich red Turkish carpeting, cherry-wood panelling, and marvellous stained-glass windows at many of the turnings. In fact so maze-like were they, it occurred to me that I might in future have need of the compass watch fob adorning my abdomen in order to locate my suite. I remarked upon the complexity of the layout to my young guide and he divulged that he carried a small map pressed flat to the interior crown of his fez to meet any moments of confusion to which he himself was prone. Nonetheless in due time (and without recourse to his map) he guided me to the door of my famous suite and deposited me therein.

The Red Parlour Suite was exactly as I had seen it depicted in artist's sketches. The walls of the spacious parlour were covered in a rich ruby-red wallpaper and the complementing rose of the thick carpet was echoed in the heavy velvet drapes. A most commodious velvet-covered settee faced an arched fireplace of white marble, while above this an oil painting of Sir John A. Macdonald looked down upon the room. A bouquet of glorious red roses graced the surface of a fine mahogany desk with delicate porcelain *objets d'art* displayed in the glass-fronted shelves above it. I could not help but feel honoured to number among the guests that the hotel management trusted not to pilfer any of these undoubtedly priceless *objets*.

The bedchamber beckoned and here, opposite another arched white marble fireplace, I discovered a canopied four-poster bed hung with folds of lush purple velvet. All of the other fine pieces of furniture in the room—the bureau, vanity, washstand, and shaving stand—all were constructed of elaborately carved mahogany and topped with white marble. I felt a sudden urge to strip to the buff and climb into the magnificent bed just to revel in the luxury of it all, but I told myself no, hold fast, Ravencroft, all in good time. A second door led to a smaller but nonetheless opulent room which I assumed was designed to be either one's servant's room or one's dressing room. It would of course serve as the latter for me.

I returned to the lovely Red Parlour and was drawn irresistibly to the deep bay window, with its wicker table and comfortable green velvet armchair, and as the lace curtains fluttered I filled my lungs with the sweet-smelling breezes coming off the harbour. The brilliant blue waters of Lake Ontario were dotted with the huge white sails of trading ships and the smaller sails of private yachts. How many hundreds of hours, I asked myself, did Sir John A. Macdonald sit in this very chair gazing out over the bay as I am now? Did Oscar Wilde find this view to his liking? I looked at the pretty wicker table at my elbow and thought: he may well have composed a poem or jotted down a line of dialogue for his next play on this table. He sat in this very chair, slept in that princely bed. This is hallowed ground. Tomorrow morning I will take my breakfast in this fine nook. In all candour, I was barely able to restrain a sudden impulse to let fly with a "whoopee!" like some half-demented ranch hand, but instead I merely said, "Yes, I fancy this suite will suit me admirably."

Just then I heard a bump on the ceiling overhead and I realized that La Divine was undoubtedly now in residence and a mere thirteen or fourteen feet above me. What was she doing? Was she rehearsing her lines or was she changing her clothes preparatory to taking some rest in her coffin? Perhaps, despite her furs, she was still cold. What if I heard a knock on my door and La Divine came sweeping into the room?

"Hello darling, please forgive a lonely French woman for disturbing you, but I am zo desperate. I have burned all ze furniture in my suite but mahogany does not throw much heat and my rooms are still cold."

"La Divine Sarah, I worship you! Please, take all the wood I possess. Indeed, take anything you desire. Perhaps you would like to burn my luggage. Egad, I would offer myself as fuel if I were not such a malodorous combustible."

"But mon cher, that will not be necessary. I will simply stay here with you. We will be zo warm together in your bed and I will be no bother."

She let her fur cloak slip from her shoulders and stood before me, half bent in supplication, wearing nothing save a transparent lace. A knock sounded at my door and I discovered the young lad who had been sent to Union Station to retrieve my bags standing in the hall with same. I gave him what I deemed to be a generous gratuity and it suddenly occurred to me that I had yet to send a telegram to my uncles informing them of my safe arrival. The boy directed me to a sheaf of telegram forms in a pigeon-hole of the mahogany desk, and a moment later he was on his way to dispatch my missive assuring my uncles that I was safely ensconced in the Arlington Hotel. Uncle Harold's underlined warning in *Tricks on Travellers* came back to me and I briefly considered depositing my money in the hotel safe, but then I thought no, one cannot predict when the opportunity to purchase a theatre ticket might arise, and I was not about to get caught short of cash. The young lad's arrival had been doubly fortunate in that it had also served to break the spell La Divine had cast over me and I thought once again of my mission. First things first, Ravencroft, I said to myself, unpack your bags so as to avoid wrinkles and secondly—arm yourself. I completed my first task in record time and set out in search of a revolver.

I knew from their frequent advertisements in the *Star* that Aikenhead's hardware emporium carried a full line of firearms and thus it was to this establishment that I directed my cabby to convey me. Aikenhead's turned out to be a full three storeys high, and when I finally located the armament department I discovered a large chamber with its walls positively peppered with rifles and revolvers of every possible description. An affable young clerk approached me, and when I confessed to a certain amount of indecision he pointed out that all their guns were recommended for accurate and handy shooting but that, if I could tell him for what particular purpose I needed a gun, he could recommend the most appropriate model for my needs. This query rather put me on the spot, and I found myself weaving a long tale about being a diamond salesman who frequently travelled abroad. I told him, among other things, that my wife was of a nervous disposition and was insisting that I acquire a revolver despite the fact that I was known for my pugilistic skills. The young clerk said he had to agree with my good wife that a gun was unsurpassable as a prophylactic against malefactors, and I soon found myself purchasing a light-weight .22-calibre specimen with "Defender" stamped upon it, and a box of one hundred bullets.

I exited Aikenhead's hardware emporium with my lethal paper parcel under my arm and turned without delay towards The Queen's Hotel. I had taken but a few steps, however, when suddenly a middle-aged woman both dubious and dirty took hold of my arm in a most familiar manner.

"Looking for something saucy, dearie?" said she, winking at me broadly and licking her lips.

I was badly startled and tried to pull away from the woman but she suddenly kissed me full on the lips and ventured a familiarity with her hand.

"Let me go!" I cried and this time succeeded in breaking her hold. Still, she persisted in her attempt to overwhelm me.

"Come on, dearie, cop your cherry? Give a girl a thrill."

The woman's love-apples were spilling out of her blouse and quivering like fine jellies, but despite her physical attributes I was determined to resist her entreaty. "Certainly not, madam!" I cried. "Get away from me or I shall call a constable!"

The woman did not take kindly to my threat and, before melting into the surging populace around us, favoured me with a string of filthy oaths the likes of which I had not heard theretofore. For my part, I was fairly in a daze and simply continued walking in the direction of the Queen's, attempting to regain my composure. Of course I had read extensively about "cruisers"—girls in the streets in search of custom—but this being my first encounter with one of them, I was rather shaken by the event—I admit it freely. A line from Carveth's *Rogues and Rogueries of Toronto* came to mind: "They sally forth by both day and night producing atrocious and singular scenes out in the street." She undoubtedly wished me to accompany her to some upholstered sewer and home of vice unspeakable, the better to rob me. *If she had not already!* For the second time that day, I shot my hand inside my coat and discovered—to my intense relief— that my envelope and my watch were still affixed to my person. Of course there was also the possibility that she maintained a plain room thereabouts and, had I accompanied her, we would simply have enjoyed love's seraphic act together, and for a moment I wondered if perhaps—but then my reason returned and I remembered the vow I made to La Divine every night kneeling before her coffin, to save myself for the finest *fille de joie* in the most exclusive sporting house of which Toronto could boast and, by dint of exhaustive tutelage therein, become a lover of astounding accomplishments. Certainly I did not see how rotting of the pox given to me by a street cruiser could be considered a part of that agenda.

When at last I passed once again through the doors into the stately Queen's Hotel, I discovered the massive lobby to be much more lively than when I had left it. A large crowd of men, mainly of advanced years and all very prosperous-looking, were milling around and talking to one another in a highly animated fashion. Indeed the string quartet in the gallery was barely audible over the babble of voices, and as I made my way through the throng I noticed that many of them were conversing in foreign languages. I was still somewhat shaken by my run-in with the cruiser woman, and in consequence I felt disinclined to cope with anything anxiety-provoking, so I elected to abjure the elevator and use the stairs to reach my suite. Nothing out of the common occurred until I reached the third-floor landing and my nose detected a scent so unusual and wondrous as to be not of this earth. I was instantly mesmerized by its pungent aroma and, no longer able to call my will my own, I began climbing the stairs to the uppermost floor—the floor on which I knew La Divine's suite was to be found. I reached the top of the stairs and found myself drawn through the maze of corridors until, without warning, I rounded a corner and found myself nose to nose with a gigantic Negro. He stood fully seven feet in height, with his massive black arms folded across his bare chest. His head was crowned by a tremendous yellow turban while ballooning orange trousers and a huge pair of Persian slippers with upturned points completed his fantastic ensemble. As I stood gaping like a hayseed, the Negro remained motionless save for his two huge eyes that swivelled in their sockets and transfixed me like two pins through a zoological specimen. I had never seen a Negro before—other than in magazines. The air was heavy with the pungent perfume that had drawn me and I heard the screech and chatter of a parrot from behind the door he guarded. After a time I found my voice and for some reason stammered: "Thank you very much sir," before turning on my heels and beating a hasty retreat back in the direction whence I had come. After a prolonged search I eventually found the stairs, and after an even more prolonged search, located my own suite. I had of course read of La Divine's famous bodyguard, but different articles offered different versions of how the Negro came to be in her service. One story had it that while on safari hunt in Africa, she had found him dying in the jungle of snake bite and nursed him back to health. Another claimed she had captured him in a tiger trap and domesticated him. What was certain was that while in Africa, La Divine had obtained a perfume which possessed an aphrodisiacal power, owing to the fact that the scent incorporated the ground-up testicles of a lion. My nostrils and clothes were now permeated with this same perfume, and I suddenly found myself in a pronounced state of bestial agitation and began thinking of the street cruiser woman's love apples. This image quickly rendered me highly vulnerable to a certain temptation, and as my imaginings became more and more wildly erotic in nature I began alternately dwelling on the cruiser and La Divine. In brief, my outrageous lust having been unleashed, I threw myself upon the velvet settee in front of the fireplace and, while Sir John A. Macdonald, the founder of our great Dominion, looked down upon me, I took my John Henry firmly in hand and abused myself with a will. After a very brief time a boiling flood of relief overtook me and I fell back exhausted. Of course I was immediately ashamed of my deviant behaviour—especially when I thought of the illustrious former occupants of the suite and the momentous decisions taken in that very room profoundly affecting Canadian history—perhaps even on that very settee—but in my defence it had to be said that La Divine's aphrodisiacal perfume had forced me to commit the vile act, and I could not help myself.

As I lay back against the cushions I took stock of my situation. I was now armed with both a revolver and a rock-hard determination to witness La Divine's performance the following night at any cost. Therefore it was absolutely imperative that I find a joy palace that very night. Unfortunately I possessed no idea where to find such a place, and in this regard my Toronto guidebooks were useless to me. As I did up my trouser-fly buttons, my only thought was that perhaps a newsboy or, better still, a savvy barman, could direct me to the proper establishment. I resolved to first put La Divine's portrait up in place of Sir John A.'s now rather reproachful gaze, and then take myself off to the Queen's bar-room and, with any luck, its knowledgeable barman.

CHAPTER V

A MEDICAL CONSULTATION OF SORTS

I opened the stout oak door to the Royal Canadian Room and left the lofty opulence of the hotel lobby for the warmth of the famous bar-room. A massive stone fireplace with logs acrackling dominated the room while mellow pine panelling and amber-shaded wall lamps did much to enhance the wonderfully cosy effect in the rustic retreat. I took up a position at the opulent mahogany bar counter and tried to think of the correct manner in which to initiate my indelicate inquiry with the barman. He was busy taking orders from several gentlemen paying their devotions to King Alcohol at the far end of the bar so I had a moment to ponder the problem. I could hardly just come right out and ask him directly, and presumably I ought to offer him a gratuity. A spontaneous check of my appearance in the magnificent mirror behind the bar counter was less than encouraging, for despite my height and fine Imperial, for some strange reason I suddenly looked alarmingly young, and it occurred to me that the barman might not even serve me an alcoholic beverage much less tell me where I might find a superb joy palace. I cursed myself for not having thought my approach through beforehand in the calm of my suite. Had I done so I might even have had a few notes jotted down to guide me.

"Good evening sir. What may I get you?" asked the barman.

Caught off guard and unprepared, I looked at him in confusion. Then over his shoulder I spotted a sign reading:

ROYAL CANADIAN ROOM
HOME OF THE TIMBER DOODLE

"I'll try one of your Timber Doodles if you please, barman," I responded. I was hoping it would take him a minute or two to concoct my Timber Doodle so as to give me valuable thinking time but he merely filled a glass with an amber liquid from a brass spigot and all I could think of to say was "Thank you so much." I had never tasted a Timber Doodle before and upon my first sip I was very pleasantly surprised to find it to be of a delicious, fruity character. Indeed it was so sweet and tasty that I wondered if I had inadvertently ordered a teetotal drink available to slake the thirst of the more pious guests in the hotel. (In retrospect, however, I need not have bothered my head over this.) I was quite cross with myself for having lost my opportunity to question the man and I saw that the only thing to do was to down my drink and attract his attention with my empty glass. I suited action to the word and moments later the barman placed a full glass before me. It was clearly time to make my move.

"Thank you so, much barman," I began. "But excuse me, I was wondering, I am newly arrived from New York City, indeed this is my first visit to Toronto and a thought just struck me. In the manner of by the by and so forth, I was wondering if you might be able to direct me to a high-class house."

"House, sir?" queried the man. "How do you mean, sir?"

"Well," I said winking broadly, "a place where ladies of good address like to meet gentleman of ditto, if you see what I mean."

I winked again. He stood there puzzled for a moment before the dawn of understanding finally broke through upon him.

"Oh," he exclaimed in full voice, clearly delighted with himself, "a brothel?"

I blanched. "Yes, but only of the very highest class."

"No sir," he said matter-of-factly. "No idea at all. But there are plenty of street girls to service you. I would suggest Wellington Street. It's just a few streets over from the hotel."

Inwardly I cursed the oaf for being so maddeningly obtuse. "No no, as I told you, I am only interested in a very high-class establishment—a joy palace if you will."

"Oh well, in that case, I'm afraid I can't help you, sir."

"I see, well, perhaps I won't bother. It is of no consequence. Thank you anyway."

The barman nodded and strode off to tend to his thirsty patrons. For my part I could not get away from the ignoramus fast enough and beat a hasty retreat to the comfort of one of the wing-back chairs placed throughout the room. Was it really possible that I had over-estimated the prevalence of such houses in Toronto, or was it that I had under-estimated their exclusiveness? I noted that my brow was bedewed and my hands were clammy. I wondered whom else I might ask. Dare I risk humiliating myself with a waiter? Or, I wondered, should I seek out the street and a savvy newsboy? Time was passing and I was floundering. To add to my agitation, I noticed that a burly old buffer in a long white beard was staring at me intently from across the room. Clearly a relic from the hirsute sixties, his beard covered the better part of his shirt front and his white hair sprang up and out in all directions. A stubby briar pipe projected from amidst his white whiskers and his moustache was stained a rather disgusting mahogany colour. He looked, in sum, like a rather demented Santa Claus. I noted a row of glasses on the table in front of him and looked away, determined to ignore the old inebriate and get back to the problem at hand. It occurred to me that I should have flashed a dime at the barman before asking my question. But then again, the doorman of the hotel might be a more "educated" person. I stole a glance back in the old coot's direction and discovered that he was still staring at me. I held his gaze for a moment in hopes of forcing him to look away in embarrassment, but to my annoyance his eyes remained fixed full upon me. Damn his drunken impudence! I thought to myself. Why do people always bother one when one is most in need of calm? Action was demanded and, without deigning to look at the fellow, I swiftly transferred my person to the chair on the opposite side of the table, thus rewarding his vulgarity with a view of my back. There now, I told myself, he will simply have to find some other unwilling subject for his impertinence. Now back to the problem at hand. The more I thought on it, the more I liked the idea of moving on to the Queen's doorman and making inquiries of him.

"Enjoying your libation, Mr. Dill?" asked a superior-sounding voice.

I looked up with a start and discovered standing beside me the aforementioned white bush of beard, with two strange eyes peering out of it. He had startled me badly and in any case I was in no mood to humour a drunken sot who, it was now obvious, thought I was someone I was not.

"Now see here," I said with authority, "I do not know who you are, nor do I care to. My name is not Dill and whether I am or am not enjoying my libation is none of your concern. Good day to you, sir."

"Come now, young man," he persisted, "do not take that tone with me. I know you to be Mr. Jeremiah Dill—my former patient in the Provincial Lunatic Asylum."

This was too much to bear. The old dotard had mistaken me for not only another person but a lunatic into the bargain. I was insulted and I did not disguise the fact.

"Certainly not, sir. You have mistaken my identity. I am Reginald Ravencroft, newly removed from the city of New York in the United States of America. Now kindly remove yourself from my presence or I shall be forced to call the barman."

The expression on the old man's face altered and for the first time he began to look shaken.

"But, but you must be Dill," he stammered. "That is to say—I can scarcely bring myself to believe it. The resemblance is astonishing. Oh my stars and garters, what have I done? And staring at you into the bargain! Oh dear, I am most dreadfully sorry, sir. Please may I presume to intrude for just one small moment more that I may explain my atrocious conduct to you?"

The poor man looked so alarmed and confused by his mistake and so very eager to make things right between us that I did not have the heart to refuse his request.

"Yes of course," I said. "Pray, be seated."

"Permit me to introduce myself, I am Doctor Marmaduke Dandy. My card."

"Thank you, doctor," I said, accepting his card and

presenting him in turn with one of mine. His card confirmed his identity.

DOCTOR M. DANDY
CHIEF ALIENIST
PROVINCIAL LUNATIC ASYLUM
TORONTO ONTARIO

I looked up at the worthy doctor and found him to be preparing to read my card by adjusting a pair of gold pince-nez upon his rather large nose, which possessed the rosy red hue and pronounced blue veins characteristic of the confirmed tippler. He was sketched on a generous plan and his waistcoat boasted many strands of pipe tobacco and assorted other wayward particles of unknown origin. I further noted that there were extensive notations in black ink on both his shirt cuffs. Indeed his entire person very much reflected the card he had given me—well worn, creased, and spotty—and I thought to myself that, if he were an eccentric old alienist in a novel by Mr. Dickens, his name would be Doctor Battyspots or some such appellation.

"Dear me, I hardly know where to begin my explanation," he said. "You see, it is all to do with my photographs. That is to say . . . no, wait, I shall begin at the beginning. As you have learned from my card, I am the chief alienist at the Provincial Lunatic Asylum here in Toronto. Are you acquainted with the science of physiognomy, sir?"

I responded in the negative.

"No, I suspected not, but do not be embarrassed by your ignorance for it is a science in its infancy. Physiognomy is the study of human character through facial configuration. I have devoted my life to the exploration of the well-known sympathy which exists between the diseased brain and the features of the face. Indeed I have this very afternoon given a paper in the ball-room of this hotel on the physiognomy of insanity. There is a convention of alienists here at the Queen's, you see."

I recalled the large group of foreign-speaking gentlemen I had seen earlier in the lobby.

"Professor Hesse of Vienna was the main speaker—he was expounding on the theories of Doctor Sigmund Freud—but I was asked to deliver a small paper on the application of photography to the physiognomic phenomena of insanity. And that is where you and the wretched Jeremiah Dill come into the picture."

"Doctor Dandy, are you saying that I possess the identical facial configurations as a madman?"

"No no—or at least—if you would but look at his photograph you would see that, while the truly telling features are in no way alike, still, from a distance and under this dim lighting, you do bear a superficial resemblance to Mr. Dill. I have it just here, his was one of the case studies I used to illustrate my paper."

And so saying he delved into a worn leather satchel and spilled out a mass of photographs onto the table. One glance at the pictures told me what a frightfully deranged crew they were. Wild, staring eyes, slavering mouths, running noses, hair standing up in sharp spikes, they were all raving mad.

"Here they are, sir, my poor lunatics, victims of outrageous lust, every man jack of them."

"Indeed," I said. "How so?"

"How so? Well sir, perhaps you are not aware of it, but it is a scientific fact that concupiscence, or lust, is at the base of all insanity. That is to say, either the giving into or the denial of lust is at the root of it all."

I blanched as I recalled the dreadful scene in my Red Parlour Suite less than an hour earlier, when I had been forced to relieve my throbbing organ on the settee under the disapproving gaze of our great nation's founder.

"Ah yes, here is the unfortunate sexual monomaniac Mr. Jeremiah Dill," said Doctor Dandy as he extracted a single photograph from amongst its ghastly fellows. "Before I show you his photograph, the examination of which I hope will explain my impertinence and gain your forgiveness, perhaps I should briefly recount his psychopathological history, and then you may judge for yourself my contention that his facial configuration corresponds to his insanity. By the way, would you allow me to order you another drink, Mr. Ravencroft?"

"Yes, by all means," I replied, "very good of you. I am drinking Timber Doodles."

The old doctor ordered my Timber Doodle and a double scotch whisky for himself and they arrived forthwith. He downed his whisky in a single draught and, thus fortified, launched into his most unusual narrative.

"I should begin by telling you that young Mr. Dill is the son of one of the most prosperous merchants in this city. As a lad of sixteen years, he was known to be clever, well mannered, a conscientious Christian, and assiduous in his studies at no less an institution of learning than Upper Canada College. In short, sir, he was in every way a very promising young man—that is, up until one short year ago, when, without warning, he began to go to the bad."

"Indeed," I said as I took a gulp of my drink.

"His deterioration was as swift as it was alarming. Uncharacteristic tardiness was closely followed by a cessation of churchgoing and increasingly vitriolic back-chat. It became known that he had taken to frequenting disreputable billiard parlours. Then it was discovered that he had been writing letters very improper in both sentiment and language to female friends of his good sisters, who naturally were wholly mortified by their brother's behaviour. Soon he was no longer differentiating between young and old females, and he once went so far as to suggest to a dowager acquaintance of his sainted mother that she should visit him in his bedchamber that they might be naughty together. In short, he was rapidly developing the rutting instincts of a goat. His inhibitions continued to weaken and correspondingly his lustfulness strengthened until finally he took to exposing his naked person to the atmosphere in general, and outraged female passers-by in particular."

"Great God!" I exclaimed.

"At that point the constabulary intervened and he was forcibly brought to me at the asylum. From the moment he was placed in my care his condition deteriorated rapidly. After some months this period of licentious excitement left him and a profound melancholy supervened."

"Are you saying, doctor, that he was bitterly disappointed at having remained virginal?"

"That I cannot say, sir. In all events, under a regimen of cold baths and the inhalation of nitrate of amyl I was successful in rousing him from his stupor, and three months ago he was released under the supervision of the Dills' personal physician and a private-duty nurse. That in a nutshell, if you will forgive the pun, is the history of the man you are about to see. Here, sir, cast your eyes on the unhappy Mr. Jeremiah Dill."

And so saying, with a flourish that I found wholly inappropriate, Doctor Dandy laid my "twin's" photograph before me. I do not consider myself unduly vain, but my lord, the horribly leering face that greeted my inspection! Such ruttish eyes! That satanic grin! I could not help but wonder, had I observed my own face in a mirror whilst abusing myself in my suite, would such an embodiment of salacious rage have returned my gaze? I dared not dwell on the thought.

"Well, Mr. Ravencroft, what say you, are not the perturbations which rampageous lust produces in the human physiognomy clearly evident? Of course, I admit now that your resemblance is quite slight, but sir, in all candour, raise your cheekbones but one half of one inch and narrow the eyes by one quarter of one inch and I would swear in a court of law that you were a sexual deviate or, at the least, a young man of prodigious lustfulness."

"Is that so?"

"I hope I have not offended you and, looking on the bright side, I think you will agree that while the photograph shows Mr. Dill to be clearly demented, it is also quite evident that he is the son of gentry. The discerning eye can read the unmistakable signs of pedigreed personage on his countenance—as can one see it in your own fine face, sir."

"Yes, quite."

"Perhaps you are shocked at the suggestion that the wealthy class is no less prone to insanity than their lessers. Of course there is a greater percentage of the unfortunate class to be found in public asylums, but I assure you the wits of the wealthy are no less disposed to go wandering than those of the poor—oh no, if anything quite the reverse is true. No, you see, the wealthy have the means to use private asylums or keep their demented family members incarcerated at home in hopes of preventing their good family name from being tainted with madness. Oh yes, I speak with first-hand knowledge and I tell you candidly, sir, the attics and basements of the rich in the Dominion of Canada from sea to sea are fairly bursting with demented relatives."

I signalled the waiter for another round of drinks.

"And you say it is all caused by lust?" I ventured.

"Young man, in my opinion the Canadian people as a whole and Torontonians in particular are the most lustful group of people known to science. And yet the ignorance of the righteous Torontonians remains steadfast. They still believe that when one refers to

Toronto as "Clubland" one is speaking only of such august institutions as the Toronto Club, and the Albany. The good and pious Torontonians are fools, sir! Such names as the Queen of Hearts and the House of All Nations are entirely unknown to them."

Suddenly my interest in the eccentric doctor increased many-fold. Good grief, I thought to myself, have I found my "savvy barman"? "Heavens, doctor," I said with feigned outrage. "Surely you are not referring to houses of ill repute!"

"Am I not, sir? By thunder, I most certainly am."

"Do you mean to tell me that you have visited these places? You know their actual locations and customs?" I ventured hopefully.

"I do, sir, and I fear you would be dreadfully shocked and appalled were I to tell all concerning the vice resorts to be found in this city."

"Oh, but really, doctor, I can hardly credit it. I mean to say, Toronto is known internationally for her saintliness. Indeed my guidebook informs me that she is known as The City of Churches."

"Churches, sir? Oh, there are many churches and necessarily many clergymen, but let me tell you this, you would be disgusted at the numbers of their fraternity—and mark you, not just the Methodists—whose outrageous lusts become completely unbridled and must needs be confined. As we speak, sir, I count no fewer than seven demented men of the cloth presently searching in vain for their wits in the Provincial Lunatic Asylum. Count them, sir, *seven!* I will spare you the ghastly details concerning the clergymen's daughters I have in my care."

"I am horrified, doctor. Shall we have another drink?"

Doctor Dandy assented with enthusiasm and I signalled the waiter. It occurred to me that the good doctor was clearly in his cups and, truth to tell, for the past while I had felt myself becoming increasingly tiddly, as if the Timber Doodles were capable of producing a delayed effect upon a person.

"But doctor," I continued, "do tell me more about these purple parlours. Why are they not closed down by the authorities?"

"Ah sir, now you have hit upon it. You have correctly surmised that the saintly city fathers cannot be wholly ignorant of these romping rendezvous and you query why they tolerate their existence. The answer is this: the pious leaders of our community do not raid these houses and arrest the wanton ladies and all therein for the simple reason that they would be arresting themselves!"

"You cannot mean it, sir!" I protested.

Doctor Dandy glanced about him as if spies might be lurking behind his wing-chair and then, leaning in towards me, spoke in a low, conspiratorial tone heavy with whisky fumes.

"Sir, I am talking about a select clientele boasting lords of industry, captains of commerce, princes of politics, to say nothing of the crowned heads of Europe and a bevy of English nobility who are wont to honour the finest houses with their presence when stopping in this city."

"Never!" I cried, just as the waiter appeared with our drinks.

The doctor downed his whisky once again in a single draught and I took a good long pull at my Timber Doodle.

"Do you know, sir," Doctor Dandy continued—clearly warming to his lewd topic, "there is one such purple parlour that has the confounded cheek to call itself The House of Moral Elevation? Oh, it is most certainly dedicated to the process of elevation, but it is hardly the morals of its members which it seeks to raise. And listen here, what would you say to a certain school I know of known as The School of Venus? Oh, do not trouble to consult the Board of Education directory, for it is not an institution of learning for which the divine scholar Reverend Egerton Ryerson would take credit."

"Sir, I will not do it," I said earnestly.

To my surprise the doctor then picked up my glass and casually drained the remainder of my Timber Doodle. He paused, seemingly gauging the seeping effect of the drink on his digestion, and then burst forth.

"Great God in heaven, man, we are talking about mansions in which sexual circuses are nightly enjoyed! Daisy Chains, Monkey Parades, games of 'boxcar'—you recall that in railway parlance freight cars are routinely coupled and uncoupled—good lord, sir, waiter girls and lewd theatricals all combining to create atrocious and singular scenes in a perpetual festival of vice!"

"Doctor I dare not believe it!"

At this point Doctor Dandy announced that he was off to the gents', and thus I had a moment alone in which to think—albeit through a mind swimming in Timber Doodles. I had no desire to linger with the strange doctor but I dared not lose this living encyclopedia of all that was lewd and depraved in Toronto. By the time he returned to his seat—weaving rather badly, I may say—I had decided upon a course of action.

"Sir," I began, "I am no end indebted to you for your most illuminating discourse on the lust of Toronto, which I find fascinating. That is to say, appalling and fascinating—from a scientific point of view—and I would like very much to repay you in some small way. Now, doctor, I am given to understand that the meals in the Maple Leaf Room here in the hotel are of a most appetizing and enjoyable character, and I wonder, would you do me the honour of dining with me?"

Doctor Dandy thought this an excellent idea and immediately consented with enthusiasm. He stuffed his hideous photographs back in his satchel, rose unsteadily to his feet, and then to my horror fell straight to the floor—landing on his posterior. I sprang to my feet, or rather attempted to spring to my feet, for in so doing I caught my foot on the table leg nearest me and I too landed on the floor of the Royal Canadian Room. Fortunately a passing waiter was kind enough to raise us both to our feet and we set out arm in arm in search of the restaurant. It had become all too clear to me that we were both in an advanced state of self-induced illumination.

The Maple Leaf Room—into which ladies were not permitted—represented the quintessence of baronial splendour, with its mahogany panelling and crystal gaseliers and huge oil paintings depicting picturesque galleons on gale-swept seas. We were seated without delay and a Negro waiter wearing white gloves appeared at our side, eager to do our bidding. The doctor, apparently a habitué of the establishment, did not trouble himself to consult his menu.

"They do a very fine porterhouse steak here in the Maple Leaf," he said rather thickly. "I most heartily recommend it to you. It is an ode to Chateaubriand himself, and, come to think of it, I generally start with the fresh trout."

I agreed immediately to his choice and watched in dismay as he summoned the wine steward.

"I have more than just passing familiarity with the Queen's cellars, Mr. Ravencroft," he said, "so perhaps you would like me to order the wines?"

I answered in the affirmative and the steward, replete with noble chain of office, arrived within mere seconds, wine card in hand.

"Good evening to you, steward," said Doctor Dandy. "I have no need of the wine card, thank you. Please be so good as to bring us a Richebourg '69 with the fish and two bottles of the

Pommard '70 with our steaks."

As we were waiting for our meal the doctor asked me if I knew Toronto well. I deemed it wise to play the ignoramus and responded in the negative.

"Well then, sir," he said. "Understand this: Yonge Street runs north up from the lake and cleaves the city in twain. That is the key to navigating this town, do you see? Knowing where Yonge Street is."

"Yes, quite," I said.

Our trout arrived at that moment and I tucked into the first morsel of food I had seen all day. Indeed we both became so absorbed in consuming what turned out to be a glorious meal that scarcely a word passed between us. The wines proved to be of such extraordinary character that I could only sit back and marvel at their beauty and grace. This was of course my initiation into the world of fine wines, and I can only say that the Richebourg '69 and Pommard '70 will for ever live on in my memory. I declined a dessert while Doctor Dandy ordered a bottle of Sandeman '63 port and, appropriately enough, tipsy-cake—a healthy percentage of which found its way into his beard. Finally he downed his fork once and for all.

"Well now, there," he said, "an excellent meal and some very sound wines to boot. I thank you most heartily, Mr. Ravencroft, for your hospitality. A very nice drop of port, do you not agree, sir?"

As it happened, I liked the warm glow produced by the fine old port very much indeed, and found myself draining my glass several times. Doctor Dandy had been looking decidedly hazy for some time, and I was intrigued as he nonchalantly rested his elbow on the table with his head in his hand and commenced staring hard at the table before him in a form of stupor. I spoke his name but to my dismay his eyes slowly closed and several staccato snores erupted from his nostrils. I signalled wildly for the waiter.

"Strong coffee please, waiter," I said. "Quick as you can."

The waiter favoured me with a knowing smile. "Of course, sir. And may I suggest a little brandy?"

"Well, I hardly think brandy is called for at this point, do you?" I said, aghast at his inappropriate suggestion.

"Well sir, if I may be permitted to say so, I have had the honour of serving the good doctor many times and I have often observed that brandy has a marvellous restorative effect upon him."

Obviously I was not about to argue with the fellow. The

coffee and brandy arrived forthwith and, sure enough Doctor Dandy was fully conscious once again very soon thereafter. To my joy, he asked me what we had been discussing.

"Brothels," I said. "The outrageously wicked brothels to be found in Toronto. Tell me, doctor, of all the many you have visited, is there one in particular that stands out in your mind?"

Doctor Dandy paused to consider my question before answering. "Not three blocks from where we now sit stands a vice resort known as The Cloister, wherein venal divinities, under the direction of a licentious abbess, regularly partake in orgies of the most bacchanalian description and immorality of such heinous character it makes my hair stand on end just to think of it."

"My word!" I exclaimed.

"Once, upon entering the vestibule of The Cloister, what singular and atrocious sight met my eyes? Can you guess it, sir?"

"Doctor, I cannot."

"A woman, comely and fully formed, completely naked, sitting casually in a velvet armchair, wearing nothing save a lewd grin."

"Never!"

"Then sir, then, as I stepped forward, in the dim light of a single candle I noted a large carrot and two potatoes arranged in her lap in a manner so highly suggestive as to leave none save a dullard in doubt as to their symbolism!"

"My God, doctor, what did you do?"

"Do, sir? What did I do? Why, I passed in to continue my research, that is what I did. I am a medical man and surely not of so weak a disposition as to be frightened away by an arrangement of vegetables—no matter how depraved that arrangement may be."

The doctor paused to light his pipe and I saw my chance.

"Doctor Dandy," I said with as much authority as I could muster. "A plan has just hatched fully formed in my mind which my Christian conscience will not allow me to ignore no matter what personal perils it may involve. I, Reginald Ambrose Ravencroft, hereby do solemnly undertake to convey, to all the Toronto vice resorts to which you can direct me, a quantity of Bibles which I will personally place in the hand of each and every wanton woman I can locate therein. There, sir, what say you to that?"

Evidently I had succeeded in shocking the doctor, for he chose his words carefully when he responded. "Mr. Ravencroft, I am overwhelmed by your industry and Christian charity but, though it pains me to say it, I must tell you that you would most definitely be wasting your time and money were you to do as you propose."

"Yes, yes. I expected you to say as much, doctor, but I remain determined in my resolve. If I can reach but one wanton woman, just one out of the hundreds, perhaps thousands, that infest this noble city, then I shall count my mission a resounding success. The location of one house and one house only is all I require of you. Perhaps you are right, to visit them all straight off might well be overly ambitious. This "Cloister" sewer in which your sensibilities were outraged by vegetables, it is nearby and sounds like an excellent place to begin. I know my duty and, sir, I shall do it. And by thunder, I shall do it this very night!"

"This very night? You mean now?" he asked incredulously.

"I mean now, sir."

"But have you a spare Bible with you?"

"Of course I do, sir, or at least, I can certainly find one somewhere in this huge hotel."

"But Mr. Ravencroft, I shall be so worried for your virtue, don't you see. How will I know that you have not fallen?"

"Doctor Dandy, I know just what I shall do. I shall write a full description of my salvation attempt and mail it to you so your mind may remain fully at ease."

The light of inspiration suddenly flooded the doctor's face. "You could visit me tomorrow at my asylum!" he cried out gleefully. "That way I could learn first hand of your adventure and I could give you a personally guided tour of my asylum. Would that please you, young sir?"

His invitation, as ghastly as it was unexpected, threw me completely off stride. I had no desire whatsoever to see the living embodiment of his photo subjects and their gruesome fellows but I heard myself saying with great gusto: "I can think of nothing I would like better, doctor. When would be convenient?"

"Why don't you join me when I drive out to the asylum tomorrow morning—say eleven o'clock?"

"Capital, doctor. Capital. I shall look forward to it. Without question. Now then, where is this Cloister sewer to be found?"

The doctor took a long pull at his brandy, hesitated, and then spoke with decision.

"You will find The Cloister on King Street, several doors

west of the corner of King and Simcoe streets."

"North side? South side?"

"North side—but really, I am still not at all sure that this is such a wise idea."

"Tosh, doctor, nothing ventured, nothing gained."

We finished our brandies and, despite the fact that we both encountered some small difficulty in rising from the table, nonetheless we did so unaided and proceeded arm in arm out to the lobby of the hotel. The lobby was crowded with a large group of formally dressed guests and it was while in the midst of this elegant throng that Doctor Dandy remarked casually and yet in a voice loud enough for all to hear, "And do not worry, young sir, you will find no rats issuing forth from the drains to molest you in my asylum."

"No, quite," was the best I could muster as I ushered him towards the exit as rapidly as decorum permitted.

The doorman summoned a hansom cab but just as the doctor was about to climb inside he suddenly turned and seized my arm.

"Take care, young Ravencroft, for God's sake take care. I remain in great fear for your virtue. These harlots know no bounds. They will stop at nothing to have their way with you, and there is no level of debauchery to which they refuse to sink. And mark you, take special care in the company of Cecily. She is a long-legged beauty, sir, with ripe, outsized breasts and flaming red tresses. In Cecily's mind the end justifies the means, and in her case the end will be to create in you a sensation of unparalleled orgiastic ecstasy. I do not believe I can state it more plainly than that. Remain resolute in your resolve. Take care that you do not fall."

"Sir, I shall remain resolute. Of that you may be absolutely certain. Good night to you, Doctor Dandy."

"Very well then. Onward cabby!" he cried.

As I watched the cab disappear down the street, I considered returning to my suite in order to freshen my moustache and under-garments, but, what with the Timber Doodles and various wines I had imbibed, I quite simply did not believe myself capable of locating my suite unassisted in the maze of hallways. I therefore immediately set out on foot for The Cloister. Earlier, when Doctor Dandy had mentioned the location of said joy palace, I had dimly recalled that there was something noteworthy about that particular junction of streets, but owing perhaps to the drink I could not immediately recall its significance. However, as I walked the short distance up York Street and along King to Simcoe Street, I remembered that the four corners of the intersection were populated by St. Andrew's Presbyterian Church, Upper Canada College, Government House, and the British Hotel, and that for that reason Torontonians referred to it as the meeting place of Salvation, Education, Administration, and Perdition. I soon reached this famous junction of streets, but as I paused to get my bearings, my hopes died. Doctor Dandy had said that The Cloister was to be found on the north side of the street, several doors west of the corner, but one glance in that direction told me that the original Upper Canada College building was the only structure on that entire block. The remainder of the block all the way over to John Street was taken up by the old college cricket grounds. Dandy—the drunken sot—had either lied to me or been so befuddled with drink that he got his streets mixed up. I decided to walk over to John Street, just on the remote chance that I was mistaken, but of course I was not. The cricket grounds were overgrown with tall weeds and looked as deserted and lonely as I felt. There was nothing I could do but trudge back towards Simcoe Street, and with each succeeding step my feeling of disappointment turned ever more to one of desperation. I had failed utterly in my quest, and come the following evening in all likelihood I would be either dead or headed to jail, and in either case I would not have participated in love's seraphic act. I felt a surge of anger well up inside me.

"Confound you, Dandy, you drunken imbecile!" I cried aloud.

Aside from Government House there was not a mansion in sight, for pity's sake. I could hear the old fart pontificating: "These houses are mansions, sir. Many are set well back from the street in their own expansive grounds." Suddenly I stood stock still as a thought as bizarre as it was attractive struck me. Was it totally inconceivable that Government House and The Cloister were one and the same? Another snippet of Dandy's conversation came back to me. "Sir, I am talking about a select clientele boasting lords of industry, captains of commerce, princes of politics, to say nothing of the crowned heads of Europe and a bevy of English nobility who are wont to honour the finest houses with their presence when stopping in this city." Was it possible that so august a personage as Sir Alexander Campbell, the Lieutenant-Governor of Ontario, was the proprietor of a joy palace dedicated to satisfying the venal appetites of international nobility and Canada's most prominent citizens? I was torn between wanting it to be so—that I might end my quest—and hating to think that the government of my province should be so debased. Then all of a sudden I realized it could not be the Lieutenant-Governor, for Doctor Dandy had said The Cloister was under the direction of a licentious abbess. But then again that could be Lady Campbell, his good wife, and obviously Sir Alexander would in fact, if not in person, be the boss of the whole disgusting outfit. What audacity! What outrageous cunning! It was preposterous, and yet, the more I thought on it, the more obvious it became. When I had asked the doctor why the authorities did not arrest the inhabitants of the purple parlours, he had said they could not do so because they would be arresting themselves. By God, it was more than just possible, it was a ghastly fact! And furthermore, this explained why he did not give me the precise address. The poor doctor was himself so appalled at his information that he could not bring himself to utter those two loathsome words: Government House! Suddenly I was running at the top of my speed towards Simcoe Street in search of the gates to the huge estate and Cecily—the woman whose sole purpose in life was to create in me a sensation of unparalleled orgiastic ecstasy. It was all falling into place as if by magic. I mean to say, could it be mere coincidence that the name Cecily is the feminine form of Cecil—my first alias? I thought not!

As I rounded the corner my heart soared as I saw that the windows of the mansion were ablaze with light. Simcoe Street was lined with elegant carriages filled with randy old satyrs awaiting their turn to enter the sweeping drive! "By thunder," I said, "we are having a riotous evening, are we not?" And so openly! It was a wonder they were not more fearful of being seen. But then again, that was the beauty of it. What harm could there be in being seen entering Government House? Just then a fine brougham passed me and by the light of its interior lamps I was able to make out the gleaming white shirt-front of some debauched old buffer, and beside him the sparkling diamonds adorning the neck of his elderly female companion.

I stopped. I reeled. A chill ran down my spine the like of which I had never experienced. Mr. Jeremiah Dill's horribly leering, pop-eyed face swam before my eyes. What were the doctor's fateful words? "I admit now that your resemblance is quite slight, but sir, in all candour, raise your cheekbones but one half of one inch and narrow the eyes by one quarter of one inch and I would swear you were a sexual deviate." Sir Alexander Campbell, the man known as The Christian Politician, a satyr and brothel-keeper? His saintly wife a licentious abbess? It was beyond preposterous, it was raving mad. Suddenly I knew what was happening to my mind. It was as Dandy had described the wretched Dill—as his mental weakness progressed, his moral sense became increasingly perverted. So fixed in my mind had my disgusting purpose become that I was not only ready but eager to believe the Lieutenant-Governor of Ontario and his good lady to be the conductors of orgies of the most bacchanalian description. I turned away from the glittering and wholly respectable scene, deeply ashamed. Then just for an instant I thought to myself, could Doctor Dandy have meant east rather than west of King and Simcoe streets? But looking eastward I was confronted by the Church of Scotland's glorious Norman pile—St. Andrew's Presbyterian Church. "Oh Willoughby," I said aloud, "for God's sake, man, give it up." There was nothing farther eastward save buildings of an obvious commercial nature and The British Hotel, which I knew from its frequent condemnation in the press to be a germ-ridden, vermin-infested sewer. And so I trudged slowly back to The Queen's Hotel, deeply ashamed of myself and full of alarm as I stared into the yawning chasm of sexual monomania.

The hotel lobby was deserted but, as ill luck would have it, just as I was midway across the marble floor the orchestra in the Ladies' Drawing Room struck up the strains of "God Save the Queen". I was unsure of what protocol demanded. I mean to say, should I stand by myself at attention in the middle of the lobby and risk looking like an imbecile or should I continue walking and risk being branded an unpatriotic vulgarian? In short, was I exempt from observing anthem protocol by the fact that I was not actually in the room in which our beloved anthem was being played? I hesitated, stood at attention briefly, and then bolted across the floor. The elevator stood awaiting my orders but it was painfully obvious that my brain was quite literally awash in drink and that the use of the perpendicular railway could only result in an intestinal catastrophe. I was therefore compelled to mount the stairs. To this day I cannot explain how I managed to find my suite unaided, but find it I did. The gas lamps had been lit, as had the fire in the parlour, and I fell headlong on the green settee in front of the warm blaze. Three dispiriting facts stared me in the face. I had failed dismally to be indoctrinated into the ways of love. I had agreed to take a tour of a ghastly asylum for the insane of Ontario the following morning. And I still had no ticket to see La Divine's performance. I gazed at the silent ceiling above me. Should I perhaps draft a note to La Divine, expressing my devotion and explaining my predicament?

CHAPTER VI

A MEETING OF MINDS

I awoke to a digestive holocaust that occasioned a moment of dreadful urgency. When I returned from the water-closet down the hall I discovered it to be well past nine o'clock in the morning. My tongue was furred like a beaver pelt and I was positively desperate for a bottle of Doctor Palmer's Pink Pills For Pale People with which to allay my profound digestive discord. I dunked my head in cold water and sat for a moment in the bay window gazing out at the misty lake. La Divine Sarah's performance was that night but seemingly I could do nothing about acquiring a ticket until the theatre opened an hour or two before the performance. The last thing on earth I felt like doing was touring Doctor Dandy's hideous asylum, but I had given my word and of course, being a gentleman, I had no option but to go. Still, looking on the bright side, it was just possible I could get another brothel address from Doctor Dandy and return to town in time to make another attempt at debauchery later that afternoon. I staggered into the bedroom and sat on the edge of my glorious bed. It was too late now for me to crawl between the lavender-scented sheets, and I thought to myself, how dreadfully unfair it will be if I die tonight without having taken advantage of the opportunity to sleep in such a wonderful bed. As I sat lamenting my situation I noticed a strange-looking gizmo resting on one of the two marble-topped tables which flanked the bed. It was a round dial about the size of an apple pie, with an arrow-shaped switch in the centre of it resembling the hand of a clock. Upon closer examination I discovered a small brass plaque on which was inscribed the following:

ELECTRO-MAGNETIC ANNUNCIATOR DIAL

Kindly point arrow to that which you desire and press the button at the bottom. Your demand will thus be instantly made known to our staff. While this patented device is generated by electricity, there need not be any fear of electrical shock or fire.

A list of virtually everything a human being might desire was printed around the perimeter of the device. All drinks known to mankind, every eatable in common demand, cigars, chewing tobacco, Eno's Fruit Salts, playing cards, city directory, chamber maid, messenger boy, barber, help get a doctor, help get police, et cetera. Truly there must have been over one hundred choices in this marvellous catalogue of necessaries. I elected to summon a maid, and to her I conveyed my wish for a bottle of Eno's Fruit Salts, a bath, a barber, and breakfast—in that order. My wishes were quickly granted and within a short time I was a new man. As I was leaving my suite for the Provincial Lunatic Asylum I recalled the clerk's words at Aikenhead's hardware emporium concerning the efficacy of a revolver as an unsurpassable prophylactic against malefactors, and I paused to slip my Defender into the inner pocket of my jacket. Better to be safe than sorry, as Uncle Harold was so fond of telling me.

Doctor Dandy's driver was waiting for me in the hotel lobby and escorted me forthwith to a closed carriage standing directly in front of the hotel. As I climbed inside I detected the smell of sherry and discovered the good doctor to be wrapped in a blanket and snoring audibly. My jarring the carriage roused him to consciousness.

"Who are you sir? What do you want?" he inquired with

some indignation upon sight of me.

"Doctor Dandy," I protested, "I am Reginald Ravencroft. We dined together last night and you invited me to tour your asylum this morning."

A look of consternation persisted for a moment before the light of comprehension burst forth. "Oh yes, of course you are. Of course you are. Now then, young man, how does this fine autumn day find you? In good spirits, I trust."

"Well, yes and no, doctor," I said, getting directly to the point. "You see, I was highly frustrated last night when I attempted to deliver Bibles to the house of ill repute to which you directed me. The fact is that you sent me to old Upper Canada College."

"Old Upper Canada College? But why ever would you go there? That is on King Street. The Cloister is on Queen Street, not King Street."

My heart leapt! "Well sir, I did have the impression that you said King Street," I said, trying to hide my elation.

"Oh dear me, did I really? I am most terribly sorry. I must admit, I do seem to be getting slightly confused as I grow older. It can be very inconvenient at times, you know."

"So the part about it being a few doors west of Simcoe on the north side still applies?"

"Oh yes, most definitely. Indeed, we shall be driving past it in a short time, and I will point it out to you if that would make you feel better."

I remarked casually that perhaps that would be best. I expected him to try once again to dissuade me from my mission but he was far too excited about my pending tour of his asylum to fret over my virtue.

"Really, Mr. Ravencroft, I cannot tell you how pleased I am to be able to show you my asylum. You have no idea how far we've come in the past half-century. Do you realize that when I returned to Canada in 1844 to help combat the ever-growing insanity in Upper Canada, all lunatics were jailed along with common criminals?"

"And you may well imagine that being shut away in a stinking dungeon is hardly likely to bring a man to his senses whose wits have gone awandering."

"Well no," I said. "Quite."

"Nor were many of the so-called patients demented in the first place. Innocent wives were confined so as to allow their lust-crazed husbands free rein with their mistresses or comely household servants. Eldest sons were falsely committed so as to forfeit their inheritance. It was simply appalling, sir. Demented persons of both sexes sleeping on straw, rats issuing forth from the open drains in their cells to molest them. Oh, I was disgusted."

I had been surreptitiously peeking out the small window beside me so as to remain aware of our location, and I now saw that we were at the all-important junction of Queen and Simcoe streets.

"Oh, excuse me, doctor, is this the street in question?"

"Street?" he asked, looking somewhat disgruntled at my interruption of his narrative. "What street? Oh yes, wait now, yes, there it is, that large red brick house set well back from the street, that is the infamous Cloister."

I stuck my head out of the window just in time to see the house in question. There was certainly nothing unusual about it, nothing to indicate that it was anything other than an ordinary domicile, but my spirits soared and I felt fully confident that finally, against all odds, I had succeeded once and for all in finding a genuine Toronto joy palace. I resolved to get through Doctor Dandy's tour as quickly as possible and visit The Cloister later that afternoon.

"Do you know what we did?" asked the good doctor.

"No sir, I cannot imagine," I said, not having the foggiest notion what the doctor was talking about.

"We began by holding an architectural design competition for an asylum to house five hundred Upper Canadian lunatics. And on what exterior model do you suppose the winning design was based? The National Gallery in London England! Yes sir, a fact, as you will soon see."

"Good gracious!" I exclaimed as I wondered what the likelihood of The Cloister being open for trade in the afternoon was. After all, one would assume that the girls would have to get some sleep sometime, and they would certainly get none during the night.

"Are you fond of riddles, young man?" Doctor Dandy asked.

"Yes, I suppose I am, as much as the next man anyway."

"Good. Answer me this if you can. What measures fifty-five feet by twenty-five feet and resides on the third floor of my asylum?"

Needless to say, I had not the slightest idea. Indeed I was loath even to imagine what might be located on the third floor of the gruesome place.

"I cannot imagine, what is it?" I asked.

"What is it, sir? Why, it is the Provincial Lunatic Asylum Ballroom!" he cried with great elation.

"Never! A ballroom in an asylum? Very progressive."

"Is it not, sir? I shall show it to you. On the last Friday night of every month we have our monthly ball, which is for the patients and their relatives, but we also have our annual Asylum Charity Ball, which the *crème de la crème* of Toronto society attends."

"A truly amazing story, doctor, and one I am the richer for hearing," I said as a ray of hope shot through my mind. To wit: perhaps such a large establishment as The Cloister would have, as it were, two shifts, a day shift and a night shift, so as not to lose valuable custom from persons such as myself who could not work a nocturnal visit into their busy schedules.

"It really is a most marvellous affair—indeed it is coming up in little more than one month's time, perhaps you would care to attend?" Doctor Dandy remarked.

"Yes, of course, if I am still stopping in Toronto, which is, alas, doubtful," I said as a cloud of doubt flitted across my hope-filled sky. To wit: would the day shift be as adroit as the night shift? That is to say, would the day girls be more in the nature of second-string girls, like the players on a baseball team? And surely the athletic Cecily would be a night-shift employee, for she could hardly be expected to be on duty twenty-four hours a day—could she?

"Ah ha!" the doctor cried as he pointed out the window. "Now there is a truly glorious pile!"

I looked in the direction indicated by his knobby finger and beheld the romantic forest of gables and towers that was Trinity University.

"Good heavens! What a magnificent sight!"

"Is it not, sir? No place in Canada so forcibly reminds me of noble Oxford as does Trinity. But now, let me draw your attention to the beneficent temple of Christian charity up ahead on your left."

I followed his gaze and saw a massive grey fortress surmounted by a golden dome. It was the Provincial Lunatic Asylum.

"Doctor, do not try to tell me that beautiful pile is your asylum!"

"Oh but it is, sir," he said, his chest visibly swelling with pride, "it most certainly is. And here is another riddle for you. What is enclosed in that glorious golden dome which crowns the pile?"

"I cannot imagine. A vacancy, I would assume," I said, wilfully forgetting my guidebook intelligence.

"My young sir, that dome contains, not a vacancy as you suppose, but, would you believe it, an iron tank housing eleven thousand gallons of water!"

"Never! Is that possible?"

"Certainly it is possible, sir. It is a fact. Each and every day water is pumped up into that glorious dome by a steam engine, and that is how we are able to offer running water and water closets throughout the asylum."

"It is all highly remarkable, doctor, quite astonishing."

For in all honesty the asylum's façade, with the huge central block flanked by the two side wings and crowned by the golden dome, really was most striking. It was only as we drew nearer and I could see the barred windows and the buff brick turned a dismal grey that the cruel reality of the institution made itself felt. We passed through the gates and proceeded up the long lane. The spacious grounds were very nicely tended to, and I said as much to the good doctor.

"Yes, I am very proud of them, Mr. Ravencroft. Those persons you see tending the grounds are lunatics from the male wards."

I noted the men he was referring to and I also noted a somewhat stranger scene off to one side. "I wonder what that fellow over there is doing, doctor. It almost looks as though he is talking to that bush and shaking its branch heartily, as one would a person's outstretched hand."

"Yes. That is precisely what he is doing. His name is Mr. Richardson and he is an excellent gardener. All is well as long as the shrubs do not turn hostile."

We continued up the drive and I saw a couple of men evidently playing some manner of wrestling game behind a stand of clematis. It may well be that I was fooled by the glare of the sun on their asylum garments, but I am bound to say that to me they appeared to be quite naked, and I deemed it prudent not to inquire as to their intentions.

We were decanted at the front door and I soon found myself standing in the asylum's cavernous main hall. It rose some five storeys in height, with an ornate iron staircase spiralling up to the successive gallery landings of the floors above. I saw no one save for two nurses who scuttled by us without comment.

"Now then," said Doctor Dandy, rubbing his hands together gleefully, "where would you like to begin—men's wing or women's?"

Each wing sounded equally gruesome to me but I saw immediately that in choosing the women's wing I ran the risk of being deemed a voyeur, and thusly I chose the men's wing. We proceeded to wind our way up the spiral staircase to the second-floor landing, where Dandy paused to select a key from a large brass ring.

"This is the Male Refractory Ward and it is here that we house our most deranged male patients," he remarked cheerfully. "I'm afraid they require constant attendance."

The door the doctor unlocked was made of highly polished oak but it might more appropriately have been studded with iron nails—the world it concealed was so wretched. The instant it opened I gagged at the stench of urine and excrement issuing forth while my ears were assaulted by the moans and screams of the demented. Ahead of us stretched a long corridor filled with male lunatics dressed in heavy grey canvas uniforms, and I noted that each man wore a chain around his waist and a padlock where normally a belt buckle would reside. Many walked slowly in circles with sunken heads, hands clasped behind them. Several stood at rigid attention against a far wall with their arms pinned to their sides, like recruits in the presence of a drill sergeant. Others huddled in the corners twitching and mumbling to no one in particular. Their heads had all been recently shaved. I fingered the butt of my revolver involuntarily and evidently my face betrayed my emotions, for Doctor Dandy immediately attempted to calm my fears.

"Oh, you mustn't be frightened of them, Mr. Ravencroft, we do not allow any lunatics with violent proclivities to roam the halls. They are all quite harmless—dreadfully demented, I grant you—but perfectly harmless."

"But they're in chains!" I remonstrated.

"Chains? Oh goodness me, no. Those are merely belts to ensure that they do not remove their trousers. Many of our lunatics are prone to exposing themselves to the atmosphere. The chain does not harm them. Come along now, don't be shy."

I watched in dismay as the doctor breezed on down the hall with a casual hand gesture indicating that I should follow him.

"Yes, they are all here: blacksmiths, artists, schoolmasters, ventriloquists, coachwrights, policemen, men of the cloth, sea captains. Ah here, sir, just look who we have in this room."

My mind revolted at this command but he was so enthusiastic about his charges that I had not the heart to refuse him. I peered through the window in the door and beheld a wretched-looking man of about sixty years curled up on a thin mattress which lay on the floor. The small cell was otherwise barren and the window had been boarded over. On the lunatic's countenance I read a mixture of intense sorrow and alarm. He had adopted a listening attitude, eyes wide open, head cocked to one side, like a confused terrier.

"You are looking at the unfortunate Professor Archibald Dundonald—formerly professor of theology at Knox College, University of Toronto. That he is a dipsomaniac, that is to say, suffering from a morbid craving for alcohol, is obvious by his chronic and indelible appearance of sottishness. Unfortunately, in Professor Dundonald's case, his dipsomania led him down the evil avenue to *paranoia hallucinatoria*—an insidious breed of confusional insanity not uncommon in brain workers. They abuse their brains, you see, and this abuse causes a malnourishment therein. This resulting exhaustion in turn causes them to seek sustenance in alcohol and leads to extraordinary constipation. A total stoppage of the bowels ensues and, in due course, raving insanity. 'Great wits are sure to madness near alli'd. And thin partitions do their bounds divide,' as Mr. Dryden puts it."

"Egad, I do begin to see," I said.

"When he was brought to us he was quite palpably insane. Indeed he was hiding out, living wild in High Park, for some weeks before a policeman brought him to us. He suffers from the delusive belief that certain members of the theology faculty at Knox College and all persons from the province of Quebec have designs on his life. These abominable fancies often take on the most outrageous character. You will note that the window in his room has been boarded over; this is to prevent him from looking out upon the asylum grounds. Undoubtedly this seems cruel to you, but it is in fact a kindness. Too often when he is allowed to view the grounds he sees French Canadian woodsmen in tuques with stubby pipes stalking through the surrounding trees, and this naturally distresses him greatly. He fears sleep because his dreams are populated by disembodied Quebec faces that howl at him and curse horribly in

French. Thus we are forced to induce sleep chemically so as to give his poor exhausted brain a much-needed rest."

At that moment we were both startled by an outbreak of screams and curses issuing from a door just down the hall.

"Doctor! Doctor Dandy! Oh please, doctor, feed it! I must have mice! It's biting me dreadfully!" cried the anonymous voice.

"Ah, he's sensed I am near. Come along, Mr. Ravencroft, and meet Mr. Albert Pie."

Much to my consternation, Doctor Dandy's manner remained as cheery as could be. In retrospect I see that, just as the surgeon grows accustomed to sawing off limbs and digits, and it is all in a day's work for the mortician to stuff a corpse's mouth with cotton batting, so too had the doctor become inured to the theatre of the raving. I followed him down the hall with great reluctance and peered in the window. The small room was empty save for a man confined in a small wooden chair by manacles at his ankles and wrists and stout iron bands around his chest and forehead. Mr. Albert Pie was distressingly young, my age or thereabouts, and entirely normal-looking save for the fact that his head was shaved and he was confined in the barbaric-looking chair. When he saw Doctor Dandy through the glass, he resumed begging for help.

"Help me! Oh God, help me, doctor!" pleaded Mr. Pie.

"We'd best go in," said Doctor Dandy.

I shuddered involuntarily but dutifully followed along.

We entered the small room and the doctor said: "Now then, Mr. Pie, calm yourself, calm yourself."

"Doctor," gasped the unfortunate man, "the pain is unbearable, they're eating me alive!"

"Yes, Mr. Pie, I do realize that, and I will tell nurse to administer some additional morphine."

"I don't need morphine, I need mice. Just three or four so they will not bite at my guts so."

Doctor Dandy turned to me. "Mr. Pie suffers from the delusion that snakes have taken up residence in his stomach. He believes that initially one slithered into his mouth and down into his abdominal cavity one night while he lay sleeping with his mouth open, but now there are several snakes living inside him. I will send nurse along directly, Mr. Pie." We exited the cell amidst a torrent of vile curses, and walked farther down the hall.

"His condition is as piteous as it is macabre," the doctor

explained. "He lives in terror of making the slightest movement for he claims that the snakes dislike having their repose disturbed and in retaliation lash out—viciously biting his internal organs. He believes that the snakes are hungry and begs to be given live mice that he may ingest the rodents and thereby assuage the vipers' hunger. When mice are denied him—for clearly such a diet is completely out of the question—he cries out for black beetles and flies. At other times he becomes enraged by his unwanted tenants and seeks to kill the intruders by beating on his abdomen with clenched fists, and when his assault only stirs up the wrath of the snakes, he then begs for the use of a carving knife or hatchet that he may kill them or, create an open wound through which they can be pulled out of their ghastly abode. Needless to say, he is extremely dangerous to himself and grossly inconvenient to others. I confess to a deal of disappointment in this case, in that about a month ago I thought I had cured him, but his improvement turned out to be only temporary."

Despite my intense feeling of revulsion, I could not help but be curious as to how one would even begin to try to cure such a bizarre case, and asked Dandy to continue his explanation.

"Ah well, you see, rather than persisting in my fruitless attempts to convince Mr. Pie that there was no snake living inside him—you recall that initially he believed there was only one snake within—I decided to play along with his delusion. I instructed one of our grounds-keepers to capture a live garter snake and one day after Mr. Pie used his commode I immediately slipped the snake into the pot along with his dirt. I cried out in jubilation that he had been right all along—there had indeed been a snake living inside him but now he had excreted it. Well, when Mr. Pie saw the snake in the chamber pot he was elated. He began jumping about the room—testing to see if there were any more snakes inside him—and lo and behold he was free from all pain. But alas, within a couple of days he suddenly reported that the pain had returned and that it was clear to him that the original snake was a female who had laid eggs in his stomach. So you see that now, instead of one snake, he has several in residence. Naturally I was greatly disappointed, but at least I was able to satisfy myself that his pain is not due to some manner of tumour or colonic stricture."

But I was scarcely listening to the good doctor's discourse, for I suddenly felt extremely weary of his ghastly asylum.

"I think, doctor," I said, "that I have seen enough for one day."

"What's that? You cannot leave yet, Mr. Ravencroft! Why, you have yet to visit the women's wing, or the ballroom or . . . or, well, I don't know what all you will miss if you leave now."

"Well, perhaps I could come back another day to finish the tour," I said in a conciliatory tone.

"Another day, sir? But what is wrong with this day?"

"Nothing is wrong with today, doctor, save that I find myself feeling very tired, and wishing to return to my hotel for a rest. I feel certain that I will be able to appreciate your hymn to Christian charity far better another day—when I am refreshed."

To my relief the doctor suddenly seemed to accept my explanation, and as he escorted me out of the building his high spirits returned.

"Yes, Mr. Ravencroft, a theatre of madness it most certainly is, but still a far cry from wet cells and attendants with savage dogs, eh what?"

"Oh, indeed yes. I leave your grand institution knowing that it is an oasis of succour for the demented and not a place of brutal incarceration as, doubtless, ignorant folk would have one believe."

"And I have your word that you really will come back to finish your tour?"

"Without doubt, doctor," I assured him.

He held the massive door open for me, we bade each other farewell, and with an intense feeling of relief I heard the huge asylum door slam shut behind me. The doctor's coachman was nowhere to be seen but fortunately the carriage was parked a short distance down the lane. My relief at being out in the open air was considerable and, as I headed for the carriage, I found my pace involuntarily quickening to a run. Then with a single bound I leapt inside the carriage and, to my horror, cannoned directly into an innocent individual of unknown identity.

"Great God!" I cried as I vaulted onto the leather seat opposite. "Sir, I beg your pardon! Do please forgive my gross impertinence. I assumed this carriage to be wholly vacant. That is to say, I believed it to be Doctor Dandy's carriage."

The young man opposite me was the most extraordinary-looking individual I had ever beheld. He was quite a small person but despite his boyish appearance he sported a gleaming gold monocle on a black velvet ribbon, an outlandishly large black hat with a soft, wide brim à la Rembrandt, and was entirely enveloped in a full-length velvet cloak of a deep port-wine hue. He looked in short, or perhaps I should say *although* short, to be a famous actor or poet or littérateur. Certainly he was a clothes-wearing man of some considerable note. I could not have said with any certainty what his age might be, for his clean-shaven face and diminutive stature placed him at about sixteen years while his monocle and highly theatrical costume placed him closer to twenty. One point, however, was indisputable, and that was that he possessed a most singular pair of eyes, in that the lids drooped slightly, thus creating a hooded, sleepy appearance, while beneath them, in violent contradiction, burned a pair of luminous green eyes—restless, keenly observant, and full of oddity. I noted that the air was rich with the scent of expensive toilet water and, unlike myself, he appeared to be completely unruffled by my blundering into him. He paused to re-adjust his hat to a rakish tilt before speaking.

"Pray calm yourself, sir," he said with a most cultured British accent. "You are not mistaken, for this is indeed Doctor Dandy's carriage. Am I to understand that the good doctor neglected to inform you that you will be sharing his carriage during your journey back to Toronto?"

"Quite so, sir," I said, "he made no mention of it whatsoever."

"Ah well, never mind, it is of no consequence. Allow me to introduce myself, I am Lord Windermere," he said as, with an effortless flourish, he produced an exquisite card upon which a royal crest was heavily embossed in gold.

"How do you do, Lord Windermere," I said. "I am Reginald Ambrose Ravencroft, Esquire, very pleased to make your acquaintance."

I was quite startled by the news that I was sharing the carriage with a real British lord—thrown off completely, as a matter of fact—and in consequence rather fumbled the presentation of my own card—although thankfully not to the extent of launching it into the air, as I had done on the train.

Lord Windermere studied it a moment and then said with rather a melancholy smile: "Alas, Mr. Ravencroft, I regret to inform you that stern words are required with your card printer. He appears to be under the impression that you are a mortician by the name of Charles Mortimer."

I will not dwell on my feeling of utter stupidity and my ensuing apology. Suffice it to say that the degree of my humiliation was appalling in its extremity. More agitated fumbling ensued and eventually I managed the supposedly simple task of presenting one's card.

"Ah," said his lordship, "I see you hail from the great metropolis of New York. What brings you northward to 'Saintly Toronto', as I believe she is known?"

"Oh, this and that, my lord. A little business, a little pleasure. I shall be stopping at the Queen's for some few weeks or more, I should imagine," I replied really quite convincingly. I then went on to reiterate my apology for sitting on him and expressed my surprise at Doctor Dandy's failure to mention his presence.

"Think nothing of it, Mr. Ravencroft," he said. "I fear it is all too typical of the doctor to have forgotten to mention my existence. He is a brilliant alienist, of course, but I have been given to understand that, sadly, he is himself rapidly losing his mind."

"Good lord!" I exclaimed. "Losing his mind? Is it as serious as all that?"

"I have been so informed, yes. Oh, but I do not condemn the poor man. Indeed it seems these days that everyone about me is losing his wits. I have been here this morning visiting my dear wife, who, I regret to inform you, is a raving lunatic."

"Oh dear, I am so very sorry to hear of it, my lord."

"Yes, it is very sad, quite heart-breaking in fact. Until our arrival here in Toronto three short weeks ago, she was in perfect health. Indeed, I think I may say, without fear of contradiction, that Lady Windermere is internationally known for both her perspicacity and her sound digestion. We set sail from Paris on the *Labynia* and docked in Montreal after an uneventful voyage. It was four days later, after having journeyed by train to Toronto, that my dear little wife promptly lost her mind. There, Mr. Ravencroft, what do you make of that?"

"Well, dear me, I really would not know. Has she ever had any . . . difficulty of this kind before?"

"Difficulty? Do you mean, was Lady Windermere in the habit of fouling her drawers and cursing like a sailor as she now delights in doing? Not to my knowledge, sir, no. It is my belief that up until her arrival in Toronto she abominated such actions as do all persons of taste and refinement—to say nothing of royal blood. Shall I tell you what I think drove her mad? It is my theory that, having just left the gaiety and *haute couture* of Paris, the outrageous dowdiness of Toronto and its people was simply too great a shock to her sensibilities. Indeed a shock so great as to have totally unhinged her reason. And thus, with the door to her mind standing, as it were, ajar, her wits were free to go awandering."

I hardly knew how best to respond to Lord Windermere's distressing frankness concerning Lady Windermere's mental instability—much less his defamation of Toronto. The best I could do was mutter, "I am so very sorry to hear it, your lordship. It must be very distressing for you to see her thusly."

"It has been very disconcerting, Mr. Ravencroft. Very disconcerting indeed," he responded.

Lord Windermere then began searching for something within the folds of his voluminous cloak, and I caught a glimpse of his black knee-high Chantilly riding boots, polished to a dazzling finish. I also noticed for the first time that across his lap lay a beautiful cherry-wood stick inlaid with ivory in a delicate ivy pattern, and possessing a gold handle wrought in the form of a stalking lion. It was without question the most exquisite specimen of its kind I had ever beheld.

"Are you one of Queen Nicotina's willing and dutiful subjects, Mr. Ravencroft?" he asked as he withdrew a tortoise-shell snuff-box from an interior pocket of his cloak.

"Yes, my lord," I said, "I am proud to number among that league, but I prefer a cigarette to snuff, thank you just the same."

He nodded in assent and proceeded to enact a flawless example of snuff inhalation. He passed his snuff-box from his right hand to his left, rapped upon the box with his extended right index finger, and then opened the lid of the box with a mannered flick of this same digit. A small silver spoon appeared seemingly from out of the ether, but actually, I believe, from up his sleeve, and he conveyed a spoonful of snuff to each nostril in turn and adroitly inhaled the grains of tobacco. For my part, I fired up a Turkish Beauty, and we both sat back to enjoy Queen Nicotina's soothing balm.

"Ah me," remarked his lordship with a sigh as he returned his snuff-box to his inner pocket, "I too enjoy a cigarette but every now and again nothing can surpass the 'Crumbs of Comfort'."

He produced a lace handkerchief, which he wore up his sleeve in the military fashion, and proceeded to dust off the front of his cloak lest any crumbs had strayed. It was then that I saw it. Lord Windermere was sporting a padlocked patient-identification chain bracelet on his exposed wrist! My mind was instantly awhirl. I was, in fact, sitting in a closed carriage with an escaped lunatic! The man was very possibly dangerous and it was clearly my duty to try to thwart his escape—if only to save my own skin. As casually as possible—given my state of agitation—I transferred my cigarette to my left hand and slipped my right hand inside my jacket and around the butt of my Defender. Then I paused to assess the situation. Three main avenues of escape appeared before me. Firstly, I could suddenly whip out my revolver and demand that the fellow return to the confines of the asylum at gun-point. Secondly, I could wait for the coachman to return—he had mysteriously remained absent all the while we were conversing—and get out of the carriage on the pretext of desiring to upbraid the man for his inexcusable tardiness and thence, once beyond the lunatic's reach, raise the alarm. Thirdly, I could simply fling myself out the carriage door and leg it to safety. The first option, while appealing to the romantic in me, seemed overly fraught with danger. I put it to myself: the man is a madman, what if he does not fear guns and hurls himself upon me—am I really prepared to shoot the fellow? Furthermore, what if he too is armed—am I prepared to die simply in order to return a poor lunatic to an asylum? In short would I not be better to leave it up to the police?

"Mr. Ravencroft," said Lord Windermere—or rather, the escaped lunatic.

"Yes sir," I responded with a start.

"Are you unwell?"

"Not at all, Lord Windermere, why do you ask?" I said, perhaps a trifle too aggressively.

"Forgive me, but I notice your brow is bedewed with perspiration and the weather hardly warrants it. Indeed I see now that your spectacles are beginning to fog. I trust you are not ill."

"Well, as a matter of fact, I have only recently recovered from a bout of influenza," I said as I quickly wiped the moisture from my brow. "You must forgive me, my lord, for I—oh, here is that confounded coachman at last." For sure enough, the fellow was lumbering down the asylum steps headed for our carriage. "If you will excuse me one moment, Lord Windermere, I am going to give that blasted fellow a good piece of my mind for keeping us waiting all this time."

"Please, Mr. Ravencroft, calm yourself," he said with a pronounced note of impatience in his voice. "I do not doubt the man has good cause for delaying our departure."

"I beg your pardon," I said, not knowing how to interpret his mood.

"Just let the fellow get on with his job," he snapped.

"I think not, my lord," I said as I began to rise from my seat.

In my excitement, I had failed to notice that the lunatic's stick was no longer lying across his lap but rather held firmly in his right hand. Suddenly I saw its tip poised in the air directly in front of my face, and in the next instant a vicious stiletto blade, about six inches in length, sprang out from the end of the shaft.

"Silence, Mr. Ravencroft. Remain seated and silent," he said, in a voice quiet yet edged with ruthless authority. His English accent was no longer in evidence.

I remained completely still, my eyes glued upon the evil blade dancing not two inches from my nose. I could smell its oiled metal surface and did not doubt for an instant that he would stab me in the throat if I were to go for my revolver.

"Please do not kill me" was the most eloquent plea I could manage.

"Remain calm—do nothing. All I require is transportation into Toronto," he responded tersely.

He struck the carriage ceiling twice with his fist and the carriage lurched forward. I deemed it wise to play the innocent.

"Really, Lord Windermere, I do not understand. I merely wanted to chastise the coachman."

"Yes, no doubt, Mr. Ravencroft, but your extraordinarily pale countenance and bedewed brow suggested to me that I had been careless and I remembered the *memento luni* on my wrist. I am afraid I found myself in somewhat of a rush this morning and could not afford the time to pick the silly little nuisance."

I opened my mouth to speak but he spoke first.

"Understand me, sir, I have killed in the past and I shan't hesitate to do so again should the need arise. You may rely—"

But I was not destined to hear the remainder of the lunatic's threat for it was at that moment that I suddenly entered a state of unconsciousness. That is to say, I fainted dead away.

Some time later, as I slowly swam back up to consciousness, my first sensation was one of movement as the carriage bounced along the rough country road leading into the city. I focused my eyes with some effort and saw the lunatic lounging on his seat, an inscrutable smile upon his face. He was toying idly with his extraordinary stick—out of which the blade still extended. I sat bolt upright and he levelled it at my chest.

"I was just sitting up!" I cried.

The lunatic started to say something but checked himself and, after a pause, put a question to me. "Will you give me your solemn oath as a gentleman not to impede my escape in any way?"

"I do so swear."

"I take it I can trust you? That is to say, you are a gentleman, are you not?"

"Every inch of me, sir. I am an honourable man and hence my word is my bond."

"Excellent. I must say that I am inclined to believe you."

He sat back against the soft leather of his seat and his stick resumed its former position lying across his legs in a casual manner. He did not, however, go so far as to retract the blade, and I did not think it to be forgetfulness that caused him to leave it protruding. For my part, I took the opportunity to freshen the points of my Imperial moustache.

"I apologize for this vulgar threat of violence upon your person, Mr. Ravencroft, but you must admit that you were about to raise the alarm, were you not?"

I hesitated, not knowing which was the safest tack to take, and finally opted for the truth. "Yes I was," I said. "But in all candour I was not so much concerned with returning you to the asylum as I was with my own safety."

"Yes, I daresay in theory you were wise to be frightened. Many of my colleagues—'Men crazed with shadows that they chase'—can be somewhat . . . unpredictable. But tell me, Mr. Ravencroft, what precisely is your relationship with Doctor Dandy?"

By this stage in the proceedings I no longer possessed the composure required for subterfuge, and thus once again I simply blurted out the truth: "We met by chance last night in the Royal Canadian Room at The Queen's Hotel and he invited me to tour the asylum, as he is very proud of his work there. For my part, I had no desire to see the ghastly place but, owing to the fact that by midnight tonight I may well be either dead or incarcerated on account of my criminal efforts to obtain a ticket to see La Divine Sarah Bernhardt's performance of *Phèdre* at the Grand Opera House, I was desperate to get the name and location of an excellent brothel, that I might become a man before either dying or going to jail, and I believed that Doctor Dandy could supply me with that information."

I sank back breathless after my outburst and, in the ensuing silence, heard a metallic click as the lunatic's blade flicked back into the interior of the shaft and he laid his stick to one side.

"Am I to assume then," said he as he withdrew my Defender from within the folds of his cloak, "that your mission to obtain a ticket to see La Divine Sarah this evening, by any means fair or foul, accounts for your friend here?"

I was surprised to see my revolver, for in truth I had forgotten all about it. "Yes," I said. "Quite right. I bought it at Aikenhead's hardware emporium yesterday for just that purpose."

"Why then, one cannot help but wonder, are you carrying it this morning? Fear of lunatics?"

"Well frankly, yes."

"Quite so," he said with a wry smile. He laid the revolver casually on the bench beside him.

"I wonder, might I be allowed to introduce myself to you once again?

"By all means. Please do."

"Belvedere La Griffin, my card," he said as he produced a card bearing his name stamped in gold.

"Enchanté," I responded. "I remain Reginald Ravencroft."

"Naturally."

I paused to examine his card and was astonished to see that Mr. La Griffin also favoured Latin mottoes.

BELVEDERE LA GRIFFIN ESQ.
CONTRA AUDENTIOR

"May I now offer you a cigarette?" he inquired. "They are Napoleons."

I assented and, with truly enviable dash, he extended an

elegant gold cigarette case in my direction and simultaneously popped open the lid by releasing the spring catch. I accepted the proffered Napoleon and reached inside my waistcoat for a match, but he anticipated my intention and dexterously withdrew one from an ornate gold match safe wrought in the shape of a dagger. He lit my Napoleon and inserted his own into a carved ivory cigarette holder before lighting it. He then leaned back against his seat, his legs crossed at the ankles—smoking with a sublime air.

Emboldened by his evident relaxation, I ventured a question. "Might I enquire, Mr. La Griffin, was your choice of Lord Windermere as an alias purely coincidental or did you intentionally assume the identity of one of Mr. Oscar Wilde's characters?"

He smiled, hesitated, and then asked, "Do you not think a cigarette a perfect type of perfect pleasure, Mr. Ravencroft?"

"I do indeed, Mr. La Griffin. 'It is exquisite, it leaves one unsatisfied,'" I said finishing his Oscar Wilde quotation without missing a beat.

It had been my desire to impress him and I was more than gratified by the shocked look on his face. He clearly had not expected me to be so well read.

"I presume then that I should take your ready quotation as confirmation that you deliberately chose the name of Mr. Wilde's character," I prompted.

To my surprise, however, he did not respond in any way save to continue staring at me with transfixed eyes. When his mouth began to gape, I grew alarmed.

"Are you ill, Mr. La Griffin?" I inquired.

In response to my question, his cigarette holder fell to the carriage floor, a spasm ran through the entire length of his body, and to my unutterable horror, he died. I sat stunned, frozen in my seat. Obviously what I had taken to be a look of surprise on his face at my completion of his Wilde quotation had been, in reality, the onset of death. I felt a rising sense of panic and a creeping nausea. I realized that I was about to vomit and sought the door handle that I might avoid fouling the interior of the carriage when, suddenly, Mr. La Griffin twitched. I started. Was it a postmortual muscle spasm or was he alive? Then he moved! Indeed, following another convulsive twitch, he slowly curled himself up in a ball on his seat like a small child—his hands forming a pillow under his head, his mouth slightly open, his eyes closed, and a quiet snoring sound becoming audible.

Good lord, I thought to myself, how incredibly odd! My next thought concerned what course of action I should take. I had given my word not to hinder his escape and therefore raising the alarm was completely out of bounds, but if I woke him up I would be guilty of wilfully aiding and abetting an escaped lunatic—very possibly a criminal act for which I could be held accountable. My inclination was simply to ignore the entire situation, but if I did nothing, that is to say, simply exited the carriage at my destination, then the coachman would unknowingly return the sleeping Mr. La Griffin to the asylum and in all likelihood he would eventually be discovered. In short, by doing nothing I would, in effect, be turning him in to the asylum authorities. I looked out the window and saw that we had long since entered the city limits and that it would not be much longer before we arrived at the Queen's. A decision was required.

My uninvited guest sighed gently and shifted in his sleep, possibly as a precursor to regaining consciousness, and I immediately retrieved my revolver and his stick from the seat opposite. He continued to sleep, however, and as I surveyed my dapper companion he suddenly appeared to me to be very vulnerable. His gold monocle had fallen out of his eye and was dangling off the seat by its black velvet ribbon, and his extraordinary hat was lying on the dusty carriage floor beside his cigarette holder. I picked them up and, as I laid them on the seat beside him I suddenly realized that I both pitied and greatly admired Mr. Belvedere La Griffin, and clearly I had no option but to awaken him and see him safely on his way. Just as I was about to rouse him, however, it occurred to me that I might as well take advantage of his impromptu nap to examine more closely his most flamboyant costume. His magnificent Chantilly riding boots were clearly made by a master boot-maker, for they could not have been larger than a size five or six, as compared to my manly size elevens, and the heels, I noted with some small amusement, were of extraordinary height—clearly in an effort to remedy his lack of stature. When I bent down to examine the soles I failed to discover the makers' signature as I had hoped to do, but I noted with a thrill that the soles were likewise varnished to perfection. I had of course read how the immortal Beau Brummel insisted that his man varnish the soles as meticulously as the uppers, so as to guarantee that he did not do a poor job on the sides. It was impossible to see precisely what La Griffin was wearing beneath his voluminous cloak so I took the liberty of lifting back one of its folds to facilitate my inspection.

A catch came in my breath as I revealed his extraordinarily fine outfit. His suit was an exquisite three-button morning affair made of a very fine grey wool cashmere, beautifully enhanced with black silk-stitched edges. His trousers were of a slightly darker grey wool material, with black satin piping running down the sides in a military fashion, and I noted that they boasted a sharp-edged crease down the front which the newly invented trouser press made possible. His collar I judged to be a Stirling Stand-up and at his neck he sported a crimson silk Ascot—its perfect folds secured by a large but by no means gaudy pearl stick-pin. His studs and links were made of gold and, to round out his costume, his hands were sheathed in fine kid dress gloves of such delicacy, such perfection of fit, that they constituted a quiet hymn to their maker. Soft green in tint, they sported a single clasp, gusset fingers, and Paris points, and were piqué sewn. As I bent my head lower so as to examine them more closely, I realized that they were lightly scented with, I believe, *eau de Jasmine*.

I sat back with a feeling of awe mixed with shame as I recalled having debated, if only for a moment, sending this bird of such fantastic plumage back to that jackal-filled cage. To the ignorant persons of this world he undoubtedly appeared comical in his swashbuckling rig-out, and I suppose there was a slight suggestion of a child who, having pillaged his grandfather's trunk in the attic, was now in masquerade as one of Mr. Dumas's Three Musketeers, but I could see beyond such a facile interpretation. Lunatic or no, Mr. Belvedere La Griffin was a genuine dandy the likes of which I had theretofore only read about. He was, in brief, a man of my own kidney, and I suddenly knew deep down in my bones that somehow, at some point before our journey together was over, I would have to summon the courage to request the name of his tailor—regardless how gross an impropriety such a request would constitute.

Suddenly he twitched spasmodically and I immediately assumed an attitude of casual repose. As an afterthought, I took up my Defender and levelled it at him. Tit for tat, I reckoned. In the next instant his eyes opened wide and he sprang up with a start, a look of confusion and alarm written on his face. He looked first at my face and then at my revolver. He was, at least for the moment, clearly nonplussed.

"Greetings, Mr. La Griffin. I trust you enjoyed your little nap?" said I, hugely enjoying this unexpected reversal in the balance of power.

My words seemed to re-orient him to his situation and his expression relaxed somewhat. "Ah yes, Mr. Ravencroft, is it not?" he said as he screwed his monocle into his eye and donned his hat.

"Precisely so. At your service," I said.

"We appear to be meeting each other repeatedly today."

"Yes, we do indeed."

"I really must apologize for my rudeness, Mr. Ravencroft. Ah, I see we are just passing Osgoode Hall. I would estimate that I have been asleep for—let me see—fifteen minutes?"

I assented and he looked directly down at my revolver, still levelled at him. He smiled wanly.

"And of course you have taken advantage of my slumbers to alert the coachman of my presence."

As he spoke I realized that it was cruel of me to toy with him in this fashion, since his very liberty was at stake and not to be made light of. Furthermore, I suddenly sensed that my little game was about to backfire upon me dreadfully. That is to say, I suspected that within the ensuing few seconds he was going to spring upon me. I returned my gun to my pocket.

"Most certainly not Mr. La Griffin," I replied indignantly. "I gave you my word not to sound the alarm and I am a man of honour, sir. Besides which, having toured the asylum, I would not care to send anyone short of a raving maniac back there. Please allow me to apologize for pointing my revolver at you, and allow me to return your fine stick. I see now that it was wrong of me to have you on like that."

Mr. La Griffin accepted his stick but, rather disconcertingly, said nothing. Indeed, his luminous green eyes stared back at me with an intensity that made me feel decidedly uncomfortable. Eventually, however, he smiled faintly.

"Apology accepted, Mr. Ravencroft. I daresay you are curious as to how I came to fall asleep in the middle of our conversation."

I admitted to being somewhat perplexed on that point.

"I regret to say that I suffer from a form of epilepsy known as narcolepsy," he explained. "As you have just witnessed, my attacks take the form of spontaneous mesmeric sleep. I need hardly tell you that they can be deuced inconvenient."

"Well yes, to say the least," I said with genuine concern. "Is there no cure for this disease?"

"Alas no, and furthermore the sleep attacks may last

anywhere from several seconds to several years."

"Good God. Years?"

"So Doctor Dandy informs me, yes. Thus far mine have never lasted longer than an hour or so."

"But for heaven's sake, I can see that your condition is dreadfully inconvenient but it hardly seems fair that you should be incarcerated in an asylum merely for falling asleep. I mean to say, that does not make you a lunatic—does it?"

"Certainly not," said he. "But on the other hand, I am, truly, as mad as a hatter, for like the immortal Edgar Allan Poe, I too am 'constitutionally secretive and nervous in a very unusual degree. I become insane with long intervals of horrible sanity'."

I could but stare at the man.

"Speaking of which, I really ought to rid myself of this revolting little article, don't you agree?" he said, indicating the lunatic identification bracelet on his wrist. I watched as he extracted a piece of bent wire from an inner pocket and opened the small padlock with the ease a legitimate key would have afforded him. He held the bracelet up before me. "Such a nuisance," he said, and casually tossed it out the window.

I sensed that we were nearing the end of our journey together and I was suddenly seized with a desire to express my admiration for him. I drew a breath and began: "Mr. La Griffin, I must tell you that I believe you to be a Self Creationist of exceptional ability. Further, that I admire your dandiacal style greatly—you are a true poet of cloth, sir, and I sit before you in awe of your apparel. If it would not be too gross an impertinence, might I trouble you for the names of your tailor, glove-maker, haberdasher, and bootmaker?"

My companion seemed momentarily taken aback by my request. He paused, weighing his words before responding.

"You are quite right, Mr. Ravencroft, your request does constitute a gross impertinence, and furthermore, why a gentleman from New York City would require such information escapes me for it is my understanding that New York is a well-tailored city. However, given my degree of indebtedness to you for not raising the alarm, I suppose I must answer you fully, although under normal circumstances I would not dream of doing so."

He hesitated as I withdrew my pocket notebook and sterling silver lead pencil with all possible speed and made ready to make the appropriate notation.

"My tailor's name is Mr. Salvatore Piccolo and you will find him at number 222 Colborne Street, next door to the Albany Club— the home away from home of the Conservative Party. As for my gloves, they constitute a collaborative effort. Mr. Michael Gregory at number 32B King Street West is responsible for the thumbs, Mr. Nicholas Fish just down the way at 42A is fingers, and Monsieur Pierre Montclaire is responsible for palms, backs, and assembling the various digits. Monsieur Montclaire is the former manager of the Paris Kid Glove Shop on Yonge Street but has since opened his own small but highly exclusive glove-making establishment on Colborne Street—across the street from Mr. Piccolo, and next door to the Dog and Duck. As to my bootmaker, Mr. Hamish Moore has that great honour and he is to be found in his shop at number 5 Leader Lane, just off Victoria Row. Finally, Mr. John Peevers, purveyor of fine hats and divers haberdasheries, is located on Church Street directly opposite the St. James Cathedral Sunday School building. Naturally you wish to know the recipe for the polish necessary to achieve such a dazzling shine on my boots, but that information I categorically refuse to divulge—indebtedness or no. I will, however, give you a hint. Are you familiar with Lieutenant-Colonel Kelly of the First Foot Guards—the patron saint of boot polish?"

I answered in the negative.

"No, I suspected as much. It is common knowledge that Lieutenant-Colonel Kelly—who, sad to say, died while valiantly trying to rescue his favourite pair of boots from his sister's flaming house—that same Kelly achieved an unsurpassed brilliance of shine owing to the fact that he mixed his secret polish with champagne before applying it to his boots. I too follow this practice, and the results speak for themselves. More than that I will not say."

"No, quite. I understand completely. But, incidentally," I ventured, "I could not fail to notice when you were curled up on the seat asleep that you also follow Beau Brummel's dictates regarding the varnishing of the soles as meticulously as the uppers."

"Oh, so you have heard of Mr. Brummel in America, have you, Mr. Ravencroft?" he responded dryly.

"But of course, Mr. La Griffin. Indeed I too attempt in my own small way to follow his precepts," I said as I sharpened the upturned points of my Imperial with two staccato twists.

"Do you indeed? But surely not in that dreadful suit?"

101

"Oh no, of course not!" I cried indignantly—my cheeks aflame with embarrassment and hurt. "But I understand your confusion. You must understand, I was compelled to buy this 'size approximate' suit owing to the fact that all my luggage was consumed in a fire in the baggage car of my train. That is why I was so eager to obtain the names of your tailor—that I might replenish enough of my wardrobe to see me through my sojourn in Toronto. No, let me be quite clear on this point, Mr. Brummel and I are completely *d'accord* in so far as we share the belief that there is quite as much vanity and coxcombry in slovenliness as there is in the most extravagant opposite. Although one must also bear in mind his warning that the severest mortification a gentleman can incur is to attract pointed observation in the street due solely to his attire."

"Ah yes," broke in Mr. La Griffin, "it is all very well for Mr. Beau Brummell to be so pure. Kindly keep in mind that he had the happy fortune to live not only in London, England, but at the height of the Dandiacal Age. Just try dressing well in holy Toronto and not drawing attention to yourself—quite impossible, I do assure you. One simply cannot help but stand out in a crowd of dowdy, frock-coated, puritanical dullards. My feeling is that, since it is inevitable that I shall, as it were, steal the show wherever I go, I may as well indulge my every sartorial whim—in addition to every other whim, of course. In short, Mr. Ravencroft, I enjoy an appearance distinct and apart from my dreary fellows."

"Well, yes," I said, "when you put it that way, I would have to agree. Dandyism is, after all, one of the decorative arts."

"Quite. 'One should either be a work of art or wear a work of art'. Now tell me, are you familiar with the writings of Monsieur Charles Baudelaire, Mr. Ravencroft?"

I responded that, regrettably, I was not.

"I see. Make it your business to read him without delay. You cannot understand Dandyism without reading Baudelaire. He will tell you that Dandyism is not, as is commonly supposed, simply an excessive love of clothes and material elegance. To the perfect dandy such matters are merely symbolic of his own spiritual perfection. Dandyism is the poetry of appearances, a quest for spiritual perfection through style. It is the last splendour of heroism in decadence. It is a setting sun and, like the star in its decline, Dandyism is superb, without heat, and full of melancholy."

"Mr. La Griffin," I said, genuinely moved, "I shall do all

that you suggest. Please, tell me how I can ever repay you for troubling to counsel me so wisely and so well."

"Not at all, Mr. Ravencroft, indeed it is I who am indebted to you—for helping me achieve my liberty. I may say that, while debts of a monetary nature have never bothered me unduly, I do detest being in a position of personal indebtedness. I believe you mentioned your fervent desire to attend La Divine Sarah's performance tonight. . . ."

My heart leapt at the implication of his words. "Yes, I am quite prepared to risk my life if necessary," I assured him.

"I must tell you that I share your devotion to La Divine Sarah, and it was because of my desire to attend her performance that I felt compelled to execute this unauthorized removal of my person from the asylum. I propose to settle my debt to you by ensuring that you are a member of that most privileged audience tonight."

My spirits soared heavenward! "I would be more than pleased to purchase from you any extra ticket you might possess," I stammered. "And you may name your price, of course."

"Alas, at this stage, I have no tickets whatsoever," he said.

My spirits plummeted.

"However," he continued, "I am a man of resource and indomitable will and, like you, I will stop at absolutely nothing to attain admittance tonight. If you will be so good as to meet me outside the Grand Opera House this evening at thirty minutes past seven o'clock, I can assure you, I will have discovered a means for us to gain entrance to the theatre."

I did not wish to sound like a Doubting Thomas but I could not prevent myself from cavilling. "Mr. La Griffin, I do not doubt your sincerity for one moment, and I beg your forgiveness in advance, but how can you be so certain? What if you fail and we are both left out in the street?"

"That is not a possibility I am prepared to consider," he said, with a deal of irritation in his voice. *"Contra Audentior*, Mr. Ravencroft—in opposition, more daring."

"Yes, quite," I said. *"Fidem Servo*—I keep faith."

"See that you do, sir. And now I note that it is time for me to decamp. One final point: rest assured that you made the correct decision when you laid your weapon aside." In the wink of an eye he leapt across the carriage and I felt the barrel of a derringer pistol pressed to my temple. "For had you not done so, you would most assuredly not have lived to see another day—much less La Divine Sarah. Until tonight, then, adieu Mr. Reginald Ravencroft."

And so saying, my companion flung open the door and leapt out of the moving carriage, leaving me to watch in helpless fascination as he set off in full stride up York Street with his gold monocle glinting in the bright September sunshine and his huge cloak swirling out around him—splendid in his hauteur. As he disappeared around the corner I sought to contain my rioting emotions until I might have a quiet moment in which to fully understand the implications of my meeting with Mr. Belvedere La Griffin. My heart was still racing wildly, but the danger was now past, and the fact remained that I had the promise of a ticket to La Divine's performance!

In any event, the next thing I knew, the carriage had stopped and the Queen's doorman was ushering me into the hotel. I went directly up to my suite and took up residence in the bay window, with a Turkish Beauty and the resolve to make some sense of it all. On the one hand I was thrilled to have met Belvedere La Griffin, for he was clearly an authentic dandy, a dévoté of both La Divine Sarah and Oscar Wilde and quite simply the most exciting person I could ever imagine meeting. I was wholly mortified by his condemnation of my fine walking suit but, on the positive side, I now had the names and addresses of the finest sartorial craftsmen in all Toronto. Then too, the promise of a ticket to see La Divine Sarah fairly took my breath away with joy—but could I trust him to fulfil his pledge? I mean to say, who exactly was he? When I thought about it, "Belvedere La Griffin" seemed a most unlikely name, and this coupled with the fact that he was an escapee from the Provincial Lunatic Asylum hardly encouraged trust in either his intentions or his judgement. Suddenly a thought occurred: was a griffin not some manner of mythological winged beast? A quick consult of my Concise Oxford English Dictionary—without which I never travel—disclosed that a griffin/griffon/gryphon is a fabulous creature with the head and wings of an eagle attached to the body of lion! It seemed incredible that on only my second day in Toronto I should meet a man who was not only a true poet of cloth but one bearing a name so similar in spirit to my own—that is to say, Griffin and Ravencroft. Furthermore, I noted a secondary definition for griffin, a type of short-haired terrier, and if ever the description "terrier-like" applied to anyone, it applied to the diminutive yet heavily armed and fearless Belvedere La Griffin. But then again, was not his name just a little too appropriate? Should it matter to me if he was travelling under an alias? Could I afford to throw any stones in that direction? And further, did the fact that he was an escapee from an asylum mean that he was a lunatic as opposed to a Self Creationist like myself? I could not answer that question with a significant degree of certainty. But lunatic or not, there was no denying that the charm of his conversation proclaimed him to be a gentleman, and in my heart of hearts I believed he was sincere in his pledge to help me. Since he was a man of his word, I could take it as fact that he would do his best to provide me with a theatre ticket. But was that not the key phrase here: "do his best"? Granting for the moment that he had both the desire and the ability to get the tickets, even so, I now saw two very large potential pitfalls. Firstly, he was a narcoleptic, and therefore subject to bouts of mesmeric sleep without warning and of uncertain duration. Secondly, he was an escaped lunatic and therefore susceptible to capture—especially given his flamboyant style of dress. No, my position was suddenly quite clear to me. As regarded Mr. Belvedere La Griffin, I should remain thrilled to have met him, but a modicum of caution was warranted. As to his condemnation of my outfit, I should rejoice in and learn from his counsel. And as for my theatre ticket, I had to assume that, despite his best efforts, Belvedere La Griffin would fail me, and that in but a few short hours I would be called upon to obtain a ticket by fair means or foul, regardless of the danger. Therefore my next move was to get to The Cloister joy palace with all possible speed, for if the opportunity to engage in love's seraphic act that afternoon was real, I had to take advantage of it.

I set about freshening my toilet posthaste, and after a short cab ride I found myself standing across the street from the notorious Cloister joy palace. The building's appearance filled me with neither lustfulness nor hope. I understood that a dingy, nondescript façade was necessary so as not to advertise the riotous orgies taking place within but, nonetheless, its appearance really was dreadfully dreary. The shades were drawn in every window, the paint had long since given up any pretence of sticking to the large wooden verandah, and bits of newspaper and assorted filth littered the muddy front yard. Then there was the still unresolved problem of night shift versus day shift—would the day-shift girls, assuming they existed, be as beautiful and friendly as the night-shift girls? Further, would the lovely Cecily be available so early in the day? But then again, given the uncertainty of my future, did I really have any option but to go inside? I felt deuced conspicuous standing there in the brilliant sunshine, gawking at a joy palace while purposeful Christian citizens swirled all about me, so I decided to walk around the block in order to sort out my thoughts and reach a final decision. By the time I returned to my post across from the house, I had resolved once and for all that I had no option but to continue down my chosen path to wherever it might lead me, and I therefore crossed the street and mounted the verandah steps. I paused before the paint-chipped door. Neither knocker nor bell chain was in evidence and no sound issued forth from within. I raised my hand to strike upon the door when suddenly I heard a voice address me.

"Willoughby Tweed," said the voice. "Whatever are you doing? Certainly the afternoon girls will be less comely than the night girls—it only stands to reason. Out of fear of being a coward, you are cowardly persisting in doing what you know to be wrong. This is not the action of Reginald Ravencroft. Reginald Ravencroft has too much faith in his destiny. He abjures moderation as his sworn enemy, security is anathema to him. Furthermore, what you are doing is an act of betrayal of Belvedere La Griffin. He has given his word that he will devise a means for you both to attend the performance. If you are incapable of trusting him, then you are unworthy of his friendship. In short, Reginald Ravencroft, *Fidem Servo.*"

I paused, but only momentarily, before turning smartly on my heel and striding back down the steps. There was only one proper course of action for me to take, and that was to ensure that I looked my very best when, later that evening, I sat in the Grand Opera House bathed in the holy light of La Divine Sarah Bernhardt. To that end, I swung my bow back towards The Queen's Hotel and set sail for the tonsorial parlour I knew to exist therein.

The Paradise Barber Shop was truly a mecca of leisurely ablutions, wherein the slightest hint of haste on the part of the barber was considered a grievous affront to the customer. In appearance it reminded me of Bingham's Palm Garden Oasis, for it too was crowded with cascading fern fronds and palm trees in brass jardinières. I took up residence in one of several tapestry-covered chairs amidst the palms and basked in an atmosphere heavy with all the smells of Araby, and filled with the chirping of happy canaries cleverly placed throughout the establishment to raise the spirits of those within. On a shelf above the heavy marble basins I noted the personal shaving mugs of regular customers, labelled with their initials in Old English letters, while at the far end of the room toupees were offered for sale to any persons whose lack of capillary adornment rendered a hair appliance necessary. A vast array of newspapers and periodicals were available for the customers' perusal and I selected the latest edition of *The Police Gazette*. On the cover of this esteemed periodical was the depiction of a buxom female person clad only in black tights, riding a bicycle, and as I surveyed her voluptuous form it occurred to me that I might have unknowingly had a near brush with disaster back at The Cloister. That is to say, what if the establishment was closed until nightfall? Had I knocked, I might well have awoken the doorman from a very sound and well-deserved sleep. What if, after cursing me and waving me away, he remembered my face and refused me admittance when I returned at an appropriate time some night in the near future? Then another thought occurred to me. Belvedere La Griffin claimed Doctor Dandy was rapidly losing his mind. What if that was indeed the case, and he either had no experience with brothels whatsoever or, at best, was wholly mistaken concerning the whereabouts of The Cloister? I decided it would be best if I stopped tormenting myself over The Cloister and, to that end, I put down my *Police Gazette* and took up the latest edition of the less sensational *Globe*. I had hoped to lose myself in a more calming article but this was not to be, for under the headline STOUT DRAY HORSES REQUIRED, I discovered a photograph taken outside Union Station of two huge wagons piled high with dozens of trunks containing La Divine Sarah's costumes and assorted necessaries. Those costumes were undoubtedly hanging up backstage at that very moment, in readiness for the sorceress and her theatrical company, while I sat basking in the smells of Araby without a ticket. I consulted father's Waltham and discovered that it was five minutes of five. It was time for me to be on the move once again. Fortunately the barber had just finished applying a dab of French *cosmetique* to my beautifully upturned Imperial, and there remained only for a squirt of bay rum to be applied to my patent-leather locks before I set off for my suite with the wonderful aroma of occult essences wafting out from my person.

I went directly to my dressing room to suit up, and it was thrilling to finally don my smart new theatre costume, but I found myself becoming increasingly agitated as the moment of departure drew near, and it occurred to me that a bracer of some description was called for before setting out. I considered going down to the Royal Canadian Room for a Timber Doodle, but in so doing I would run the risk of bumping into Doctor Dandy, and I did not feel myself to be up to that event. Then in a flash I remembered reading during the course of my research a quotation from Boswell's *Life of Samuel Johnson* in which Doctor Johnson was quoted as saying that claret is the liquor for boys and port is for men, but he who aspires to be a hero must drink brandy. It was but the work of a moment to issue my request via the wonders of my Electric Annunciator, and shortly thereafter a waiter appeared at my door bearing a decanter of Rémy Martin upon a silver tray, accompanied by a large crystal snifter. I poured a stiff measure of the golden liquid into the snifter and, after taking care to cradle it in my cupped hands so as to warm the old cognac, I took a sizeable draught and basked in the warm glow it produced. It was wonderfully soothing, and as I surveyed myself in my dressing mirror I felt compelled to speak.

"Reginald old lad," I said, "this is the most important night of your life. There is no room for failure tonight, no second chance. Tonight you must act like a man and, if required, a hero."

And so saying, I downed the remainder of my Rémy Martin and donned my opera cape and topper. My revolver was stowed in my trouser band and my inheritance pinned to my coat lining. My date with destiny was nigh. At long last I was off to the Grand Opera House to see my saviour—La Divine Sarah Bernhardt.

CHAPTER VII

MY ADVENTURE AT THE THEATRE

I elected to walk the short distance to the Grand Opera House to gain time in which to further steel myself for action. In spite of Belvedere La Griffin's promise of a ticket, I had to assume that he would fail me and therefore the onus was still on me to find a way into the theatre—by hook or by crook. It being just past the dinner hour, the streets around the hotel were largely deserted, and thus it came as a terrible shock to me when I rounded the corner onto Adelaide Street and found it jammed with hansom cabs and private carriages competing to deliver their glittering charges to the entrance of the theatre. For some reason I had simply assumed that the vast majority of the audience would arrive closer to the hour of performance. As I drew nearer to the magnificent theatre I saw that the crowd of happy theatre-goers was so dense that it would be impossible for me to get near the entrance, and that the odds of locating an individual person amidst such a throng, and in particular the diminutive Belvedere La Griffin, were very slim. Furthermore the elegant mob was so animated and blind to my existence that the thought of trying to get the attention of an isolated play-goer and making an offer to purchase his ticket seemed completely out of the question. My brow was completely bedewed with perspiration despite the coolness of the September evening, and the knowledge that I was carrying a revolver only made me feel more ridiculous. Everyone in the crowd looked so excited and happy, I had to wonder how I could have even considered robbing another human being of the opportunity to see La Divine. I debated forcing my way through the crowd to the box office, but I knew it would be a wasted effort, for there could not possibly be an extra ticket. Then I thought, no, I must at least inquire, so that I will not be haunted for the rest of my life by the thought that, had I taken the trouble to ask, there just might have been a single ticket turned in. And so, I fought my way through the mob to the door of the theatre only to have my progress halted by a cockaded doorman who informed me that the performance was sold out and that, since the tickets were non-refundable, none would have been turned in to the box office. There was nothing I could do but move aside and fight my way back against the stream of persons pressing in relentlessly against me. I was angry and desperate and, in truth, I was very much afraid that I was about to break into tears of rage in front of everyone. But then one faint glimmer of hope managed to peep through the black clouds of my despair. Since it was virtually impossible for me to locate Belvedere La Griffin in the crush, perhaps if I isolated myself, stood apart from the crowd, he would find me.

I quickly made my way across the street from the theatre and there, much to my disgust, I discovered a group of some dozen or more dowagers walking up and down in single file protesting La Divine's presence in their saintly Toronto. The lead protester carried a sign reading, "Send the theatrical whore back to Babylon," while another's read, "Behold I was shaped in wickedness and in sin hath my mother conceived me." One of them, who was sporting a large wooden crucifix, started chanting, "Repel the stranger within our gates." That I was angered by their behaviour goes without saying, but I could not allow myself to be distracted by their revolting antics. I stood off to one side and surveyed the crowd for Belvedere La Griffin but I held little genuine hope in my heart. If he was in the crowd—that is to say, not captured or asleep—and if, against all odds, he had somehow managed to acquire two tickets, then in all likelihood he had seen that our finding each other was an impossibility and had simply gone inside by himself to enjoy the performance. And even if he was willing to make the effort to find me, he was hardly likely to enter the glare from the gas lamps lighting the entrance and risk being spotted by one of the constables attempting to maintain order in front of the theatre. I continued to scan the throng of play-goers across the street for my comrade, but before long the crowd thinned out to the point that I could say with certainty that Belvedere did not number among the few persons remaining to enter the theatre. A dreadful fact stared me squarely in the face. Unless I took immediate and decisive action of some kind, I was not going to see La Divine Sarah perform. I had sworn to myself that if necessary I would risk my very life to gain admittance, and yet somehow I was standing dressed in my fine new opera clothes on the wrong side of the street. Could something as pathetic as shyness account for why I had not even *tried* to purchase a ticket from a member of the crowd? Was I merely a charlatan, a Balls Falls hayseed lost in the big city? Suddenly a plan as desperate as it was audacious sprang fully formed into my mind. In a few moments, when nearly everyone had entered the theatre, I could approach the doorman and claim to have found a billfold that I insisted on giving to the manager, Mr. O.B. Sheppard himself, so that I knew for certain it would be safe. Once shown into Mr. Sheppard's office, I could force him at gun-point to have two extra seats set up in the theatre that we would both occupy for the duration of the play. At the conclusion of the performance, I would do my best to disappear into the crowd and thereby escape incarceration. Action was clearly the order of the day. I slipped my hand inside my opera cloak and grasped the butt of my revolver. The remaining few persons were entering the theatre. My moment of truth was at hand, and as I withdrew my revolver from my trouser waist I felt a sudden surge of joy as I realized that yes, Reginald Ravencroft *né* Willoughby Tweed really was willing to risk everything for one crowded hour of glorious life. More than that, I was prepared to be a hero! I drew a deep breath, squared my shoulders, and took one last look up at the noble Union Jack flying above the theatre. And there, high atop the Grand Opera House tower, stood Belvedere La Griffin—his tall silk topper outlined against the darkening sky and his long opera cloak flapping wildly about him as he waved his arms to attract my attention. Oh, how my heart soared with relief! I immediately waved back to him and started to cross the street towards the front of the theatre, but he motioned for me to go down Grand Opera Lane at the side the theatre. I did as directed and stood looking up at the eaves of the soaring roof, but from that vantage point I could see nothing of him. Then suddenly an object plummeted from the sky and very nearly hit me on the head. Upon inspection it proved to be a weighted silk handkerchief. I untied the knot and found within the folds a piece of roof tile and a personal card. The card belonged to one "Herbert Musket, Esq." There was a note written on the inside of the handkerchief. It ran:

Reginald Ravencroft, Esq.
Please be so good as to enter the theatre without delay and present the enclosed card at the reservation wicket where they are holding our tickets. You are to pass yourself off as Mr. Herbert Musket. Explain that your father, Henry Musket, will be unable to attend tonight's performance and has authorized you to use his tickets in his stead. Once you have secured the tickets, however, on no account go directly to the seats indicated thereon. Rather, wait for me in the shadows under the first balcony. I shall be along as quickly as possible.
Belvedere La Griffin, Esq.
Contra Audentior

I legged it for the theatre entrance the instant I finished reading the note, and moments later found myself amidst the gay throng in the perfumed warmth of the foyer. It hardly seemed possible that this was the same foyer I had befouled with my vomit only the day before, and in the back of my mind I could not help but wonder whatever had become of my fine new bowler. However, I had no time for idle speculation and so I screwed up my courage and presented myself at the reservation wicket.

"Good evening to you," said I. "Herbert Musket—my card. My father is unable to attend tonight's performance due to an untimely illness and I will be using his seats this evening."

"Yes, Mr. Musket," said the clerk with scarcely a glance in my direction. "We received your telegram this afternoon and have been holding your tickets as directed."

He then calmly placed two translation brochures and the two precious pieces of stiff red cardboard in my white-gloved hand and I walked away with them—as easy as that. I deposited my opera cape, topper, and stick with the cloak-room attendant, obtained a pair of opera glasses from the rental counter, and entered the magnificent inner temple of the Grand Opera House. The sight of it fairly took my breath away. Before me stretched a galaxy of winking fairy lamps illuminating a riot of ruby-red velvet and gilt ornamentation. A dazzling crystal sunburst gaselier hung suspended from the centre of a spectacular dome upon which dozens of cherubs cavorted amidst lofty white clouds. I gaped wide-eyed at the massive proscenium arch—all richly frescoed in burnished gold leaf—and the luxurious private boxes filled with Toronto's nobility. My excitement knew no bounds as I saw the flashing eyes set in fair faces, the dazzling white shoulders, the sparkle of diamonds, the flirting of fans, and the wonderfully nobby uniforms looped with gold braid and peppered with medals that adorned many of the ladies' escorts. Statesmen, politicians, merchant princes—all of Toronto's Four Hundred were in full attendance. From out of the shadows, I felt a hand on my arm.

"Good evening, Mr. Ravencroft," said a voice.

I started perceptibly and looked down to find Belvedere La Griffin standing beside me. He had shed his cape and topper and I noted with admiration that his evening clothes were of the most exquisite cut, and that he was sporting a green carnation in his lapel à la Mr. Oscar Wilde. The intended effect was subverted however by the addition of an over-sized black moustache which, regrettably, made him look very much like a diminutive lion tamer.

"Good evening, Mr. La Griffin. How are you?" I asked somewhat awkwardly.

"How am I? Oh, fully clothed and in my right mind. Well, fully clothed at any rate. I trust the acquisition of our tickets proceeded without incident?"

"Absolutely, yes. The man hardly even looked at me. I can never thank you enough for getting me a ticket."

"Don't mention it, old man. I think we can now consider ourselves to be square—as far as my debt to you is concerned."

"Oh no," I said. "Now it is I who am in your debt. I confess I had given up all hope of finding you."

"And I had all but given up hope of attracting your attention. I hesitated to lob roof tiles at you for fear that those protesting philistines might see me and draw the attention of the police. As it was, I felt it only prudent to don this ridiculous moustache."

"Yes, I see. But tell me, is it wise for us to just sit in someone's seats? I mean to say, won't Mr. Musket have us thrown out when he arrives?"

"Most unlikely, dear boy. I suggest you trust me on that point. I further suggest we claim our most excellent seats while there are still many patrons in the aisles to screen our entrance. I cannot afford to be spotted by the authorities at this juncture."

With those words we left the safety of the shadows and joined the river of beauty and fashion flowing down the centre aisle. To my astonishment and delight, we did not stop until we reached the second row of the Orchestra. Mr. La Griffin indicated that I should occupy the velvet armchair second in from the aisle and he took up residence in the chair nearest the aisle. There was nothing save one row of seats and the orchestra pit between us and where the Eighth Wonder of the World would be appearing at any moment. I tucked my rented opera glasses into my jacket pocket and hoped my benefactor had not noticed them. I was, I confess, somewhat concerned as to how it was that we were sitting in such fine seats.

"My word, Mr. La Griffin," I remarked lightly. "These seats rank as the finest in the house. How ever did you manage it?"

"With little difficulty and great pleasure, Mr. Ravencroft. However, I think it best that I postpone recounting my amusing little tale until after the performance. Though I scarcely know you, my intuition tells me that you will enjoy your excellent seat the more if you remain in ignorance concerning its origin. Suffice it to say that, had I possessed but one more hour in which to work, I am confident I would have succeeded in securing us a private box."

A middle-aged man in evening clothes loomed up at Belvedere La Griffin's side.

"Good God, Herbert! What are you doing here?" he demanded.

I flinched but my companion remained impassive. "I do beg your pardon," he said casually. "You are. . . ?"

"Kindly do not take that superior tone with me, Herbert Musket. You know very well who I am."

"Do I?" asked my companion. He paused to adjust his

monocle and surveyed the man. "Oh yes, of course, it's Picket, is it not? Mr. Ravencroft, allow me to introduce Mr. Archibald Picket, my father's business partner. Picket, may I present Mr. Reginald Ravencroft of New York City."

"Good evening sir," I said as I rose from my seat and extended my hand. Mr. Picket hesitated and then shook it with thinly disguised irritation.

"Herbert, are you aware that the seats you and your friend are occupying belong to your father and myself?"

"Yes, so I understand. Alas, father will have no use for his fine seat tonight as urgent business has called him out of town, and I rather fancy you may wish to follow his example."

"Urgent business? I know nothing of any urgent business."

"Ah well, now on that point I really cannot comment except to say that, if memory serves—and you know it so rarely does—father said something about a rather disastrous fire and, I believe, explosion. But you know, in his distress the poor old trout was stuttering and stammering something shocking and I could scarcely understand a word he said. He kept wringing his hands and repeating the word 'ruined'."

"Great God! Did he say where the fire was?" demanded Mr. Picket.

"Yes, yes he did. It was in . . . oh, now where was it? Could it have been Hamilton?"

"Hamilton! Dear God, we've got thousands of dollars' worth of ammunition in our Hamilton warehouse!"

"Or was it Ottawa?" Belvedere mused.

"Neither the warehouse or its contents are insured!"

"Ah well, there you are. I fancy that would explain his panic, would it not? Yes, I do seem to recall him asking that I instruct you to join him immediately should I happen to bump into you. Personally I think it a deuced shame you shall miss—"

But Mr. Picket could no longer hear Belvedere's words, for he was legging it up the aisle for all he was worth. For my part, I hardly knew where to look. Was it really possible that Belvedere La Griffin was in reality Herbert Musket? My heart went out to him but I hardly knew what to say. Then suddenly it came to me.

"Mr. La Griffin," I said, "I was wondering, at the risk of being impertinent, might I be allowed to address you as Belvedere henceforth? You will find that I can be relied upon to answer to the name Reginald."

"Certainly, Reginald, by all means."

"It is a pity about your father's fire," I remarked.

"Fire? What fire would that be, Reginald?"

I could but stare in shock as I realized the extent of his machinations.

"Oh, you mean in Ottawa—or was it Hamilton? No matter. Yes, I took the liberty of dispatching a telegram to my dear father a few hours ago informing him of the most untimely conflagration. I can read that little musket man like a book—that is to say, a penny dreadful—and I knew that his miserly nature would preclude his having insured the warehouse and that I could count upon his greed to put him on the first available train."

"But surely he is going to be dreadfully angry with you— isn't he?" I ventured.

Belvedere turned to me with a rather impish, self-satisfied grin. "Well yes, off hand I should think he will be *deuced* annoyed with me. Most assuredly. Would not you be?"

"I would be furious."

"Perhaps I should explain something to you, Reginald. My father is an odious little boor, a man of little breeding and still less imagination. His presence here tonight would have been nothing less than a disgrace. And, I may say, ditto for Mr. Archibald Picket. Together they enjoy a reputation as being the two most boring men in all Toronto, and believe me, that is no mean accomplishment. The idea of La Divine Sarah's wondrous beam being cast upon the likes of them is nothing short of obscene—especially when their presence here tonight would have prevented the attendance of our most worthy selves. I suggest that you think no more about it— unless of course your sense of honour compels you to vacate the rather fine seat you are presently warming."

"Oh no. That will not be necessary. But I am curious on one point: what manner of business is your father in? Mr. Picket mentioned ammunition."

Belvedere paused and then started to laugh quietly to himself. "Well, if you can believe it, my father owns Musket Munitions. The little musket man manufactures guns, Reginald. Guns! Really it's too funny."

I did not know how best to respond to my companion's mirth concerning his own father so I fell to studying my translation brochure. As I read La Divine's name I was nearly overwhelmed by the enormity of the moment.

"You know, Belvedere, in all honesty I can scarcely believe that I am about to see La Divine. You may find this difficult to believe, but she quite literally saved my life when I was a youngster."

"Really, how so?"

"Well, through her example of Self Creationism. You see, at the time it was my intention to kill myself."

"Fascinating. We share a past predilection towards self-destruction—except mine, of course, is not so very past."

"Right now, at this precise moment, La Divine is sitting alone in her dressing room, wholly absorbed in the contemplation of the tragedy she is about to endure. Silent tears are coursing down her cheeks as she wills herself to feel, nay live, the tragedy of *Phèdre* in all its heart-breaking detail."

"Yes, quite. You are of course referring to her habitual solitary preparation for *Phèdre* as described in her interview in *The Strand* last year. I seem to recall the interviewer saying that it is rare for her to finish a performance of *Phèdre* without fainting at least twice."

"Yes, and weren't you shocked when La Divine said she consulted an eminent surgeon about having a living tiger's tail grafted onto the end of her spine?"

But Belvedere La Griffin was not destined to answer my question, for at that moment the excited chatter throughout the theatre ceased abruptly as the house lights dimmed and the orchestra struck up "God Save the Queen". When we resumed our seats, the house lights went out and total darkness engulfed us. Two thousand souls waited in terrible suspense. The ruby-red curtains parted and, as the gas lights came up, King Hippolytus and his mentor Theramenes walked on stage.

The story told in Racine's play is as simple as it is moving. It revolves around Queen Phèdre, who, while her husband King Theseus is off at the wars, has developed an uncontrollable sexual passion for her stepson, Hippolytus. She is herself revolted by her incestuous feelings, and when the play opens she has decided to commit suicide rather than degrade herself and her family. Soon, however, King Theseus is reported killed, and Phèdre is overcome by her lust. She confesses to the innocent Hippolytus that she craves his love. He is appalled, and when Phèdre sees that he is disgusted by her love for him, she begs that he run his sword through her heart. This he flatly refuses to do—not wishing to stain his hands with her filthy blood. Then suddenly the reports of King Theseus's death prove to be false as he returns from the wars a triumphant hero. Phèdre is terrified that Hippolytus will tell his father of her incestuous overtures. Her loyal old nurse, Oenone, rushes to her and begs that she accuse Hippolytus before he accuses her. Phèdre does not possess the requisite evil to do the deed herself, but she allows the nurse to tell Theseus that it was Hippolytus who tried to outrage Phèdre and not the other way around. Theseus believes the nurse and the innocent Hippolytus is executed. Phèdre—racked by remorse and ravaged by self-loathing—takes a slow-acting poison. As the play ends, she creeps on stage and, after confessing her heinous crime to Theseus, dies.

First we watched as Hippolytus and a friend discussed the fate of Theseus, who was off at the wars and had not been heard from for too long a time. They left the stage and then, without warning, a tiny, half-demented woman crept on stage. Incredibly, I did not realize that I was looking at La Divine Sarah until she spoke. But when she spoke, she did so with the most haunting voice that ever enchanted human ears. I was instantly mesmerized, lost, transported by this ethereal princess. Her confession to Hippolytus of her vile love for him was excruciatingly moving. Hers was a soul on fire, devoured by insatiable lust and crushing guilt. I cringed but sat transfixed, unable to look away. How Hippolytus resisted her powerful seductiveness was unfathomable to me, for her allure was simultaneously mystical and sensual. As the tortured and terrifying Phèdre followed her fate to oblivion I felt myself growing ever more faint with emotion, until eventually I lost consciousness for several moments. As I returned to my senses, I saw her kneeling before Hippolytus with her arms outstretched, writhing in agonized longing, begging him to slay her.

"This frightful monster must not now escape. Here is my heart. Here must your blow strike home. . . . Or if it's unworthy of your blows, or such a death too mild for my deserts, or if you deem my blood too vile to stain your hand, lend me, if not your arm, your sword. Give it me!" cried La Divine.

The hypnotic force she unleashed upon the audience was not unlike that used by snakes on helpless rabbits, and I suddenly understood how in real life she could tame savage jungle cats with ease where less adept trainers were devoured. When she learned of

Hippolytus's execution her voice rang out in such anguish as to send an icy shiver through me, and in her appalling grief her tears flowed with devastating realism. In fact, I learned later that her terrifying effect compelled many women in the audience, and more than a few men, to escape to the foyer in order to compose themselves in mid-performance.

Finally, after she took the poison, Queen Phèdre's death scene with all its devastating pathos was upon us. The candle of her life was burning low and the fatal fire which the gods had ignited in her loins was finally, fatally extinguished. As she spoke her final words I was sobbing audibly, and when I heard a horrible choking sound I turned and, through my bleary eyes, saw that Belvedere La Griffin too had quite lost control of himself.

"It was I, Theseus, who on your virtuous, filial son made bold to cast a lewd, incestuous eye. Heaven in my heart lit an ill-omened fire. . . . I have instilled into my burning veins a poison. Already it has reached my heart and spread a strange chill through my body. Even now only as through a cloud I see the bright heaven and the husband whom I still defile. But death, robbing my eyes of light, will give back to the sun its tarnished purity."

The curtain fell but the tragedy was so terrible a reality that we were all held immobile in the clench of its spell, awestruck, stupefied, incapable of applauding. The theatre remained deathly silent until suddenly two thousand souls rose as one and pandemonium broke loose. The curtain rose and the supporting cast swept onto the stage to take their bows. Wild applause greeted their arrival and I noted that the grease-paint on each of their faces was smeared by the real tears they too had shed. When they left the stage the tumult continued undiminished. We waited. An eternity passed. Where on God's earth was she? And then La Divine Sarah appeared before us. She took a few hesitant steps but, to our horror, she tottered and swooned. Fortunately her leading man happened to be standing close by in the wings and, with a valiant leap, caught her in his arms. He held her a moment and then led her to the centre of the stage. The applause became frenzied, with the audience shouting and cheering and stamping their feet. La Divine stood alone, her head sunk on her breast, her arms dangling at her side. She had not only given us her heart and soul, she had given us her blood. After a pause, she shot her arms straight out to the sides exultantly. The effect was explosive. The audience went berserk! I personally was virtually incoherent! A blizzard of floral tributes of every hue and genus known to mankind filled the air and carpeted the stage around her, and I cursed myself savagely for coming to the theatre empty-handed. Suddenly, to everyone's amazement, hundreds of white doves were flying wildly about the theatre. As we read in the newspapers the following day, University of Toronto students— ardent Sar-adorers all—had smuggled the birds into the theatre and loosely tied sonnets and love poems to their necks. Their intention had been for the doves to circle gracefully overhead while their romantic messages fluttered down at La Divine's feet. It was a very pretty thought, but unfortunately the doves were terrified by the lights and noise and began loosing messages of a much less romantic nature upon the heads and shoulders of the ecstatic audience. I was myself splattered on both shoulders but fortunately my head was spared. La Divine Sarah blew a kiss to her worshippers and swept off the stage. The tumult continued unabated and within moments she returned for her first ovation. In all, La Divine was called before the curtain twenty-three times, and each time she reappeared she was applauded to the echo. Sometimes she bowed like a queen, other times she acknowledged the acclamations with a languid wave of her ivory hand. For myself, I cried "Bravo!" until my ragged vocal cords refused to obey my commands and I was forced merely to clap my hands and stamp my feet with every remaining ounce of energy I possessed.

Finally, long after the dazzling house lamps had been turned up, the theatre manager was forced to mount the stage and beg the audience to cease applauding and go home.

I turned to Belvedere but discovered that he had slipped away at some point. For my part, I was so overcome by La Divine's astonishing performance that I found myself moving in a daze along with the crowd seeking the front doors of the theatre. Outside the theatre, brass-buttoned porters were attempting to organize the carriages and cabs for the departing theatre-goers. I joined a stream of pedestrians heading I knew not where, and had gone some distance when it suddenly occurred to me that, were I to station myself outside the stage door, I might gain one more glimpse of La Divine. I knew the door to be located down Opera House Lane and when I arrived there I discovered a group of at least one hundred persons gathered with the same purpose as myself. I tried to spot Belvedere but I was unable to see him. Two burly police constables emerged from the stage door and ordered us to clear a path from the door to the waiting carriage in the lane. After we complied with the constables' wishes, a "Sar-adorer" stepped out of the crowd carrying pink rose petals in his upturned opera hat and scattered them on the ground upon which La Divine's precious little feet were about to tread. Her Negro guard was next to appear, followed closely by Mr. Jarrett, and finally the sorceress herself stepped out and smiled shyly at her worshippers. This time the crowd stood in awed respect rather than cheering wildly, and in the hushed silence that greeted La Divine's appearance, a young girl stepped forward with a modest bouquet of violets. La Divine bent and took the flowers from the child's hands and kissed her lightly on both cheeks before walking quietly over the rose petals to the open carriage door. Then, just as she accepted Mr. Jarrett's proffered hand, I heard a voice call out to her. "Sarah, you saved my life!" She stopped and looked me full in the face. Then, with a sly grin, she purred, "But of course, dahrrling," and disappeared into the darkened carriage.

The crowd was slow to disperse. We were all stunned by her presence but no one more so than I. The most magnificent woman ever to inhabit the planet had smiled and spoken to me. I wandered aimlessly down Grand Opera House Lane and out onto Adelaide Street hearing her precious words over and over—numb with the miracle of it all. I found myself at Yonge Street and suddenly I knew what I must do. To simply return to the Queen's and attempt to enclose my joy within the walls of my suite was out of the question. It could only end in my smashing the furniture or leaping from a window. A passing policeman provided me with the information I needed and, in no time at all, I had located a livery stable, roused the owner, and was thundering along Front Street on the back of a fine stallion heading for open country. My mount, "Chocolate" by name, was clearly overdue for a good sound gallop, and his exuberant spirit perfectly matched the raging euphoria I felt within. At one point I remembered my revolver and emptied all six chambers into the air whilst whooping like a demented Indian. On and on we raced down the moonlit road until finally, as we neared Sunnyside Beach, Chocolate slowed of his own accord to a canter and finally a walk— as did my mind. It was a delicious fall night with a gentle breeze blowing in off the lake and the full moon reflected high above it. Could it be that a mere forty-eight hours ago I had been lying in my bedroom on the farm looking up at this same moon? There was no denying that my life was nothing short of charmed.

Chocolate and I turned for home and, as we made our way through the leaf-strewn streets, I repeated the verse I had memorized so many years before.

Happy is the man who can say,
Tomorrow do thy worst,
For I have lived today.

It was early morning when I sought the balm of sleep within the folds of my glorious lavender-scented sheets.

CHAPTER VIII

MY MISSION BECOMES CLEAR

I slept long and deep that night, and when I finally left the healing arms of Morpheus I awoke knowing with absolute certainty that my triumphant destiny was assured. I could not possibly fail in my plan to infiltrate Toronto's high society for the simple reason that La Divine Sarah Bernhardt really and truly was watching over me. She had confirmed this fact outside the stage door by her reaction to my assertion that she had saved my life. "But of course, dahrrling" was her very matter-of-fact response. She exhibited no look of confusion, no startled surprise, just a sly smile. In short, she *recognized* me! She *knew* me. All those years of praying to her image in my bedroom and later in my Church of Self Creation—somehow, in some occult manner beyond my understanding, she had been listening to my prayers and guiding me towards her through a complex scheme of signs. She had caused me to see the notice in *The Globe* announcing her appearance in Toronto, which had led me to the Royal Canadian Room in search of a savvy barman, which had led me to Doctor Dandy, who in turn had led me to Belvedere La Griffin and thence to the theatre and my rendezvous with her at the backstage door, where she could personally counsel me. What she said to me was, in effect, "Yes, Willoughby, I have been watching over you and yes, I will continue to guide you. It is your job to *Fidem Servo*—to maintain your faith in my protective power over you and be receptive to all the signs I will send to illuminate your path, no matter how obscure they may be." It was obvious that now, with my faith permanently embedded in my being, I had only to go forward fearlessly with my grand design to become a leisured gentleman of means. I began by passing a glorious week shopping by day, dining long and well in the early evening, and theatre-going by night.

My first and by no means unwelcome priority had to be the acquisition of a proper wardrobe, and since all of Belvedere's sartorial craftsmen were located within two blocks of each other in the fashionable King Street West area, it was to this, Toronto's original avenue of commerce, that I began what was to be the first of many wonderfully happy days spent among dry goods. Toronto's King Street was deemed to be the counterpart of London's Oxford Street, and well could I believe it, for lining its noble sides eastward from Yonge Street all the way over to Market Street were extravagant confections of cast iron and carved stone boasting plate-glass windows crowded with a profusion of fine clothing, rare antiques, jewels, exquisite porcelains, and every kind of fancy goods one could desire. G.R. Renfrew and Co., furriers to the Queen, Nordheimer's, China Hall, Victoria Row, and The Golden Lion, with its huge stone lion rampant atop the roof some four storeys high—they were all there, lined up for my inspection. The strolling crowds of a sunny morn, men about town collecting an appetite before lunch, beautiful women in elegant carriages, handsome young blades on horseback full of dash and go—this was my glittering new world.

My quest for a superb wardrobe began with Belvedere's tailor, Mr. Salvatore Piccolo, whom I found to be a courteous and dapper Italian man of about fifty years. His establishment was elegantly appointed in every way—the walls being lined with bolt upon bolt of the finest materials, neatly ensconced in shelves of black walnut, while three elaborate brass gaseliers provided brilliant illumination and a most impressive aura of refinement. I mentioned

Belvedere's name right off the bat so as to establish my bona fides and Mr. Piccolo remarked that Mr. La Griffin was indeed a most particular and knowledgeable client. I then went on to explain the concealment of my nudity with such a bourgeois horror of a ready-made suit, owing to the fire aboard the baggage car of my train from New York City, and was rewarded with a look of both relief and pity on the fine man's face. Over a period of some four hours, Mr. Piccolo and I studied the artists' sketches contained in two large leather folios and fingered dozens of bolts of cloth. During my perusal I took care to salt my conversation with no fewer than seven quotations from Beau Brummel on the art of sartorial adornment, and at least five additional ones from Oscar Wilde, so as to leave Mr. Piccolo in no doubt concerning my worthiness. Indeed I continued my discourse on fashion during the exhaustive measuring of my person, and I sensed that the noble tailor was highly impressed with my acumen. We concluded our session with my commissioning seven suits of clothes and an ermine-lined opera cape, and he requested that I return in five days' time for my first fitting. As I turned to leave his establishment, however, Mr. Piccolo cleared his throat and, with a noticeable degree of embarrassment, requested that, should I see Mr. La Griffin in the near future, I would remind him of the amount of money owing on his account. I thought quickly and said that I had quite forgotten that Mr. La Griffin had asked me to settle his account on his behalf. When I inquired as to the sum involved, Mr. Piccolo mentioned a figure which fairly took my breath away. Indeed at first I thought he must surely be pulling my leg—but when I guffawed appreciatively and he remained stony-faced I realized my error, and handed over the outrageous sum.

The establishment of Mr. Hamish Moore, bootmaker extraordinaire, was next at hand, followed by Monsieur Pierre Montclaire, master of the glove. He in turn sent me on to his colleagues, Mr. Gregory for thumbs and Mr. Fish for fingers. Mr. John Peevers, hatter and haberdasher, came last, and while on Church Street I had the great pleasure of examining Toronto's glorious Anglican pile—St. James' Cathedral. As I admired its graceful spire rising, as I happened to know, some three hundred feet skywards above the earthly throng, I was treated to the sound of its beautiful Westminster chimes ringing the hour. It was time I returned to the Queen's if I was to bathe before dining and attending the theatre that night, and so I retraced my steps along King Street in search of a hansom cab. As I passed the huge windows of The Golden Lion, however, I came to a dead stop. Displayed on a small dais therein was an oriental smoking robe the magnificence of which took my breath away. It was made of flowing green silk, with a pattern of writhing tobacco leaves embroidered in heavy gold thread upon it, and ringed with gold tassels around the bottom. Before I knew it, a handy sales clerk was explaining to me that the unique robe was made in Persia using twenty-four skeins of silk and in excess of one hundred and fifty feet of gold thread. When I asked the price he quoted a sum of money capable of sustaining me at the Queen's for some weeks, and for a moment I began to wonder if perhaps I should get a grip on my spending. But when the clerk suggested that the addition of a Greek cap of green Morocco leather embroidered in gold and a pair of red Turkish slippers with upturned toes would wholly round out the ensemble, I suddenly found I was powerless to say no, and I was assured that my precious outfit would be delivered to my hotel by express tricycle within the hour. Of course, my new smoking costume demanded that I pay a visit to Raleigh's Tobacco Emporium, several doors up the way, with its life-sized wooden carving of the famous knight standing on the sidewalk outside the front door. Raleigh's proved to be truly a mecca to Queen Nicotina's subjects, with one side of the emporium devoted to the reigning monarch of smoke—king cigar—the other side given over to prince cigarette, while cousins pipe, snuff, and chewing tobacco held court at the rear of the store.

When I rejoined the throng of fashionable shoppers on King Street I carried a heavy paper parcel containing a box of Pall Mall cigarettes, a cigarette holder in scrolled ivory, one cigar case in fine-grained Morocco leather, one carved meerschaum cigar holder, one sterling silver cigar clipper, and a box of fifty Shakespeare Half-Perfecto cigars. I turned once again towards the Queen's and it occurred to me that my parsimonious Uncle Harold would have me forcibly confined in Doctor Dandy's lunatic asylum if he knew of my outrageously extravagant smoking costume. Still, the deed was done, and if I expected to be accepted as a true gentleman, I had to look the part. Thinking of Uncle Harold put me in mind of writing my uncles, and I altered my course so as to pass The Arlington Hotel in which, it may be remembered, my uncles believed me to be residing. It was but the work of a moment to saunter into their writing room and purloin a few pages of the Arlington's stationery.

When I finally returned to the Queen's I stopped at the reception desk just on the off-chance that Belvedere had sent along a note explaining his abrupt departure from the theatre or, possibly, simply saying good-bye, but the clerk responded in the negative to my inquiry.

That evening I had the intense pleasure of attending Gilbert and Sullivan's *Pirates of Penzance* at the Toronto Opera House. (At first I was of two minds concerning the morality of attending one of their operas because I had read of their vicious lampooning of Oscar Wilde in *H.M.S. Pinafore,* but when I recalled Mr. Wilde's famous dictum regarding the fact that the only thing worse than being talked about is not being talked about, I decided he would approve of my attendance.) As it turned out, the opera was marvellous from beginning to end and I eagerly joined the happy throng in applauding it with enthusiasm. I had half hoped to see Belvedere in attendance, but despite arriving early and posting myself at the entrance of the theatre so as to survey the patrons as they entered, I saw no sign of him, and when I checked once again with the reception desk upon my return to my hotel, there was no message awaiting me.

Late that night, as I sat smoking in front of the fire in my glorious new smoking costume, I ruminated on my adventure with Belvedere at the Grand and thought to myself how strange it was to think of Belvedere La Griffin being Herbert Musket. Herbert Musket was such a drab, plebeian-sounding name, I found it quite impossible to imagine addressing Belvedere as such. At the same time, though, I took comfort in the fact that, like me, he had felt compelled to create a new, more appropriate identity. It was also interesting that we were birds of a feather where killing ourselves was concerned—the one distressing element being his allusion to the fact that his last suicide attempt was quite recent. I hoped with all my heart that he too was somewhere safe and warm before a cheery blaze.

The following day I had set aside as the day I would finally visit the store I had been shopping in via correspondence for all those many years, the shrine to which all visitors to Toronto eventually find their way, "The Palace Store of Toronto"—Eaton's! I had of course seen the exterior of the store depicted on the cover of my catalogues for years, but still I was unprepared for my first sighting of that vast commercial emporium. Covering almost an entire commercial block, it was the biggest retail pile in the entire Dominion of Canada, and boasted the largest plate-glass windows in all Toronto.

As I stepped through the massive glass doors I was staggered by the profusion of dry goods, for it is one thing to see thousands of articles listed in the pages of a catalogue, but quite another to find oneself standing at the edge of a vast sales floor surrounded by a stock so immense its value can only be estimated. In truth I felt myself to be quite overwhelmed by it all, and I welcomed the arrival of a floor-walker to guide me through the bewildering acres of dry goods. He represented himself as being a Mr. Swan, and I thought to myself, yes, Mr. Swan appears to be a man of good address eager to conduct me to my desired location, exactly as the advertisements in *The Globe* assured me he would be. When he inquired as to which department he might have the honour of escorting me to, I responded, "Men's Toiletries, please," for I had decided in advance of my arrival to investigate the efficacy of the new "safety" razor with a view to possibly purchasing one of the same. (The debate had been raging in the papers for months concerning the use of a safety versus the usual straight razor, with proponents of the safety citing reliability and ease of use while opponents called them unmanly.) Mr. Swan introduced me to Mr. Lawrie, the head of the Men's Toiletries Department, and I immediately asked his opinion on the safety controversy.

"Young man," he said, "I will not mince words nor cloud my meaning with verbal subterfuge. Are you aware that in a recently held competition sponsored by Yardley's Soap, Mr. Teddy Wicks—champion barber and strongman—shaved ten men with a Star Safety Razor in one minute fifty-eight seconds thereby winning the contest and a prize of one hundred dollars?"

I admitted that I was ignorant of such a feat.

"Are you also ignorant of the fact that the Star Safety is personally endorsed by no less a man than Oliver Wendell Holmes?"

Once again, I admitted that I was in ignorance.

"Well sir, let me simply say that it is a known fact that many men with dash and go will use nothing but a Star Safety and that used in conjunction with a cake of Yardley's Shaving Soap—endorsed by no less a man than Phineas T. Barnum—you cannot achieve a closer, faster shave. Furthermore, as Mr. Barnum himself has pointed out, to use a cheap soap substitute may well cause blood poisoning by applying impure animal fats to the tender cuticle of the face."

Mr. Lawrie had me firmly in his power by this time, and

very soon thereafter I was the proud owner of not only a Star Safety Razor and a cake of Yardley's Shaving Soap, but also a fine ivory-handled shaving brush, a white china shaving mug crafted by the English firm of Royal Doulton, with genuine gold accents, and a fine travelling toilette case in genuine lizard containing divers combs, brushes, files, scissors, and other grooming implements. As he assured me that I was now fully equipped to deal with any errant hair or whisker, it occurred to me that Mr. Lawrie might well be just the fellow to recommend a good curative for troublesome eruptions of the face. Upon inquiry I was informed that Flagler's Skin Enhancer had been established beyond the possibility of doubt or cavil as the most efficacious remover of warts, pimples, and flesh-worms. I thanked him for his advice and passed on without troubling to ask what precisely a flesh-worm might be, or if, in his expert opinion, I possessed any.

I spent many happy hours wandering the aisles of the vast emporium and made many additional purchases, including a pair of round tortoise-shell spectacles imported from France. They were reputed to be the latest in dash and go, and without question an immense improvement on my rather old-fashioned wire spectacles. When at last I was ready to pay for my purchases I was most interested to observe first-hand Eaton's famous cash boys in operation. The instant I handed Mr. Lawrie my money, he yelled, "Cash! Come cash!" and proceeded to raise a small flag with the number five emblazoned on it up the length of a four-foot-high flagpole attached to his counter. A moment later a young lad in a smart blue uniform appeared, took my money from the clerk, and returned from parts unknown within a minute or two with my change. As I exited the grand store, it felt strange to have immediate possession of my goods after years of waiting three weeks for my order to arrive. Now I was able to buy anything I desired directly, and free to do so at any time I liked.

Over the ensuing week I was constantly on the go—shopping and sightseeing by day and attending the theatre by night. I was very keen to visit the Massey Music Hall, which had only just opened, and I spent a most enjoyable evening within its exotic Moorish interior attending a recital given by the Toronto Mendelssohn Choir. During the first half of the programme the choir sang several very beautiful pieces from the classical repertoire, and after the interval, the celebrated whistling soloist Miss Laura McManis joined the choir for what proved to be truly a virtuoso whistling performance. In the course of the evening one could not help but notice the many pretty faces gracing the audience, and the fact that Miss McManis herself possessed an extremely comely form. In fact I found myself imagining at some length what she would look like without the annoying intervention of clothing. I had been aware all week that, like Phèdre, I had an inner passion that could not be long ignored, and after Miss McManis's performance I resolved to return to The Cloister as soon as my new wardrobe was completed.

Along with Massey Music Hall, the Bijou Theatre quickly became a favoured haunt of mine, for in addition to having dancing girls, they also offered two different plays each evening. "The Bad Girl of the Family", "Bertha the Sewing Machine Girl", "Fifteen Years of a Drunkard's Life", "Petticoat Perfidy"—I saw them all. I also had the great pleasure of visiting that "Shrine of Flora", the Palm House Pavilion—a mammoth crystal palace located in the lush grounds of the Allan Horticultural Gardens. It was there, amidst the towering palm trees, that I delighted in hearing Miss Pauline Johnson, the well-known Indian poetess, recite her poems, followed by a lecture by Professor Alphonse Ryan, who attempted to answer the perennial question: is there a distinctly Canadian character?

By mid-week I still had not heard from Belvedere La Griffin, and as I contemplated how best to spend my day, something—or Someone—told me that if I were to take a tally-ho tour of the city and keep my eyes peeled I would be sure to spot him. In this assumption I was, alas, mistaken, but nonetheless I did enjoy a delightful tour of Toronto. We—that is to say, eleven fellow tourists and I—departed The Queen's Hotel high atop an open tally-ho carriage driven by a footman fancifully attired in the livery of the previous century who duly conveyed us around the core of the city and then up Yonge Street all the way to the village of Yorkville, where the horses were changed before our return journey. It was heaven to me to finally see all the most unique buildings of Toronto, like Gooderham's triangular-shaped Coffin Block and the soaring Confederation Life Association Building—not to mention the glorious Bank of Montreal with its Beaux Arts design—but it was the mansions of Toronto's first families that really thrilled me to the very core of my soul. "Euclid Hall", the Gothic pile on Jarvis Street belonging to Mr. Hart Massey, of farm-implement and bicycle fortune—so baronial with its tower and battlements. "Lampton

Lodge", former home of the founder of *The Globe* newspaper, Mr. George Brown, who had been murdered ten years previously by a disgruntled employee of his newspaper. Then on to St. George Street, with all the great red Romanesque Revival houses so suggestive of French *châteaux* with their rounded towers, huge arches, and massive walls of stone and brick. In these fantastic villas lived the likes of George Gooderham—owner of the largest distillery in the British Empire, and even Timothy Eaton himself. I could but stare and wonder which of these mansions I would some day call my own.

The latter part of the week I spent with my tailor, bootmaker, and glovemaker, engaged in first, second, and, in the case of Mr. Piccolo, third fittings. He more than lived up to his reputation as a wizard of the needle, and upon leaving his establishment I was confident that I numbered among the smartest-dressed men in all Toronto.

I had decided earlier in the week to postpone my trip to The Cloister until I could wear one of my spiffing new outfits, and thus on Saturday, when I finally took possession of my new wardrobe, I set Monday night as the night Miss Cecily would lead me through love's labyrinth—the Sabbath being clearly out of the question for both practical and moral reasons.

Sunday evening I enjoyed practising poses and suave lines of dialogue in front of the mirror, but later that night, as I was reclining on the settee before the fire wearing my magnificent Persian smoking robe and cradling a double brandy, my thoughts returned once again to the fate of Belvedere La Griffin. I could understand his need to escape back up to the roof of the theatre before the crowds clogged the aisles, but I found it most peculiar that he had not bothered to even bid me good-night. Could it be that he was so overcome by his emotions that he was incapable of speech? But then could he not at least have waved good-bye? And surely the gentlemanly thing to do would be to write me a note of explanation or even stop by the hotel to express his apology. He knew perfectly well that I was stopping at the Queen's. The plain fact was that I missed him dreadfully. He was the only kindred spirit I had ever known, and whereas before meeting Belvedere I had been alone but by no means lonely, now that he had deserted me, I felt very much adrift. It seemed such a shame, for together we could be haunting the tailor shops and brothels and fine restaurants and theatres and having enormous fun. His knowledge of the world in general and

Toronto in particular so vastly exceeded my own—he could be my mentor as well as my friend. As for my contribution, I could provide both appreciation of his talents and ample funds if needed. It seemed so unfair. So devilishly, fiendishly unfair, and it hurt me to think that he held me in such low esteem that he could not even trouble himself to write me a brief note to say good-bye.

I sat staring into the glowing coals while I pondered the matter and the more I pondered, the more incomprehensible the whole affair seemed to be. Belvedere La Griffin was first and last a gentleman, on that I would stake my life, and a gentleman simply does not slip away from another gentleman without saying good-bye or at the least offering an explanation and an apology at a later date. But that being the case, where was his apology? Was he incapable of sending one? Where indeed was Belvedere? Was he strapped in a tranquillizer chair in the Provincial Lunatic Asylum, screaming to the heavens? Or, having lived to see La Divine Sarah perform, had he felt there was nothing left worth living for and hanged himself? Could he be lost in a mesmeric sleep? As my thoughts wandered, a terrible sense of foreboding crept over me. I felt it growing stronger until suddenly the candle upon the mantle shelf guttered and went out. I sat looking at the smoking wick and a sickly cold sweat began seeping out of my every pore. I knew then, in my heart, that Belvedere La Griffin was dead. I also knew that I was responsible for his death, for had I not allowed him to escape from the asylum he would still be alive. But then again, how could I reconcile his demise with the fact that La Divine Sarah was constantly watching over me and guiding my every move? Could it be that she deemed it necessary to sacrifice Belvedere's life that I might obtain a ticket to see her? I had to admit it was a possibility. Guilt and sadness weighed down upon me. Were it not for Belvedere I would have missed La Divine's performance. Indeed, I would very possibly be lying on a marble slab in the city morgue with a mist of cold water constantly washing over me to retard the process of putrefaction. I bent my head in deepest shame and I wept. But it was too much to bear, and through my tears I reminded myself that, had I not aided him in his escape, he would never have seen La Divine, and, like me, he had been more than willing to sacrifice his life in order to bask in her wondrous light. I watched as, one by one, the glowing coals in the grate slowly died. But just then another thought occurred to me. Could it be that he was not dead, but wounded and in desperate need of my assistance? Possibly Mr. Musket, upon finding his warehouse in Hamilton still standing, realized that Belvedere was behind the ruse and telegraphed the Toronto police, instructing them to arrest his lunatic son as he attempted to sneak out of the Grand Opera House. The police had been waiting for him after the performance and he had been wounded in flight by a bullet, or perhaps was forced to leap from high atop the theatre roof onto some soft substance like hay in the back of a wagon, and, while not killing himself, had suffered severe internal damage and was now lying near death holed up in his rooms—wherever they might be. Or on a less fanciful note, possibly he was merely lost in a mesmeric sleep in his rooms and slowly dying of starvation. In either case, it was highly probable that he was desperately in need of my assistance. Suddenly my mission was clear to me. Doctor Dandy was my only link with Belvedere and so, like it or not, I had no choice but to go back to the Provincial Lunatic Asylum to learn what I could of Belvedere's fate. If, pray God, he was still at large, I would have to find a way to either trick or persuade Doctor Dandy into giving me his address, and thereby go to his aid. Of course, it was unlikely that he would seek refuge in his own rooms, for that would be the first place the police searched, but still, he might have inadvertently left behind some clue as to his present whereabouts. I had no idea how I would accomplish my mission, I only knew that I would give my all to save the life of Belvedere La Griffin.

CHAPTER IX

REGINALD RAVENCROFT TO THE RESCUE

B y eleven o'clock the following morning I had tracked Doctor Dandy to his office in the Provincial Lunatic Asylum, and he was nothing short of delighted to see me again.

"My dear Mr. Ravencroft, I cannot tell you how pleased I am that you have kept your promise to return and complete your tour. This may shock you but there are many visitors who do not return. And how fortunate that my meeting over at the Asylum for Victims of Misplaced Confidence was rescheduled for tomorrow morning, or you should not have found me here. I am on the Board of Governors, you know. So many comely and naïve young mothers, all of whom have, in their naivety, given themselves to unscrupulous men."

"Victims of lust," I ventured.

"Victims of lust, yes, just so. Now then, young sir, away we go to the Women's Grand Hysterics Ward, eh what? I want you to meet Mrs. Wells. She has only just joined us here and she is as classic a case of post-connubial mania as I have ever seen. The mania is caused by outrage to virgin modesty on the wedding night, you see, and Mrs. Wells now believes herself to be Joan of Arc."

"Fascinating, doctor, I look forward to meeting her, and I am also hoping to meet Lady Windermere, who I understand has joined your family of lunatics quite recently."

Doctor Dandy fixed me with a look of consternation.

"Lady Windermere? I am not aware of a lunatic of noble blood in residence at this time. Might I inquire how you came to learn of her, Mr. Ravencroft?"

"Quite simply. Lord Windermere told me himself. Good heavens, doctor, you must remember Lord Windermere. It was at your invitation that he rode back to town with me in your carriage when I first visited the asylum."

"At my invitation? That is absurd, sir. I have never even heard of a Lord Windermere—much less met the man."

I extracted my bill-fold and showed him his lordship's card. As he read it, Doctor Dandy's look of consternation was replaced by one of satisfaction.

"Tell me," he said, "by any chance is Lord Windermere a young man of about nineteen years, and slightly under five feet in height?"

I responded in the affirmative and he opened a drawer in a tall oak filing cabinet and withdrew a paper folio.

"Is this Lord Windermere?" he asked as he handed me a photograph of Belvedere.

I confirmed his suspicion and he addressed me with authority.

"Mr. Ravencroft, I must inform you that the individual who shared your journey is no lord. He is, or was, an inmate of this asylum named Herbert Musket, and is currently at large."

"Good heavens!" I said in feigned outrage, secretly overjoyed to hear that Belvedere had not been recaptured. "You don't mean to tell me I rode all the way into Toronto with an escaped lunatic! My God, doctor, I might have been killed!"

"Calm yourself, Mr. Ravencroft, calm yourself. Herbert Musket is not a dangerous lunatic, or at least not under normal circumstances. Of course he can be violent when thwarted, but not where innocent persons are concerned. To understand Mr. Herbert Musket we must look back to his early childhood when he attempted to murder his father."

"What!" I cried in genuine alarm.

"When he was but a lad of nine years, Herbert's mother hanged herself from a beam in the family carriage-house. Herbert, for reasons I have been unable to ascertain, believed that his father drove his mother to commit suicide. In retaliation, he attempted to kill his father one morning while Musket Senior was eating his breakfast. Being a foreigner you will not be familiar with the name Henry Musket, but he is a very well known manufacturer. He owns Musket Munitions and his factory on Gerrard Street is one of the largest in all Toronto. Henry Musket possesses a large personal collection of armaments both antique and contemporary, and numbering among his collection at the time of which I speak was a brass cannon hailing from the American Civil War. He fancied this large item of ordnance as an article of lawn ornamentation and it sat in front of his house on St. George Street. Little nine-year-old Herbert somehow managed to pivot the cannon and fire it at the dining room in which his father was eating breakfast. It was a remarkable feat for a lad of his size and years, but what he did not know was that the barrel of the cannon was cracked. When he fired it, the barrel exploded and Herbert's hands and a large portion of his body were very badly burned. Indeed, it is a wonder he did not lose his hands altogether. It is also a wonder that Henry Musket was not killed, for the cannon ball blew the dining room to atoms and, had he not been called away from his breakfast by a domestic problem, he too would surely have been blown to bits. The upshot of it all was that Herbert spent the better part of a year recovering from his wounds in the Hospital for Sick Children. No criminal charge was laid because Henry Musket preferred society to see it as an accident or, at worst, a childish prank that, well, back-fired. His dead wife had tainted the family name with madness quite enough for his liking and he was not about to publicly add Herbert to the list. It was towards the end of his convalescence that Herbert attempted to follow his mother to the grave via the same route—that is to say, he hanged himself. Fortunately he was cut down in time and revived, but he added some very severe rope burns to his list of disfigurements and he bears the scars to this day. Immediately following his suicide attempt, Herbert was packed off to Victoria College in Cobourg as a full-time boarder and he remained there for some years before being expelled for duelling. Through his father's connections, he was next admitted to Upper Canada College which he attended for two years before once again being expelled—this time for the manufacturing and selling of gin to his school-mates. Since that time I believe he has been living largely by his wits and on substantial credit."

"And how came he here?" I asked.

"He was brought to us about two months ago after a second suicide attempt. He slit his wrists in the bathtub of a suite at The Rossin House Hotel. Happily, however, he must have had second thoughts, for he was discovered lying unconscious out in the hallway. After being sent to the Toronto General Hospital, he was brought to me so that I might ascertain if he was still a danger to himself. In the course of my psychologizing him I came to discover that he not only suffers from periodic bouts of severe melancholia, he is also a narcoleptic."

Belvedere had of course told me all about the nature of his disease, but I could not inform Doctor Dandy of that fact and thus I had no option but to allow the doctor to continue. At one point he told of a case where a narcoleptic soldier fell asleep during an actual bombardment and, after having slept for over a week, had to have a tooth drawn in order to be force-fed. I thought of Belvedere sound asleep somewhere, slowly but inevitably starving to death.

"Observe that photograph well, Mr. Ravencroft, for Herbert Musket's psychopathology is stamped upon it. Note his most extraordinary eyes—full of oddity, are they not? The bilateral lid ptosis which so often characterizes the mania—that is to say, drooping of the eyelids—is deceptive for these languid eyes belie a volcano of mischief. Observe the wide forehead, indicative of a truly impressive intelligence, and the sensitive mouth—how many sobs are etched on that mouth, I ask you?"

The photograph in my hand was gruesome to behold. Clearly it had been taken when Belvedere was heavily drugged and I was sure he would be furious if he knew of its existence. I felt ashamed of myself for participating in such a revealing discussion concerning the intimate private history of his life.

"You can see how invaluable the photographic studies of my patients are in a case like this. The Toronto constabulary are in possession of this photograph and we expect to have Herbert back in our care very soon. And come to think of it, now that we know he is travelling under the name of Lord Windermere, his capture should come about all the sooner."

"You believe him to be dangerous then, do you?" I asked.

"Dangerous to others? No. Dangerous to himself? Most definitely. I believe it is imperative that we find Mr. Herbert Musket before he has another fit of suicidal monomania and carries out his fatal purpose. Hospitalization is essential in his case—very probably for the rest of his life."

"And tell me, Doctor Dandy, is Mr. Musket a victim of lust like so many of your patients?"

"Lust? Of course he is, but in his case it is his denial of lust which is muddying the waters of his mind. It is my belief that he is profoundly embarrassed by the many scars he bears and believes that women would be repulsed should he reveal his naked body to them. Hence he must abjure all women and crush his natural lustful feelings. But lust cannot be for ever denied. It builds up within the loins of men. Some men respond by forcing their attentions on women—Herbert responds by losing consciousness. But now, enough of this. Come along and meet the unfortunate Mrs. Wells and her sisters in the Grand Hysterics ward."

Doctor Dandy crossed to the door, but just as he reached for the handle, the door opened and a nurse handed him a telegram. As he read it, I turned the paper folio lying open on the desk to face me and quickly scanned the opening page of Belvedere's medical history.

"Oh, confound it all," Doctor Dandy said. "Nurse, summon the wagon immediately."

On the third line down the page, I found what I was looking for. "Last Known Address: #3 Phoebe Street, Toronto."

"Is something wrong, doctor?" I asked.

"Yes, I am dreadfully sorry, but we shall have to postpone your tour of the female wing, Mr. Ravencroft. This telegram informs me that the mayor of Toronto has just had some manner of mental collapse. He has barricaded himself in his office and, believing himself to be a bomb, is threatening to blow himself up if everyone does not leave him alone. My presence is requested most urgently."

I expressed my regret and, taking care not to give my word to resume my tour at another date, I took my leave of the good doctor and his house of horrors. As I sank back on the leather seat in my hansom cab, I did so with a deal of satisfaction, for I now not only had Belvedere's address, I also had proven that Belvedere La Griffin was not the only person clever enough to send a bogus telegram. Reginald Ravencroft would most decidedly *not* be touring the women's wing of the Provincial Lunatic Asylum that day or any other day—thank you just the same.

Number 3 Phoebe Street proved to be a large, red brick house surmounted by a many-gabled roof and tower. A dense growth of English ivy covered most of the exterior and it was set well back from the street in its own grounds. It had obviously been a fine house in its day, but it now possessed an air of faded grandeur. I rapped upon the door with the iron knocker and, after a time, the door opened and I was confronted by a rather imposing dowager. Like the house, she too possessed an air of faded gentility.

"Good afternoon," I said. "I apologize for disturbing you. My name is Reginald Ravencroft and I am looking for my good friend Mr. Belvedere La Griffin. Would he be at home, by any chance?"

"No," said she, drawing herself up to her maximum height. "He would not. I have neither seen nor heard from Mr. La Griffin in nearly three months and his rent is dreadfully in arrears. Should you succeed in locating him, I would be grateful if you would tell him that Mrs. Flowers must receive all moneys owed immediately or I shall be forced to rent his rooms and sell his belongings in lieu of payment. I do not wish to be unkind but he does take advantage. I am a widow and I count on the rent from the upper rooms to put food on my table."

I leapt to Belvedere's defence without hesitation. "Yes, I understand, Mrs. Flowers, but it may interest you to know that the unfortunate man has been in hospital these past few months recuperating from a near-fatal accident involving an overturned hansom cab. You may be sure that it was never his intention or desire to cause you any pecuniary distress. Indeed I am sure he will be most upset to hear of your condition."

Upon hearing my shocking news, the good Mrs. Flowers was most agitated, and volunteered that a disreputable-looking old man with a filthy white beard had been around representing himself as a doctor and asking if Mr. La Griffin was at home. She had not liked the look of him one bit and had sent him on his way with a flea in his ear. I told her she was quite right to have done so and gave her the happy news of Belvedere's recovery.

"I am pleased to report that my friend's condition has greatly improved," said I. "Indeed, it was my understanding that he had been discharged several days ago—hence my calling upon him at his rooms. In any event, Mrs. Flowers, you may be sure that Mr. La Griffin will be returning home very shortly."

I then inquired as to the precise amount of rent owing and, when she quoted a figure, I instantly paid the sum and advanced her the rent money for the forthcoming month.

"And now," I said, "if you don't mind, I would like to go up to his rooms so that I may see that they are in readiness for his return. I assume you possess an extra key."

Mrs. Flowers bade me wait in the vestibule while she fetched the desired key and I found myself sharing the walnut-panelled room with a huge grizzly bear standing upright on his hind legs to a height of over seven feet. One of his massive paws was outstretched and on it balanced a silver salver, obviously intended as a repository for calling cards. As Mrs. Flowers returned she found me staring up at the beast.

"Colonel Flowers was a great white hunter, you know," she said wistfully.

I accepted the key and ascended the sweeping staircase to the second-floor landing, where a wall and door had obviously been added so as to create a private suite of rooms. I unlocked the door and slipped into the darkness of Belvedere's private domain. It was deathly still. When I struck a match I discovered myself to be standing at the head of a long hallway with many closed doors leading off it.

"Belvedere?" I called out in an urgent whisper. "It's Reginald Ravencroft."

I heard not a sound. I called out again but received no response. Suddenly I wanted very much to turn on my heels and flee, but the finer part of me knew it was my duty to investigate each and every room, no matter who or what might be lying in wait for me. I made my way along the hall. The first four doors revealed empty rooms and I began to wonder if somehow Belvedere had managed to clear out his belongings without Mrs. Flowers' knowledge. Upon opening the fifth door, however, I discovered a fantastic room decorated to suit the taste of the most wanton voluptuary—the oriental lair of Belvedere La Griffin. Heavy tapestry curtains blocked out most of the daylight and, rather than advertise my presence to the outside world by opening them, I lit a candle in a large brass holder wrought in the shape of a dragon. Belvedere had transformed the entire room into an oriental tent by draping striped fabrics from the middle of the high ceiling out to the corners of the room. The room centred around a large oriental divan nestled amidst towering plumes of dried grasses in huge blue-and-white porcelain vases. Over-lapping Persian mats covered the floor of the fantastic tent and an entire wall was adorned with curved swords and spears and other ancient Eastern implements of slaughter. The wall opposite was filled with books—many in padded Morocco leather bindings— and a brief inventory revealed a predominance of poetry, with Edgar Allan Poe and Charles Baudelaire most prominently displayed. A Cairo table stood in front of the bookshelves and on it sat an oversized phonograph machine with a full forty-two-inch brass "Grande" flower-horn, complete with extension crane to support its length and considerable weight. By comparison it made my Uncle Jasper's inexpensive Harvard Talking Machine with its little twelve-inch tin horn look like a child's toy. The titles on the wax cylinder records lined up beside the phonograph were also of a very different description from those of my uncle. Belvedere possessed no comic talking records such as "The Laughing Coon", or "Two Rubes in an Eating House", or for that matter any selections from the Important Speech Series like "Lincoln's Gettysburg Address" or "Talmage on Infidelity". Rather, his records seemed to be of a more romantic nature, with song titles like "I'm Wearing My Heart Out for You" and "She's Just a Little Different from the Others That I Know". Suddenly I felt a wave of guilt wash over me. Belvedere was clearly not in the room—asleep, dead, or otherwise—and I had no right to be examining the contents of what was obviously his *sanctum sanctorum* in such detail. Of course, I had to complete my inspection of his suite to be sure that he was not languishing within, but I withdrew from his Persian parlour with the resolve to make the remainder of my search as brief as possible.

The next door revealed his bedroom, which boasted red-and-black-striped velvet wallpaper on walls and ceiling alike. It was furnished solely with a huge canopy bed standing in the centre of the room, which, with its carved oak headboard rising up to the ceiling and acres of heavy purple drapery to enclose the sleeper within, appeared to me to be of antique British ancestry. The mattress of the bed was a good three feet off the floor and a stool with two steps was positioned to aid in one's ascent. It struck me as slightly absurd— even humorous—to think of little Belvedere mounting the steps and lying hidden within the vast bed, but I reminded myself that Belvedere La Griffin was diminutive only in body.

There was but one room remaining to investigate and I knew it could only be his dressing room. It proved to be a long rectangular room and, like the bedroom, was furnished in a spartan fashion—at least in comparison to his Persian paradise. The dressing-room furniture consisted merely of two massive mahogany armoires fully fifteen feet in length on opposite walls, and an equally large gilt-framed mirror taking up most of the wall at the far end of the room. A very fine oil portrait of Beau Brummell graced the wall to the left of the door, while on the right hung a portrait of a man I did not recognize but subsequently came to know as Monsieur Charles Baudelaire. The centre of the room was empty save for a thick Turkey carpet covering the floor. Each armoire possessed four separate compartments and it was to these that I was now irresistibly drawn. I discovered that all four compartments in the first armoire were devoted to wearing apparel. Suits of every hue and cut, nightwear, daywear, outerwear, neckwear, hose, undergarments, hats, gloves, and footwear—everything a clothes-wearing man could desire was to be found within the massive cupboard. I then turned to the second armoire and discovered in the first compartment an extraordinary array of walking sticks held horizontally by little brass clips against a plum velvet background. My eyes fastened on one in particular—a long ivory specimen with a head set with three large turquoise stones. I felt as though I had seen it before, and suddenly I realized that it was an exact copy of Honoré de Balzac's famous stick as detailed in the *Illustrated London News* some years back. The second door revealed another extraordinary collection, but one of a very lethal variety. Dozens of revolvers and knives lined the walls of the compartment, and I thought to myself that despite Belvedere's disdain for his father, he had obviously inherited Musket Senior's love of weaponry. I noted two empty spaces amidst the revolvers and was speculating as to their significance when suddenly I was interrupted.

"What are you looking for, Mr. Ravencroft?" demanded a voice.

I reeled around to find Mrs. Flowers standing in the doorway, and when I had recovered my composure sufficiently, I explained that I was merely making sure everything was in order. I detected an element of suspicion in her manner but I could not leave without dashing off a note of warning to Belvedere, just on the off chance he should return to his rooms. It ran:

Belvedere
Beware. Doctor Dandy has supplied the police with your
photograph to facilitate your capture. Take care. Your face is
known.
Your friend,
Reginald Ravencroft
P.S. Please excuse the liberty, but I settled your debt with
Mrs. Flowers and your rent for October is also taken care of.

My hansom cab was waiting for me at the curb as per
instructions, and I informed the cabby that I wished to be conveyed
to Victoria Row on King Street West. As I sat back in the cab I was
unsure just how I should feel. On the positive side of things, I had
determined that Belvedere was not under restraint in the asylum or
starving to death in his rooms. On the negative side, however, I had
failed to locate him and I had seen nothing in his rooms to indicate
where he might be. (Although what I had hoped to find, short of an
open map with a large arrow scrawled upon it, I do not know.) I also
found Doctor Dandy's story regarding Belvedere's attempted murder
of his father quite alarming. I mean to say, I thought the filching of
his father's theatre tickets was audacious, but that was just a mild
transgression compared to blowing up the family dining room. But
then again, if Mr. Musket truly was responsible for Mrs. Musket's
suicide, then Belvedere was simply exacting a just revenge. Also, at
the time he was only a child and children tend to think in very black
and white terms. Then there was the doctor's diagnosis of Belvedere's
suicidal condition. My inclination was to dismiss it out of hand,
despite his previous attempts to kill himself, but of course I was not
a doctor. It saddened me to think of the many scars Belvedere's finery
concealed. It was very confusing and disappointing, for it seemed
that all I could do was keep an eye out for him in the streets of
Toronto, but I had little hope of ever spotting him in such a vast
metropolis. Beyond that, it was time I got on with my own life, and
the next step in my quest for a suitable bride was my tutelage in the
timeless art of love. To that end I decided then and there to begin
my lessons at The Cloister, in Cecily's alabaster arms, that very night.
I spent the remainder of the afternoon "doing Yonge Street",

as the saying went, including a most enjoyable visit to Britnell Book Shop, where I acquired the newly published *Memoirs of Sherlock Holmes*. Then I returned to the Queen's and, after a long leisurely soak and a visit to the Paradise Barber Shop, I continued to the Maple Leaf Room, where a Fricandeau of Veal aux Petit Pois, along with a very sound Bordeaux wine and several brandies served to steady my nerves wonderfully for the rigorous evening ahead of me. I next confronted the all-important question of what to wear to my initiation into the pit of passion, and eventually, after having tried on all of my fine new suits several times, I chose my new dinner suit, or "tuxedo", as they had been recently dubbed. I thought it only prudent to adopt a pseudonym for the evening, and I therefore did not pack any calling cards upon my person. Cecily would simply have to take me at my word that my name was Guy Islingworth. As for funds, it struck me as reckless to take all of my remaining inheritance and so, after dithering for a time, I cut the stack of bills roughly in half and slipped one wad into my bill-fold. Finally I stepped before the mirror to survey my finery, and I thought to myself how proud father would be to see me so nattily turned out. I picked up his malacca stick and touched it to the brim of my "New York Style" topper.

"Good night, father," said I. "Tonight I become a man!"

CHAPTER X

LOST IN LOVE'S LABYRINTH

I instructed my cabby to deposit me down the street a ways from The Cloister and as I walked the remaining distance I was greatly relieved to see that, while the large windows in the vice resort were all in darkness, the red glass of the transom window was brightly lit from within. As I was about to turn up the walk, however, a lad of about ten years leapt out of a bush and blocked my path. He wore a dirty tweed cap and talked with a cigarette dangling out of his mouth.

"Lookin' for a lady, mister?" he asked.

I was both taken aback and annoyed by his interference, and furthermore I thought it highly improper to discuss matters of a delicate nature with a child.

"Certainly not," I said. "I am going to visit a friend. Now kindly get out of my way."

"Can't visit your friend without a membership card and the

password."

"Do you work here?" I demanded.

"That's right, I'm Billy the lighthouse. I let Big Sue know if there's cops comin' around and help gents that are lost find the house."

I was of course appalled that this mere child was a recruiter for vice but clearly I had no alternative but to follow his lead.

"And you sell membership cards?" I asked.

He answered in the affirmative and proceeded to sell me a card for the princely sum of two dollars.

"Give three quick raps on the door," he added. "Then when Big Sue opens the window, ask her if she has any fresh bacon—that's tonight's password, see?"

I offered perfunctory thanks to the lad, mounted the steps, and executed three sharp raps on the door as per instructions. I waited. Silence. I continued waiting. I debated rapping again but stopped myself from doing so for fear of breaking the "three raps" knocking code. Suddenly, just as I was about to seek enlightenment from the boy, a judas window in the door opened and two little eyes peered out at me.

"What can I do fer ya?" asked a woman, none too cordially.

"Good evening," I said. "I was wondering, have you any fresh bacon this evening?"

"Any what?"

"Fresh bacon," I said with some annoyance. "The young lad in the bushes—Billy the lighthouse—told me that was tonight's password."

"Password? Ah fer Christ's sake!"

She closed the window and I heard several bolts shoot back. Then the door opened and I was confronted by a giant of a woman, well over six feet in height and weighing somewhere in the vicinity of three hundred pounds. Her cheeks were spotted with at least half a dozen black moles while on her upper lip she sported a growth of long black hairs that many a young man would be proud to call his moustache. Clearly I was addressing Big Sue.

"Where is he, that give ya the password?" she demanded.

I indicated the stand of bushes whence Billy had leapt and the huge woman pushed past me out onto the verandah.

"Get outa here, ya lit'le sh-t!" screamed Big Sue at the indicated shrubbery.

There was a violent rustling of leaves and we watched as Billy the lighthouse ran off giggling down the street and into the night.

"Dirty lit'le sh-t," she remarked. "Here ta get yer cherry copped, are ya sonny?"

"Certainly not," I said, summoning all the haughtiness I could muster. "I am from New York City and I have come to see what sport the ladies of Toronto can give me. I am doing a comparison, as you might say."

Big Sue grunted and led the way into the dimly lit vestibule. I noticed a pistol protruding from a black holster on her huge hip and a stubby leather bludgeon hanging off her wrist by a thong, rather like an evil little purse. The naked receptionist with a suggestive arrangement of vegetables that Doctor Dandy had described was nowhere to be seen but, on the positive side, I could hear a piano playing a jolly music-hall ditty and a great deal of laughter and merriment coming from within. I fingered the two dollar's worth of cardboard in my pocket.

"I don't suppose you have any interest in the membership card the boy in the bushes sold me," I said, trying desperately to resist the natural impulse to stare at her hirsute upper lip.

"Membership card?" she snorted with contempt. "Sh-t! Don't tell me the little bastard stung ya for a card too? How much?"

I told the great fat woman fifty cents.

"Jesus Christ! Listen, ya got two choices—all-nighter or up and down with one of the girls. What'll it be?"

I indicated that a relatively brief dalliance was all I desired and she proceeded to pull out a fistful of coloured ribbons from a bulging pocket. She extracted a blue one and, before I could protest, she pinned it with a violent stabbing motion onto the fine silk lapel of my tuxedo jacket. I queried her action and she explained, in her own quaint vernacular, that it was a colour-coded system of payment. I was to pay her in advance and the colour of my ribbon indicated to the lady involved in my visit what manner of service I was entitled to.

"That'll be twenty," said she flatly.

I paid Big Sue the money she demanded and she instructed me to go on into the parlour.

"The girls all know what to do," she added, somewhat gratuitously.

"Yes, quite. But say, can you tell me if Cecily is working this evening?"

"Sure, just go right on in" was her only reply.

Thus far, my reception had failed dismally to live up to my expectations in terms of erotic vegetables or even common courtesy, but when I entered the large front hall it was obvious that The Cloister, while not being the finest sporting house in the land, as Doctor Dandy had led me to believe, was nonetheless a far cry from a hot-sheet hotel on Bedbug Row. Virtually every item of decor, from the carpet and wallpaper to the furniture upholstery, was done up in a rich ruby-red colour, and I noted a row of brass coat pegs along one wall wrought in the shape of very long and highly erect male members. The music and laughter were all coming from a large room through an archway, and when I had hung my hat and coat up on one of the naughty pegs, I moved on to investigate within.

I found the parlour to be crowded with licentious libertines and a bevy of women in various stages of undress. Their costumes ranged from low-cut gowns and Japanese kimono wrappers to ribbon-trimmed nightgowns that left little to the imagination. No one person seemed to be in charge of the proceedings, and I could only assume that I was supposed to catch the eye of the girl I fancied and rely on her to do the rest. As to how I should go about locating Cecily, I had no idea whatsoever. In lieu of a plan, I leaned against the woodwork in the archway and, after inserting a Pall Mall cigarette in my ivory holder, I struck what I hoped was a nonchalant stance. In the far corner a young man with a large moustache was providing some wonderfully jaunty piano music, but I noticed for the first time that the male patrons of the establishment were not of the highest calibre of persons. There was a good two dozen of them sitting on the chairs and settees arranged against the walls—some with girls on their laps, others shooting hot glances about the place—and many of their number seemed coarse and even filthy. That is to say, there appeared to be few, if any, real gentlemen among them. Certainly I was the only one present wearing a formal suit of any description, much less the latest in tuxedo cut, and it occurred to me that at the earliest opportunity I might be wise to surreptitiously stow father's rather showy timepiece safely in my trouser pocket. I was just thinking to myself how handy a madam would be to guide a person along when Big Sue grabbed my arm from behind.

"Get on in there, bud, show's about to start," she said.

"Oh yes, well, quite" I said as she marched me over to a settee already crowded with persons.

"Make room, boys!" commanded Big Sue as she wedged me in between two disreputable-looking fellows. I would have apologized to them for my intrusion but neither one took any notice of my arrival. The chap to my right was occupied in exchanging lewd winks and lecherous gestures with a red-haired woman across the room, while the other fellow was busy kissing a girl on his knee. To say that I felt dashed awkward sandwiched between them is to understate— I admit that freely. Then I noticed a very comely-looking young lady dressed in a black corset affair on the opposite side of the room, and the instant I caught her eye she rushed over and threw herself upon my lap.

"Sure and would ya be lookin' for somethin' hot and sticky then?" she asked in a thick Irish brogue.

Her corset amply advertised her bountiful figure and I was sorely tempted by her charms, but I recalled reading that Irish joy-girls are savagely wicked in their sexual acrobatics and thought I should perhaps learn to walk before attempting to canter. And besides, I was still intent on finding Cecily.

"Well yes, I am," I said, "but to be honest I was hoping to find Cecily. Is she here tonight?"

"Cecily? Never heard of her."

"Well, perhaps I'll just sit here awhile anyway. But thank you very much for the offer," I said.

"Suit yourself I'm sure," was all she said before going to sit on another fellow's lap.

At that point the piano music ceased abruptly and Big Sue waddled to the centre of the room clapping her hands.

"Quiet down! Quiet!" she yelled. All right, let's go girls, make a parade, make a parade!"

The piano music started again and all the unattached girls commenced parading around the room in a single line. Big Sue remained in the centre of the room running the show.

"Pick a baby, boys! Don't get stuck in your seats! Pick a baby!" she cried.

Right away men started yelling and pointing to indicate which girl they wanted, and when a girl saw a fellow pointing at her, she dropped out of the line and ran to sit on his knee. It was clearly time for me to make a decision. I had little or no hope of identifying Cecily amidst the confusion and if I didn't soon act I would be left with the least comely woman in the house. Just then, into the room walked a tall, raven-haired beauty, with wonderfully full red lips and breath-taking curves. To the north of her thin waist she wore naught but a little red satin vest while to the south she sported lacy black drawers, black stockings with pink garters, and high-heeled slippers. My eyeballs were out on stems as I stared at the magnificent breasts spilling out of her low decolletage. She walked directly over to me and took up residence in my lap.

"Hello honey, my name's Pansy," she purred. "What's your name?"

"Archibald Picket," I said, in my agitated state completely forgetting my Guy Islingworth pseudonym. "I'm very pleased to meet you, Pansy."

She threw her arms around my neck and I noted her wonderfully bushy armpits—no doubt indicative of the lush foliage to be found on a more intimate part of her person. Then she smiled broadly at me and revealed two solid gold teeth at the front of her upper row.

"Like my teeth?"

"Yes. Very much. They must have cost a great deal of money."

"Of course they did, but I wouldn't know exactly how much. They were gifts from admirers."

"Very smart indeed," I said.

She asked how it was she had never seen me in The Cloister before and I explained that I was from New York City and was just passing through Toronto en route to the gold rush in British Columbia. Then, with neither preamble nor warning, she planted a passionate kiss full on my lips, and after my initial shock I met her salacious advance with a will. When, gasping for oxygen, we eventually broke apart, she begged me to slip my hand inside her little red satin vest and feel her ripe tomatoes. I needed no coaxing to seek out the glorious orbs, and as I stroked them, she slipped her little hand down my trousers and commenced fondling that most private part of my person.

"Oh kiss me, kiss me Archie," she begged.

Long, swooning kisses ensued, and all the while my hand ranged freely about her bosom while her hand did its mischief. My limb had long since grown dreadfully hard and I thought to myself: my lord, I am inflamed with coarse lust and we have yet to leave the settee! I panted and squirmed under Pansy's relentless fondling but she appeared to be unaware of my rising fever. Then, as wonderful tingling spasms pervaded my entire being, I discharged copiously into my trousers and she ceased her wanton gyrations.

"Oh Archie," she said, "it's so crowded down here, won't you come upstairs and be bad with me?"

"Yes of course," I said. "With great pleasure."

Pansy led the way to the foot of the stairs and then suddenly turned to me. "Oh daddy, can we have some champagne sent up? You know, I just hate a cheapskate who won't treat a girl like a lady."

I assented without hesitation and, after gesturing to a waiter, she began her slow sashay up the sweeping staircase. I followed as in a dream, my eyes glued to the swishing half-moons before my face. I was finally ascending a staircase to love's labyrinth. I followed Pansy down a long hallway past many closed doors until finally she stopped and motioned me into a room at the end of the passage. The bedroom was small and furnished simply with a large brass bed and walnut bureau, but there was a lovely pink glow in the room cast by an oil lamp with satyrs chasing nymphs painted upon its pink glass shade.

Once we gained the other side of the bedroom door, events happened rapidly. First Pansy detached the blue ribbon from my lapel and threw it in amongst a jumble of identical ribbons in the top drawer of the bureau. When I queried this, she explained matter-of-factly that she saved all the ribbons she earned and exchanged them for cash at the end of each week. Given that it was only Tuesday and there were dozens of ribbons in the drawer, I surmised that business had been brisk, to say the least, and decided not to query her on the subject any further. I had hoped we might get to know one another a little better before getting to the business at hand, but the moment my ribbon was safely stowed with its colourful fellows Pansy crossed the room and embraced me passionately.

"Oh, I'll bet you're a devil with a girl," she said.

I owned that there might be some truth in her supposition but I hastened to assure her that I was a gentleman first and last. A knock sounded on the door and Pansy opened it to reveal a Chinese waiter with our bottle of champagne and two glasses on a tray. After an awkward pause I realized that I was expected to pay for the wine immediately, and I did so forthwith. It proved to be wildly expensive, but I did not begrudge the extra cost for I felt I would be the better for the Dutch courage the wine would provide.

Pansy opened the bottle and filled the glasses.

"Down the hatch!" she cried.

"Cheers," I said and downed my wine in a single draught.

Pansy however took one sip and spat out her wine in disgust.

"Horse piss!" she cried. "What the h-ll! You'd think they could tell a gent when they see one. You know what they've done, don't you? They figure you're some kid who can't tell the difference between good wine and bad, so they fill up a good bottle with horse piss. Well they won't get away with it—not with you they won't."

I watched as she strode over to a brocade bell-pull hanging on the wall beside the bed and gave three short jerks upon it.

"There," she said, "they'll know what that means. Oh lordy— I've just come over queer."

Whereupon—much to my intense embarrassment, not to mention disgust—Pansy pulled an enamel chamber pot out from under the bed and nonchalantly made violent use of it. All I could do, short of fleeing the room, was to suddenly develop an intense interest in the wallpaper pattern. I had simply assumed that one would repair to a twinkle-house should the need to vent one's bowels arise, or, if the use of a thunder-mug was unavoidable, at least do so in a condition of privacy. In any case, by the time the Chinese waiter appeared with another bottle of bubbly Pansy had finished her business and we proceeded.

"Happy days!" she cried.

I echoed her cry and once again downed my glass in a single draught. The odd thing was that, for all her fuss about the poor quality of the first bottle, I could discern no difference between them. But Pansy was of another mind.

"Now that's what I call real champagne," she said as she refilled my glass.

I obediently downed my wine, and looked up to find Pansy slipping off her little red vest.

"Oh daddy, won't you give my boobies a great big kiss?" she said, waggling her huge breasts at me.

I did not require a second invitation, and in an instant I had my lips glued to the rosy teat of one of Pansy's magnificent orbs.

"Oh, you're such a naughty little boy," she said. "Sucking at mummy's titty. Don't stop."

I continued my employment with gusto and felt my head growing lighter and lighter. I looked up at her face and, although my spectacles had misted over, I could still make out her features, and she too was now clearly inflamed with unbridled lust. It was a scene out of the pages of *Forbidden Knickers*—the book Uncle Jasper kept in the drawer of his night-table—and here was I cast in the role of Sir Randy Lavender, the lust-crazed satyr. My mission had been to debase myself thoroughly, and now, under Pansy's artful guidance, I knew I could not possibly fail.

"Let's move over to the bed, Archie. I must have you now" I heard her say, but as I turned to comply with her request an alarming dizziness came over me. I staggered and felt myself slowly sinking to my knees. The room was spinning wildly out of control and I reached out for Pansy standing high above me but she was no longer there. Then for an instant my vision cleared and I saw Big Sue and a man with a sweeping jet-black moustache standing just inside the door, while directly above me stood a short, thick-set fellow with straw-coloured hair and a battered topper. He smiled at me and revealed the three yellow stumps which constituted his teeth. Then he slowly raised a length of wood high above his head and brought it down upon my skull with all the force at his command. Instantly thousands of startled birds flew upward and then . . . all was blackness. I had come a nasty cropper.

CHAPTER XI

MY GUARDIAN ANGEL APPEARS

I am submerged in a thick warm liquid. It is wonderfully soothing. Although I am entirely immersed, I am not drowning—I simply do not need to breathe. Gradually I become aware of a pungent odour seeping into the silent, black void. I think to myself: how strange, I know this smell is a part of me and yet I have forgotten what it means. The odour grows in intensity and is now almost nauseating. I feel a sense of panic rising within me. Am I going to suffocate? Where is the smell coming from? How can I stop it? It brings a bitter, metallic taste with it. I sense the colour white all around me and suddenly I know that the odour is my father and I am not immersed in warm liquid, I am lying deep down in my warm feather mattress. I am back in my bedroom in Balls Falls and Father is preparing a medicine for me. It is ether I smell, for Father's white coat always smells of ether. In a moment I will ask him if Mother can come up and see me now.

Gradually I became aware of a cool dampness on my forehead, a rhythmic stroking. My eyes opened involuntarily and I made out the fuzzy outline of a human face wrapped in black cloth. I struggled to bring the image into focus and slowly I made out the features of an old nun. She looked very cross at first but then she smiled.

"Hello my boy," she said. "Welcome home."

I looked into her kind eyes, wondering who she was and what I should say to her. Then I shifted my weight and an excruciating pain stabbed at my head. I fell limp. Darkness closed over me once again and I sank back down into the merciful warmth.

When I next regained consciousness I discovered that I was lying in a narrow white cell. The room and everything in it—the iron bed, the locker, and the dresser—everything was painted white. There was a strong smell of ether and I felt sure that I was in a hospital although I had no recollection of how I had been injured. My head ached and upon investigation I discovered it to be swathed in bandages. A nun came into the room and told me that I was in St. Michael's Hospital on Bond Street. I was to lie still and she would fetch the doctor. A short time later a man with a pointed white beard came into the room and informed me that he was Doctor Fitzpatrick. I asked him what had happened to me and how I came to be in his hospital but he insisted on taking care of the medical side of things first, and after consulting a temperature chart that was hanging from the foot of my bed, he began his examination. What is your name? Where do you live? How many fingers am I holding up? Who is our queen? I answered the questions to his satisfaction, although I very nearly made a blunder when he asked me my name and just for a moment the only name I could remember was Willoughby Tweed. I asked him how long I had been in hospital and when he enlightened me I could only blink in astonishment.

"You have been here with the Sisters of St. Joseph for eight days," he said. "It seems clear that you are the victim of some act of wanton violence and we are very curious to learn what happened to you. All we know is that eight nights ago one of the sisters answered the night bell and found you lying in a coal wagon. You were naked save for an overcoat wrapped about you and you had obviously been very badly beaten. Upon further investigation we discovered that you possessed a considerable quantity of water in your lungs. To be frank, we were very much afraid you would die."

The memory of The Cloister and the treacherous Pansy came rushing back to me. I felt an overwhelming need to be alone with my thoughts and I resolved to end the interview as quickly as possible. Doctor Fitzpatrick was asking me if I remembered being on a boat or near water.

"Yes, I remember now," I said. "I was walking along by the Yonge Street docks and some thugs attacked me. They beat me up and I suppose they threw me in the harbour afterwards."

He then asked me if I would recognize these thugs, and when I answered in the negative he questioned me about being wheeled to the hospital and asked if I had any idea as to the identity of my guardian angel. I responded by closing my eyes and feigning sleep and I soon heard the door close softly behind the good doctor.

A moment later the full horror of my loss washed over my mind like blood. I had been stripped of everything. My fine new tuxedo and Piccadilly shoes, my new smoking appliances—dear God in heaven, even Father's watch and signet ring! His gold studs and ruby stick-pin, his malacca stick, my New York style silk topper, my new tortoise-shell spectacles—all gone for ever. And then of course—my money. What was I to do with less than half of my inheritance? And there was my bill at the Queen's to be settled as well. It was so profoundly humiliating! I saw Pansy laughing while she waggled her love-apples at me. I saw the moustachioed man and the stubby little runt who hit me. They drugged me, of course. The second bottle of champagne was doped. The three short tugs on the bell-pull was the signal—"They'll know what it means," Pansy had said. I was flattered by all that malarkey about me being a gentlemen who deserved the special wine! My fine clothes had rendered me conspicuous amidst the rabble and I had been blithering on about being from New York City en route to the gold rush in British Columbia. Perhaps they hoped I was foolish enough to carry my prospecting money upon my person, and I did not disappoint them. I thought of Uncle Harold's admonitions and the warnings in *Tricks on Travellers*. And where was my guardian angel, La Divine Sarah, when the evil Pansy and her henchmen tried to kill me? After speaking with La Divine at the backstage door I had thought I was invincible. There was no point in going to the police. I had no evidence and they would undoubtedly tell me I had got what I deserved for frequenting a vice resort. My Toronto life was over. I had lost my money. All my dreams were still-born. In fact I had lost everything except that which I most wanted to lose—my virginity. And where was I to go? How could I face my uncles? Did I dare make up some fantastic tale about being robbed on the way to stowing my money in a bank? Reginald Ambrose Ravencroft was dead and it occurred to me that perhaps Willoughby Tweed should join him in oblivion. I felt my strength ebbing away. Gradually the balm of sleep pervaded my being.

I was awakened by the sound of an explosion. It was night and the room was lit solely by a single gas jet on the wall above my head. Without my spectacles all objects in the room were fuzzy and I had great difficulty distinguishing shapes.

"Who's there?" I called out.

A match flared down at the foot of my bed and a figure lit a cigarette.

"Good lord," I exclaimed. "It's you!"

"Good evening, Reginald. You'll have a glass of champagne, of course," said Belvedere La Griffin.

I stared at him in astonishment—quite literally refusing to believe my own eyes.

"How can you be here?" I said—more to myself than to my visitor. "You have no way of knowing I am here."

"My dear Reginald," said Belvedere as he walked around the bed and handed me a fluted champagne glass, "I knew you were here for the simple reason that I brought you here. Who else do you suppose would wheel you all the way up Church Street in a coal wagon?"

"You brought me here?" I asked incredulously.

"Why of course, old boy. I've just told you that."

My mind refused to believe my senses and I was growing more and more agitated.

"How did you get in here?" I demanded. "It's pitch-dark outside. It's the middle of the night. They wouldn't let you in so you cannot be real."

Belvedere apparently sensed that I did not share his amusement at my confusion, and adopted a conciliatory tone.

"Reginald please, do calm yourself. Drink some of your fizz and I will gladly tell all."

I took a sip of the sparkling amber liquid and made a noise of appreciation. Belvedere smiled with satisfaction.

"Excellent, dear boy, I felt certain it would not be wasted on you. It's the Krug '74, of course. Are you familiar with the '74 vintages?"

I confessed I was not.

"Ah well, briefly, in 1874 the grapes were so ripe when pressed that the wine they yielded possessed a darker shade of gold than is usual and also a slightly pink sheen. Hence you can always spot a true '74 by its streak of mahogany. That it is one of the truly magnificent vintages goes without saying. But now let me see, getting back to the matter at hand. You wish to learn how I gained entry to this dreary establishment. Nothing simpler, I broke a tiny window at the rear of the hospital, searched for a door with your name on it, *et voilà*—here I am. And as I said, I knew you were here because it was I who deposited you on the doorstep."

"But how on earth could you have happened upon—"

"There there, calm yourself and allow me to explain. After you left my rooms I read your note and—"

"Wait, you were there—in your rooms on Phoebe Street?"

"Certainly, old man—hiding up in the tower. Of course I did not know it was you in my rooms until I heard you and Mrs. Flowers conversing, and I couldn't very well come down to join you because I could not risk alerting Mrs. Flowers to my presence. So I watched you from the tower window as you left, came downstairs, read your note, and I wished to thank you for your warning and for taking care of that tiresome matter of my back rent. It seemed prudent to wait until dark before going to your hotel, but as my cab drew up to the Queen's whom should I see departing in a hansom but your good self. I instructed my cabby to follow you but he lagged behind and when we finally caught up you were entering that dreadful brothel. Well, as I said, I really was most eager to thank you and to learn any additional news concerning my pursuers, so I decided to wait in the cab for you to conclude your 'business'. Well, I waited and I waited and I got bored and I took a little stroll, and whilst wandering down the lane at the rear of the house I chanced to see two louts loading your decidedly limp body onto a wagon and driving away into the night with you. Well, I mean to say, what could I do? I ran back to my cab, followed their wagon over to the pier at the foot of Jarvis Street, behind Roger's Coal Yard, and arrived just in time to see them pitching you into the water."

I stared at Belvedere in horror as I fully realized how close my brush with death had been.

"Fortunately they assumed you could be counted upon to drown without any further encouragement, and they departed without further ado. That left me just enough time to confiscate a small skiff, row around the pier, and haul you out of the water. Incidentally, those shiners of yours really are dreadful but do not despair, I know a black-eye artist who can fix you up in no time at all. Anyway, where was I? Oh yes, so off I went in search of my cab only to discover that the oaf of a cabby had left me stranded. I ran back to you—you were lying buck-naked on the pier, bleeding profusely and covered in slime—and I looked around for an alternate mode of conveyance. Unfortunately the best I could produce was that damned coal wagon—weight approximately two tons. I knew St. Michael's to be the nearest hospital and I had no option but to trundle you up Church Street—cabbies being loath to accept slimy naked fares. I deposited you at the side door and waited in the bushes to see that they took you in. You understand I would normally have brought you inside, but as I am on the run, I thought it best to remain anonymous."

"I owe my life to you," I said with incredulity. "Without your heroic intervention I would be a putrefied corpse decomposing at the bottom of the bay. Belvedere, how on earth can I ever repay you?"

"Repay me? Don't be absurd, dear boy. All in a night's work, as it were. Only too glad to be of assistance. Have some more fizz and a gasper. You'll find that with the Krug '74 your enjoyment will grow as the contents of the bottle diminishes—unlike so many other so-called 'fine vintages'."

Belvedere refilled my glass and lit my cigarette and an awkward silence set in. It was as if by chatting on merrily without pause he had sought to save me from having to confront the horrible reality of what they had done to me. Finally I could bear the silence no longer.

"They stripped me," I said. "Beat me, stripped me naked, and threw me in the harbour."

"Yes."

"They took my father's watch and signet ring and all my money and now I shall have to go home. My real name is Willoughby Tweed. I am not wealthy and I do not come from New York City. I am just a hayseed from Balls Falls. My parents are dead and it is my inheritance that funded this sojourn to Toronto. My attackers stole over half of my inheritance from me and now, what with all my purchases and high living and my bill at the hotel, I have practically nothing left. I am a penniless fraud. My debt to you is so colossal that I cannot possibly repay you and for that, among many other things, I most humbly apologize. As it is, I have no alternative but to go back to Balls Falls and—well, I don't know what—live with my uncles and get some manner of job."

Belvedere paused, seemingly to absorb the full implications of my outburst.

"Let me be certain I fully understand you," he said slowly. "Are you seriously telling me that you intend to slink home leaving the outrage perpetrated upon your person unavenged?"

"Yes," I said. "I am. I have no alternative."

"They came within an ace of killing you!" he cried with barely controlled fury. "Had they used a knife or pistol on you instead of a bludgeon I could not have saved you. These people are leprous beyond all loathing. They are not human beings, they are human grubs that must be trodden underfoot like the slimy revolting things they are. There can be no mercy in this affair, Reginald. It is a matter of honour now. They must be repaid in their own coin, and with considerable interest. It simply goes without saying that you will be exacting a terrible revenge upon them. Before you are finished there must be at least one dead man floating in the Toronto harbour!"

Belvedere broke off his outburst and looked away—clearly in an effort to regain control of his emotions. Then he continued in a more light-hearted tone.

"Good heavens, Balls Falls, the very idea. Living like some manner of bumpkin. Why, just imagine, you would forever remain ignorant of the new line of needle-toe pumps Pickles Shoe Parlour has just received—unthinkable!"

I smiled at his attempt to lighten the moment, but nonetheless I had to be honest with him.

"Belvedere," I began. "I understand and appreciate what you are attempting to do for me, truly I do, and I would love nothing more than to do as you suggest, to grind them under foot and retrieve that which is mine, but you must understand that I do not possess the . . . expertise to do so. I cannot simply grab my revolver and go in shooting."

"Well, of course you can't, you fool," he snapped impatiently. "They would cut you down instantly." He paused and chose his words carefully. "Is it true to say that it is not the heart you lack for revenge, but merely the funds and experience in such things? Is that what you are saying?"

"Yes, that is what I'm saying."

"Well then, for heaven's sake, old fruit," he exclaimed, "why ever did you not say so in the first place? My word, for a moment I actually thought you were telling me you are a coward. Now then, tell me this, did you see who beat you, would you recognize them?"

I answered in the affirmative and told Belvedere my sorry tale from start to finish. By the conclusion of my account I could tell that his feelings of outrage threatened to overwhelm him.

"They will pay," he said softly. "They will pay with their blood. I couldn't see the faces of the men who threw you into the harbour but I saw them in silhouette, and one of them was the lout wearing the battered topper who struck you down, I am sure of it. As of now, he is a dead man who simply has yet to be informed of the fact."

Suddenly I felt a wave of fatigue envelop me, and apparently Belvedere noted this for he abruptly changed tack.

"But enough of that for now. Obviously you are decidedly *hors de combat* at this time, but your condition will soon improve and when you are fit and hungry for blood we shall plot our strategy. In the meantime, I brought you some reading material to keep the tedium at bay. *Les Fleurs du Mal—The Flowers of Evil*—by Monsieur Charles Baudelaire—one of the greatest if not the greatest poet ever to put verse on paper, and certainly a clothes-wearing man of enormous importance—as I believe I mentioned to you during our fateful meeting in Doctor Dandy's carriage. He was compelled to leave home at the tender age of thirteen years, due to the fact that his father drank only Burgundy wines whereas Charles was a Bordeaux man. From him you will learn much that must needs be known about life, death, and, most important, style. And for a little light reading, I have brought you the latest issue of Grip's *Comic Almanac*. Allow me to quote from the cover just here: 'If you have the blues, if you expect to have the blues, or if you know anyone else who has the blues—buy it.' End of quotation." He laid the book and almanac on the bed beside me. "Oh yes, and this trifle—I almost forgot."

Belvedere whisked a pocket puff from his suit jacket with the flourish of a magician and laid it across my chest.

"*Pour vous, Monsieur Ravencroft, avec les compliments de Madame Sarah.*"

I picked up the dainty lace-edged handkerchief and beheld the holy words *"Quand Même"* stitched in blue thread in the upper left corner.

"My God," I exclaimed softly as I inhaled La Divine's intoxicating perfume once again.

"The scent from that hanky should have you on your feet in no time, but do take care, for you know of course that her perfume possesses a strong aphrodisiacal power owing to the inclusion of the testes of a lion."

I began to protest that I could not possibly accept a gift of such incalculable worth but he dismissed my arguments out of hand.

"La Divine Sarah was kind enough to receive me in her dressing room after her performance, and I presented her with a pear-shaped pearl on a gold chain to represent the tears she drew from me. And she, in turn, gave me that handkerchief, that I might dry my tears. I was of course overwhelmed by—"

Belvedere suddenly went silent as raised voices and the sound of running footsteps came from the hallway.

"I think perhaps it is time I took my leave, old boy. How fortunate that your room is on the ground floor."

I watched as he scooped the glasses and empty champagne bottle into a dark leather satchel. He then raised the window, and inserted one leg through the aperture.

"We shall meet at the Queen's when you are discharged, and in the meantime I shall make a few discreet inquiries on my own."

"But wait," I broke in, "how will you know when I get out?"

"Fear not, I will know. And know this also: together we will cut your assailants down without mercy, on that you have my solemn oath."

And with those words, Belvedere La Griffin disappeared through the window into the night. I turned off the gas to the jet above my head and lay back in the darkness, clutching La Divine's hanky to my nostrils. I felt numb, but whether with excitement or fear I could not say.

Doctor Fitzpatrick insisted on my remaining in hospital until I had fully regained my strength, and each day under the watchful eye of Sister Dorothy I was encouraged to walk a little farther through the grey halls of the hospital. I sent a note to The Queen's Hotel informing them of my situation so they would not think I had skipped out on the bill, and I requested that they send over one of my new day suits that I might be clothed for my eventual return. A pair of spectacles was found for me and when my head bandages were removed I was finally allowed the use of a mirror. The black-eye specialist Belvedere had mentioned would need all possible skill to hide my horrible disfigurement. In due time a police constable came to take information and I repeated the story I had told Doctor Fitzpatrick about being assaulted by waterfront thugs that I could not identify. The constable cautioned me not to walk down by the docks alone late at night and went away without further comment.

When I thought about my midnight caller—as I often did—I was struck by how profoundly Belvedere's manner had changed from my past acquaintance with him. He seemed so relaxed and chatty—it was difficult to believe that he was the same person who had threatened me with a stiletto blade and a derringer in Doctor Dandy's carriage. Of course I would never be able to repay my debt to him—first for enabling me to see La Divine perform, then for saving my life, and finally for giving me the precious handkerchief La Divine had given to him. It was without question the most generous gift anyone had ever given me, and even now, as I write these lines after so many years have passed, when I hold it to my nose I can still smell La Divine's intoxicating scent.

As the days passed I relived my assault at The Cloister hundreds of times, and gradually my feeling of shock turned to anger and my anger to a smouldering rage. I made up dozens of different scenarios but they all culminated in the same central act: first the humiliation and then the complete obliteration of the malevolent little man who had beaten me. The end of every story found him cowering on his knees before me, blubbing like a baby for mercy, my loaded revolver pressed against his temple. "Ta-ta old son," I would say, just before splattering his brains all over the wall. As for Big Sue and the abominable Pansy, I hated them intensely for betraying and humiliating me. I loathed them. I wanted to hurt them terribly but unfortunately one could hardly splash a woman's brains against a wall and still call oneself a gentleman. I imagined, as an alternative, threatening them, making them dreadfully afraid, so afraid that they fouled their filthy knickers and begged me for forgiveness. They had to know beyond any doubt that in the end I was the victor and they the vanquished.

And yet, as the time of my release drew near I found that my desire for revenge was being slowly tempered by my fear of the sort of men who could kill a fellow as cold-bloodedly as my attackers. To them, the taking of a human life was simply a business decision, a reflex. They were not distracted by empathy for their victim's suffering. They were practised in their evil art, and fearless. I was not unafraid and I did not believe Belvedere to be wholly unconcerned with his own safety either—despite what he might say to the contrary. I also felt that there was little or no chance of my ever retrieving Father's jewellery. It would be long since sold off to someone and so what manner of revenge was left to me? My attackers were guilty of attempted murder, they had not succeeded in killing me, and yet Belvedere said that someone must be floating dead in the harbour before our work was done. That sounded like murder to me.

But then again, I had to ask, could I live with myself if I went crawling back to Balls Falls? Would I not be forever consumed by the need for some form of revenge? In the end I decided to leave it in the hands of my Fate Goddess. If, when I was released, Belvedere had what I considered to be a feasible plan that did not involve killing anyone, then I would join forces with him. But if that was not the case or if he had decided to let the penniless hayseed from Waybackyonder fight his own battles, then I would have no choice but to return home in defeat.

CHAPTER XII

BELVEDERE HATCHES A PLAN

I t was late one afternoon—nearly a full two weeks after my admittance—when Doctor Fitzpatrick informed me that my bed was needed and that I was to be discharged within the hour. My eyes were still horribly discoloured and the thick scabs on my forehead and scalp had yet to fall off but I was not displeased to leave the hospital.

I instructed my cabby to stop briefly at the post office on Adelaide Street and as expected, I discovered a letter from my uncles. In it they expressed surprise and concern that they had received no further word from me since my telegram announcing my safe arrival, and I quickly dashed off a note explaining my silence. I told them that I had only just moved into a clean Christian boarding house run by a kindly old dowager named Mrs. O'Reilly when the house was raided by the police and everyone, including Mrs. O'Reilly and myself, was arrested for white slave trading. It then came to light that kindly Mrs. O'Reilly was, in reality, the notorious white slaver Brigitte O'Dooley of Chicago. Eventually my name was cleared but unfortunately, while languishing in the dank cells of the Don Jail, I had contracted jail fever, and I required nursing by nuns for some weeks. I explained that while in hospital I had made the acquaintance of a fellow patient named Mr. Belvedere La Griffin, who informed me that he was in need of an honourable gentleman to share the cost of his suite of rooms, and I had immediately volunteered for the post. In future, therefore, my uncles should address all correspondence to me in care of Mr. La Griffin at number 3 Phoebe Street.

That done, I proceeded on to the Queen's without delay, for I longed for the quiet and comfort of my Red Parlour Suite. Upon opening the door to my suite, however, I discovered the air to be blue with tobacco smoke and through the haze I spied Belvedere La Griffin lounging on the settee in front of the fire reading my copy of *The Memoirs of Sherlock Holmes.*

"Good afternoon, Reginald old man. Come along in, do," said he with a languid wave of his hand. "I trust you do not object to my having made use of your fine suite during your absence—such a waste—so forth and so on."

I assured him that I most certainly did not object and that indeed I was only too pleased to be able to offer him all the hospitality at my command.

"Do help yourself to a drink, won't you?" he said, indicating an exquisite mahogany tantalus housing three crystal decanters on a side table. "How are you feeling?"

I poured myself a glass of what I took to be sherry and sank into the wing-back chair adjacent to the settee.

"I suppose on balance I feel—utterly despondent," I answered. "I am in ruins both facially and financially, and had I been thinking clearly in the hospital I would have instructed the Queen's management to pack my belongings and rent this suite, for I can no longer afford to live here. As it is, were I to pay my bill today I would have barely enough cash to get me back to Balls Falls."

"Good God, you're not back on this returning to Balls bloody Falls nonsense again, are you? After our discussion in your hospital room I simply assumed you were prepared to fight back. Now it appears you really are nothing but a snivelling little coward."

"I am not a snivelling little coward!"

"Well then, are you or are you not game for the fight?" he demanded.

"Yes and no!" I cried defiantly. "Of course I want revenge on my attackers, and of course I want to regain my father's heirlooms and my money, but I categorically refuse to be part of any plan that involves the wilful murder of a human being—even the malignant little maggot who struck me down. On this point I am resolute!"

Belvedere opened his mouth to respond but immediately closed it and, with an obvious effort of will, forced himself to regain control of his emotions. I watched as he removed his monocle from his eye and slowly polished the lens on the lapel of his fine cashmere suit coat before replacing it in his orbit.

"Allow me to apologize, Reginald," he said quietly. "I presume too much. You are quite right, of course. We must be realistic in this matter and confine ourselves to killings of a financial nature only. I assume you are at least up to that?"

"With all my heart. What is your plan?"

"My plan is as yet in its infancy and therefore somewhat unformed."

"I do not take your meaning," I said bluntly.

"My plan is to acquire some working capital in the near future—in fact this very evening—and thus buy ourselves valuable time in which to formulate our Main Plan. And before you agitate yourself, let me assure you that tonight's little adventure does not involve your attackers and is only technically of a criminal nature. I propose to secretly visit my father's house tonight and remove some of my own possessions, that I may pawn them and thereby raise the needed funds. As I told you at the theatre, my father and I do not enjoy a comfortable relationship, and it is most unlikely that the old toad would let me in if I were simply to arrive at his doorstep—particularly after our having so recently filched his theatre tickets. And if we were to go tomorrow when he is off at his factory, then Wilson, his butler, would deny me entry. So if I am to return to his house it is necessary that I do so under cover of darkness."

"You mean you propose to burglarize your own father's home."

"To burglarize a premise is to break into it and steal something, I propose merely to effect a clandestine entry and remove a few things I left behind. Your part in the affair will be simply to act as 'lookout' and to help me carry some items which are rather heavy. May I count on your assistance?"

"Yes, you may," I said.

"Excellent. Now then, I fear there is something I really must point out to you before we go any farther with our plans—something you are not going to like—concerning your fine Imperial moustache. It is my sad duty to inform you that your most admirable Imperial must be ruthlessly slaughtered."

"What?" I cried. "Out of the question!"

"No, I am sorry, old boy—your very life depends upon it. Should your would-be assassins recognize you, they will make a proper job of killing you and leave nothing to chance. As it is, they assume you to be dead and therefore are not looking for you, so the removal of your Imperial should alter your appearance sufficiently to grant you complete anonymity."

"I can grow a beard," I countered.

"No, I'm sorry. It would take far too long, old son. We must strike soon, not weeks from now."

"I can wear a false beard!" I cried triumphantly.

"Again, no, that will not do. You would draw more attention than you seek to avoid. For example, what would the management of this hotel make of your sudden alteration? Besides which, I myself must wear just such an appliance in order to evade the police, for you must have noticed how quickly Archibald Picket saw through my false-moustache disguise at the Grand Opera House. With the hirsute pair of us stalking the town we would enter the area of farce."

I drew in a deep breath, and with the exhalation I accepted the fact that he was right. My Imperial moustache—that which I had tended so lovingly—was doomed.

"Yes, you are of course perfectly correct," I said. "I had planned to bathe and visit the Queen's barber before having my dinner and I shall instruct him to remove it then."

"Stout fellow," he said. "Now then, after you have washed away the hospital stink and been properly groomed, I propose two courses of action: firstly that we visit my acquaintance the black-eye specialist, and secondly that we enjoy a fine meal together. Normally I would suggest a bird-and-bottle supper at McConkey's to celebrate your return to the fray, but tonight I think a private alcove at the St. Charles would suit us better. You will find the fare at the St. Charles to be of a highly enjoyable character."

I agreed to Belvedere's agenda and he then surprised me by announcing that it was time for him to gather up his few belongings and return to his Phoebe Street rooms. I offered him the bed in my dressing room, indeed I insisted upon his remaining indefinitely as my guest, but he would have none of it.

"No, thank you, Reginald. I had planned to return to my lair tomorrow in any case and I am generally better for my own company. You needn't worry, I am sure the authorities will not think to return to Phoebe Street after all this time, and besides, I can come and go via a fire ladder that leads to my dressing-room window. That side of the house is entirely screened by trees so I needn't fear detection. Indeed, the existence of my secret exit played a large role in my taking the rooms in the first place. It has been my experience that one can never be too careful where exits are concerned."

It was useless to argue with Belvedere, and I could do nothing but watch him pack his clothes and gather up his tantalus and various other bits and pieces. He then donned a large false beard.

"Really this appliance is too tiresome. The ridiculous part is that I very much doubt my capture ranks highly on the authorities' list of priorities. After all, as I understand it, I am deemed to be a danger to myself only, and not to other persons, but still—one never knows—an over-zealous young constable etcetera—so precautions must be taken. I shall be waiting for you in a hansom cab in front of the hotel at precisely eight o'clock. Until this evening, then. . . . "

I wasted no time ordering my bath and taking myself off to the Paradise Barber Shop, for I reckoned that the sooner I despoiled myself of my Imperial, the sooner I could get on with the remainder of my life. My barber—God bless him—protested vehemently when I gave him his lethal orders, but I insisted and with two strokes of his razor my Imperial was gone.

Eight o'clock found me in front of the hotel and within one or two minutes Belvedere's cab appeared at the curb. He instructed the cabby to convey us to number 6 Albert Street.

"We are headed for the home of Mr. Alfred Shaughnessy. He is a former trainer of professional pugilists and a true artiste in the field of bruises."

I wondered whether he would be open for business at that late hour, and I voiced my concern, but Belvedere just chuckled to himself. "Oh yes, for me he will be open. One way or another I have sent Alf a good deal of business over the years."

I waited in vain for a comment from Belvedere regarding my naked upper lip, and it was not long before our cab drew up before a rather dismal-looking frame house on Albert Street. On a rusty iron bracket over the door hung a sign which read "Black Eyes Cured". No welcoming light shone from the windows.

Belvedere applied his fist to the door several times before we heard the bolt shoot back and there appeared an elderly little sprite of a man sporting a rather inflamed bulbous nose on his grizzled face.

"Who's there? What the h-ll do ya want?" growled Alf Shaughnessy.

"Good evening to you, Alf. It is Belvedere La Griffin. I have a friend here in urgent need of your skills."

My companion's words worked a wonderful transformation on Alf, for suddenly he was all smiles and amiability.

"Ah, b'God, is it you then, Mr. La Griffin, with a shaggin' great beard onta yar face?" inquired Alf in a thick Irish brogue. "Come you in, come you in, sur."

"Thank you, Alf," said Belvedere. "Meet my friend Mr. Reginald Ravencroft."

Alf Shaughnessy and I exchanged greetings and he led us down a short hall to the kitchen at the rear of the house, where he bade me sit at the kitchen table. He then lit a bright oil lamp hanging overhead and examined my eyes closely.

"Ah, sure 'tis a pity you didn't get him to me sooner, Mr. La Griffin," Alf remarked. "It's been two weeks or more since them marks was made."

"Quite right, Alf," said Belvedere. "But my friend was in hospital and for a time there was some considerable doubt as to whether he need ever concern himself with his appearance again."

"B'Jesus, I can well believe that, sur. The bruise of a blow is as plain as print to me, Mr. Ravencroft. You've been kicked tree times in the mug by some shaggin' bastard wearing round-toed boots. And I'll tell ya you're lucky for that, if he'd a been wearin' them needly toes he'd 'a pulped yer eyeballs like two grapes. Shaggin' bastard split yer head open too, I see."

Alf selected half a dozen jars of dark ointments from a shelf and fell to work. His touch was surprisingly gentle and, with the exception of a slight burning sensation, I felt no pain whatsoever as he rubbed the various salves one after the other into the discoloured skin surrounding my eyes. I considered asking him what was in his ointments—just to break the silence, as it were—but I didn't want to risk being rebuked for prying into matters that did not concern me. Then Belvedere spoke up.

"Have you been getting lots of trade, Alf?"

"Oh b'God, I can't complain. Boys will always be boys. A course I'm always busiest round Christmas and New Year's Day, and the week after blessed Saint Paddy's day I'm workin' both the day and the night time too.

Alf finished off his ministrations and held up a small hand mirror. "Will that do ya, sur?"

I looked into the glass and saw to my joy that my disfigurement was scarcely perceptible.

"Good God, Mr. Shaughnessy," I said, "you're a wizard."

"Yes indeed, well done. Let's celebrate with a little of the Irish, shall we?" said Belvedere as he withdrew a bottle of Bushmills from an inner pocket of his cloak. Alf did not require a second invitation, and downed two glasses of whisky as quickly as Belvedere could pour them.

"You know, Alf, it's a terrible thing when a man cannot even visit a brothel without fearing for his very life," Belvedere remarked casually. "Do you happen to know The Cloister, on Queen Street near Simcoe?"

Alf downed another drink and pondered Belvedere's question a moment.

"Cloister? Never heard of it," he said. "Wait a bit, you must mean Big Sue's. Oh, sweet Jesus, you never went alone ta Big Sue's sin parlour ta dip yer pen—tell me it ain't so!"

I could only smile wanly as inwardly I cursed that befuddled old imbecile Doctor Dandy.

"Yer a damn fool fer that, Mr. Ravencroft!" cried Alf with a great cackle and another tip of his glass. "If you've tangled with Big Sue 'tis a wonder there's anything left of ya." He paused to fire up a malodorous pipe with an equally offensive sulphur match. "That Big Sue is a terror. Some joker gives her trouble, why, she slugs him a good one and grabs his ear between her teeth and drags him ta the door. Then, if the poor fool struggles, like as not she bites his ear clean off and puts it in a jar of alcohol behind the bar kept for that purpose alone. Ya get what I'm tellin' ya, Mr. Ravencroft—she keeps her trophies in pickle!"

A chill ran threw me as I pictured the glass repository for her grisly mementos. I was indeed lucky to be alive.

Belvedere spoke up. "Another glass, Alf?"

Alf held out his glass to be refilled. "Tanks."

"So you're saying, then, that this Big Sue owns the brothel—is that right?" asked Belvedere.

"Oh now, I never said such a t'ing, Mr. La Griffin. All I said was that it was called Big Sue's. No, Sue is bouncer and general factotum is all. It's Little Dave Goody she's runnin' it with, and they work for Dan the Dude Dougherty. Yuv surely heard of Dan the Dude Dougherty—boss of the Dead Dog Gang?"

"Tell me, Alf," I interrupted, "this Little Dave Goody fellow you mentioned, would he be a short, stocky ruffian with straw-coloured hair and three stubby teeth—wears a battered topper?"

"Ah sure, that'll be Little Dave. A bandy-legged little ape of a fella. He's a notorious needle-jabber—cocaine mostly, but they say there's no drug Little Dave ain't tried. I once sat near him at the Wheat Sheaf. He got a glass a whisky and added a dozen or so drops of liquid camphor to it. Then he threw it back, and while his body was still racked by the crash of the beverage he plunged a hypodermic needle full a cocaine right through his shirt sleeve inta his arm. Sure and the nerve of the little bastard. Do ya not remember a few years back the police discovered a butchered human cadaver hanging by a hook in front of a butcher's on Lombard Street, along with the deer and bear carcasses? They blamed it on medical students but I know for certain it was the work of Little Dave Goody. In fact, I even know the name of the fella on the hook!"

Alf hooted at the joke of it all.

"That is the man that assaulted me," I said.

"Oh, dear sweet God in heaven, if you're not Irish yuv sure 'nough got the luck of the Irish, for if Big Sue is evil incarnate then Little Dave Goody is the very divil hisself. Why, compared to his usual, all he give ya was a wee tap and a poke—just enough to put a shanty on yer glimmer. Normally he delights in usin' spiked iron knucks and puts bits a axe blade inta the soles of his fightin' boots. Yer lucky he weren't wearin' them fightin' boots when he stamped ya. And them knucks are fearsome vicious things too. I seen a man once who'd tangled with Little Dave's knucks, the flesh on his face was ripped clean off. B'Jesus, Mr. Ravencroft, you're the best-lookin' victim of Little Dave Goody to be found in all the land."

"You say he works for Dan the Dude Dougherty, Alf. What manner of man would he be then?" asked Belvedere.

"Dan the Dude is the Beau Brummel of the Toronto underworld. Tall and slim is he, and very dapper—always arrayed like a lily of the field. He has a great fondness for brightly coloured waistcoats and sparklers. His fingers and shirt front are ablaze with them—just like Diamond Jim Brady. And he's ever so particular about his whiskers. A shaggin' great moustache—jet black it is— sweepin' way out ta the sides so long he can tie the ends together under his chin if he so desires. But he likes his liquor and his face is heavily pocked. His weapon of choice has always been the straight razor, but what really puts the fear of God inta men's hearts when he's around is his tool for the purpose of gouging out eyes. I'm told it's made of copper and worn on the thumb, and they say he performs this manoeuvre with great neatness and dispatch."

"There's one other man I'm curious about," said Belvedere. "He's short like Little Dave but heavier, and wears a pork-pie hat."

"Oh, now I couldn't be tellin' you that for a dead cert, but I fancy that would be Piggie O'Neil. He's a fat little fart of a man with a great brown birth-mark on his cheek. I suppose you'll be wantin' ta know where you might locate these lads?"

"We would indeed," said Belvedere. "We've a little score to settle, as you can see."

"Well, if you're determined, Little Dave Goody is often to be found at Big Sue's—course ya know that—but last I heard the Dead Dogs' principal place of meetin' was the Black Bull Tavern on Queen Street. I know the 'tender there—Bullet Malloy—he does a good trade from them Dead Dogs."

"Excuse me," I broke in, "I'm curious, why do they call themselves the Dead Dogs?"

"Well now, the way I heard it, they used to call theyselves the Gas House Gang on account a how their headquarters was in a house next ta the gas-works on Berkeley Street and they all stank of the gas. But then one night Little Dave give a dinner party for all his pals. Everyone includin' hisself ate heartily and praised the unusual flavour of the roast but only Little Dave knew the origin of the joint a meat. Well sur, a little while later he goes out and when he comes back in he's got the big black head of a Newfoundland dog on the end of a pike, and laughin' sure to wet hisself!"

Alf collapsed in a fit of hilarity while I felt distinctly ill. Belvedere looked grim and rose to signal our departure. He pressed a dollar bill on Alf along with our thanks.

"You fellas want to watch yerselves, them Dead Dogs is divils. When they fights, ears and eyes are highly regarded as souvenirs of an interestin' occasion," said Alf as we took our leave.

When we regained the interior of our cab Belvedere chuckled to himself. "Well, I should call that a very profitable stop, wouldn't you?" he said.

"Yes indeed. And you were absolutely correct about Alf's artistic talents."

"Oh, I took it for granted that he could work wonders with your eyes, but I could only hope that he would know the names of the personnel at The Cloister—or rather, Big Sue's."

"And yet, to be honest with you," I said somewhat hesitantly, "I do not see how we are really that much further ahead. I mean to say, we now know the names of our enemies and the location of their usual place of rendezvous, but I fail to see what it is we are to do from here. Where do we start, and to what end?"

Belvedere brushed aside my concerns with an impatient wave of his hand. "As I told you, we can only proceed one step at a time. Our Main Plan will reveal itself eventually. At this stage our aim is to get some fine food and sound wines into you to wash away the hospital slop you have been forced to consume these past few weeks. And as to where we shall begin, we shall begin at the St. Charles Grill."

We spent the remainder of our journey in silence except for when we passed the construction of the new city hall. The excavation was complete and steam-powered cranes sat on the property ready to resume their task of lifting the huge blocks of sandstone into place. I remarked upon the beauty of Romanesque Revival architecture—of which the city hall was to be a splendid example—but Belvedere would have none of it.

"I detest so-called 'Romanesque Revival' architecture," he said petulantly. "It should all be ground to powder and sent back to Chicago where it originated."

I did not pursue the topic further, and shortly thereafter we left the cool night air behind us and stepped into the warm, rose-tinted atmosphere of the St. Charles Grill. Our private dining alcove proved to be one of several candle-lit snuggeries in the restaurant and we were seated in easy chairs of luxurious depth. The maître d' informed us that our waiter would be with us directly and then left us, drawing the heavy brocade curtains behind him to ensure our absolute privacy.

"I trust this is to your satisfaction?" asked Belvedere.

"Of course, yes indeed, it's wonderfully rich and cosy. I was not aware that such private facilities existed."

"Oh yes, several of the finest restaurants in the city boast private dining rooms and alcoves, but none more relaxing than the St. Charles. I like to think of it as the Canadian equivalent of Oscar Wilde's Café Royal—except of course that, with the exception of our good selves, there is no one on the premises worth knowing."

Our waiter slipped silently through the curtains and made a gentle inquiry as to our pleasure. I asked Belvedere if he would take complete charge of our meal, as he was an habitué of the establishment, and he assented with good grace. Soon thereafter the waiter reappeared with two plates of grilled oysters on thin sterling silver skewers and our first bottle of wine.

"Incidentally, Reginald," said Belvedere. "Since your experience with fine wines is limited, I have deliberately chosen vintages that, while by no means being weak, are nonetheless of a delicate character. Indeed, if you would care to sample some of the excellent Johannisberg '79 before you, I feel sure you will discover it to be so light as to be almost feeble, but so charmingly feeble as to be quite lovable."

I did as he bade me do and was immediately rewarded as the amber wine thrilled my senses. My companion looked on in eager anticipation.

"Belvedere," I said, "I possess neither the experience nor the vocabulary to adequately praise this wine. I can only say that it possesses an ineffable charm."

"Bravo, Reginald," he said. "You are so right. It is a wine of great character and delicacy—so gentle and sweet, on the brink of the grave yet unafraid."

We consumed our oysters, moved on to clear soup, and followed this with Tenderloin of Beef, Larded, aux champignons and a bottle of Nuits-St.-Georges '65.

Belvedere eagerly sampled the Nuits-St.-Georges and again waxed poetical. "Ah now, there you are! Burgundy *in excelsis!* Perfection in a wine glass. A faultless wine with a great breed."

Whereupon he fell upon his tenderloin with a will. For some reason I had expected him to pick rather fussily at his food, like a reluctant sparrow, but nothing could have been further from the truth. Indeed he tore into the beef and vintage burgundy with a gusto that was little short of alarming. At one point I paused in my consumption to remark upon his formidable appetite, but he cut me short.

"No, I'm sorry, Reginald, but I wonder if you would do me the courtesy of refraining from speech during the actual eating of our meal. Brief, sporadic exclamations of appreciation are allowed but sustained chatter simply will not do. I find it most distracting and one's meal invariably ends up cooling to an unacceptable degree."

"Yes, quite. I apologize" was the best I could muster in answer to his stern rebuke, and I remained mute throughout the Wild Duck with Currant Jelly and the Mousse of Salmon à la Victoria. Finally he touched the corners of his mouth lightly with his white linen napkin and inquired as to whether I had a preference for dessert or *gâteaux assortis*.

"Thank you, no," I said stiffly. "I could not possibly eat another bite."

"Oh dear, what a shame. You don't object if I. . . . "

"No no, please do."

And with that I watched him consume a large piece of French layer cake followed by a generous bowl of Baked Fig Pudding in Madeira Wine Sauce. Finally, as we sat over our coffee and Courvoisier, Belvedere produced his leather cigar case and offered me a Cuban specimen which I accepted with thanks. I was still smarting from his censure for my talking during dinner, but as I savoured the warm cognac a wonderfully soothing narcosis enveloped me and I felt my spirits quietly descending into a gentler mood. Belvedere leaned back in his chair and drew long at his cigar.

"By the by, Reginald," he said, "I've been meaning to ask you. What's the news from Gilbert the Filbert—the Colonel of the Nuts?"

My look betrayed my confusion at his reference.

"My former keeper—Doctor Marmaduke Dandy. In your note you mentioned a photograph that he has seen fit to give to the constabulary. I was not aware that my photo had been taken. Did you see it?"

I confessed that I had.

"And? A good likeness, would you say?"

"No. I would not call it a flattering image. It is obvious that you were very heavily drugged when it was taken."

"I see. And did he see fit to tell you something of my colourful past?"

"Yes," I admitted. "He told me that you tried to blow your father up with a cannon and have attempted suicide on two occasions."

"Quite so. The odious Musket Man drove my mother to her death. She hanged herself in the carriage house—too neat to do it in the house, damn her. And I felt it only right that he follow her to oblivion. How was I to know the bloody cannon was cracked?"

"Well no, quite. How could you?"

"And yes, I admit there have been occasions when I have longed to dig myself a good deep grave in a soil thick with snails and rich as grease, and sleep in oblivion like a shark in a wave."

"You have longed to join *le mort joyeux*, the gladly dead," I said, so as to prove to Belvedere that I recognized his quotation from Baudelaire's poem "Le Mort Joyeux".

"Quite so. You enjoyed *Les Fleurs du Mal* then?"

"I thought it exquisite. I am indebted to you yet again."

"Think nothing of it. Tell me, before you were robbed at Big Sue's, what was your overall goal in life?"

"Perfectly simple. To become a votary of pleasure and quaff the purple cup of life to the very dregs."

"To dedicate your life to the constant search for delicate joys and exquisite sorrows?"

"Quite so."

"And now, unless we can reclaim your funds and a good deal more besides, your life is not worth the living. Correct?"

"In a nutshell, yes."

"As you are no doubt aware, I too am currently undergoing an advanced case of pecuniary distress, only my situation is even more desperate than yours. You at least still have some funds remaining and, with proper manipulation, substantial credit at your command. Incidentally, I assume you can cover the bill here tonight."

"Oh yes, most definitely," I assured him.

"Sadly, I have been totally bereft of dollars for some three or four months and have now exhausted all sources of credit. That of course is another reason why it is so important that our mission tonight to liberate my few pitiful belongings should not fail. Money is indispensable to anyone who makes a cult of the passions. Not that I aspire to money for its own sake; I could cheerfully make due with infinite credit. I mean to say, how else can we hope to live on in the memory of the commercial classes if we pay our bills?"

"Well, quite," I said simply—not feeling the need to confirm that yes, I recognized the Oscarism.

"Although you must understand that I am not averse to the accumulation of dollars—provided of course that it does not entail any work on my part."

"Certainly not," I agreed.

"But enough of chat. It is time to act!" Belvedere cried.

I reached for my timepiece and was reminded by the vacancy in my waistcoat pocket that, thanks to Little Dave Goody and Dan the Dude Dougherty, I no longer possessed such an article. Belvedere consulted his own fine gold specimen.

"Yes, my dear papa should be nicely tucked up in bed by now. Just time for a toast, I fancy," he said.

He jerked the bell-pull and when the waiter appeared he ordered two more beakers of brandy and, as an afterthought, requested that his silver flask be filled with the golden nectar as well.

"The night air is damp this time of year and I fancy we will be glad of a little liquid warmth before this night is through," he remarked.

When the waiter returned with the flask and our brandies, Belvedere raised his beaker.

"Reginald Ravencroft, I give you—revenge!"

"Revenge!" I cried, and we tipped back our brandies together.

CHAPTER XIII

UNLAWFUL ENTRY

B y the time we left the cosy confines of the St. Charles Grill it was past ten o'clock and a chilling fog had begun to roll in off the lake. I assumed we were in need of a hansom cab but Belvedere headed off down Yonge Street, saying only that he had already arranged for our mode of transportation. He led the way to Goforth's Livery Stable on Wellington Street and took possession of an open wagon with a large mare hitched to it, and I deduced that whatever it was we were about to liberate was of a bulky description.

Once we were under way it became clear that the fog was thickening by the minute. The two oil lanterns on the wagon did nothing to light our way, and I thought to myself what a good thing it was that Belvedere knew where he was going, for the gas lamps lining the streets of Toronto were equally ineffective at penetrating the foggy night. At one point, he reined in at an intersection and bade me hold up one of the wagon lanterns that he might decipher the street sign, and we discovered that we had travelled northwards up as far as College Street. At this distance from the heart of the city, there was not another conveyance to be seen or heard at that time of night—not even a hansom cab. We continued on in the quiet gloom until, after a time, Belvedere broke the silence.

"Do you think me insane, Reginald?" he asked casually.

"Certainly not," I said.

"I find it amusing that I am deemed to be insane by alienists like Dandy. If you want to meet a madman, look no further than my father. He is not sane, he possesses neither the imagination nor courage to be a sane man. He is a *type* of man. He is an 'upright citizen'. Where I possess individuality, eccentricity, daring, and panache, he exists in a perpetual state of habit, conformity, hypocritical piety, and fear. In my view the hallmark of lunacy is consistency. To be consistent is to be insane. I am completely unfettered by consistency. Consistency is a confession of failure. I act by improvising, life is more amusing that way."

"I couldn't agree more, Belvedere. As Oscar Wilde tells us, it is quite absurd to divide people into the sane and insane. People are either charming or tedious. If I may quote: 'To be sane according to the vulgar standard of sanity is quite easy. It merely requires a certain amount of sordid terror, a certain lack of imaginative thought, and a certain low passion for middle-class respectability.' Unquote."

"Yes, quite. Well said."

"Thank you," I said, flushed with pleasure at my companion's approval.

Belvedere shivered and withdrew his flask. "Have a bracer, old man. This damp air is really quite chilling."

I accepted his kind offer. The spreading warmth of the Courvoisier was wonderful, and I drew long at the sterling silver receptacle before continuing.

"I mean to say, I well recall back in Balls Falls how confused I became when I was attempting to understand the implications of Self Creationism as exemplified by La Divine Sarah. At first it seemed that by choosing a new identity for myself I would be living a lie, but, in time, I understood that that was all wrong. I came to see that central to the act of Self Creationism is the realization that truth is only that which the majority of persons agree upon. The fact that 'reality' is highly mutable, that it can in fact be altered at will, does not make it any the less valid, because of course it never was fixed or immutable in the first place."

"But of course, old man. 'Insanity' is merely a method by which we multiply our personalities, and what on earth can be wrong with that? Nothing whatsoever."

"Precisely so."

"I suppose Dandy mentioned my most recent suicide attempt?" he asked.

"In passing, yes, he did."

"A few short months ago I was determined to quit this world in expectation of a better life hereafter or, failing that, at least one in which people are better dressed. I felt I had to die for I was guilty of ennui and, as you are doubtless aware, ennui is the one crime for which there can be no forgiveness. I rented a suite at The Rossin House, enjoyed an exquisite meal with the choicest of wines, and opened a vein in the bath. It was delightful in every regard save for the fact that I lost consciousness and the bath overflowed. Water dripped down through the floor into the suite below, causing the plaster ceiling to fall, and I was discovered."

"Good heavens!" I exclaimed.

Belvedere tittered. "Of course, my name is blood at the Rossin."

"Well yes, quite, it would be."

"Perhaps you are familiar with a short story by Mr. Robert Louis Stevenson entitled 'The Suicide Club'?"

I answered in the negative.

"I recommend it to you highly. Essentially it concerns the refusal to allow one's life to become a slow, laborious trudge to the tomb—as are most men's lives. Its central thesis is that life is a stage upon which to play the fool, but only for so long as the part amuses us. When life ceases to be amusing we should quit the stage, and find the back stairs to liberty."

"Yes, I do see," I said.

We lapsed back into silence and I watched as the huge dark houses loomed up out of the fog. Slowly a feeling of apprehension rose up from within me and, although I knew Belvedere would heap scorn upon me for voicing my concern, I could not resist the compulsion.

"Belvedere," I began, "are you quite sure this is such a good idea? What if we are taken for common burglars and shot?"

"Yes, I intended to raise that very subject with you, Reginald. Both my dear father and Wilson, his butler, are rather inclined to shoot first and ask questions at a later date. So we really must be extremely quiet. I cannot impress that point upon you too strongly. Also, should something go wrong, simply run for your life. Do not concern yourself with my whereabouts or well-being. There will not be time for either of us to be concerned with the other. If you can get clear of the house, then you should be all right. This fog will cover your escape and all you need do is run like blazes. From there, simply find your way back to the Queen's. Now, are we clear on that point?"

I nodded in dumb, or rather, numb assent. He was telling me that should trouble arise it would be every man for himself and I should not look to him for any kind of assistance.

"But look here, Belvedere," I heard myself saying, "I don't know whether you read yesterday's *Star*, but in it was the account of a recent trial in Cobourg for armed house-breaking. The man received fifteen years' hard labour in the Kingston Penitentiary for the robbery and twenty lashes of the whip for carrying a gun. What I mean is, should we get caught, your father wouldn't actually insist upon a criminal charge of house-breaking being laid against us, would he?"

"Rely upon it as you do the rising of the sun."

"But you're his son, his own flesh and blood!" I protested. "And besides, we'll only be taking what already belongs to you. How can you be charged with taking what is rightfully, indeed legally yours?"

"When we get inside we will have to remove our shoes so as to avoid making too much noise. As you will see, there is not so much as one rug or carpet in the entire house to silence our footfalls. My father believes floor coverings to be both effeminate and collectors of disease-carrying dust."

I thought of Belvedere's luxurious Persian parlour, smothered in cushions and tapestries and oriental carpets.

He smiled wanly. "Can you even begin to imagine how much that man detests me?"

I could think of no suitable answer to his question and so I did not attempt one. Shortly thereafter we crossed the intersection of St. George and Bloor streets and Belvedere urged the mare up a darkened lane and reined in.

"I think it wise to leave the wagon here and walk the remainder of the way," he said. "Before we go, I believe there is just enough brandy left for a final toast."

He poured himself a measure into the flask cap and handed me the flask.

"*Contra Audentior,*" he said.

"*Fidem Servo,*" I replied.

With that, Belvedere extracted a large carpet-bag from underneath a tarpaulin lying on the back of the wagon and I heard the unmistakable clink of tools. Then, after extinguishing the wagon lamps, we slowly made our way through the fog back out to the street and along some distance, until Belvedere touched my sleeve and motioned for me to follow him through a small iron gate and up a gravel path. The gravel proved to be alarmingly noisy under foot, and we soon veered off and approached the front of the house across an expanse of lawn. I found myself wondering if the fateful cannon with which Belvedere had attempted to murder his father was still somewhere on the grounds, but I saw no evidence of it. The Musket residence proved to be a lofty brick pile of the Romanesque Revival school of architecture, which explained why Belvedere had so roundly condemned the style when I said how much I admired it. The verandah boasted a great round stone arch set on heavy pillars, and as we drew near to it Belvedere told me to wait under a tree off to one side while he tried his latchkey in the front door. An ornate iron gas lantern hung above the verandah arch and I could see Belvedere in its dim yellow light as he tried in vain to gain entry. A moment later he was by my side once again.

"It's bolted," he said. "I knew it would be but I had to be sure. We'll try the conservatory."

We crept through the darkened garden around to the side of the huge house and crouched before the tall, multipaned conservatory door. Belvedere gave a twist on the doorknob but it refused to turn.

"Wonderful! It's locked!" he said in an excited whisper.

"What? What is good about the door being locked?"

"Because now we shall have to break in—just like real house-breakers!"

He opened his carpet-bag, and withdrew a bull's-eye lantern and various other tools of the nefarious trade.

"Here, hold the lantern while I light it. It's a good night for creeping around unseen, but a poor one for house-breaking."

"How do you mean?"

"Well obviously, the fog is good because you can easily disappear into it, but for house-breaking one wants a stormy night with great gusts of wind that will cause windows and shutters to rattle. That provides an excellent cover sound. Any noise we might inadvertently make would be ascribed to the wind."

"Perhaps we should wait then. Postpone our adventure until a windy night comes along," I said, with no hope whatsoever that he would heed my absurd suggestion.

"Generally speaking, the conservatory is the favoured location for forced entry by house-breakers," he continued. "The doors always contain glass panes, and it is usually located on the side or rear of the house and therefore hidden from view from the street."

"Really?"

"Oh yes, even the most casual reader of *The Police Gazette* will tell you that."

While I shone the lantern's thin yellow beam upon the door, my companion painted one of the small door-panes with glue out of a blue bottle and then pressed a sheet of brown paper onto the glass—leaving the corners turned outwards. Then he ran a glazier's diamond around the glass an inch or so from the edge of the paper. He gave the pane a light bunt with his fist and pulled the paper away by its edge. The glass adhered to the paper and he held it up triumphantly before my eyes.

"Very smartly done," I said.

"Nothing to it. And you know, it has just occurred to me that fly-paper would be a good deal more expedient for this purpose—I must try that sometime."

He quickly put his paraphernalia back into his carpet-bag and passed his arm through the hole in the glass. I heard the lock snap open and with his free hand he twisted the doorknob. It twisted but the door refused to yield to his push.

"Damnation," he muttered.

"What is it?"

"He's put bolts on this door as well—top and bottom, I'll wager. I shall have to cut out two more panes."

And that is exactly what he did. The top pane proved to be a little more difficult because he couldn't reach it unaided, and I was obliged to go down on all fours and offer my back as a step-stool. Eventually, his efforts were rewarded as the second bolt slid back and the door swung in upon its hinges. Belvedere chuckled to himself and I suddenly felt sick with fear. It was time to cross the threshold of safety and into the conservatory. He turned to me.

"Still with me, old man?" he asked, with perhaps a hint of mockery in his voice.

I looked at him and just then, from out of the fog, we heard the Upper Canada College tower clock strike the midnight hour. I found both my courage and my voice.

"Lead on," I said.

We passed inside and immediately removed our shoes, which I assumed we would just leave by the door to be collected upon our departure, but Belvedere was more far-sighted than I.

"Put your shoes in your pockets, Reginald," he said in a low whisper. "We must keep them with us at all times. Should this line of retreat be cut off, we will have to leave the house by another route."

I felt my hands go clammy.

Having grown up in the house, Belvedere knew its geography intimately, and events happened quickly. He led the way and within moments I found myself in a large panelled dining room. Then, from out of his satchel, he removed a black cloth sack and instructed me to hold it open. For a moment I was mystified, but my feeling of confusion quickly changed to one of shock and dismay as he began filling the sack with items off a long side table. When he had told me that he wanted to pick up a few personal articles, I had never for one moment dreamt they would include the family silver! Serving trays, a wonderfully ornate coffee set, soup tureen, flatware—he quickly wrapped each piece individually in bits of cloth and slipped them into my sack. Then he was on his knees before a huge mahogany sideboard. The lock on the right-hand cupboard door was the object of his fascination, and in a trice he had a ring of assorted keys out of his magic bag and was trying each key in succession in the lock. On his fifth attempt, his efforts were rewarded with a sharp metallic click and the door swung open to reveal a dozen or more wine bottles laid down in the customary manner.

"Well now, then," he remarked with a barely suppressed chortle. "Isn't that a pretty sight?"

Another cloth sack appeared, and once again I held it open as he filled it with additional swag. By the time the last bottle was inserted I was more than ready to leave the Musket premises.

"For God's sake, Belvedere. We must—"

Belvedere seized my arm as a night-shattering creak came from the hallway. Someone was up and about the place! He covered the beam from his bull's-eye lantern and we remained rooted to the spot listening intently for the slightest sound.

Finally I heard him whisper, "Grab a sack and follow me."

I did as directed and followed him through a side door into a butler's pantry. He closed the door after us and we remained standing stock still in the pitch dark—once again straining to detect any ominous sounds. With every passing second I knew in my heart that the door was about to burst open, and I could only pray that they would recognize Belvedere and hold their fire. The house was totally silent.

After several minutes, Belvedere drew me close to him. "Remain here," he whispered. "If you hear a commotion, run for your life."

"Wait, where are you going?" I demanded.

But he was already on his way through the doorway and I could only watch in horror as the door closed behind him. There then ensued a hellish, creepy period of time during which I stood immobile in the inky darkness of the butler's pantry, sick with fear. Should I be discovered, it would mean either instant death or fifteen years' hard labour, and at that stage I did not know which eventuality I most feared. The minutes crept by. The house remained completely silent until suddenly I heard a thudding sound from the floor above me. What that could mean, I hardly dared speculate. In the next instant I was seized with an overwhelming desire to run away—simply to run through the house until I found a door leading outside and flee into the foggy night. In truth, had I not been paralysed with fright I do not doubt that I would have done so. Then I heard several sharp creaks from somewhere nearby—certainly on the same floor that I was on. An arm slipped around my neck from behind and a hand covered my mouth! I struggled desperately.

"It's me, Reginald!" Belvedere said.

I ceased struggling and he released his grip. I was nearly dead of fright, and very angry.

"Great God almighty, what are you doing!" I cried out—fortunately still in a whisper.

"I'm sorry. But I couldn't risk startling you upon my return and causing you to bolt or cry out aloud."

"Egad, you scared me! Where did you come from?"

"There is a door at the other end of the pantry. But never mind that. Follow me."

Before I could answer he was on the move once again, and I had no option but to follow him. We tiptoed across the large hallway and into the library. In a trice he was kneeling before a large black safe. His satchel was open and his bull's-eye lantern in his hand. For my part, I was shocked speechless that we were not beating a retreat.

"Hold the light on the dial," he commanded.

Numb with shock and consternation, I simply obeyed his command and watched as he adjusted his monocle and set to work on the dial of the safe. At first he spun the knob with great authority and appeared to know the combination, but each time he dialled it and pulled on the lever, nothing happened.

"Damn him to h-ll!" he cursed. "The old blow-arse has changed the combination." Then he laughed quietly to himself. "I guess he knows his little boy better than I thought he did. Well all right, we'll see. The safe is sitting on castors and the wagon can take the weight, so we will just have to take it home where we can use a little 'dinah' on it at our leisure."

I leaned my weight against the safe. It didn't move, and had there been enough light in the room for him to see my face, Belvedere would have seen me gaping at him open-mouthed in astonishment.

"Belvedere, what are you saying?" I hissed at him. "This is ridiculous! That safe must weigh at least a thousand pounds. We cannot possibly push it all the way back to the wagon—and even if we could—how would we lift it up onto the back? It's impossible!"

Belvedere remained silent for a moment—apparently digesting my words. "All right. Hold the light on the dial again," he said at last.

I focused the beam and watched as he prized the dial off with a thin jemmy. Then he went over to a desk, found a piece of white paper, and, placing the round dial upon the paper, traced its outline with a pencil. When he had cut out the circle of paper, he returned to the safe and began putting the dial back on the door, but with the paper cut-out inserted in between the dial and the door to the safe. But he stopped.

"Wait," he said, "I've forgotten the grease. Quickly—where can I get some grease? There must be—yes, give me the light."

I watched as he prowled around the room before stopping at the swivel chair behind his father's desk. Then, bending down, he smeared some of the grease from the chair's screw shaft onto his finger. Finally, he returned to the safe, rubbed the grease on the inside of the pointed indicator knob, and put the dial face back onto the safe's door.

"There, I daresay there's more than one way to fleece a skinflint," he said. "You see, when my dear father next opens the safe, he will unknowingly reveal the combination, for the greased dial indicator will trace out the combination in grease on the concealed paper. Now let us get out of here while we still can."

It was a suggestion I wholly supported, and we immediately retraced our steps to the conservatory. When we arrived at the doors, however, I was surprised to see a medium-sized seaman's chest sitting off to one side.

"Here, grab a handle," said Belvedere. "It would hardly do to leave without our treasure chest, now would it?"

I took a hold and we crept through the fog towards the wagon—each with a sack of swag in one hand and a handle of the sea chest in the other. For my part, I had a horrible premonition that we were about to discover a vacancy where once the wagon had stood, but fortunately it remained precisely where we had left it. Belvedere covered our booty with the old tarpaulin and, with a flick of the reins, we were on our way home.

"A job well done, I'd say," he exclaimed gleefully.

But no sooner had the words left his mouth than he let out an ejaculation of despair and reined to a stop. "My carpet bag! I left it at the conservatory door. I must go back for it."

"What?" I cried.

But before I could mount further protest Belvedere disappeared into the fog and, for the second time that night, I found myself alone, waiting impotently for events to unfold. When he finally returned with his precious satchel and we got under way, I was more than ready to let loose a torrent of abuse upon his head.

"Great God in heaven, Belvedere, it's all very well for you to be so jolly but I have been treated most unfairly. You duped me! You duped me cruelly! I have been an innocent participant in a most ignoble activity—a base act of common thievery. You told me that you were simply picking up some of your own possessions, but I fail to see how your father's silver and bottles of wine can be deemed to be your property. And what if we had been caught? Indeed we are hardly out of the woods yet. Should a policeman stop us, we will both end up in the Don Jail. I mean to say, damn it all, had you come right out and asked me to assist you in your thieving, well, I suppose I might have consented, but I call it damned ungentlemanly of you to take advantage of my trusting nature. There. I have stated my case. What have you to say for yourself?"

"Damnation, I believe the fog is beginning to lift. I rather hoped it would see us safely home," he remarked matter-of-factly. "But yes, in response to your accusations, as I understand it, the thrust of your outburst is two-fold. Firstly that I lied to you and secondly that our activities tonight are in themselves highly discreditable. 'A base act of common thievery' and so forth. Well now, concerning the latter point, I do not mind in the least being called a thief, but I take great exception to being termed a common thief. A most uncommon thief, I should hope."

"Call it what you will, but thieving can hardly be considered the act of a gentleman."

"My dear Reginald, do calm yourself, of course it can. I mean to say, if one were to commit some gross act—farting at table, say, or wearing a cravat with a Dragoon collar—well, quite obviously one would be justifiably deemed a boor. But the appropriation of certain goods—"

"Thieving," I corrected.

"Very well, thieving, if you insist. See here, it all depends on whom one robs and with what degree of panache one executes the annexation. Now tonight, I have had the great pleasure of reducing the wealth of my father and increasing the financial status of our good and noble selves. Furthermore, as I recall, your conscience did not inconvenience you terribly when you knowingly enjoyed my father's theatre seat several weeks ago."

"No. That's true," I admitted.

"As for your ridiculous insistence upon thieving not being the act of a gentleman, it occurs to me that one element you have neglected to take into account is the manner in which the ill-gotten gains are spent. I would remind you that it was to raise capital to fund our campaign of revenge on your behalf that we went aburgling tonight."

"Yes," I said. "I do appreciate that fact."

"Had you known we were going out tonight to do a spot of thieving, you would have been highly agitated. If anything, you should be grateful to me for sparing you the worry concomitant with the threat of being jugged or shot."

I felt he had more than made his point and I sought to bring my dressing down to a conclusion. "You are of course completely correct in all you say, Belvedere, and I do appreciate all your efforts on my behalf. Please allow me to apologize. I spoke without thinking. I'm sorry."

"Think nothing of it, old man. The subject is closed."

The fog was now lifting quite quickly, and as we drove down Spadina Avenue it occurred to me that, to a police constable, two gentlemen in evening clothes driving an old wagon through the city in the middle of the night would surely appear highly suspicious. Mercifully, our trip passed without our encountering any representatives of the law, and in due course Belvedere reined to a halt in the lane behind Mrs. Flowers' house.

"And here we are, home safe and sound. Do come up and have a celebratory snifter, old man," he said. "I am afraid the chest is too heavy to carry up the ladder, so we shall have to risk using the stairs. Needless to say, stealth is essential."

We crept up to his rooms and Belvedere turned up the gas in his Persian parlour and lit a most welcome fire. He then poured us both brandies and invited me to lounge on an oriental cushion in front of the fire while he laid the swag out on the floor for our inspection. The pieces of family silver were of undoubted quality.

"Rather fine, wouldn't you agree?" he asked.

"Of course, yes, exquisite."

"Perhaps you would like to examine the monogram."

I did as he bade me do and was surprised to see the letter "B" artistically etched into the silver, and not the expected "M" for Musket. Belvedere anticipated my surprise.

"Yes, Reginald old son. 'B' as in Beaumont—Mother's maiden name, you know. Such fine silver would of course come from her people—French Huguenots, incidentally. To allow that oaf of a Musket man to retain possession of it was quite out of the question. The silver is now in its rightful home and here it shall remain always."

I blanched visibly as my diatribe concerning his pilfering his father's silver resounded in my ears.

"Belvedere," I began, "do forgive me. I assumed—well, obviously I assumed it belonged to your father."

"Don't trouble yourself on that account. You may take conciliation in the fact that these bottles of vintage port wine most definitely belong to the old trout, and he will be livid when he discovers they have taken wing. And now, perhaps you would be interested in seeing what I have in this chest?"

With one motion Belvedere lifted the lid of the chest and spilled its contents out on the floor before me.

"Behold!" he cried. "Booty from my wicked childhood!"

I gaped in astonishment as hundreds of watches and other pieces of jewellery spilled out over the oriental carpet.

"My god!" I exclaimed. "Wherever did you get them all?"

"Oh, I've collected them over the years from my various school chums. Much of it I won at the poker table and the remainder I accepted as payment for bottles of a certain beverage called Strip Me Naked which I manufactured and sold to my schoolmates at Upper Canada College. It was a horrible gin-like concoction, the tipple of the *mobile vulgus,* you understand, but all the fellows thought it great fun. Through an unfortunate misunderstanding, however, some of their parents got wind of my little operation and, what with this and that, I found it expedient to stow this chest under the eaves in dear Father's house. When I left you in the pantry tonight, I stole up to the attic and retrieved it. I must say it is quite gratifying to see it after all these years."

"Good lord. How many do you reckon you've got?"

"I can tell you precisely—look here."

He pointed to an area of the cloth lining on the underside of the lid. Looking very carefully I could make out the faint remains of many columns of figures inscribed in lead pencil.

"You see, here is the final total," he said. "Under 'stick-pins'—48. 'Watches'—162. 'Rings'—72. And under 'cufflinks'—94."

I marvelled at his possessing such daring at so tender an age and inquired as to how much he thought it would all fetch.

"One hundred dollars at the minimum, I should think, possibly as high as two hundred and fifty—there is a good deal of gold in that pile. And actually, I wonder if you would do me a small favour?"

"Certainly. You have only to name it."

"I wonder if you would mind pawning my booty for me? What with Doctor Dandy and his henchmen scouring the city for me, I think it best that I limit my public appearances as much as possible—especially given that pawn shops are more often than not under surveillance by the police."

I agreed to his request without hesitation and he instructed me to take the jewellery to Green and Co. Pawnbrokers on York Street.

"Oh, but not immediately," he added. "I shall need to clear the way, as it were, so wait until I notify you that it is time for you to perform your little errand. Here, hold on—you're in need of a good watch, take whichever one strikes your fancy. Please, I insist, as a memento of our little adventure."

I did not need to be asked a second time and, after much deliberation, I selected a heavy gold specimen—wonderfully engraved in an art nouveau pattern of entwined roses. Then I noticed the thin grey light filtering through a gap in the curtains. I remarked upon the lateness of the hour and Belvedere asked if I would mind returning the horse and wagon to Goforth's livery on my way back to the hotel. I took his question as my cue to leave and, a short time later, I found the mighty Mr. Goforth already bent over his anvil, shaping horseshoes. I paid him off and walked the remainder of the way through the early morning. Finally, as the first rays of sunlight began to show, I stowed Belvedere's booty in my dressing room and crawled—weary to the bone—into my luxurious bed. I fell instantly into a deep and dreamless sleep. We had indeed made a night of it.

CHAPTER XIV

QUEEN'S PARK AND ARTISTIC FLATULENCE

When I returned to consciousness I was amazed to discover that I had slept both the day and evening through and it was nigh on midnight. Obviously the exertions of the past night—following hard on the heels of my release from hospital—had exhausted me utterly. Certainly it had been a night like no other in my experience and, while I was very frightened throughout the entire adventure, I had to admit to enjoying a certain retrospective thrill at our felonious foray. Belvedere La Griffin was, to say the least, a most extraordinary fellow, and when in his company one could expect extraordinary events to ensue.

One thing I had not failed to note, however, concerned his version of the events at The Rossin House during his latest suicide attempt. Doctor Dandy had said that he was discovered lying unconscious in the hallway outside his suite—obviously a voluntary attempt on Belvedere's part to prevent his own death—whereas Belvedere claimed that he had been saved accidentally due to his bath overflowing. You understand I was not faulting Belvedere for promoting a little fib, for after all, he was a Self Creationist *par excellence*, but nonetheless I found it interesting. On a whim I retrieved my stash of funds, counted it, and estimated the amount of my hotel bill to date. My suspicions were at once confirmed. I had passed the point of being able to settle my bill in full, and that meant I could not move to cheaper lodgings or even a less opulent room at the Queen's, for to do so would arouse suspicions concerning my solvency. My fate was clearly in Belvedere's hands. I returned to my bed and, once again, sought the balm of sleep.

I awoke the following morning feeling greatly refreshed and much more optimistic in general. Even my eyes were less repulsive-looking, and with the application of some of Alf's magic potion I began to look distinctly human. Outside, a wonderfully sunny September day called out to me, and I wasted no time requesting that a horse be made ready for a canter in the park. I donned my new Chantilly riding boots and spiffing Nottingham green riding costume, and shortly thereafter found myself stepping smartly along University Avenue towards the iron gates of Queen's Park astride a showy chestnut mare by the name of Wendy. I felt as if I had been magically transported to the Champs Elyseés for all around me the elegant carriages of Toronto's high society were rolling up and down "the Avenue" and thus creating a truly Parisian air.

Queen's Park provided a magnificent oasis boasting over one hundred acres of velvety green sward graced by ancient elms, weeping willows, and various other noble botanical specimens. It was further enhanced by such glorious architectural piles as the University of Toronto and the new Ontario Parliament Building. On that particular September day, the trees were ablaze with the colours of autumn and luminous white clouds drifting across the deep blue sky created a scene much like a Constable painting.

It being a Saturday, the park was richly populated with folk seeking the fresh fall air and divers hawkers of chestnuts and ices and the omnipresent hurdy gurdy men. I took great pleasure in trotting hither and thither along the winding paths, nodding hello to small clumps of people picnicking and to the nannies sitting on iron benches with perambulators containing their precious cherubs of the home beside them.

There was music in the air and I drew up opposite the band shell to enjoy the music of Strauss and survey the colourful scene around me. When the band paused for some refreshment, my attention was drawn to a well-dressed, elderly man standing on a wooden box delivering a heated lecture to the crowd assembled around him. I had of course read of Speakers Corner in London's Hyde Park, but my guidebooks had failed to mention such a place in Queen's Park. I was curious to hear what the man was saying, so I secured Wendy's reins to an iron hitching post and joined the throng about the speaker. I was shocked by the thesis of his discourse.

"I know very well you do not wish to know it, but I am a fully qualified physician and I am telling you this for an out and out medical fact," said the speaker. "There is no greater threat today to the health of our populace than the riding of bicycles. All around you are people suffering from Kyphosis Bicyclistarum, which is nothing less than the postorial dorsal curvature more commonly known as Bicycle Hump!"

"How much are the horse breeders paying you, doc?" shouted the man in front of me.

"Oh no, nothing of the kind, sir. I look out at you good people today and everywhere I look I see sufferers of Bicycle Face staring back at me. It is the result of constant strain to preserve equilibrium while cycling and, once fixed upon the countenance, can never be removed. Indeed, many of my male patients have been forced to grow very unbecoming full beards to hide their deformity while, for female victims of Bicycle Face, I can do nothing except advise the constant wearing of a veil. Yes sir, you may take it as fact!"

"Phooey!" cried a lone voice in the crowd.

"Phooey to you, sir," answered the doctor. "Why only last week I addressed—or rather attempted to address—the League of Canadian Wheelmen and, as I stood on the podium, I gazed down in horror on the multitude of disfigured faces before me. I tell you the crowd was positively peppered with pop-eyes, projecting jaws, and bent necks. I also saw hundreds of cases of chronic Bicycle Twitch."

A crowd member blew the medical man a piercing raspberry.

"As for you women, you so-called bicyclettes, I have spoken to you as a man of science but I am likewise a Christian and let me tell you, a woman awheel is an independent creature free to go whither she will, and an invitation to every rude man to make insulting remarks of a personal nature. Many of you ladies think it is smart to wear bloomer costumes. Well, I am here today to tell you that a woman in bloomer cycling costume is shadier than the elms. I personally witnessed a bloomerette pedalling along Jarvis Street not two days ago who—when a dignified and elderly man made remarks to her regarding her garb—dismounted from her iron steed and assaulted the elderly gentleman with a clenched fist. I am happy to tell you that I played a role in getting that young woman arrested and fined on charges of disorderly conduct, assault, and resisting arrest! And as for cycling on the Sabbath—the Sunday Wheel should be prohibited by law, for it is a desecration and secularization of the Lord's Day! Why do you suppose they call those cyclists who thrive on excessive speeding 'scorchers'? Why do they call the paved area between streetcar rails where these scorchers ride the 'devil strip'? Yes, and I know what they are saying. They are saying that the wheel today is king in Toronto. Well, all I can say to you—and remember, I am a fully qualified medical doctor—all I can say to you is—beware! You have been warned, and don't come crying to me when you discover yourself walking like an ape and looking like one as well! I thank you, ladies and gentlemen."

The doctor stepped down amidst more cries of "Phooey!" along with a smattering of applause. He was immediately replaced by a clergyman who launched into a fearsome tirade against the operating of Toronto streetcars on Sunday, and that was my cue to mount up and continue my ride. It occurred to me that at some point during my visit to the park a typically swarthy little man might approach me with a view to selling me a naughty French postcard or nature study, or even a novelette, but no such person presented himself and I was above making inquiries—no matter how discreet. But nonetheless I enjoyed a most entertaining afternoon including an amusing Punch and Judy show, and I headed for home in a mood of great buoyancy.

My light-heartedness was not destined to remain with me all the way back to the Queen's, for as I passed The Kensington Hotel a most appalling sight drew my attention. Chained to the iron fence running along the front of the hotel was a man of about sixty years who had been stripped bare to the waist and had had his trousers cut off at the knee, while around his neck hung a sign reading "Deadbeat". I divined that this unfortunate man had been unable to pay his bill and had been apprehended attempting to leave the hotel. I had never seen such a pathetic sight and, needless to say, I could not help but wonder if he was a sign to me of what lay ahead if I failed to acquire some funds. I of course felt dreadfully sorry for the poor man and, not wishing to increase his embarrassment, I rode on past him pretending not to notice his existence. Other passers-by were not so discreet, and I had not gone twenty feet before I heard the unmistakable sound of taunting children. I turned Wendy around and saw a half-dozen or more of them laughing and jeering at the poor fellow. They had begun chanting the word "deadbeat" over and over, and one impudent little beggar was actually poking at the tethered man with a pointed stick. The poor fellow was plainly terrified of the little beasts and was begging them to leave him alone. I was aghast and, before I really knew what I was doing, I charged Wendy at the ruffians and they fled the scene amidst many hoots and hollers. No sooner had I chased them off than a tall, moustachioed member of the constabulary came strolling up the street. I stopped the policeman and informed him that young children had been taking cruel advantage of the unfortunate man chained to the fence. Furthermore I asked him if in fact this act of bondage was a legal action. I was rewarded for my inquiries with a rather nasty grin that revealed two rows of diseased brown teeth, and a terse comment.

"Well he shoulda paid his God damn bill, shouldn't he," he said, and with that this guardian of the law brushed past me and continued his relentless search for evil-doers.

Of course I was disgusted by both his indifference and his belligerence, but there seemed to be little else I could do. I wished the unfortunate deadbeat well and bade him good day. When I returned to the Queen's I found a telegram at the reception desk awaiting my arrival. It ran:

Reginald,
I wonder if tomorrow afternoon you would be so good as to perform the little errand in York Street we discussed. If the proprietor should ask you how it is you have such a quantity of jewellery (and I very much doubt that he will), simply say that your father, who recently passed away, was a jeweller. As to the money, press him to give you $250 and under no circumstances accept less than $100. Also, I have it on very reliable authority that there is a certain china figurine for sale in his establishment that he has greatly undervalued.

The figurine in question is green in colour, stands approximately eighteen inches high, and depicts an archer of the Medieval period. It is to be found on a display shelf just inside the door. Do not question the man concerning the item or prolong the transaction in any manner as I do not want him to examine it closely and thereby notice its antiquity and consequent true value.

Thanking you in advance,

Belvedere

P.S. If it is convenient, come to my rooms tomorrow night at ten o'clock.

P.P.S. Best to use the window entrance, I think.

I was in a rather shaky condition as I read the telegram for, truth to tell, the episode with the hotel deadbeat had upset me dreadfully. My few remaining funds were dwindling fast and I had no claim whatsoever on even a portion of the money to be raised from pawning Belvedere's booty. Which left me wondering how on earth I was to live. In the end I decided the best thing I could do under the circumstances was to take myself off to the Bijou Theatre for an evening of light entertainment, and that is precisely what I did. The programme began with a charming little farce entitled "Love Laughs at Locksmiths" and was followed by a succession of remarkable novelty acts. First the Human Anvil delighted in having huge rocks broken over his chest and then the Elastic Lady defied the human vertebrae in her sinuous twistings and Sandow the Strongman frolicked with cannon-balls. But by far the most astonishing act of the evening was a French comic artist calling himself Le Petomane. In the playbill he was dubbed "the nightingale of the famous Moulin Rouge" and so naturally I assumed him to be a singer. As it turned out, I was only partially correct in that assumption. The master of ceremonies phrased it thusly:

"And now, ladies and gentlemen, all the way from the Moulin Rouge in Paris, France, warbling from the depths of his trousers, Le Petomane—the famous singing arsehole!"

My fellow audience members and I watched in shock as a very dignified-looking gentleman with a large moustache walked alone on stage and bowed majestically in our direction. His costume was singular in that he wore a short black jacket of the kind favoured by waiters, bright red breeches, white silk stockings, white gloves, and patent leather pumps. He began by explaining in a heavy French accent that God had granted him the power to breathe through his anus, and that by storing up air inside his body he could, and indeed would, produce all manner of sounds at will. He announced his first effect.

"And now for you, ze sound of ze dressmaker tearing two yard of ze cotton."

He then turned his back to us, bent forward at the waist, placed his hands on his knees, and let go with a fart that not only duplicated exactly the sound of tearing cotton but lasted a full fifteen seconds in duration! From that moment onwards Le Petomane had us in his power. He treated us to the sounds of rolling thunder, a trombone, a violin, a dog with his tail caught in the door, the timid little fart of a young girl, the hysterical fart of a mother-in-law, and on and on. On many occasions the laughter grew dangerously near to hysteria, and I noted uniformed nurses standing at strategic spots throughout the theatre ready to give aid to persons overcome with hilarity. To close his act, Le Petomane left the stage for a moment and returned with a rubber hose several feet in length and inserted it into his rectum through a hole in his trousers. He then attached a small flute to the free end of the hose, and played several jaunty sea shanties upon it. Le Petomane was cheered and applauded wildly and he rewarded his enthusiastic fans by returning to the stage for an encore performance. He brought with him a low stool, a water pitcher, and a large tin basin. He placed the basin on the stool, poured a large quantity of water from the pitcher into the basin, and lowered himself onto the basin of water. We sat in hushed expectation as he sat perfectly still—seemingly doing nothing whatsoever. Then, slowly, he rose to his feet and, to the delight of all assembled, loosed a jet of water from his backside a full twenty feet into the wings! The audience went mad—many members literally falling down on the floor with laughter—while I found myself to be temporarily sightless due to my tears of hilarity.

My jolly evening served to raise my spirits no end, and as I lay in bed that night I thought once again of the pitiful hotel deadbeat outside the Kensington, and I resolved to fear not—to press on, trust in Belvedere, and generally *Fidem Servo*. Tomorrow was another day and I would begin it by returning to fashionable King Street and replacing all the fine clothes and accoutrements the Dead Dogs had stolen from me. A life of security had to remain anathema to me. I would soldier-on, unheedful of petty concerns.

CHAPTER XV

THE WAR CABINET MEETS

B y the following morning I was perhaps a little less sure of myself but nonetheless I kept my resolve, and by late afternoon my new clothes were ordered and I had replaced all my lost smoking tackle. Next I transferred Belvedere's booty into my club satchel and proceeded on to York Street, where, under the customary three gilt balls, I discovered a sign reading "Green and Co. Pawnbrokers". As I entered the shop I witnessed a scene out of the pages of a romantic novel. A respectable-looking, middle-aged woman who, going by her black "widow's weeds", I judged to have recently lost her husband, was in the process of pawning a gold locket and two silver candlesticks. These constituted, quite obviously, her last few possessions of any value, and now that she had fallen on hard times, and with a large family to feed, she had no alternative but to sell them. My heart went out to her and she reminded me that unforeseen destitution is far from being an uncommon event in this life. When she left the premises I stepped up to the cage, housing a man I took to be Mr. Green. He was a most taciturn fellow, short, rather poorly dressed, and in need of a shave. His manner of discourse was most perfunctory.

"Good day to you, sir," I said.

"You have something to pawn?" asked Mr. Green—if indeed he was Mr. Green.

"Yes sir, a quantity of jewellery," I said as I passed the satchel over the top of the cage.

He set about examining the loot with an eye-glass.

"Twenty dollars," he said.

"What?" I cried. "Ridiculous. I shall not take one cent less than two hundred and fifty."

"Ninety-five."

"Two hundred and seventy-five."

We glared into each other's eyes.

"One hundred and fifty," he said.

"Two hundred and fifty and that is final."

"One hundred and fifty-five or get out!" he shouted.

"Done."

He left me waiting at the counter for a short time and then returned with my money and a paper sack full of brass pawn redemption disks. I bade him good day and walked to the door but, as I reached for the handle, I exhibited sudden interest in an archer figurine on the display shelf and asked how much he desired for it.

"Dollar fifty."

"I'll give you one dollar," I said.

"Done."

I passed a dollar through the cage bars, placed my purchase in my satchel, and bade Mr. Green a very pleasant afternoon.

Ten o'clock that night found me standing in the dark at the foot of the fire ladder running up the side of Mrs. Flowers' house to Belvedere's darkened dressing-room window. I had my satchel with me and that made the climbing of the ladder rather awkward, but nonetheless I soon reached the top and knocked gently on Belvedere's window. I waited. Nothing. I reapplied my knuckles to the pane and paused. No sight nor sound of Belvedere. I raised my fist to strike yet again, but just then the window slid up silently and a face appeared.

"Good evening, Reginald," exclaimed Belvedere. "Come in,

won't you? Do forgive my tardiness. I was listening to my phonograph and quite forgot the time."

Belvedere took my club satchel from me and helped me climb in the window. His dressing room was in complete darkness and he led the way through to his cosy Persian parlour, which was lit by fully dozens of candles in an array of oriental stands and wall brackets, and warmed by a cheery blaze in the grate. Soothing orchestral music came from the huge horn of his phonograph and the air was heavy with the smell of incense. Belvedere was resplendent in a blue satin brocade Persian robe, a purple fez, and purple upturned slippers not unlike my own, and looked completely at home as he took up residence on his Turkish divan. On the floor beside the divan stood a huge brass hookah pipe fully four feet in height, with a long, coiled tube ending in an ivory mouth-piece. He began puffing on the apparatus and, as he did so, the water in the base of the pipe made a burbling sound. After a minute or so he removed the ivory mouth-piece from his mouth, looked at me rather dreamily, and then suddenly seemed to remember my presence.

"Oh, make yourself comfortable, old man, please. What do you fancy? Some port perhaps? Help yourself, won't you—the decanter is just behind you there on the papier-mâché table."

I poured myself a glass of port and sat on a camel stool in front of the fire. The warm glow produced by the old port and the hot-house heat of the room were most welcome, for it was unseasonably cool weather for the time of year and my journey in the hansom cab had chilled me to the bone.

"How do you find it—the port, I mean. To your liking?" Belvedere asked.

"I find it . . . delicious."

He raised his own glass and breathed deeply. Then he took a small sip and followed this by a slightly larger draught.

"Yes, the Sandeman '63. There's no other port like it in existence. A charm so difficult to define. Luscious and delicious, with an eel-like satiny body, robust but not even a hint of brutality, and as if that were not enough—oh, how does it go?

> Stolen sweets are always sweeter,
> Stolen kisses much completer,
> Stolen looks are nice in chapels,
> Stolen, stolen, be your apples.

I mean of course that this lovely port wine that we are enjoying is that which we purloined from my odious father. Oh, and speaking of stolen, just throw this on the fire, will you, Reginald, it's getting a bit chilly in here."

Belvedere reached under a large silk pillow behind him and withdrew a brown paper folio of the type used in business to file papers. He passed it over to me and I was shocked to see the name "Herbert Musket" written on the cover. One glance inside confirmed that I was holding in my hand Belvedere's medical file from the Provincial Lunatic Asylum.

"I slipped in just after three o'clock this morning and removed the dreary little object. I should think it will burn rather well."

I tossed the folio into the flames and watched its rapid consumption. As the last of it burned, a sudden suspicion crept over me that someone was watching me from the shadows in the far corner of the room. I wheeled around and came face to face with Oscar Wilde to the life.

"Good lord, it's Oscar," I exclaimed.

"Hmm, yes. Please," said Belvedere with a wave of his hand inviting me to examine the object.

I rose and discovered it to be a large bronze bust that was Oscar Wilde in every detail.

"Do you like it? It is by Mr. Frederick Dunbar," he said. "I bought it at the Art Institute in Montreal some years ago. I think it rather fine."

At his prompting I remembered reading about the exhibit in *Saturday Night* and seeing an illustration of this very bust. In fact I vividly recalled envying the undoubtedly exotic person who purchased the work—never daring to dream that I would some day call that person friend. The bust was resting atop a stout marble table and beside it sat a very large pair of men's buckled black evening pumps under a glass dome. My curiosity was piqued.

"Forgive me, Belvedere," I said, "but these buckle pumps, are they in some way connected to Mr. Wilde?"

"Only in so far as they are Oscar's own pumps. He gave them to me."

"Are you saying that you know Oscar Wilde personally?" I asked—my voice filled with incredulity.

"Certainly, dear boy. It was some years back—three or four, I suppose. I met him when he was in Toronto delivering his lectures on the Decorative Arts at the Grand Opera House. Indeed, we dined together at McConkey's. Now, mind you, I am not claiming to have dined alone with Oscar, we were in a party of a dozen or more persons—local artists and littérateurs for the most part—but nonetheless, Oscar spoke brilliantly and I enjoyed myself no end. As to how I came to be in such august company, the explanation is quite simple. There was a vulgarian who persisted in heckling Oscar during his lecture. I stood it for as long as I could but, finally, I felt compelled to silence the oaf by slapping his face with my glove."

"Do you mean to say you challenged the fellow to an actual duel?" I asked.

"Of course I challenged him to an actual duel. Is there any other kind of duel? The man was becoming increasingly abusive and left me no other option. Well, in any case, Oscar overheard our exchange and intervened. The fellow I dearly wanted to gut with my blade was ejected from the theatre and Oscar insisted that I join his party for a midnight supper at McConkey's after his lecture. Naturally I was only too charmed to accept his kind invitation. Over supper he told me he could tell at a glance that I was one of Toronto's foremost fashionables, and that he pitied me having to live in such an artistic wasteland as Canada. I of course agreed and said how I wished I could walk in his shoes. To my astonishment, he quickly responded, 'And so you shall, my lad,' and presented me with the pumps right off his feet. I was overwhelmed by his generosity, and I suggested a trade—his pumps for mine—but my pumps being a full six sizes smaller than Oscar's, he declined my offer and insisted I take his along with me as a memento of the evening and a reminder always to walk in the path of beauty. One day I feel sure I shall look to find they have sprouted little gossamer wings on the heels."

I could only stare at my friend in awe.

"But enough of the past, let us return to the present day. Tell me how you got on at Green and Co."

I returned to the camel stool in front of the fire and removed the archer from my satchel.

"Your *objet d'art*, sir," I said as I handed Belvedere the figurine. "And the sum of one hundred and fifty-five dollars! He tried to cheat me into taking only twenty but I wouldn't hear of it."

"Excellent, Reginald. Well done." He tucked the roll of bills into a side pocket in his robe without bothering to count it. "We should be feeling very pleased with ourselves, for events are unfolding exactly as they should. Thanks to my larcenous youth and your excellent haggling skills, we now have some essential operating capital."

I flushed with pride at his words of praise.

"But of equal if not greater importance," he continued, "thanks to Alf Shaughnessy we know who our enemy is and where he is to be found. That is to say, Little Dave Goody and Dan the Dude Dougherty at the Black Bull Tavern. I wonder if you are aware that this notorious tavern is but four blocks from this very room? Indeed, it is highly likely that as we speak the men who attempted to kill you are there drinking at your expense."

Belvedere paused to puff on his hookah while I pondered his observation. As I stared into the fire the idea of the Dead Dog Gang in the flesh did not fill me with enthusiasm. I looked up at the sound of metal on metal. Belvedere was now sitting cross-legged on the divan, slowly, or rather, lovingly drawing the blade of a long rapier back and forth along a steel—not so much honing the edge as caressing it.

"Let us take stock," he said, "compare the strengths and weaknesses of the opposing armies. Obviously they have a great deal more battle experience than we and their troops vastly outnumber us. However, we must not overlook the one huge advantage we possess. We, and only we, know that a war has been declared. We alone possess the priceless advantage of the surprise attack. They assume you to be dead and the matter finished. Having butchered your fine Imperial, we are assured that they will not recognize you, and therefore we are free to watch them. We also possess intelligence, ruthlessness, and wills forged in iron. I propose that tomorrow we begin a programme of clandestine observation of the infamous Black Bull, and with luck, the Dead Dogs themselves. We shall thereby learn the extent of their criminal operations, their habits, strengths, and weaknesses. Obviously our overall aim is to devise a way to rob them. Would you mind handing me that copy of *The Telegram* lying on the floor?"

I did as requested and watched as Belvedere extracted a single sheet of newsprint and held it out at arm's length. He then took the rapier he had been honing all the while and slowly sliced the page in half.

"Yes, very nice," he remarked. "You could shave a man with that edge—and a good deal more besides."

He handed the rapier to me and I examined his work. He was not exaggerating, for it was literally as sharp as a straight razor. I noted that it was out of a sword-stick and that the handle consisted of an ivory knob carved in the shape of a woman's head.

"Here is the shaft," he said. "Take it as a gift in thanks for the kindness you have shown me. You'll find it a useful item to have about your person."

He handed me a rosewood shaft and I inserted the three feet of razor-sharp steel into it. As I held the stick in the palm of my hand I discovered it to be much heavier at the bottom end than the top.

"Yes," he said, "it's weighted with buck-shot as well. So handy when one suddenly finds oneself in need of a bludgeon."

"It is exquisite, Belvedere. What can I say except thank you? I shall always treasure it."

"My pleasure, old boy. May you use it in good health. As I recall, you also possess a revolver. Beginning tomorrow you must carry it on your person at all times, for let us not forget that these are evil beings we are up against. Should they somehow recognize you or in some other way tumble to our purpose, they will try their best to cut us down without the slightest hesitation. We must be well armed against that eventuality."

He opened a silver box and offered me a Turkish Beauty, which I accepted with thanks. While he lit one for himself I contemplated his sombre warning and, though I hated myself for being a coward, still my overwhelming feeling was one of fear. As I knew all too well, the Dead Dogs were indeed evil beings, and in my heart I also knew that I was no match for them. I swallowed hard and wished the room were not so infernally hot.

"Belvedere," I said through a cloud of smoke. "I do not feel . . . that is to say. . . . Forgive me but I am no longer certain I can do this—take them on, I mean. They frighten me terribly. I have never been in a fight and I know in my heart that I am no match for them."

I braced myself for Belvedere's inevitable tirade but, strangely, he remained completely at ease.

"But of course you are, Reginald," he remarked matter-of-factly. "You have already bested them once today."

With one deft movement he seized the figurine and decapitated it against the oak leg of the divan. I watched in amazement as he up-ended it and half a dozen glittering diamonds tumbled out onto the Turkey carpet.

"Great God," I cried in astonishment. "Those are diamonds!"

Belvedere smiled. "But of course. What else?"

"But how did you know they were in there?"

"Very simply, Reginald, that is where I put them. It's well known that Green and Co. remain in business by selling stolen goods brought to them by the major criminal gangs of Toronto, and I should be very surprised if the Dead Dogs do not number among their suppliers. Indeed, you may be sure that it is out of their establishment that your father's watch and signet ring have already been sold. I decided that it was only fitting that Mr. Green should fund our campaign of war. Yesterday, posing as a diamond dealer from Montreal, I visited the shop to examine their merchandise. They had some very fine diamonds on display—all of which you may be sure have been prized out of ring settings and stick-pins stolen from hapless persons like yourself. I dared not risk merely slipping some into my pocket lest he note their absence before I left the premises, so I employed a trick detailed in the most recent edition of *The Police Gazette*. When Mr. Green was busy with another customer, I simply put the diamonds into the bottom of the figurine and stuffed my handkerchief in afterwards to hold them inside and keep them from rattling. *Et voilà*. Those diamonds are of the highest quality and doubtless worth at least four hundred dollars. So you see, Reginald, we most certainly can beat the nefarious Dead Dog Gang at their own game. It merely requires patience and intelligence."

I held one of the diamonds in front of the fire and the flashing colours sent a thrill through me.

"Be in no doubt, Reginald," Belvedere continued. "People such as you and I are in a perpetual state of war. The enemy is three-fold. On the most mundane level, the Dead Dogs and their ilk, who would cheerfully smash our heads and pocket our watches. Then come the Methodists and alienists and sundry other philistines who delight in breaking the imaginations of persons who live for beauty and Self Creation. And finally there is that most formidable of opponents—life itself, with all its repetitiveness, its practical demands, its corrosive solitude, odious ennui, inevitable illness and death. However, we must not give way to despair as I have done in the past, for we are not unarmed in this war. For the slimy louts with their iron knucks and heavy boots we have pretty little derringers and razor-sharp sword-sticks. For the pious philistines—indifference and barbed wit coupled with outlandish dash and flair. And finally, to fight the boredom and stagnation—music, poetry, fine food and drink, and, most essential of all, the life-sustaining thrill of desperate deeds of derring-do. And now please join me in a toast. To risk!" cried Belvedere as he raised his wine glass. "For risk is to life as brandy is to soda—essential!"

"To risk!" I cried.

We clinked our glasses and both took long pulls at our port.

"Now then," Belvedere continued. "I suggest we commence our surveillance of the Black Bull tomorrow afternoon. You will find me positioned in a closed carriage directly across the street from the tavern at precisely two o'clock. And may I remind you to come fully armed. Should we be spotted we will most assuredly have to fight for our very lives. It simply would not do to be taken alive by the likes of Little Dave Goody and his Dead Dogs."

"No, I do see that, very definitely yes," I said.

On that ominous note we concluded our discussion of war tactics, and shortly thereafter I took my leave via the dressing-room window. Later, as I lay safe in my warm bed, I found sleep to be an elusive friend. "For God's sake, Reginald," I told myself, "whatever else you do, do not let them take you alive!"

CHAPTER XVI

THE FETID BOWELS OF THE BULL

The following afternoon I arrived at the appointed place and hour to discover a black brougham carriage parked opposite the Black Bull. No coachman was to be seen at the reins, and for a moment I hesitated to knock upon a side window lest it be the wrong carriage, but when I finally did so the window blind moved slightly and the door opened to admit me. I found Belvedere inside the plum-coloured interior, with his false beard upon his face and an open copy of *Tailor and Cutter* upon his knee. He did not look pleased, and I ventured a gentle inquiry as to his general state of being.

"Bored," he snapped. "This endless waiting is too tiresome. Do you know, in the time I have been stationed here watching that odious tavern, not a single lout has entered or exited the premises? Am I to spend the remainder of my life sitting in a hired carriage staring into nothingness?"

As it was just eleven minutes past the hour of two o'clock, I found myself somewhat confused by Belvedere's complaint.

"I take it, then, that you arrived earlier than anticipated—before two o'clock?" I asked.

"Certainly not. I said two o'clock and I meant two o'clock," he responded testily.

Clearly my companion was in an irascible mood, and I sought to relieve his burden of inactivity, and the atmosphere in the carriage in general, by offering to take over the surveillance while he enjoyed his *Tailor and Cutter*. He accepted my offer, and for a period of ten or more minutes I scanned the street for my attackers while he perused an article on the Prince of Wales's latest hat. A short time later, however, Belvedere cast his periodical aside.

"Very well then, we shall have to go in," he cried in exasperation. "I had hoped to avoid actually entering the filthy sewer, but if we must then we must."

I felt a chill run through me.

"Is that really wise?" I asked. "I mean to say, I know my missing Imperial alters my appearance considerably but is there not still a fairly strong likelihood that one of their number may recognize me?"

In answer to my question Belvedere reached into a side pocket and extracted a small blue jar of glue, and what proved to be a Vandyke style beard. "I realize that, when I persuaded you to butcher your fine Imperial moustache, I said that your wearing a false beard was out of the question. However, in situations where you are deliberately rubbing shoulders with gangland villains, I believe an exception should be made," he said. I applied the hirsute appliance and was pleasantly surprised at its flattering effect.

"Now then," he said. "I see you have your new walking stick with you. I assume you have your revolver on your person."

"Of course."

"And you have checked its load?"

I removed my Defender and passed it over to him, that he might satisfy himself that I was not a complete imbecile.

"Excellent," he said. "I too am well armed."

"I wonder," I heard myself saying, "will we not look a little conspicuous in our fine clothes amid the rabble?"

"Undoubtedly, but I believe we will be taken for a couple of sports in search of low women," he replied.

Privately I questioned that assertion, but I had little choice other than to follow him as he decamped from the carriage and picked his way across Queen Street, trying to avoid the heavy carriage traffic and the steaming road apples. When we gained the opposite side of the street, he stopped abruptly.

"Remember, Reginald," he said, "we cannot allow ourselves to be taken alive in this tavern. Therefore at the very first sign of aggression towards us we must open fire."

I would have liked to discuss that point further, but before I could protest, he strode onward and disappeared through the door of the Black Bull.

The instant I entered the tavern I was nearly overpowered by the stench of urine, sweat, and cheap cigars that polluted the atmosphere. It took several moments for my eyes to adjust to the dim interior, but when at last I could see clearly I discerned a long, ill-lit room with a low ceiling of heavy oak beams and a rough bar counter running almost the entire length of one side. A large wooden sign was affixed to the wall above the bar.

EVERYTHING TO EAT AND DITTO TO DRINK
PIES OF UNDOUBTED CHARACTER

Below this sign were nailed the head and skin of a huge black Newfoundland dog, and its presence certainly left one in no doubt concerning which Toronto gang called the Black Bull "home". About a dozen toughs were lounging at rough wooden tables scattered around the room but neither Little Dave Goody nor Dan the Dude Dougherty numbered among them. Belvedere led the way towards an empty table at the rear of the room and, in traversing the tavern, we discovered that the floor was covered in a soggy mixture of sawdust, tobacco juice, urine, and several pools of vomit. While I waited at the table, Belvedere ordered drinks at the bar counter from a man who, judging by his bizarre cranial development, could only be the "Bullet" Malloy that Alf Shaughnessy had mentioned. Mr. Malloy was himself, quite obviously, a filthy drunkard. Belvedere returned with two large glasses filled with an amber fluid.

"Whisky?" I asked.

"In name only. It is called Squirrel Whisky but it is actually rectified oil of turpentine—ideal as a solvent for varnishes but I cannot recommend it as a beverage—not if you value your stomach or your sanity. Just pretend to drink it."

I took a tiny sip and discovered it to be wholly noxious. We settled back to await further developments, but almost immediately I became aware of raised voices coming from two men playing cards beneath a sign exhorting the patrons not to discharge firearms on the premises. Their voices rose steadily in a volley of curses until, without warning, one of the men—a swarthy giant of a man—reared up and dashed a heavy crockery spittoon against the other man's skull. Lumpy brown slime exploded over the victim's head and he fell to the floor like a piece of lead. I looked at Belvedere. He was sitting bolt upright with his hand inside his coat pocket in readiness. His eyes shone with the brightness of fever.

But nothing came of it. No one else in the bar, including Bullet Malloy, deigned to take any notice of the assault and the huge aggressor merely gathered up the few pennies on the table and joined some other louts at a table closer to the entrance. As he lumbered over to the table, I noted thick bunches of black hair growing out of his ears and additional tufts sprouting from his huge nostrils. I looked back at his prostrate chum. His head was a mass of blood and brown scum. There was no movement or sign of life that I could detect.

"They're drinking Bingo," said Belvedere. "It's a punch compounded of whisky, hot rum, camphor, benzine, and cocaine sweepings. It comes guaranteed to provide a case of delirium tremens with every glass."

He nudged my arm.

"Observe Creepy and Crawly just walking in."

I followed his gaze. Coming through the door were two heavies—one wearing a so-called "turtle-necked" sweater and chequered cap while the other one sported a dirty sack suit and a battered pork-pie hat. A dog paw hung from both their watch chains in lieu of a conventional fob.

Belvedere inclined his head in my direction.

"The short, fat one with the pork-pie hat and the birth-mark is the vile Piggie O'Neil—Little Dave's chum."

The sobriquet of the lout in question was indeed apt. Slovenly, squat, with a fat, pasty face and a snub nose—his entire being cried out of the porcine. I noted the large brown birth-mark on his cheek—much as if someone had spilled iodine upon it. Piggie was obviously very intoxicated for, as he crashed onto a chair, his head immediately pitched forward and hit the wooden table before him with a resounding thud. He didn't move, and his companion merely slumped into the chair beside him. I stared at this malignant little pig of a man and pictured him with a hold on my legs, casually flinging me into the inky blackness of the bay. I imagined myself slowly rising from my seat, withdrawing my Defender, and sauntering over to him. "Good night, Piggie," I would say just before calmly pressing the barrel of my revolver to the back of his head and squeezing off a lethal round. It would be so simple. There was even some doubt in my mind as to whether his companion would do anything about it. I could easily imagine him simply getting up and moving to another table, just as the big man with the hair growing out of his ears had done. Belvedere's voice brought me back to reality.

"Come along, Reginald, we had best be on our way," he said. "Unless we consume our drinks, Bullet Malloy will wonder what we're up to."

His words roused me from my evil reverie and we departed the Black Bull without incident. Outside, the dazzling sunshine and fresh autumn air hit me with force and I realized I had been breathing as shallowly as possible in the malodorous haven of the lawless.

"Climb inside, Reginald," Belvedere said. "I will drive us."

I did as directed and shortly thereafter we pulled up at North's Carriage Livery, at the corner of Nelson and Simcoe streets, where Belvedere returned the brougham and engaged a hansom cab. As we threaded our way through the congested streets, I was still struggling to come to grips with the squalor and violence of the Black Bull.

"Do you think he was dead?" I asked.

"Who? The man with the nicotine shampoo? I certainly hope so. I do not doubt that Toronto would be the better for one less Bingo fiend."

I remained in the dark as to our destination until finally we reined in outside Pember's Turkish Baths and Hair Emporium, opposite Birks on Yonge Street. After our sojourn into the fetid bowels of the Black Bull, there was no need for explanation.

"Best to remove our beards first, I fancy," said Belvedere. "Simply would not do to have them peeling off in the steam bath."

I did as directed and we entered the exclusive ablutionary establishment. To my surprise, Belvedere left me just inside the door, explaining that due to his escaped lunatic status, it would be safer for him to bathe privately. He suggested that I would enjoy the public cleansing programme offered by Pember's, and I proceeded on to a series of four steam rooms of ever-increasing temperatures interspersed with wonderfully reviving cold needle douches. It was an extremely high-toned establishment, elegantly fitted up and handsomely furnished in white marble, and I did not doubt that the spectral faces looming up from out of the steam belonged to many of Toronto's greatest financiers and merchants. From the last steam room I was led to the medicated shampoo immersion tank, then into a mineral bath, then to the massage tables in the hot room, then to the marble plunge bath, which I was informed constituted the largest of its kind in Canada, and finally ended my programme in the towelling room. When I went to get dressed I discovered that my clothes and footwear had been likewise cleansed, and this news came as something of a relief for I did not doubt that the stink of the Black Bull had rendered them conspicuous. There remained only the hair emporium to visit, and it was there that I rejoined Belvedere.

Several hours after our arrival, we left Pember's Turkish Baths and Hair Emporium and both Belvedere and I declared ourselves quite restored and wildly hungry. We dined that night at the home of Toronto's *le beau monde*—McConkey's Restaurant. It was truly the last word in luxury and refinement—listing among its many attributes the fact that it was the first restaurant in the city to possess electric lamps—and my memory of the Partridge Fantaisie consumed therein remains to this day one of my most cherished. Then it was off to the Grand Opera House and a performance of Brandon Thomas's *Charley's Aunt,* which we both enjoyed intensely. By unspoken agreement, we did not discuss Piggie O'Neil or Little Dave Goody or any of the other revolting Dead Dog parasites until after the theatre, when we repaired to Le Chat Noir for a quiet drink. Belvedere seemed to me to be ominously pensive.

"We must take great care, Reginald," he said after a time. "Having seen their lair and some of the goings-on within it, I think you will agree, now more than ever, that these Dead Dogs are indeed ugly, brutal men. Indeed, I see now that we were unwise to enter the tavern, for the violence therein is often random and, as you pointed out, we certainly were conspicuous among such a grotesque gathering of louts. To return a second time could not help but draw unwanted attention to ourselves. Furthermore, it is clear that our surveillance would serve us better later in the day, and I propose that we resume our covert observation tomorrow afternoon around four. Before then, however, if you should like to accompany me, I find I really must pay a call on Mr. Piccolo, for I am in desperate need of some new waistcoats. Perhaps you would like to meet me at his shop tomorrow afternoon at, let us say, two o'clock?"

I assented with enthusiasm, for I was overjoyed at the prospect of accompanying such a poet of cloth as Belvedere La Griffin to his tailor. We agreed that a final beaker of brandy was in order and shortly thereafter we bade each other adieu until the following day.

CHAPTER XVII

THE BLOODIED PIT

I made a point of arriving at Mr. Piccolo's establishment in advance of Belvedere, for I knew he was unaware that I had settled his account with his tailor and I wanted to be present when the two men met. However, I was to be disappointed in that Belvedere seemed to take for granted the fact that Mr. Piccolo greeted him warmly and made no mention of past moneys due before further sums of credit could be offered him. Indeed I was further surprised by the fact that Belvedere was measured for nothing save a mocha-coloured frock coat, a green brocade waistcoat, and a pair of canary-yellow spats, while I, under his guidance, ended up ordering a total of seven waistcoats, four pairs of trousers, and eleven shirts.

We continued our promenade eastward along King Street, stopping here and looking there, until we came abreast of the St. Lawrence Coffee House. Belvedere suggested we go inside for a cup of coffee and perhaps a scone before taking up our post outside the Black Bull, and I eagerly agreed, as I was feeling rather peckish myself and I knew our surveillance might well be a lengthy one. The St. Lawrence turned out to be an admirable little coffee house, richly panelled in oak, with a cheery blaze burning in a rustic stone fireplace adding to its warmth. We were seated in the bow window looking out onto the street, and I must say I felt very comfortable watching the passing parade of fashionable shoppers from our snug point of observation. Our waiter quickly supplied us with steaming mugs of coffee and a plate piled high with muffins and assorted sticky buns and we both attacked them with a will. At one point I was surprised to see Belvedere unscrew the silver knob of his walking stick and pour an amber liquid from the shaft of the stick into his coffee. He turned to me.

"Touch of brandy, old boy?" he asked.

I accepted with thanks, and when at last we had devoured the plate of eatables, we ordered more coffee. While I continued to observe the ever-changing scene outside, Belvedere chose to read one of the numerous newspapers which hung on wooden rods. Evidently there was a most amusing article therein for he began to chortle to himself.

"Good Lord, listen to this, Reginald. A certain Professor Rowberry of number 14 Elm Street has placed an advertisement. Whom does it remind you of? 'If your head measures only nineteen inches around, you are a partial idiot. Liquor will affect you easily, so will tobacco. You cannot understand grammar, mathematics, nor even play a game of checkers right. Bring me photos or tintypes of any persons and I will tell you their character free of charge.' What say you, should we take Professor Rowberry a photograph of Little Dave Goody?"

But I failed to respond to Belvedere's question, for my attention had been drawn to a tall, slim man with a ferocious jet-black moustache and a bloodless, deeply pocked complexion. He wore a wide-brimmed black felt hat, and with his sunken cheeks and piercing eyes deeply set beneath thick black eyebrows, he put me in mind of Mr. Bram Stoker's ghoul named Dracula. I was musing to myself that he might well be an actor in costume when he turned and a shaft of sunlight caught the large diamond stick-pin blazing in his black satin scarf. A catch came in my breath. I was looking at the Beau Brummel of the Toronto underworld—Dan the Dude

Dougherty!

"Egad," I remarked quietly. "Dan the Dude Dougherty just walked by."

Belvedere stiffened and cast his newspaper to the floor.

"Which way?"

"He's gone now. He's walking eastward."

Belvedere was out the door within mere seconds, with me chasing after him, one arm in my coat and the other searching for the other sleeve. King Street was still crowded with late-afternoon shoppers and at first we could not see our quarry, but eventually I spotted his big black hat and, after a brief run, we fell into step about fifteen feet behind him, amidst the crowd.

"Great God almighty, I cannot believe our good fortune!" said Belvedere as he fought to keep pace with Dan the Dude Dougherty's long strides.

"Indeed yes. But what is it exactly that you think we should do now?" I asked.

"Well, we follow him, of course. See where he goes. Learn what he's doing," he said, slightly out of puff.

Just then Dan the Dude Dougherty stopped at the front of a cab rank and climbed into a hansom. We had no option but to do likewise. I left the issuing of instructions for our cabby to Belvedere.

"You are to keep pace with the cab that just pulled out," he said. "But on no account are you to overtake it."

The good man apparently saw nothing odd in these instructions and we fell in behind the Dude's cab.

"My God, what a stroke of luck!" Belvedere cried. "We might have spent days waiting outside that sewer of a Black Bull. And you are absolutely certain it was him?"

"Absolutely certain."

"Excellent! Oh yes, we shall have some fine sport with these fellows—you mark my words."

We continued following the cab eastward along King until we reached Frederick Street. There we turned northward past the Toronto Newsboys' Home and travelled up as far as Duke Street, where we turned eastward past Christie's Biscuit Factory.

"Not the most savoury part of town," Belvedere remarked. "I wonder—"

Before he could finish his remark, the Dude's cab reined in to the curb in front of a disreputable-looking tavern called the Craven

Heifer. It occupied a brown, two-storey frame building opposite Heintzman's piano factory. Belvedere immediately rapped twice on the ceiling of our cab with his stick to indicate that we too wished to stop.

We watched in silence as Dan the Dude Dougherty dismissed his cab and strode into the Craven Heifer.

"What now?" I asked.

"Here, put this on," said Belvedere, handing me my Vandyke beard. The Dude dismissed his cab so we may assume he intends to stay inside for some time. You have your Defender—correct?"

I answered in the affirmative.

"Excellent. Let us get out and take a look around. Perhaps we can see in a rear window. Give the cabby fifty cents with the promise of fifty more if he waits for us up the street a short distance—however long we may be. We may need to leave the area in considerable haste."

Personally I was none too keen on this plan but, before I could protest, Belvedere was out of the cab and heading down the lane that ran along the side of the Heifer. I gave the cabby his money and instructions and hurried after Belvedere. When I caught up with him he was standing in the lane at the rear of tavern, which, surprisingly, was jammed with carriages. More significantly, these carriages were not just plain wagons and drays, as one would expect to find in that part of the city, but fine broughams and phaetons as well. Indeed there was a group of a dozen or more smartly turned out coachmen standing together enjoying a smoke and a chat. I looked at my companion.

"Judging by the fine carriages behind the saloon, we need not fear looking conspicuously respectable," he said. "Clearly there is a sporting event of sorts going on inside the Heifer and it has drawn a very moneyed crowd. I suggest we join them without delay."

As per usual he did not wait for my assent, but rather headed off back up the lane to Duke Street and the front entrance of the tavern. When we stepped through the door we were confronted by a plain bar-room similar to the Black Bull in furniture and layout but, mercifully, far less malodorous. It was empty save for the bartender and it was obvious from the uproar coming from the floor above us that the sporting event Belvedere had surmised was already in progress. My heart sank. It could only be a dog-fight or cock-fight and I had no desire to witness either savage contest. The bartender took us in with a glance.

"Up them stairs, gents," said he without preamble.

The scene that awaited us at the top of the stairs beggared description. The entire second floor consisted of one large room arranged like an amphitheatre, with tiered wooden benches filled with shouting men rising one above the other around the sides. They presented a rare mixture of rich and poor humanity, for men who undoubtedly numbered in the criminal fraternity of the city sat beside the bankers and brokers whose houses they might well be looting later that very night. It was obvious by the shouting and cursing and exchanging of money that a bout of some description had only just ended. The object of their attention was a pit about eight feet square in the centre of the room enclosed by a three-foot-high wire fence. It was difficult to see clearly, as the room was dimly lit by smoky kerosene lanterns, but nonetheless I could tell that the wooden floor of the pit was deeply stained with blood. As there were no feathers in evidence, I concluded that we were attending a pit-bull terrier fight. We could not see Dan the Dude Dougherty amidst the throng, and I followed Belvedere as he climbed up to a space on one of the uppermost benches that we might gain a better vantage point. I noted for the first time that men toting cudgels resembling half-length baseball bats wrapped with strands of barbed wire were posted strategically around the room—presumably to quell any disruptions that might ensue.

After a time, a short man wearing a bowler hat and leather gauntlets stepped up to a large barrel that was standing beside the pit. He carefully lifted the stiff wire screen covering the barrel and, employing a long-handled instrument resembling a pair of curling tongs, proceeded to fish out the contestants one by one and deposit them inside the pit. When he had counted out the requisite number, there were twenty huge grey wharf rats darting around the pit. Next a side door opened and a wealthy-looking elderly gentleman came pitching into the room, pulled by a bull terrier on a short chain leash, snarling and snapping frantically as he smelled his rodent prey.

"It can smell the rats," said Belvedere.

"Quite."

With the arrival of the terrier a fury of betting erupted all around us.

"Two dollars says he kills them all in fifty seconds!"

"I'll take that one!"

"A dollar on the dog in forty!"

"Make it forty-five!"

"Done!"

And so on. The betting ran high and it was some few minutes before all wagers had been arranged and recorded. Finally, time was called and, without further ado, the dog was thrown into the ring. The instant his scrambling paws hit the floor the rats panicked and huddled in a terrified, writhing grey mass in one corner of the ring. The sports surrounding us became excited almost to a frenzy as the dog grabbed rat after rat, shook it in its jaws, and cast its bloodied, lifeless carcass aside. Hooting, screeching, cursing, and stamping filled the room until I feared the tiered benches would collapse. But amazingly enough, the slaughter in the pit was over almost as soon as it began, and we were soon informed that it had taken precisely forty-eight seconds for all twenty rats to be slaughtered—slightly more than two seconds per rat. This news brought another onslaught of curses and cheers as, all around us, money changed hands. One man protested that the proprietor was intentionally putting in all the biggest rats at once, while another man complained that the rats were all just little babies. The pit-bull terrier was forgotten momentarily, and I noted that he was taking advantage of the opportunity to dine at will upon his disgusting prey lying lifeless around the pit.

We sat through four more such contests, using a variety of dogs and differing numbers of rats, until finally the barrel was empty and there could be no more sport that day. More than one of the fevered spectators was for pitting the dogs against each other, but the dogs' owners were not so foolish as to risk the life of their dogs on one bet when they were making so much money as ratters. Then a man jumped up and proposed a game of 'chuck, and another fellow chimed in that he had trapped a woodchuck that very morning and could go home and get it and be back inside of ten minutes. The crowd thought this an excellent idea and the man was urged to get back with the unfortunate creature as quickly as possible. Meanwhile a short, scrawny little lout jumped up and offered to bite the head off a live mouse for ten cents and ditto a live rat for twenty-five cents—assuming they could find a live specimen on the premises for him to decapitate.

Belvedere rose to his feet. "I believe that is our cue to leave," he said.

I was not about to argue. Our cabby was waiting for us a short distance down Duke Street, and Belvedere told him to pull up across the street from the Craven Heifer and await further orders. When we had taken up our position I raised the topic of Dan the Dude Dougherty.

"Am I to assume that you too were unable to spot Dan the Dude Dougherty among the crowd?" I asked.

"Yes, that was most curious. I methodically scanned every row of patrons and yet I failed to spot him. I wonder, is it even remotely possible that somehow he divined that he was being followed and went in the tavern just to throw us off the scent? Little Dave Goody may well have been there as well, but as I have only seen him from a distance in the dark of night, I was unable to identify him either. I take it you did not see him."

I answered in the negative.

"Well, we may yet get lucky and spot him when he comes out of the saloon—assuming of course that he has not already left. Oh good lord! Here comes the 'chuck."

I followed his gaze and saw the little beetle-browed fellow who had volunteered to get his woodchuck scurrying along the street carrying a cloth sack which obviously contained the ill-fated animal. A morbid curiosity overtook me and I could not resist asking what exactly a game of 'chuck might entail.

"Well, if you must know, they put a woodchuck, or failing that a raccoon, under a box and set a terrier to fetching it out and ripping it apart. Dreadfully gruesome, but of course the sports are very fond of it. Oh, by the by, I did recognize one face in the crowd, Detective 'Basher' Beavis of the force."

"A policeman?" I asked incredulously.

"Really, Reginald, your naivety appalls me. Of course a policeman. Why do you suppose you almost never read of the local rat and cock pits being raided? It would hardly do to arrest a police officer for illegal gambling—to say nothing of the Toronto gentry to be found upstairs in the Heifer—now would it."

I conceded the point and we waited outside the saloon for the better part of thirty minutes before men began emerging from the front door and the carriages from the back lane. Alas, neither Dan the Dude Dougherty nor Little Dave Goody nor even Piggie O'Neil numbered among them, and it was clear that our vigil had been for naught. Belvedere announced that he was in no mood to resume our surveillance of the Black Bull that day and, in the end, we opted instead for an exquisite bird-and-bottle supper at the Maple Leaf Room of The Queen's Hotel, and afterwards attended a delightful comedy at the Toronto Opera House entitled *You Can't Marry Your Grandmother*. Before parting for the night we agreed to rendezvous opposite the Black Bull once again the following afternoon.

CHAPTER XVIII

A SHOCKING DISCOVERY

I did not sleep at all well that night—several times waking with a start as I felt huge grey wharf rats crawling over my face and nipping at my lips. In the end, I lit the candle on my bedside table and somehow the light served to keep the revolting rodents at bay. It was nigh on noon when I awoke, and I elected to spend the time remaining before my appointment with Belvedere enjoying a long leisurely bath, followed by a sumptuous late luncheon in the comfort of my bay window overlooking the sparkling waters of Lake Ontario.

When at last I returned to our point of rendezvous on Queen Street, I gave a light knock on the carriage window so as not to startle Belvedere and climbed inside. He immediately inquired as to how I had slept.

"Not well," I responded.

"Rats?"

"In abundance."

"Yes, ditto here. Most distressing. But back to business—I arrived early and have now been watching that abominable tavern for over an hour. I have seen precisely nothing. If it were not for the fact that we saw Piggie O'Neil and the other Dead Dog in there the other day, I would be inclined to suspect that the gang had found a new place of congregation."

Suddenly a thought occurred to me.

"Perhaps we should focus our attention on Big Sue's joy parlour. After all, we know for a fact that Big Sue will be there, and Alf said she runs the place with Little Dave Goody, so, sooner or later, Little Dave must show up there."

Belvedere paused to consider my suggestion before replying.

"Yes. I agree," he said at last. "At least it will be a change of scene. You might as well stay in the carriage, I will drive us over."

He decamped and I felt the carriage rock as he climbed up on the box. A moment later, however, the door opened and he leapt back inside.

"Dan the Dude Dougherty," he said breathlessly. "He's walking this way—far side of the street."

I peered through the window curtain and, sure enough, the Dude was heading straight for the door of the Black Bull. For the second time in twenty-four hours, I was looking at the man who routinely gouged out men's eyeballs—the man who had actually gone so far as to invent a tool to facilitate the procedure.

"What now?" I asked.

"I'm not sure. We will wait a bit but, if he doesn't come out within half an hour, we will have to risk going inside one more time. With luck we will be able to eavesdrop on his conversation—possibly even overhear him planning a robbery."

But once again Dan the Dude Dougherty surprised us. Belvedere's words had scarcely left his mouth when I saw the Dude come out of the tavern and stride across Soho Street towards an elegant brougham with burgundy wheels and a banding of mother-of-pearl running around its sleek black body. A liveried coachman sat up upon the box but took no notice as the Dude approached the carriage and climbed inside.

"Who in God's name could that carriage belong to?" Belvedere said. "Surely it's not his own."

"Perhaps it's some wealthy sport who owes the Dude money

for a gambling debt," I ventured.

"Possibly," he said thoughtfully.

We waited in suspense for about five minutes before the Dude emerged from the carriage and walked directly back into the Black Bull.

"Who should we follow?" I asked. "Dan the Dude or the carriage?"

"Why, the brougham, of course," Belvedere responded impatiently as he slammed the door behind him.

He whipped up the horses and we began winding our way through the streets of Toronto on the tail of our Mystery Man. It was wildly exciting and, frankly, I was relieved to be leaving the environs of the Black Bull and Dan the Dude. After a time, we turned onto York Street and Belvedere reined to a halt. I peered out the window just in time to see a tall, dark-haired gentleman of about fifty years with a Vandyke beard step out of the brougham and walk briskly up the steps of an imposing sandstone and brick building. I could see a discreet brass plaque mounted on the wall beside the door but my myopia precluded my reading it at that distance. I was about to decamp when Belvedere bounded into the carriage.

"My God, did you see where he went?" he asked, all excited.

"Yes, he went into that large pink building, but I am unable to make out the name on the plaque."

"That pink building, my dear boy, is nothing less than the Toronto Club!"

"Oh yes, I see," I said, rather confused by my companion's great excitement. "But Belvedere, how does this help us? I thought Dan the Dude Dougherty and Little Dave Goody constituted our main concern."

Belvedere rolled his eyes in exasperation.

"Good heavens, man, don't you see? Anyone who is a member of the Toronto Club must be a wealthy and highly respected member of society. He is probably on the boards of half a dozen corporations in this city. So the question of utmost moment is: what in God's name is Mr. Respectable doing having a clandestine meeting in a closed carriage with the most notorious murderer in all Toronto? For all we know, he might even be in league with Dan the Dude. He could be the money and brains behind the Dead Dogs!"

"Yes, I suppose that's a possibility," I said. "But hold on, what if he's merely a victim? For example, what if Dan the Dude is blackmailing Mr. Respectable over some indiscretion and we merely witnessed the pay-off?"

"Oh, for God's sake, Reginald!" Belvedere shouted. "What does it matter? We are on the trail of something important—I feel it in my bones!"

"Well yes, quite, I do see that, of course," I responded—my feelings smarting under the force of his rebuke.

"I just wish I had gotten a good look at him, but he was through those doors in an instant," Belvedere continued. "I tell you it is vital that we learn the identity of that man. I suppose we could wait for him to come out and then shadow him until he goes home— the owner of any house in Toronto can be identified through the city registry. Or we could risk going inside."

"Isn't that a bit—"

"Yes, that's it," he said as he opened the carriage door. "I cannot possibly endure any further delay."

I scrambled out after him and caught his arm as he was mounting the steps.

"But how are we going to get in?" I demanded.

"I suggest you not concern yourself with that. If you want something to worry about, worry about my father being in residence tonight," he replied.

A tall figure loomed up in front of us the instant we stepped through the bevelled glass doors into the exclusive club.

"Good evening, gentlemen. May I be of service?" asked the figure.

"Yes. MacIntosh, is it not?" said Belvedere.

"Yes sir. How may I serve you?"

"I am Herbert Musket. My companion—Lord Tweed—and I are meeting my father, Henry Musket, for drinks. Has father arrived yet?"

"No sir, Mr. Musket has not been in all day."

"Oh lordy, poor papa," said Belvedere, turning to me. "It's his mind, you know, he's not been the same ever since that ridiculous mix-up with the police. Imagine if you can, Lord Tweed, mistaking my dear old father for a certain fellow given to exposing his private parts to female passers-by!"

"Preposterous!" I exclaimed—trying to inject a discernible British accent into the one word.

"Still, I imagine he will join us eventually. We will wait in the library, MacIntosh," said Belvedere.

"Very good, Mr. Musket. If you and his lordship would be so kind as to sign the guest register. . . ," said the noble servant.

We did as directed and I drank in the wonderfully rich atmosphere created by the mahogany panelling and pink marble pillars in the grand front hall. Clearly one could expect to meet and mix with only the wealthiest of gentlemen within this privileged sanctum. Belvedere of course took no interest in the atmosphere of the club, and we proceeded directly along the hallway to the library. It was a wonderfully baronial room—book-lined, naturally—with sofas and chairs upholstered in scarlet leather providing an oasis for those serious about their comfort as well as their privacy. Ten or more gentlemen were scattered about the long room and at first glance our quarry did not appear to number among them, but then I spotted him sitting by himself at the far end of the room, half hidden by a large fern. A snifter of brandy sat beside him on a small side table and he was enjoying a cigar with his edition of *The Globe*. Belvedere suggested we sit at a distance lest he recognize our faces at some future confrontation, and we settled ourselves into two leather armchairs of luxurious depth at the opposite end of the room.

"I take it then that you do not recognize him?" I asked.

"No, damn it, I do not—that is to say, I know his face but I cannot for the life of me put a name to it. He ranks very highly in the city and is most respectable—you can be sure of that."

A steward silently appeared at our side, bowed, and inquired if he might get us something from the bar.

"Yes," said Belvedere. "Scotch and a splash, please, and—Lord Tweed?"

"Oh yes, ditto—if you would be so kind. Oh, and a cigar—if you have such an item about the place."

Our drinks and cigars arrived with astonishing speed and Belvedere signed a chit for them.

"There's no sign of your father then?" I asked.

"Who? Oh, Father—no, I can't say as I see him. Of course that's not to say he isn't elsewhere in the club."

"But is that likely? I mean to say, does he usually come to his club at this time of day?"

"Almost invariably, yes. But let me ask you a question. In your opinion, does our Mr. Respectable, as we have dubbed him, appear agitated?"

"Well no," I said, "I should say quite the reverse. He seems to be a man completely at his ease."

"Yes, I agree. Rather unlike a man who has just paid an exorbitant amount of money to a nefarious blackmailer or settled a huge gambling debt."

We sat back to observe our quarry, who gave every appearance of being settled in for quite some time.

"My word," I remarked after a while. "What a very fine gentlemen's club this is. It has long been my aim to join both the Toronto Club and the Royal Canadian Yacht Club. I gather from my reading that most gentlemen come here of an afternoon to escape their wives and enjoy a spot of good manly conversation and perhaps a game of billiards."

"Ridiculous," Belvedere said flatly. "Wherever did you get such an absurd impression?"

"Well, from Lady Gay's society column in *Saturday Night*—among other places," I said with authority.

"My dear Reginald, I hate to be the one to disillusion you, but the sad fact of the matter is that the Toronto Rich all live in large dreary houses reading scripture and damning to perdition everyone outside their own church. They are all appalling bores with mean, mercenary minds. It is my boast that I excite contempt and ridicule from many of their number, for I am a man of imaginative dress and in consequence they automatically deem me to be morally bankrupt. I mean to say, just look at them. These are the palsied old imbeciles you aspire to shoot billiards with of an afternoon, and engage in manly conversation? A greater collection of old farts, crusty dotards, and congenital idiots one is unlikely to encounter."

"That's a bit hard, surely," I said, bristling at his curt dismissal of my aspirations.

"Hard? Look at that wizened old peanut sitting next to the palm tree—Mr. Jonas Switter by name—no chin and cheats at cards. The man is famous for holding prolonged conversations with his horse. And next to him, Professor George Watham—master of Greek at the University of Toronto and a brilliant scholar. Such a shame his organ is half eaten off by the pox. He'll be joining my club within the year."

"Your club? Which club is that?" I asked.

"Why, the Mad Hatters' Club on Queen Street West, of course. And thus far I have refrained from mentioning the crazed guardians of public morality. Look at that cross old turtle asleep in the corner. That is the ever so pious Reverend Alistair Macpherson. His idea of an exciting evening is to read scripture for several hours and round it all off with a ripping great weep before bed. On weekends I understand he varies his routine by mercilessly berating his servants for hours on end. He was openly declared a bore years ago and deserves to be preached to death by wild curates. I am surprised you have not read of him, for he is one of the founding members of the Toronto Sabbatarians, whose aim it is to make every Sunday as melancholic a day as possible. They have been so successful in their endeavours that, through the Sabbath Observance Laws, it is literally a criminal offence for children to play outside of their homes on a Sunday, and ditto for their parents. It is all true, Reginald, so you needn't look at me like that. The citizenry of Toronto is constantly harassed by these odious fanatics and their vile 'morality laws'. Only last month three members of the Toronto Golf Club were given stiff fines for playing their decidedly quiet game on a sacred Sunday afternoon. One hears of families hidden behind drawn curtains illicitly playing checkers on padded boards to avoid detection. Oh yes, the pall of Methodist conformity hangs over us all in this Sea of Puritanical Banality, this . . . this Toronto!"

Just then our attention was drawn to Mr. Respectable at the end of the room, who had raised his hand to flag down a passing steward. For a moment I dared hope that he was preparing to decamp but no, he was merely requesting another brandy. I turned to remark upon this event to Belvedere and discovered to my horror that, although his burning cigar remained clutched in his fingers and his monocle was still screwed into his eye, my companion was fast asleep! I immediately stubbed his cigar out in the large crystal ashtray at my elbow. I could feel the beads of perspiration spurting forth from my forehead. Was he simply dozing or was he in one of his mesmeric trances? I gave his shoulder a discreet shake but he did not utter so much as a moan. Questions of the utmost moment assailed me. How long would he remain asleep? Three minutes? Three hours? Three days? There was no way of knowing. And what was I to do about Mr. Respectable? I looked about me wildly. Fortunately there were several other men dozing in their armchairs, and I took some comfort in the fact that Belvedere would not draw any undue attention to us, at least until closing time. But what then? Obviously I could not abandon my friend, but what was I to do? Then it occurred to me that perhaps I could tell the management he was ill, and demand assistance in getting him into our carriage and so home to his sick-bed. I began to relax somewhat after coming up with this workable plan but my ease was short-lived, for our quarry was folding up his *Globe* and preparing to leave. I could not abandon Belvedere and yet somehow I had to learn the man's identity. I could think of only one course of action, and I summoned a nearby steward with a wave of my hand.

"Another scotch and a splash please, steward," I said in a hushed voice. "Oh and, by the by, before my chum drifted off, we were engaged in a friendly disagreement. He maintains that the gentleman just rising across the room is Mr. William Thackeray, the publisher of *The Toronto Star*, while I maintain he is Thomas Hardy, the president of the Bank of Montreal. Do you by any chance happen to know the man's identity?"

Whereupon the steward informed me that both my friend and I were mistaken, for the gentleman in question was Mr. Augustus Madox—the prominent Toronto financier.

He then scurried off to do my bidding while I watched the illustrious Augustus Madox depart the scene. For my part, my mind was reeling at the identity of our quarry for I knew full well from my study of the society pages that Mr. Madox, in addition to being one of the wealthiest men in Toronto and a pillar of both church and community, was also the chairman of the Police Commission!

I felt wildly pleased with myself for acting so decisively to discover his identity but, in the meantime, I was still in something of a pickle. Belvedere had begun to snore audibly and there seemed to be nothing for it but for me to continue to affect an air of normalcy. Accordingly, I went over to the large circular library table in the centre of the room and selected a copy of *The Dominion Illustrated* from a pile of periodicals. An hour passed, and then several more. Belvedere remained comatose. Shortly after nine o'clock the last of our fellow library dwellers departed and I realized that I would soon have to put my plan into effect for removing Belvedere from the premises and getting him safely home. I had no idea what time the club closed for the night and it occurred to me that I might as well go in search of the steward to question him on this point.

"Where the blazes is he?" Belvedere demanded.

I leapt with a start at his sudden words.

"What? You mean our Mystery Man?" I asked.

"Of course I mean our Mystery Man—Mr. Respectable," Belvedere responded testily. "Who else could I possibly mean? Now where is he? Don't tell me you just let him walk out of the club?"

Belvedere was genuinely angry and, when I saw the hole he was digging for himself, I felt even more pleased with myself. I saw no need to stem his flow of abuse just yet.

"Well yes, I'm afraid I did," I responded. "I could hardly tear off after him and leave you alone here asleep, could I."

"Of course you could have! Damn it, Reginald, I—good God, there's Father!"

Belvedere vaulted out of his chair with one motion and I followed closely on his heels. I managed one brief glimpse in the direction of the hall and saw a short, grey-haired man of about sixty years looking very severe in a high-buttoned black frock coat, topper, and pince-nez. He did not appear to have spotted us, so we legged it into the billiard room. Fortunately we had the room to ourselves.

"Well well," Belvedere remarked, "Father's arrival makes for an interesting situation, I must say. The doorman is certain to alert him to my presence. Care for a game?"

But no sooner had we selected our cues from the rack on the wall than the door burst open and there stood Mr. Henry Musket and his partner, Mr. Archibald Picket—both men looking absolute daggers at Belvedere.

"So you're skulking in here, are you, Herbert?" cried Mr. Musket.

The violence of his tone shocked me, for his demeanour and gruff voice were those of a strapping six-footer, not a man of five feet in his boots.

Belvedere remained the soul of studied indifference.

"Ah, Father," he drawled as he lined up a billiard shot, "what a treat to see you again."

"I have just been speaking to MacIntosh and he informs me I am meeting my son here for drinks tonight," said Mr. Musket, clearly seething. "I was not aware of that fact—especially in view of the fact that I do not have a son."

"Well, you know MacIntosh," Belvedere remarked, "he tends to get his names confused."

Henry Musket was growing ever more red in the face and I could tell that he was finding it difficult to keep his temper in check. He shot his hands behind his back and puffed out his chest in a pompous, military fashion.

"Enjoying my port, are you, Herbert?" he asked with much sarcasm.

"Port? What port would that be, Father? Oh damn, missed it. Your shot, Reginald."

"The port you stole from my house along with my silver—that's what port," he sneered.

"Really, Father, that is as fine a bit of twaddle as any impaired imagination could conceive. The only thing I have ever relieved a man of is his wits," Belvedere replied.

Mr. Archibald Picket spoke up at this point.

"I believe that is the man who was with Herbert at the Grand Opera House when they stole our seats, Henry," he said, pointing an accusatory finger in my direction. I felt myself blush.

"Is that a fact?" said Mr. Musket. "And what might your name be?"

I opened my mouth to speak but Belvedere was too quick for me.

"My friend's name is none of your concern. If you have a quarrel, it is with me and me alone. I suggest, if you have anything intelligent to say, that you say it and leave us to get on with our billiards."

Mr. Musket seemed to draw back—the better to survey his son from head to foot—while Belvedere produced his cigarette case and offered me a gasper, which I accepted. He lit one for himself.

"Just look at him, Picket," said Henry Musket, "Mr. Smart Alec, strutting about in peculiar clothes smoking women's cigars. You are disgusting, sir! I am ashamed to have you using my name!"

"Good lord," Belvedere calmly replied, "small fear of that."

"Confess it, you contemptible whippersnapper, you spend your evenings languishing in Chinese noodle parlours and worse!"

"Oh, dear me, Reginald, did you hear that? Chinese noodle parlours! Wherever next, I wonder. Church basements?"

"You are nothing but a clot of passions, fierce and blind," shouted Belvedere's father, his voice choked with rage. "You haven't a redeeming feature in all your filthy character. You possess so vile a nature that the English language does not supply words to describe it. You're a whisky sucker and a loafer. Your conduct is not only rude but revolting. You are a stench in the nostrils of this community!"

Silence. I tensed, awaiting Belvedere's horrendous rejoinder, but to my astonishment he remained utterly calm. Indeed he appeared not to have heard his father. He carefully potted another billiard ball and only then did he turn to face him.

"I am sorry, Father," he said quietly, "I fear you are slightly too subtle for me. Am I to understand that you take exception to my conduct?"

Henry Musket's countenance turned from a violent shade of red to an alarming purple. Evidently he perceived that, as far as Belvedere was concerned, he had just pompously loosed off a volley of blanks. He paused, as if trying to come to a decision. Then he suddenly raised his clenched fist and took a step towards Belvedere, but Mr. Picket grabbed him by the arm. Everyone in the room knew a line had been crossed.

"Don't waste your breath on the boy, Henry," said Archibald Picket. "It is a waste of lather to shave an ass. He's sure to get his just deserts in the end."

Belvedere very carefully laid his billiard cue across the table to signal that the game was at an end. I stiffened, as did Henry Musket. Father and son stood glaring at each other. A strange expression had come over Belvedere's face. When he spoke his voice was flat, unemotional, and as cold as iron.

"Shall we say dawn, tomorrow, High Park? I assume you would prefer pistols."

A large vein running from Mr. Musket's hair-line to the bridge of his nose had risen up and was pulsing. Suddenly, with one movement, he whipped a crumpled ball of paper out of his coat pocket and hurled it at his son. Belvedere, showing extraordinary dexterity, caught the missile and held it in his clenched fist.

"Your bar chit, sir!" Mr. Henry Musket cried.

Whereupon he spun on his heel and quick-marched out of the billiard room with Mr. Picket following close behind.

I looked at Belvedere, not knowing what to say or do.

His face was a study in murderous rage—at least so I thought—but a moment after the door slammed behind Picket, he burst into gales of uncontrolled laughter.

"My good God, Reginald, did you see that little Musket man's face? Did I not tell you puritanical humbug stalks in stifling horror among us?"

"Belvedere, you were masterful!" I cried as I took in the situation. "Nothing short of brilliant! He sought to draw you out, to cause you to degrade and humiliate yourself through an unseemly display of temper, but through an astonishing display of self-control, you rendered him ridiculous."

"Yes, I believe it did go something like that."

"You steadfastly refused to sink to his level of vulgarity."

"Precisely."

"But you weren't really serious when you called him out, were you? I mean to say, what would you have done if your father had accepted your challenge?"

"What would I have done? Why, I would have met him on the field of honour, of course—what else would you expect me to do?"

"No, but you wouldn't have actually tried to kill him—again I mean—would you?"

"I would have defended myself to the best of my ability and, as my father is a crack shot, I would not be able to risk merely wounding him. If you think for one minute that I would allow that odious blow-arse to scatter my brains all over High Park, you are quite mistaken. Oh, but you needn't worry, that isn't the first time I have called him out—far from it. But the silly little poltroon will never meet me. It's too tiresome. But *c'est la guerre*. And now I'm weary of this game and this place. Let us away."

And with that he potted the crumpled bar chit into one of the webbed billiard pockets and we took our leave of the august Toronto Club.

I was hoping Belvedere's anger and disappointment at our failure to identify Mr. Respectable would return and, as it turned out, I had not long to wait. We both climbed up on the box of our carriage and had just begun our journey homeward when he turned the conversation back to that very subject.

"Damnation, it annoys me no end that we failed to learn the identity of Dan the Dude Dougherty's illustrious chum. God only knows how much longer it will be before they meet again, and we shall have to keep the Dude under observation indefinitely. The fact is, Reginald, that you let the side down dreadfully."

I sat in silence, allowing my indignant companion full rein.

"I mean, for God's sake, all you had to do was make a discreet inquiry. I do appreciate that you are new to this game and you were nonplussed by my sudden slumber, but really, you must learn to think under pressure. Wait a minute!" Belvedere cried as he reined to a sudden halt. "That silly little Musket man must have addled my brain. All we have to do is return to the Toronto Club before it closes for the night and ask the steward the name of the man who was sitting in that chair. As long as we get to him tonight, he will not have forgotten."

I spoke very calmly, very deliberately.

"Belvedere, old man, if I may be allowed to interject, it may interest you to learn that the man we have been following is no less a personage than Mr. Augustus Madox."

"Never! You're absolutely certain? I mean, you inquired?"

"But of course."

Belvedere opened his mouth to make a remark but he checked himself and sank back against the leather seat, the better to survey me. I returned his gaze defiantly but, despite my best efforts to prevent it, a grin slowly crept across my face.

"You only had to ask," I said, smiling broadly.

"Please accept my apology, Reginald," he said in a deadly earnest tone. "I underestimated you. I apologize."

"Apology accepted," I said, savouring the moment.

"But now answer me this. Of all men, why in God's name would Augustus Madox be waiting outside the Black Bull to keep a rendezvous with the likes of Dan the Dude Dougherty?"

"Is it conceivable that they are in league together?"

"Of course they are, Reginald. They must be! And ironically, Augustus Madox is therefore extremely vulnerable, for his reputation is everything. Any proven connection between himself and the likes of Dan the Dude Dougherty would destroy him utterly."

"And he is all the more dangerous because of his vulnerability," I pointed out.

"Oh yes, absolutely. He possesses the power that only extreme wealth can buy—to say nothing of the ruthlessness of the Dead Dog Gang, and doubtless the protection of certain unscrupulous members of the police force as well. He is a very dangerous man. If we are to get the better of Augustus Madox we shall have to tread softly. Very softly indeed."

"I am surprised you didn't recognize him right off, when you seem to know every other prominent figure in Toronto by sight," I said.

"It was the beard that fooled me. It must be newly grown. I'd have recognized him immediately had he remained clean-shaven."

Belvedere paused, then grinned. "You know, old fruit, that was really very naughty of you to lead me on like that about Madox."

"Yes," I said, "I am afraid it was, rather."

"And my father suddenly appearing like that! Good lord, whoever next? Had we remained any longer on the premises, I don't doubt the bearded lady would have shown up eventually! But you did well tonight, and I think we should repair back to my rooms. I believe I finally have a plan."

Once Belvedere saw me settled in front of his fireplace with a brandy, he went off muttering to himself in search of I knew not what. Several minutes later, he returned and handed me a magazine opened to a particular page.

"*Saturday Night*, December of last year," he said. "Read that."

The headline at the top of the page read, "GALA CHRISTMAS BALL AT ST. LAWRENCE HALL," and the account below went on to detail the names of all the dignitaries attending the elegant affair, and to describe the ladies' gowns and accoutrements. About half-way down the page I came to what was undoubtedly the pertinent passage.

> Mr. Augustus Madox, noted Toronto financier, philanthro-
> pist, and chairman of the Police Commission, was in
> attendance with his charming wife. Mrs. Madox drew many
> delighted stares in her stunning blue silk taffeta gown which
> we understand she purchased in Paris France during a recent
> trip abroad. Adorning her gown was the famous Star of
> Kambara diamond, which is of fabulous dimensions and set
> in an artistic gold brooch. This piece is but one in Mrs.
> Madox's famous collection of jewels.

Belvedere stood before me impatiently, awaiting my response, but, truth to tell, I was unsure how I felt. Obviously he was about to propose that, one way or another, we purloin the Madox jewel collection. Finally I could no longer pretend to be a slow reader, and set the magazine aside.

"Let me first ask you this," I said. "How on earth would we ever get our hands on them?"

"Couldn't be easier, old man. We simply burgle his house just as we burgled Father's. Of course we will have to break into his safe, and that could present a few small difficulties, but perhaps Alf

Shaughnessy could help us out with a little know-how and some special tools. Alf is a very resourceful sort of man and I daresay, if he cannot help us directly, he can at least provide the name of someone who can."

I was not impressed by the analogy between this fresh audacity and the burgling of his father's residence, for it seemed to me that, compared with this, the burgle of his father's house had all the criminality of a quilting bee. But suddenly an inspiration struck me.

"Perhaps we could just quietly sneak into Madox's house and slip a piece of paper behind the safe's dial, as you did with your father's safe. Then we could sneak back a week or two later and bag the jewels without having to break the safe open or involve anyone else."

Belvedere didn't look too impressed with my inspiration.

"Unfortunately, Reginald, there is a fatal flaw in your otherwise inspired suggestion. I paid a return call to Father's house the other day, when he was away at his office, and discovered that the paper-behind-the-dial trick doesn't work. Father had opened his safe since our nocturnal visit but the paper was merely smeared with grease."

"Oh, I see. Well, that rules that out."

"But you have got the spirit of the adventure and I am convinced we are at least on the right path. I mean to say, what other options do we possess? We could shadow Dan the Dude Dougherty and his Dead Dog henchmen until the cows come home and I do not believe we would be any further ahead. I had hoped to discover a central repository or 'stash' for their loot which we could burgle or rob at gun-point, but thus far all we have discovered is the location of their favourite rat pit. No, I believe fate has shown us the way by drawing our attention to the fact that Augustus Madox is in league with Dan the Dude Dougherty."

The mention of robbery at gun-point suddenly made the idea of a quiet, stealthy burgle more appealing to me. Indeed I rather fancied the image of myself as a "masher burglar", knight errant of the jemmy and swagbag.

"In short then, we would be joining the thieving fraternity of 'swells'."

"Precisely, old sport, precisely. We would become, at least for one night, 'box men cracking a crib'. Now then, obviously our opening move in this new game must be the scouting out of the Madox residence, to get the lay of the land and see what, if any,

238

special protective devices he maintains. I know at one time he lived in a mansion on Queen's Park Crescent, but I will of course make certain of that. It would hardly do to go burgling the wrong house."

Suddenly a very real concern assailed me. "But wait, " I said, "how can we be sure that he keeps the jewels on the premises? Perhaps he keeps them in a safe-deposit box at his bank."

"No, absolutely not. It is hardly likely that a man with the protection of both the police and the Dead Dogs would inconvenience himself in that way. If for no other reason, it would be a matter of pride with the man."

I saw his point instantly. If nothing else, we could count on the jewels being there for our plucking.

"So the scouting out of Madox's house is our next concern," he continued. "Tell me, do you by any chance possess any proficiency in the riding of a bicycle?"

I admitted that I possessed none whatsoever.

"I see. It occurs to me that the wheel—being silent, easy to conceal, and swift in heavy traffic—might very well be our favoured mode of transportation during this adventure. Most handy for the scouting out of a house as well. Yes, tomorrow morning you must take yourself off to one of the numerous bicycling academies to be found around the city and learn the art and science of wheeling. There is a bicycle shop on Bay Street called Comet Cycle which looks to be a reputable firm. I suggest we meet there at three o'clock and purchase our iron steeds without delay."

I agreed to his proposal most eagerly, for the prospect of mastering a wheel thrilled me greatly. It seemed that while I was in Belvedere La Griffin's orbit, anything was possible.

CHAPTER XIX

OUR DATE WITH DANGER IS SET

By ten o'clock the following morning I was shaved, watered, and fed. The Queen's concierge recommended the Massey Riding Academy, operating out of the Victoria Rink on Huron Street, and I set off at once to enrol. The moment I stepped through the huge, iron-studded doors, my ears were assaulted by a deluge of tootings as hundreds of would-be "scorchers" circled the track, trying desperately to master their vicious steeds. My instructor, Jimmy by name, was about the same age as myself, but despite our equality in years he addressed me as "Mr. Ravencroft" and "sir" at all times. At first it seemed rather unfair that I should be calling him Jimmy while he was so respectful of my person, but his deference seemed to come naturally to him and, after a time, I began to quite enjoy it. We began my instruction on a fixed "trainer bicycle"—that is to say, a stationary bicycle, the wheels of which revolved on a set of rollers. I remarked that I was surprised at the number of students attending the academy and Jimmy volunteered that Toronto had gone "bicycle nuts" and that there were over ninety stores selling wheels—not counting all the clothing and cigar stores selling them on the side. He then requested that I mount a large three-wheeled tricycle, and I began my tutelage on it by pedalling in small circles around him. After this, he stood on the back axle with his hands on my shoulders and told me to enter the flow of traffic on the track circling the arena. I did as instructed and, to my delight, discovered that I possessed a natural bicycling ability. Apparently Jimmy also sensed my talent, for we had made but four revolutions of the arena when he shouted over the din of horns that I should pull off to the side as the time had come for me to mount my first real bicycle. Before I did so, however, he strapped a stout leather instruction belt with a large iron ring attached to it around my waist, and he held onto the ring as I began my first flight on two wheels. Needless to say, I was somewhat wobbly at the beginning—in fact despite Jimmy's best efforts to hold me upright, I succeeded in locating the floor several times, but eventually my natural sense of balance prevailed. In no time at all I was whizzing around the track with Jimmy sprinting along beside me, and finally whizzing all by myself.

Upon successful completion of my course I received an impressively printed graduation certificate replete with the Massey Academy wax seal, and when I left I gave Jimmy a handsome tip. He in turn gave me a tip, in the form of a warning.

"Look here, Mr. Ravencroft," he said. "I don't know if ya know it, but watch yerself when yer alongside cabs and wagons. Them teamsters and cabbies, they hate us cyclists with a terrible passion. It's nothin' for them to spit tabacca juice all over ya or lash out at ya with their whip. Some ah them'll even swerve their horses into yer path, and a chum ah mine was kicked right off his wheel by a Eaton's delivery man. I even heard of a coachman in Montreal who shot six cyclists stone dead. And it's no better in the countryside. There's bushwhackers out there just waitin' for Sunday cyclists, and all manner ah repair depots who think nothin' ah sprinklin' carpet tacks and wee bits ah broken glass along the roadway for half a mile around their establishments. So take care. And happy wheelin'."

I thanked Jimmy for his rather alarming warning and bade him adieu.

Later that afternoon, Belvedere and I met in front of the

wheelery on Bay Street. The shop sign hung out over the sidewalk and boasted an artistically rendered painting of a man astride an old penny-farthing cycle. Below this were the words:

COMET CYCLE—FRED TURNER, PROP.
"For men may come and men may go, but we roll on for ever."

The proprietor, Mr. Turner, was decked out in a shocking red-and-white checked suit and proved to be as loud in manner as he was in dress. Belvedere literally stiffened and drew back a step as he greeted us, and for a moment I feared he would bolt.

"Gentlemen, let me tell you that the wheel today is king in Toronto!" he cried. "Why, do you know, only the other day a reporter for *The Telegram* stood on the corner of King Street and Yonge between the hours of six and six-thirty p.m. and counted no fewer than three hundred and ninety-five bicyclists! I tell you, gentlemen, we are witnessing a revolution in the way we live, and it is due entirely to the steel fairy you see before you. In the past year, iron steeds displaced some forty thousand horses in Chicago and twenty thousand in Toronto. In the U.S. of A., the consumption of cigars is decreasing at a rate of one million a day and the annual consumption has fallen some seven hundred million since the cycling craze began— the figures being unavailable for Canada at this time."

"Most remarkable, Mr. Turner," I interjected. "We are interested in buying two bicycles."

"Very good sir, and if you've been reading any of this twaddle about bicycles being injurious to your health, I will tell you flat out here and now, as God almighty is my witness, that these so-called doctors are in the pockets of the anti-cycling league of merchants. Tailors, haberdashers, shoemakers—they're all losing money because everyone is awheel and not wearing out their apparel like they used to. Piano manufacturers likewise are up in arms, because there's no one at home any more to play a piano so why spend all that money on one? And worst of all, religious leaders hate cyclists because church attendance has fallen right off. Now, this model here is a Massey Deluxe, and to you I can recommend no other. The Massey Company, as you are doubtless aware, has until now been known solely as the manufacturer par excellence of farm machinery. Now, however, this giant of industry has turned its skilled hands to the design and manufacture of the finest wheels money can buy."

"Yes," I interjected, "I am myself a recent graduate of the

Massey Riding Academy."

"Are you, sir? Excellent. But you needn't take my word alone on this account—after all, it could be argued that as I am a purveyor of these fine bicycles, my judgement is biased. So I would draw your attention to these endorsements mounted here on the wall."

Mr. Turner indicated three large, coloured lithographs of famous wheelmen astride their iron steeds, and pointed to each in turn.

"Wheeling Bill Minor of Ottawa, who set last year's distance record of thirty-one thousand, five hundred and sixty miles. Scorcher Adolf Hubech, who pedalled two hundred and forty-seven centuries in one year—a century, as you gentlemen undoubtedly know, being one hundred miles in one day. And last but by no means least, Shorty Duff, who last year rode from Vancouver to Toronto in a mere sixty-four days—and gentlemen, may I remind you that Shorty has but one leg! All of these extraordinary wheelmen use and whole-heartedly endorse the Massey Deluxe you see before you. Indeed I can safely say that most, if not all the cracks and scorchers in Canada use Massey cycles, and on this fine wheel you will have such a turn of speed as to be able to confidentially accept brushes with all comers. But actions speak louder than words, gentlemen. You, sir, perhaps you would like to take her for a spin?"

Unfortunately it was me that Mr. Turner was addressing with that last suggestion, and although I had no desire to make a fool of myself before him and Belvedere, it seemed I had little choice but to comply. Accordingly I mounted and rode to the far end of the establishment and back. All went surprisingly well until I attempted to dismount and discovered that the wheel beneath me did not possess any mechanism for stopping. When I picked myself up and apologized for demolishing his rubber-tire display, I queried Mr. Turner on this point.

"Brakes? A needless adjunct!" he cried. "Trust me, sir, you are far better off without them. If brakes are used, a cyclist never really learns to control his steed. He relies abjectly on the mechanism and consequently never becomes proficient in the flying dismount."

I turned to Belvedere in hopes of learning his thoughts on the matter, but discovered him to be staring abjectly out the front window. Clearly I was in sole control of the venture.

"Tell me, Mr. Turner," I said, "what do you make of the stories one hears of enraged cabmen and teamsters, and bushwhackers in the countryside?"

"In a word, sir? Phooey! Utter twaddle! There is one thing and one thing only that you need have any concern over, and I have the remedy for it right here."

He stepped over to a long glass display case and extracted a peculiar-looking revolver.

"Sir, I am holding in my hand nothing less than the world-famous, patented Dog Paralyser Pistol. It is constructed of the finest India-rubber and is capable of shooting a jet of ammonia twenty-five feet. Not only that, it may be fired twelve times before reloading is required. Sir, it is my opinion that every person in the land should rise up and call the inventor of the Dog Paralyser Pistol holy. Why, would you believe it, I recently read of a man in Edmonton who gunned down a would-be bank robber with this very pistol?"

Clearly it was time to make a decision regarding our purchase, and I looked for Belvedere to discuss the matter with him. I found him in the rear of the establishment, examining a display of bicycle lamps. When I questioned him as to whether I should buy those particular bicycles and, if so, whether they should be delivered to my suite, he responded with impatience.

"Of course you should buy them. And have them sent around to the Queen's immediately. Also purchase one spare tire and two of these Eureka Patented Cycle Lamps. We desire the ones with the Japanned finish, not the nickel-plated. I must depart before I am overcome by the stink of rubber tires. I shall await you outside."

I paid Mr. Turner and instructed him to deliver two Massey Deluxes, two Eureka Patented Cycle Lamps in Japanned finish, one spare tire, and one Dog Paralyser Pistol to my suite at the Queen's. Mr. Turner responded with effusive thanks and pressed upon me a complimentary sheaf of sheet music for three popular wheeling songs of the day, namely: "Mamie, My Bicycle Girl", "Get Your Lamps Lit", and "Bicycle Built for Two".

"And remember," he added jovially, "don't be drinkin' heavy when you're awheel, for the Massey Deluxe is great on the curves but she's no good on the rye-tangles!"

I managed a small guffaw and exited the shop without further comment. Belvedere was standing outside on the sidewalk.

"I must leave you now, Reginald," he said, "for I have much to do before tonight. I shall call for you at your suite at six o'clock and we will cycle out to Madox's house to commence our reconnoitre. Good-bye."

Obviously Belvedere had no desire whatsoever to discuss the matter with me, and I could only watch as he hailed a hansom cab and left me standing alone on Bay Street. I was nonplussed momentarily, but an instant later I saw that I had been given an excellent opportunity to spend the remainder of the afternoon browsing among dry goods, and with a wave of my hand I was ensconced in a hansom cab headed for Simpsons and wherever else my fancy might lead me.

I returned to my suite around five o'clock laden with packages and discovered the gleaming red bodies of our Massey Deluxe wheels standing just inside the door. They were truly beautiful specimens, and I noted with admiration that Mr. Turner had affixed a shiny brass disk reading Comet Cycle to each cross-bar.

Belvedere arrived shortly past six o'clock, sporting the nattiest wheeling costume it had ever been my pleasure to behold. On his head he wore a burgundy wool jockey cap with smart black leather sun visor. Below this, a short Norfolk-style jacket in dark chocolate-coloured tweed, with burgundy extension cuffs that set off a tan cotton shirt with turn-down collar and a black silk necktie. This colour theme was continued with knee breeches of the same brown tweed material as the jacket, constructed so as to button around the leg just below the knee. Adorning his calves were burgundy knee stockings of fine wool and a smart pair of brown bicycling shoes.

"Well," he said, "how do you like it? The Norfolk jacket is made to button close around the neck, and the pumps are Ridemphast bicycling shoes with elastic-spring sides."

I chose my words carefully, for I knew how keenly sensitive he was regarding his appearance.

"All I can say to you, Belvedere, is that, of all the modish wheelmen I have seen about Toronto, you have without doubt achieved the highest level of smartness and go."

"Excellent. I am inclined to agree with you. Do try on your own outfit."

I noticed for the first time that he had deposited a large box on a side chair and, taking it up, I retired to the dressing room to do as he directed. My outfit proved to be an exact ditto of his save that the chocolate-brown-and-burgundy colour scheme was replaced by a striking charcoal-grey and midnight-blue. It fit me to perfection, and I returned to the sitting room to receive his verdict. He surveyed me for several moments, bade me turn around, counselled me to straighten my black silk tie, and finally announced that he was completely satisfied.

"There was no time to get Mr. Piccolo to run us up some outfits, and of course I could but guess at your sizes, but one develops an eye for such things," he said.

For my part, I was nothing short of thrilled by my spiffing new costume, and deeply honoured to be guided by Belvedere's superior sartorial acumen. And my outfit really did fit to admiration —even the Ridemphast bicycling shoes.

"Yes," he continued, "the inspiration came to me today, in that tiresome little bicycle shop, of all places. I had been wondering what manner of burgling outfits we should adopt and these seemed to be, if you will forgive the expression, tailor-made for the job. Dark in colour, plenty of pockets, close-fitting so as to avoid rustling sounds and snags when inserting oneself through small apertures, and of course they will look completely natural given that we will, in fact, be upon wheels. Should we get caught inside the house, I daresay the fellows will still be more than pleased to gouge out our eyes and stamp us to death, but *c'est la guerre*—at least we shall die fashionably dressed. But now it is high time we were awheel, for it's a long ride all the way up to Queen's Park Crescent and we must be there before dark."

Once outside the hotel, Belvedere lost no time in giving me a flawless demonstration of the running mount before tucking his head down in a scorcher's crouch and cutting loose along Front Street, his short little legs pumping away for dear life. I was a good deal more restrained in my approach but, once I succeeded in mounting my steed, I eventually achieved a slow but steady rhythm to my pedalling. I lost sight of him many times during the course of our journey but he kept reappearing, so I suppose he was doubling back to check on my progress. It was a long ride all the way up University Avenue for so recent an academy graduate as myself, and I was not sorry to reach its termination at Queen's Park, where I found Belvedere sitting under a tree awaiting me. He offered no apology for riding off ahead of me in such a show-boat fashion, and I asked for none.

"This road here is Queen's Park Crescent and, as the name implies, it curves around the perimeter of Queen's Park. Here is my plan. As we are leisurely pedalling past Madox's house, I will stop and examine my tire in such a way as to suggest that I have a flat. You will likewise dismount and, while examining my tire, together we will surreptitiously learn the lay of Madox's land, and possibly even sneak up closer to his house and peer in a few windows."

We still had some little distance to ride, and as we did so Belvedere impressed upon me just how firmly entrenched in Toronto high society was Madox.

"Look at these villas that surround him, Reginald. This one here is Judge Young's. That one up there with the pillars is Judge Osler's. Major Skaliotis is behind that hedge and Christie the biscuit baron lives just around the corner. And there is our goal."

At this point Belvedere came to a sudden halt by executing a superb flying dismount. I, regrettably, was not so fortunate, for I encountered destiny in the shape of a deep rut in the road-bed and parted company with my Massey Deluxe. As I became airborne, I remember thinking how sad Jimmy, my erstwhile instructor, would be to see me dismounting in so indecorous a fashion. I landed on my back with considerable violence but, upon rising, found that I had not injured myself seriously. An immediate examination of my fine new wheeling costume revealed that, while very dusty, it was not torn or damaged in any way. I next turned my attention to my bicycle, and it too seemed to have escaped significant damage. Belvedere did nothing to hide his irritation.

"Good lord, Reginald, stop making a spectacle of yourself. The idea is to avoid drawing attention to ourselves, not to collect a crowd."

"Yes, quite so. What's this then, a punctured tire?" I demanded in a loud voice.

We were standing in front of an ornate iron gate that blocked the entrance to a shaded carriage drive and continued in the form of a high, spiked iron fence surrounding the property. From what I could make out at that distance, the Madox mansion was a very grand red-brick pile covered in thick ivy and boasting a fine pillared portico framing the front entrance. Light shone hospitably from the mullioned windows and whispering pine trees adorned the velvety lawn, which more closely resembled the surface of a billiard table than a patch of mere vegetation. I peered through the bars of the gate and a thrill coursed through me as I espied the elegant black brougham with the burgundy wheels and mother-of-pearl banding standing in the drive beside a coach-house.

"Yes," said Belvedere in what was, I thought, rather too strident a tone of voice, "I am afraid it is punctured. Oh well, George, let us be off."

Whereupon he hoisted his bicycle up to his side and strode off manfully down the street. When we were a safe distance away, he stopped.

"This is most regrettable," he said. "I assumed we would be able to get into the grounds and learn a good deal of the house geography, and in particular determine if it possesses a conservatory, but that is not possible."

"No, unfortunately not. But at least the pine trees and shrubberies afford us some cover."

"What? Oh yes, quite. But the locked gate and spiked fence are a nuisance. But never mind that now, let us return to my rooms; I have put together some charming little items that I think will amuse you."

A short time later, we hid Belvedere's wheel behind some hay bales in the carriage house at the rear of Mrs. Flowers' house and made our way up the ladder to his dressing-room window. Once inside his suite, he led the way down the long hallway to one of the rooms not normally in use, and turned up the gaselier. Beneath the light fixture stood a long rectangular table. A length of green baize had been laid over it and, judging by the lumpy surface of the baize, there were many small items concealed beneath it. Belvedere took up a position at the end of the table, adjusted his monocle, and gripped the edge of the baize.

"And now—*voilà*!" he cried, as he jerked the baize off the table with one motion to reveal a most curious assortment of tools. "Thanks in large part to Alf Shaughnessy, I invite you to behold if you will—a complete selection of burgling tools! The glazier's diamond, sheet of brown paper, and glue bottle you of course already know from our last job. I will also be adding fly-paper to this inventory as per my previous inspiration. And these small jemmies will be at the ready just in case we have to force the window."

He pointed to a dozen or more skeleton keys on a wire hoop.

"Here we have our 'twirls'—both 'straights' and 'splits' and here are our forceps, screwdrivers, miniature brace and centre bit, keyhole saw, stout cutting knife, chain stirrups, corks, wrenches, and oil squirt-can. These little fellows here are our wedges and the gimlets with which they are screwed into the floor."

He indicated a stack of small, innocent-looking wooden wedges and the aforementioned screw gimlets.

"You see, when one has successfully made one's way to the room in which the object of one's desires reposes, in our case a safe, one firmly inserts a wedge under the door and screws it to the floor using a gimlet. Thereby, should someone be alerted to our presence and attempt to enter the room, he will be prevented from opening the door while we are afforded the opportunity to escape via a window. In addition to which, they can also be used to block one's line of retreat. Now then. If we should have to escape out an upper window, then this ladder made of whipcord will greatly aid our descent. One merely ties this end to a stout piece of furniture, radiator, or doorknob."

I nodded in agreement.

"And now we come to the safe-breaking implements. Firstly, our heavy-weight jemmies."

The pry bars he pointed to were three in number and of varying lengths and thicknesses. He picked up the longest of the three.

"This jemmy is called the Alderman. As you can see, owing to its length, it unscrews into three smaller sections for ease of transportation. The next in size is known as the Lord Mayor, and finally we have the Common Councilman. Jemmies of this sort are of course used primarily to prize open the doors of safes. Then there is our sledge and hardened steel centre-punch. I am hoping that these two simple tools will be all we need to open the safe. Apparently, if the safe is of the appropriate age and manufacture, all one need do is knock the spindle off the face of the door with one carefully aimed blow. Then one puts the tip of the centre-punch at the spot where the spindle was attached and whacks it. If one performs this procedure correctly, the door will swing open. Unfortunately, however, if one does not strike the safe at *precisely* the correct point, the lock jams in place and the door is permanently sealed. You will note that I have cut our spare bicycle tire into twelve-inch strips. I shall wrap the spindle with these strips of rubber to cushion the sound of the hammer blows. The question of blowing up the safe remains moot at this point. Obviously we cannot blow open the door of a steel safe in the dead of night in a private house without rousing the household. Of course, there is always the possibility that Madox uses a small wall safe that we can dig out of its framing and cart off with us to blow up at our leisure, but I think that fairly unlikely. Therefore, I have postponed the purchasing of any 'dinah' until we know we need it."

I asked him how he proposed to carry all these tools and he pointed to two dark canvas knapsacks at the far end of the table.

"We will adapt our Eureka Cycle Lamps for use as dark lanterns, or 'bull's-eyes', as they are called by the felonious fraternity. This I will achieve by covering the surface of the glass lens entirely with dark paper except for a pin-hole in the centre. The beam from a thusly constructed lantern is very bright but confined to a small area and it has the added advantage that, with the tip of one's finger, one can screen off the aperture if danger threatens. And finally there is the question of suitable weaponry. Naturally we will both be carrying our revolvers, but I feel that something with a louder report is required to discourage pursuit. To that end, I have added a large Colt revolver for you and an equally large piece of ordnance for myself. I have suitable leather holsters for us as well. Also, in the event that we are pursued, we may well feel the need of a rifle with which to fire accurately from a distance. To meet this potential need, this afternoon I visited Eaton's and purchased two of these patented bicycle rifles."

He held up a leather pouch about a foot and a half in length and proceeded to draw out sections of a collapsible rifle.

"As you see, it can be fired as either a pistol or a rifle, measures a mere eighteen inches when folded, weighs less than two pounds, and can easily be strapped to the cross-bar of one's bicycle."

"Very handy," I remarked. "Most ingenious."

"Isn't it, though? Now, in addition to our firearms, we will both also carry a black-jack, or 'handy-andy' as they are known in the trade, just in case we need to silently render someone unconscious. The stiletto knives are merely added insurance. Unfortunately we cannot rule out the possibility of our being captured and a search being made of our persons. In an effort to remain armed despite such an eventuality, we will also each be carrying one of these cigars."

Belvedere picked up one of two large, rather stale-looking cigars and pointed it in my direction. An instant later a vicious-looking blade shot out its end.

"Pretty, is it not? Questions?"

I asked whether we would be wearing our false beards but he

dismissed this notion out of hand as being firstly undignified and secondly impractical.

"No, we cannot be perspiring and itching relentlessly. Alf Shaughnessy would have us smear a layer of Bixby's Best Blacking on our faces, but that is out of the question for reasons too obvious to state. Rather, we shall don these fetching little numbers."

From I know not where—some concealed pocket, I suppose—with the panache of a conjurer Belvedere produced two black silk eye-masks and held them up for my examination.

"Are they not exquisite? I had Mr. Piccolo run them up for me while I waited. I told him we were off to a costume ball."

We both immediately donned our masks and I must say that, despite the fact that my myopia demanded I wear my spectacles outside my mask, I still looked spiffingly dangerous in my natty jockey cap and bicycling suit. And as for Belvedere, he could barely contain his glee. Of course the question of paramount importance to me was the exact date of our burgling. For some reason, I had been assuming it would not take place for several days or perhaps a week, but on that point, as on so many points, I was in error.

"Oh no, Reginald, certainly not," Belvedere said in answer to my query. "No, we must strike tomorrow night. There are three reasons for this. One: we are experiencing clear skies and a full moon and, under these meteorological conditions, the city has a policy of lighting only the street lamps deemed to be essential to the public safety. We therefore will be operating in a degree of darkness usually only found in the country-side. Two: it is a week-day, so we can expect the household to be abed earlier than, say, on a Saturday night. And three: I can think of no reason to postpone the joy of retribution and sudden wealth. So there you are. Let us repair to the Persian parlour and raise a beaker."

When the candles and the fire in the parlour were lit, Belvedere poured us each a brandy.

"To tomorrow night's adventure! With nerves of steel and the stealth of a cat we cannot fail!" he cried.

I echoed his sentiment, if only in words, and agreed to return to his rooms at midnight the following night in my freshly laundered cycling garb. As I made my exit through his dressing-room window, he advised me to practise my bicycling.

"Oh, and one word of caution, old sport," he said. "In the course of your practice, should you inadvertently knock some innocent pedestrian down in the street, resist the temptation to turn around and return to offer an apology. It has been my experience that people in that situation are given to being somewhat unreasonable and in some cases even insolent."

I assured him I would follow his advice to the letter, and mounted my Massey Deluxe for the ride back to the Queen's.

Later, as I lay in my bed staring at the canopy above me, I attempted to master my conflicting emotions. There was no question that Belvedere was an accomplished tactician and resolute adventurer, but for some reason I had a terrible premonition that our criminal endeavours were destined to be dogged by folly and catastrophic mishap. And though I blush to admit it, my thoughts returned to the fact that I had yet to become a man, and that, should things go wrong the following night, I would be confronted by prison or death— and still be a virgin. But this time there was no question of my going off to another brothel. The thugs of Toronto had had more than enough sport with my person. It was time for me to get my own back on them.

CHAPTER XX

ON THE EDGE OF THE ABYSS

I kept my promise to Belvedere to hone my bicycling skills, and in fact I spent the entire afternoon awheel, for it occurred to me that the most efficacious way to practise for our late-night ride was actually to make the complete journey from my hotel up to Madox's estate and back again. Unfortunately, I was unable to wear my smart new bicycling costume as it was off being cleaned, but I felt I cut quite a dashing figure astride my Massey Deluxe in my new cashmere walking suit, Chantilly riding boots, and bowler hat. When I came to Madox's estate I took care not to linger in front of his gates, but I did manage a quick peek in at it, and I admit to feeling a thrill of fear course through me at the thought of Belvedere and me creeping around in that very house in a matter of hours. Unfortunately, during my return ride I parted company with my bicycle while in full flight on two separate occasions, and I was extremely provoked with myself for tearing both knees out of my lovely cashmere suit. I also had cause to recall Jimmy my instructor's words of warning, for I was the recipient of a most impolite remark from a Simpson's delivery wagon driver whom I accidentally inconvenienced when my Massey Deluxe took it upon itself to swerve into his path. But despite these small set-backs, overall I was pleased with my efforts, for I felt my wheeling ability improved steadily throughout the afternoon— particularly my flying dismount.

I was deuced stiff after my second successive day of wheeling and, as I had time to kill anyway, I decided to take myself off to Pember's Turkish Baths and Hair Emporium to soothe my aching joints. As I lay soaking in the hot shampoo immersion bath, I found myself wondering how Belvedere was preparing himself for tonight's adventure. Then, following that line of thought, I suddenly asked myself what I would do if, God forbid, he should fall asleep in the middle of our burgle. I could hardly leave him to the mercy of Madox and his Dead Dogs, and yet, short of lifting him over the high spiked fence and carrying him home on my shoulders, there did not appear to be any other option. Then a thought occurred. If I were to take a flask of brandy along with me and Belvedere should fall asleep, I could carry him outside the house and leave him lying just inside the fence. I would sprinkle him with brandy and if he was discovered before waking up he would be taken for a harmless inebriate who, believing himself to be locked out of his own estate by some negligent groundsman, had scaled the fence and passed out due to excessive drink. Of course I would stand guard over him from the other side of the fence throughout the remainder of the night, just to be sure no dog or other marauding animal interfered with his person. Then, in the morning, I could present myself at the gate, say I had been out looking for my brother-in-law and, having just located him on the other side of the fence, would now like to retrieve him and take him home to his distraught wife. I felt considerably better for having come up with such an ingenious plan and, what with Pember's healing ministrations, I was quite the new man by the time I took my leave of the ablutionary establishment.

When I returned to the hotel, I headed straight for the Maple Leaf Room and enjoyed a hearty meal of steak and potatoes. It was odd, when you think of it, that I could eat at a time like that—that is to say, mere hours before wilfully putting both my life and my liberty in great peril—and yet a strange calmness had overtaken me, a calmness that I had never before experienced and did not understand. Everything had an unreal, rather dreamlike quality to it, and only in retrospect did I recognize the sensation for what it was: numbing fear. But as I say, at the time I congratulated myself for being so calm and brave.

I spent the remainder of the evening on the settee before the fire reading *The Memoirs of Sherlock Holmes*. Of course I had already read the thrilling stories when they appeared in *The Strand Magazine*, but nonetheless, in addition to providing a wonderful diversion, they also served to put me very much in the mood for felonious adventure, and before I knew it, it was time to suit up and be on my way. Before leaving, I took care not to carry any form of identification on my person and made a point of taking my flask full of brandy for Belvedere, my Defender for protection, and La Divine's handkerchief for luck.

The moon was full and the sky clear, just as Belvedere had forecast, so I had little difficulty seeing the roadbed during my ride over to his rooms and, in the main, I was pleased with my bicycling performance. Belvedere was noticeably solemn as he opened his dressing-room window to admit me, and I followed him in silence back down the hallway to the spare room in which the burgling tools had been laid out the previous evening. As before, the sole piece of furniture in the room was the long rectangular table, but it now wore a starched white linen cloth with a crystal wine decanter in the centre and divers weapons at each end. The decanter was filled with red wine and flanked by two crystal goblets and two silver candlesticks, while in front of these lay our black silk eye-masks. The window curtains were open and a shaft of silver moonlight shone into the room and seemed to slice through the decanter, much like a theatre spotlight. The juxtaposition of white linen, sterling silver, and crystal beside the heavy grey shapes of the revolvers and the other weapons was most striking—in fact highly romantical. Clearly the table had been arranged so as to create the appearance of an altar, and Belvedere—fully rigged out in his bicycling costume including jockey cap—was to play the role of priest. He took up a position before the table.

"Please, Reginald, lay your Defender alongside its fellows that it too may be blessed," he said.

I laid down my gun and watched as Belvedere enacted a ritual reminiscent of a holy medieval blessing for knights departing for battle.

"The Lafite '62 in the decanter before you has been waiting for over thirty years for this precise moment. It is a wine of extraordinary character and delicacy and can justifiably be called the quintessence of all the finest wines the earth has ever given to mankind, just as La Divine Sarah, the ultimate dreamer and weaver of spells, can be said to represent the zenith of Self Creationism. Therefore, it is not beyond bounds to think of this wine as being, in effect, blood from La Divine Sarah's veins. That the decanter sits illuminated by a shaft of moonlight is far from accidental in that, to every person who worships the power of imagination and Self Creationism, the moon is a holy entity. To the Hindu the moon is the god Varuna; to the ancient Greek, Selene; to the Romans, Juno Lucetia; but to us poor Canadians it is simply Lord God. Thus when we, as disciples of the moon, employ the words lord or god, we refer to the powers of creationism."

He paused to pour some wine into one of the crystal goblets and then passed it over our masks and each of our weapons in turn as he spoke.

"Lord, we accept that you are both the primary symbol and the source of imagination, and ask that everything upon this table be blessed by your beams. Let our bullets find their mark and our blades find their flesh, for tonight, guided by your divine light, we keep our date with danger and go to battle the forces of darkness and banality. We ask that you bless these savage tools that they may repel those who would gouge out our eyeballs and stamp our flesh to nothingness, and defend us from all other perils and dangers of this night."

He turned to me.

"Reginald, I would ask you now to take this goblet and hold it aloft while I recite a brief prayer."

I did as directed and Belvedere poured wine into the remaining goblet. He held it up in front of him.

"O lord, we beseech thee, lighten our darkness and, by thy great strength, deliver us from the sword and the bloody fang of the dog. Amen."

"Amen," I echoed.

"We will now don our newly blessed weapons. You will note that I have procured leather holsters in the western cowboy style for our Colt revolvers. You should conceal your Defender, black-jack, stiletto blade, and cigar-knife within the pockets of your burgling costume. We will wait until we reach Madox's before putting on our silk eye-masks."

I stowed my weapons and was greatly gratified by the dashing effect the cowboy holster created.

"And now, let us drink the blood of La Divine Sarah," Belvedere said as he raised his chalice.

"*Quand Même,*" he said.

"*Quand Même,*" I replied.

I sipped the glorious wine and swallowed it straight down, whereas Belvedere held his in his mouth before swallowing—the better to savour its astonishing character.

"Yes," he said finally. "The Lafite '62. So gentle, on the brink of the grave, yet unafraid. Light, almost feeble, yet so charmingly feeble as to be quite lovable."

"I too am overwhelmed by its character," I said. "The Lafite '62 is a wine that truly maketh glad the hearts of man."

"Well put, Reginald. I suggest we leave the remainder of this extraordinary liquid for our return, for there is no finer wine on this earth with which to celebrate a great and noble victory."

Suddenly I was seized by an inspiration.

"Belvedere," I said. "One moment. It would please me greatly if you would agree to carry La Divine's handkerchief for luck during our adventure."

"Of course, Reginald," he answered. "But only if you agree to wear Oscar's dress pumps, that you too may not put a foot wrong tonight."

I looked at my companion. "I would be honoured beyond measure to do so," I said.

As luck would have it, Oscar's pumps were only slightly too large for me and, with the addition of some crumpled newspaper, they fit well enough to make the wearing of them practical. We retrieved Belvedere's Massey Deluxe from behind the hay bales in the carriage house, threw our knapsacks over our shoulders, and the next thing I knew, our moonlit journey into danger had begun.

By unspoken agreement we pedalled in silence, and we had travelled quite some distance before I suddenly remembered the topic I had yet to broach with Belvedere. I edged my bicycle up abreast of him.

"Belvedere," I began, "it occurs to me that there is one

eventuality which we have yet to discuss, and that is the possibility that you may fall asleep during our burglary. Now, I have given considerable thought to the matter and I believe I have come up with a solution. Should that catastrophic event take place, I will be unable to lift you over the fence, but what I can do is carry you out of the house and leave you just inside the gate sprinkled with brandy from my flask. In this way, should you be found, they will assume you are merely an innocent gentleman who, having had too much to drink, has scaled the wrong fence and passed out. I would remove your weapons and all other incriminating paraphernalia from your person, and stand guard over you throughout the remainder of the night from outside the gate. In the morning, I could pretend to 'find' you, and then simply carry you off to safety."

Belvedere continued pedalling in silence a moment before responding.

"It is very decent of you to concern yourself with my well-being in this manner, Reginald. But I fear your plan is unworkable. Madox and his men would never believe that a man in such an advanced state of drunkenness could scale a ten-foot-high spiked fence. To be captured alive is unthinkable, for my inevitable death would be as brutal and debasing as the fiends could devise. Therefore, should I fall asleep, you must kill me without further ado. No, do not shrink back! Consider it a kindness. You cannot risk shooting me in the head, for in so doing you would undoubtedly raise the household and be caught yourself. I am sorry for your sake but you will have no alternative but to quietly slit my throat and quit the scene as quickly as possible. And now that I think of it, should I die tonight, you are most welcome to clear out my rooms and use or sell any or all of my possessions as you see fit."

I swallowed hard at his ruthlessly practical words. He was, as usual, quite correct.

"Fear not, Belvedere. You may rely upon me as you do the sun to rise of a morning," I assured him, although I knew in my heart that I would sooner slit my own throat than that of my friend.

"I know I can, Reginald. And I thank you for your steadfast loyalty," he said.

To dwell on the topic would have been not only upsetting but in poor taste, so I slackened my speed so as to fall back into line behind his bicycle and bring our distressing conversation to an end. When we reached Queen's Park Crescent, Belvedere suddenly leapt off his wheel and motioned for me to do likewise. I followed his direction and it immediately became apparent that my flying dismount was still far from flawless, for once again I made a spectacle of myself. Of course, at that early hour of the morning there were no spectators to concern oneself with, and Belvedere had the decency to refrain from commenting.

"Now, what's the hour?" he asked as he consulted his timepiece. "Two o'clock, excellent. We shall walk from here. Stay directly behind me and remain silent. When we scouted out the house yesterday I noted a stand of lilacs to the right of the gates. We will conceal our bicycles behind them."

I nodded in agreement, muttered, "Right you are," and we continued on Indian file. The lilacs provided an excellent place of concealment both for our bicycles and for ourselves and, as we peered through the iron fence, the moon cast her white light over the grounds and the mansion. I felt my heartbeat gathering speed.

"Do not despair, Reginald," said Belvedere—somehow sensing my fear. "'For here is the charming evening, the criminal's friend. It comes like an accomplice, with stealthy tread.'"

I recognized the quotation from Monsieur Charle Baudelaire, although I could not recall the name of the poem in which it originated.

"*Iacta est alea*," I said.

"Quite so, old sport. The die is most certainly cast, for he who desires, but acts not, breeds pestilence."

"*Fidem Servo*," I said.

"Quite."

Belvedere took off his knapsack and withdrew three lengths of chain, each about ten inches long and possessing small iron clamps on the ends. These clamps he proceeded to screw onto two adjacent fence rails, thus creating an ingenious ladder of chain rungs. He then climbed to the top of the fence and impaled half a dozen wine corks on the tips of the iron spikes. Over these corks he draped a length of black cloth, and returned to the ground.

"Before we go in," he said, "I must impress upon you the need for not only stealth but speed. Even if we do not make any unfortunate noises, there is always the possibility of servants conducting regular patrols of the house and grounds during the night. Be on your guard at all times."

"I understand. You may rely on me."

"Excellent. And now, time for our masks."

We put them on and he extended his hand that I might shake it.

"Best of luck, Reginald," he said.

"And to you, Belvedere," I said as I pumped his hand.

And with that he was up and over the fence, with me following close on his heels.

CHAPTER XXI

THE FANGS OF THE DOG

We both adopted sneaking postures the instant we hit the ground and, with knees bent, we loped stealthily across the lawn and around to the side of the mansion. We were of course hoping to find the glass doors of a conservatory, but here we were disappointed, for nothing even resembling such a room was to be found. Finally, after having twice circumnavigated the house, Belvedere crouched beneath a rear window in a patch of deep shadow.

"Shield me while I light the lamps," he said.

I positioned myself so as to block the momentary flash of light as he lit our two Eureka Cycle Lamps, and a moment later he peered through the glass to determine which room we were about to break into.

"This will do nicely," he said. "It's the dining room."

I watched as he quickly covered a pane of glass with fly-paper and cut out a section. He reached in to turn the lock but, to my surprise, he stopped and retrieved his lantern, that he could examine the mechanism more carefully.

"Great God in heaven, it's wired!" he said.

"Wired? You mean with electricity?" I asked incredulously.

"Yes, I regret to say I do."

"Good heavens," I exclaimed. "Fancy that."

I sank back on my haunches. Our date with danger was over just as it was beginning for clearly we could not overcome this obstacle. I was immediately flooded with a mixture of relief and regret—the former being by far the stronger. Belvedere remained motionless and silent—evidently loath to admit failure.

"Belvedere," I said at last. "You've done your best. We must 'put this crime off to a more convenient season.' There's nothing for it now but to leave."

"Leave?" Are you mad? There are at least two other options open to us and I am just deciding which to try first."

I fell silent while he cogitated.

"I have decided," he announced at last. "We shall try to effect a portico entry. According to *The Police Gazette*, home owners usually put alarms only on their ground-floor windows, in the naive belief that their upper windows are beyond reach and therefore inviolate. Follow me."

The portico over the front entrance was an ornate affair boasting four white columns and ivy-covered trellis-work on each side. My immediate concern centred on whether the trellis could support our weight but, before I could even voice my anxiety, Belvedere scampered up the trellis like a monkey. As he disappeared from view, I felt my nerve beginning to desert me, so I quickly followed after him lest I become paralysed with fear. I found him crouched on the roof of the portico, peering through the small panes of a Palladian window with his lantern. To my way of thinking, the rustling ivy leaves on the trellis acted as a horticultural alarm that might well have roused the household, but when I said as much to Belvedere, he dismissed my concern with a wave of his hand.

"Never mind that," he whispered. "Look at this, the window opens onto a large central hall. We couldn't ask for better luck—and observe, if you will. . . . "

He shone his lantern on the bottom of the window. It was raised a good two inches! In the next moment he slipped his hands under the window and slowly raised it a foot or more. Silence.

"We'll wait here for sixty seconds before entering," he said. "Once inside, stay close behind me."

I nodded in agreement and withdrew my Colt revolver to check its load. All six chambers housed lethal missiles. The moments ticked by as we sat poised to cross the point of no return. Then, in the wink of an eye, Belvedere flattened himself on the roof and slithered through the open window into the darkness of the interior. I hesitated only an instant before following his example. We both lay motionless on the floor, listening with every fibre of our beings for any telltale sound of movement or alarm from within. All was still save for the tick-tock of a longcase clock apparently located in the downstairs hall. Belvedere rose to his feet and silently lowered the window to its original position. The moon—our protectress— poured her beams through the large window at our backs and flooded the upper hall with her cold light. We could make out the top landing of a wide staircase about twenty feet directly in front of us, and various doors off the hall—some open, others closed.

Dear God, is there any place so still as a household in the dead of night? Every sound, the rustle of one's clothing, even one's breathing seems amplified to an unbearable degree. To sneak undetected through an unfamiliar house with all the lamps extinguished and only the moon and a dim lantern to light your way demands the courage and stealth of a jungle cat. Huge dark shapes and shadows loom about, while the legs of tables and chairs lie waiting to trip you. Then there are the natural creaks and groans of a house made of wood and plaster. And how does one know that the entire household is sound asleep? How many family members or servants are lying in their beds wide awake, unable to sleep, sensitive to the slightest rustle or creak? Is there a sick child requiring medicines at odd intervals throughout the night? All of these questions flitted through my brain.

Suddenly the snarl of a dog rent the air! I tensed for the attack, but the snarling turned into a loud, steady snoring sound echoing throughout the hall and I realized it was of human origin, and issuing from the open bedroom door not five feet away from us. My relief was immense and yet, at the same time, it was hellish unnerving to be reminded that members of the household were sleeping within mere inches of our position. All five of my senses were uncommonly alert, at their peak of sensitivity, when without warning a horrendous bong echoed throughout the house and the snoring ceased abruptly. Then two more bongs rang out as the clock downstairs informed one and all that the hour of three o'clock was upon us. Once again we remained rooted to the spot, frozen in silence, listening for any sound of movement and desperately praying that the man's snores would resume. It had grown so quiet that I could hear my watch ticking clear through both its metal casing and the heavy tweed of my smart Norfolk bicycling jacket. A match flared in the snoring man's room just along the hall from us! I heard Belvedere's sharp intake of breath, followed instantly by the withdrawal of his Colt revolver from his cowboy holster. I withdrew mine as well, and discovered the palm of my hand to be slippery with sweat and my limbs literally limp with fear. The light in the bedroom remained constant and I concluded that the striker of the match had lit a candle. As the seconds ticked by, some sixth sense warned me that a figure was about to loom up above us from out of the bedroom with a shotgun levelled at our faces, but we could only await our fate. There was nowhere to run and nothing to hide behind, and we dared not risk opening the window and retreating for, at such close proximity, we could not help but be heard by whoever was awake in the bedroom. Then, to my immeasurable relief, from the illuminated bedroom came the sound of someone evacuating his bowels into a thunder-mug! Never would I have imagined that such grunting and sighing and breaking of wind could be such sweet music to my ears. The man was obviously somewhat stopped up, for his attempts at complete evacuation continued for some little time before eventually, with a muttered curse, he gave up the cause and we heard the creak of the bed-springs as he returned to his bed and extinguished his candle. After only a few minutes his breathing slowed and became more rhythmic and, in no time at all, he was snoring lustily once again. I heard Belvedere return his Colt to its holster and he leaned so close to me that his lips brushed my ear.

"That's our cue. Follow me," he whispered.

We crept along the hall and made our way downstairs, taking care to place our feet on the edge of the treads, so as to cause the minimum of creaks. The moonlight scarcely penetrated the downstairs hall so we were obliged to uncover our bicycle lanterns to explore the topography of the house. There were six closed doors opening off the hall and I waited as Belvedere proceeded to peer into each of these rooms in turn. The last door he tried did not yield to his pressure, and he motioned for me to join him.

"This will be the master's study and I'll wager his safe is within. Wait near the bottom of the stairs and listen for any untoward sounds while I pick the lock," he said.

I took up my post and watched as he knelt and extracted his ring of skeleton keys. He tried each key in turn, while I prayed he would not accidentally drop them on the hardwood floor and thereby raise the alarm. The lock proved to be a stubborn mechanism but, after many attempts, it gave way with a sharp metallic snap. Belvedere slipped through the open door and I followed after him. One glance around the moonlit room confirmed that his assumption was correct, for we were standing in Madox's study and in the corner stood a huge black floor safe! In all honesty I scarcely dared to believe our luck—or rather Belvedere's skill at housebreaking—and he could scarcely contain his glee.

"By God, Reginald, just look at it! It's exactly like the one Alf Shaughnessy said should yield to a sharp spindle strike! Now then, quickly, while I find some candles, you draw the curtains and wedge the door. And don't forget to put the black cloth under it."

I set about my tasks with all speed and, when I had finished securing the door against intruders, I rejoined Belvedere at the safe to assist in any way I could. He had placed two candlesticks on the floor in front of the safe door, wrapped the spindle with the strips of rubber bicycle tire, and was just fetching out the small sledge hammer.

"Hold the candle up closer to the dial, Reginald, and keep it perfectly still," he commanded.

I did as ordered and tried my best to prevent the candle from shaking. Belvedere adjusted his monocle and slowly raised the hammer. Then, with one precisely aimed side-long blow, he knocked the spindle clean off the face of the safe!

"Good God," said Belvedere, "it worked. Quickly—listen at the door."

I ran to the door but heard no sounds of movement or alarm and returned to the safe. Belvedere had the pointed centre-punch positioned at the spot where the spindle had been. I had not forgotten that, if the punch was not aimed at precisely the right spot, it would jam the locking mechanism and the safe would be permanently sealed. In the next instant we would learn our fate. The suspense was palpable. It was to be all or nothing.

"Hold that candle steady, damn you," he snapped at me.

Then, without further hesitation, he raised his hammer and struck the end of the punch with a resounding ping. I wanted to run to the door immediately to see if the blow had roused anyone but I could not tear myself away. I simply had to see if it had worked.

"Well, what's it to be then?" he asked. "Rags or riches?"

I held my breath as he reached out, grasped the handle resolutely, and gave it a turn. The door to the safe swung silently open upon its hinges. I stared in amazement. Not only was the door open, the safe was filled to bursting with all manner of velvet-covered jewellery boxes, and bundles of bonds.

"Belvedere, you've done it! It's so jammed with loot, it's a wonder it didn't burst of its own accord!" I cried in a huge whisper.

"The door, Reginald. Listen for sounds of movement," he commanded.

I ran to the door and listened with all my might for any sounds of alarm but seemingly all remained silent throughout the house. I gave Belvedere the all clear sign and he motioned me back to the safe and told me to hold open his black sack while he filled it with gems. Oh, the sight of Belvedere emptying box after box of glittering jewels into the sack! At the back of the safe he came across a tin money-box, and I stared wide-eyed as he reached back to draw it out. Then in one sickening instant the room echoed with a metallic *ka-ching* sound and Belvedere cried out in pain. He bit into the folds of his jacket sleeve in a desperate attempt to stifle his agonized cry, and in a trice I was on my knees shining my bicycle lamp into the interior of the safe, frantically trying to see what had happened.

"What is it, Belvedere?" I cried.

"It's a trap," he gasped.

I saw his bloodied wrist caught in the iron fangs of the evil device. He had hold of the trap with his free hand and was trying desperately to pull it out of the safe.

"Great God, it's bolted to the interior of the safe," he said. "I'm done for, Reginald. I'm done for!"

I stared at him in horror. Madox the master-fiend had designed the heinous trap to catch and hold a man to await his pleasure. At that moment we heard shouts from somewhere inside the house, and the sound of heavy footsteps from the floor above us. I lunged inside the safe and grabbed hold of the trap's saw-toothed jaws in a desperate attempt to prize them open, but they were immovable!

"It won't open Belvedere!" I cried.

"Let me look!" he yelled.

I withdrew my head and shone the light for him.

"It needs a key. Where's my ring, Reginald?"

I tore through his knapsack looking for his ring of skeleton keys amidst the various tools, and finally found them. He snatched them from my hand and started desperately trying key after key in the small aperture, but by now both the trap and his hand were slick with blood and the keys kept slipping from his trembling hand. It was all too hideous for words.

"Let me do it!" I cried but just then the voices grew louder and someone began kicking at the door. The wedge and gimlet appeared to be holding but it was only a matter of seconds before the door gave way.

"It's hopeless, Reginald," Belvedere said quietly. "Take the swag and run for it."

I looked at him in disbelief, my vision blurring with tears.

"Never!" I cried as I withdrew my heavy Colt revolver and levelled it at the door.

"No, Reginald, that's not the way."

I looked back down at him.

"Take these—quickly," he said, as he pulled out his black-jack and stiletto knife.

I took his weapons from him but stood frozen in astonishment—the more so as I watched him withdraw his own Colt and deliberately toss it on the floor beyond his reach. Belvedere La Griffin had deliberately disarmed himself!

"What are you doing, Belvedere?" I demanded.

"Trust me, I have a plan. Now run for your life!"

"I can't just leave you!"

A horrendous crash followed by the sound of splintering wood came from behind me. I stared at Belvedere—my face a study in fear and confusion.

"Run, you fool. Run!" he shouted.

It was hopeless. If I didn't make a bolt out the window within the next few seconds I too would be caught. I looked him full in the face.

"Run!" he screamed.

In the next instant I was up on my feet and at the window. I threw back the curtains and tried to raise the sash but it was locked. I looked for the locking mechanism but my spectacles were fogged with moisture and I couldn't see it.

"The chair, Reginald! Use the chair!" cried Belvedere.

I grabbed the desk chair and hurled it through the window just as the head of an axe came crashing through a panel of the study door. Then with one motion I dove through the window opening, and was up and running immediately upon hitting the ground. I ran blindly, unaware of direction until suddenly I saw the fence up ahead, and within seconds I was scrambling up to its spiked top. I had one foot over the spikes when a force within me stopped me dead. I looked back at the house. There was gaslight blazing from several rooms upstairs, and from the study in which Belvedere lay awaiting the merciless pleasure of Madox and his thugs. Suddenly I found myself running back to the house at the top of my speed— my Colt Special in my right hand, my Defender in my left. Plan or no plan, leaving Belvedere to fend for himself was not in the cards. I simply couldn't do it. I reached the side of the house, crept along the wall until I was right beside the study window, and arrived just in time to hear a man with a commanding voice instructing someone to check the window. I dove to the ground directly beneath the window just as a man's head and shoulders appeared above me. I could only hold my breath and stare up at the underside of his chin. Had it occurred to him to look directly down the three feet to the ground, he would have found himself looking into my face and the barrels of my guns. But instead he retracted his head and I heard him report back.

"I can't see anyone out there. Should I go after him, sir?"

"No, don't bother, Roberts. I don't doubt we can persuade this little fellow here to tell us the name of his friend," said a man I assumed to be Madox.

The instant I heard his menacing words I had to know what was going on inside the room, so I screwed up all my courage and peered in over the window sill. Two men, both wearing dressing-gowns, were standing over Belvedere. One of them was Madox and the other man, Roberts, I took to be Madox's butler or valet, for his gown was of high quality and he was of good appearance. Madox was pointing a large pistol down at Belvedere and held Belvedere's Colt in his other hand.

"Search him!" ordered Madox.

Roberts stepped forward upon command and rifled Belvedere's pockets.

"No. He has no more weapons, sir," he said.

My heart skipped a beat as I suddenly remembered Belvedere's derringer, which he had undoubtedly concealed in the safe. This was the plan he had referred to. His sang-froid was terrifying!

"Well, well. So you thought you could rob me, eh, my little man," said Madox with a sneer. "Well, it takes more than a jemmy and a jaunty little outfit to rob me! What's your friend's name?"

Belvedere remained mute. Without warning Madox leapt forward and kicked him with all his might. I heard Belvedere involuntarily cry out in pain and I began to tremble. I had to act! Rivulets of sweat were running down the small of my back, and my teeth were chattering so much I feared they might hear them. Madox said something but I couldn't make it out, due to an alarming ringing sound in my ears. The two brutes towered over Belvedere, laughing.

"Not quite so clever now, are we?" Madox continued. "With all the publicity surrounding my wife's jewels, I deemed it only prudent to maintain this decoy safe down here, but to date you and your chum have been the only ones stupid enough to try to rob me. I must say I'm gratified to see how well the trap works. Roberts, remind me to congratulate Dan on his most ingenious device."

"Yes sir," said Roberts. "Should I get the police or a couple of the lads, sir?"

"Oh, I don't see any need to trouble the authorities with this little sneak. It's simpler just to let the boys dispose of him. Hitch up the trap and fetch Dutchie Hughes."

"Very good, sir. I will be as quick as I can," said Roberts as he left the room.

Suddenly a woman's voice called down from upstairs. "Is everything all right, Augustus?"

"Yes, perfectly fine," Madox shouted. "Just a silly misunderstanding. Go back to bed. I shall be up shortly."

Madox laid the revolvers on his desk and extracted a switchback knife from one of the drawers. He returned to Belvedere and the long, evil blade leapt out of the knife.

"Now then, let's have that mask off. I like to watch a man's face as I slit his throat," he said as he stepped towards Belvedere.

I saw in a flash that within the next few seconds Belvedere was going to shoot Madox dead and then, if he could not get free, turn the gun upon himself. It was imperative that I take control of the situation. I was sick with fear but nonetheless I raised my Colt and aimed it at Madox.

"Stay where you are!" I shouted—rather more loudly than I intended.

Madox started violently and stared at me and my Colt revolver in disbelief.

"Hurry!" Belvedere shouted.

I climbed in the window as quickly as possible, while taking care to keep my gun levelled at Madox at all times.

"Now look here—" Madox began.

"Shut up! Drop the knife and back away," I demanded.

Madox hesitated but then complied.

"On your knees. Turn around. Crawl to the wall and put your face against it with your hands in your pockets," I said, and again Madox did as ordered.

I rushed to Belvedere's side. His appearance had altered alarmingly, for he was deathly pale and glistening with perspiration. I noted his derringer cupped in his free hand.

"Get the key, old boy," he said.

"Where? How will I find it?"

"Madox, you fool!" he shot back at me.

"Yes, of course," I said and went over to Madox. "Where is the key to the trap?"

"Roberts has it," he replied.

I ordered him to take his hands out of his pockets and put them up against the wall. Then, with the barrel of my Colt pressed against his cranium, I searched each pocket in turn. Nothing. I noted that my hands were caked with Belvedere's blood and trembling badly.

"He doesn't have it," I said to Belvedere. "What should I do now?"

"He's lying. His stiletto—put the blade to his eye—quickly!" Belvedere ordered.

I grabbed Madox's switch-back knife up off the floor and in a trice the tip of the vicious blade was pressed to his right eyeball.

"Tell me now or I'll pulp it," I said quietly.

"In the Chinese vase on the mantel shelf," he answered.

While Belvedere kept his derringer trained on Madox I ran to the mantel and removed the small iron key from the vase. I handed it to Belvedere and in no time he had unlocked the trap, but still he remained pinned, for the jaws of the trap would have to be prized apart by two strong hands.

Belvedere addressed Madox for the first time.

"Mr. Madox. You are going to come over here, reach in, and open the trap—now!"

Madox turned and crawled over to the safe on his knees, with my Colt at the back of his head and Belvedere's derringer levelled at his face.

"I am going to put the barrel of this gun in your mouth and if this trap is not open in fifteen seconds I will blow the back of your skull off. Understood?"

"Yes" was all Madox said as he reached in for the trap.

I pressed the barrel of my Colt to his spine and I heard him gag as Belvedere fulfilled his promise and began to count. This action apparently provided admirable incentive, for he had only reached the number five when we heard the jaws of the trap spring open. I ordered Madox back to face the wall on his knees and Belvedere withdrew his arm. I was appalled to see how much blood he had lost. The thick tweed material of his jacket sleeve was a soggy crimson mass at the wrist—as was his deer-skin glove. Clearly the veins in his wrist had been severed and the blood was flowing freely. I snatched up the black cloth that I had earlier put under the door and tied a tourniquet around his wound.

Belvedere turned to Madox. "Where are the genuine jewels?" he asked.

"What do you mean? You've got them," said Madox.

"Slit his throat and we'll leave," Belvedere said calmly.

"They're in a safe upstairs in our bedroom," Madox cried.

Belvedere hesitated a moment before issuing his next orders. "Roberts will be back with help any second now," he said at last. "Therefore we don't have time to get the real jewels. Since we cannot take the jewels with us, we shall have to take Madox instead. The problem is that it will take too long to hitch up the brougham. Mr. Madox, offer a solution instantly or I'll shoot you dead."

"I, I don't know," Madox stammered.

Belvedere pulled back the hammer of his revolver and I shrank back involuntarily—awaiting the explosion.

"There is a wagon in the carriage house that our kitchen maid uses to go to market early in the morning. It's a very simple rig," said Madox.

Belvedere turned to me. He was ghastly pale and I noticed blood dripping from the tourniquet into a crimson pool on the floor.

It would not be long before he lost consciousness.

"My weapons . . . I must have my weapons," he said thickly. "I daren't wait here with Madox while you hitch up the wagon, in case the men return."

"Remain seated for the moment, old sport," I said with authority. "You must conserve what little strength you possess. We dare not risk getting separated, so we will all go to the carriage house together."

Madox had remained mute throughout this discussion of his imminent abduction, and I sensed that he was confident Roberts and Dutchie would return in time to save him. Either that or he was waiting to overpower me once Belvedere had passed out. To prevent this occurrence, I grabbed a length of our black burgling cloth and bound his hands behind his back. Then I added a noose to his neck and tied the ends of it to his bound hands—thus forcing his back to bend like a bow. This event set him to protesting strenuously, so I added a gag to his trussing. When I turned back to Belvedere I discovered that he had slumped against the safe and was no longer conscious. I was on my own and both our lives depended on my actions. If I failed to act decisively Belvedere certainly would soon be dead, either at the hands of Madox's boys or due to loss of blood.

A moment later the three of us were en route to the carriage house—Madox stumbling along in front of me, Belvedere over my shoulder. I was shocked at how little he weighed. Mercifully, we did not encounter anyone during our brief journey, and the horse and wagon were there just as Madox had said they were. I laid Belvedere on the wagon seat and lashed Madox down on the flat bed of the wagon with a length of rope. Then I set about harnessing the old mare to the wagon as quickly as possible. I was about half-way finished when I heard the grating sound of the trap coming up the gravel drive. I knew that the moment Roberts discovered our absence they might well come over to the carriage house, and therefore my best tactic was to make a break for it. Never had my fingers been so deft. They virtually flew over the straps and buckles of the harness. As yet I could not hear any sounds of the men approaching, and I prayed they were searching for us throughout the house. I climbed up on the seat and was about to whip up the mare when it suddenly occurred to me that, even with a head start, we couldn't outrun their light trap with our heavy wagon. We needed an advantage.

All I could think of doing was severing their harness, so I

climbed down and crept around to the front of the house. The trap stood under the portico in a pool of gaslight and, as I approached it, I could hear raised voices from within the house. It took all the courage in my possession to enter the pool of light, for I knew that the front door could fly open at any moment. When at last I reached the horse, I felt in my jacket pocket for my stiletto. It was gone! Then I remembered my cigar-knife, and set to work on the main harness strap. I had only just begun sawing at it when the voices from within the house grew louder and I knew the men were coming. I was out of time!

I legged it back to the wagon as fast as I could go, and with a flick of the whip we lurched out of the carriage house and down the gravel drive towards the open gates. I knew our departure would immediately alert those within the house and sure enough, when I glanced back, Roberts and another man—presumably Dutchie Hughes—came dashing out onto the steps. I urged the mare on faster, but we were nearing the end of the drive and I dared not go too fast or we would never make the turn into the street without overturning. A second later several gunshots savaged the stillness of the early morning, and I heard a loud *twing* as one of the lethal missiles struck the iron fence. I had no choice but to urge the mare on even faster, and a moment later we careened around the corner onto Queen's Park Crescent. The wagon tipped up on two wheels and out of the corner of my eye I saw Belvedere slipping sideways off the bench towards certain death. Though I was already struggling desperately to hang onto the reins, I had no option but to grab hold of him with my right hand. I felt certain we were both about to be chucked from our precarious perch, but miraculously the wagon righted itself and we went rattling down the avenue. I urged the old mare into something approaching a gallop and the wagon bucked wildly over the rough surface of the roadbed. Suddenly shots rang out again, and I looked back to see the trap in hot pursuit, while lights began appearing in house windows up and down the street as terrified homeowners peered outside. I knew the mare couldn't keep up that speed indefinitely and it was obvious that the light-weight trap was gaining on us. I no longer had any idea in what direction we were heading or where we were. I knew only that our mad flight through the streets of Toronto couldn't last much longer, and I doubted that I had sliced through the leather harness strap deeply enough to cause it to snap.

Clearly I had to find a way to return fire, even though I had the reins in my left hand and Belvedere's sleeve in the other. I attempted to rouse him by shouting his name and shaking him but it was useless. I threw my right arm around his shoulders and transferred the reins to my right hand. That left my other hand free to draw my Colt and commence blazing away over my shoulder. I emptied all six chambers in this fashion and then repeated the exercise with my Defender, but still the trap kept gaining on us and the air hissed with flying lead. One of Belvedere's bicycle rifles would have been most efficacious at that moment, but they were still in their leather pouches hanging from the crossbars of our bicycles back behind the lilacs. If my Fate Goddess did not intervene in the next few moments, we were doomed. And then, in a blaze of inspiration, I remembered my Patented Dog Paralyser Pistol, wedged in an interior pocket of my bicycling jacket. I ripped it out and began wildly loosing jets of ammonia rearwards in the general direction of the trap. Moments later I heard the frenzied cry of their horse, followed by frantic shouts and a horrendous crashing sound. Obviously the ammonia had found its mark in the eyes of the unfortunate beast, and our pursuers were suddenly *sans* transportation and *hors de combat* in general.

When we had put a good distance between ourselves and the wreck, I reined in and the mare, her heaving flanks positively smoking, slackened her pace to a walk. I had to gather my wits and take stock of the situation. The danger of being overtaken was past for the moment but we were still far from being out of the woods. I consulted my timepiece and discovered to my horror that it was nearly five in the morning. Dawn would be upon us shortly and I had no idea where we were, what direction we were heading, or where we should go—even had I known how to get there. Furthermore, we had lost the light of the moon and I could not make out the street signs in the pitch-darkness. Our situation was dire. Madox's bound and gagged presence in the back of the wagon was a source of great concern, but the question of the utmost moment was, where could I get medical attention for Belvedere? Going directly to the nearest hospital was out of the question, for soon the police would know of Madox's abduction and they would alert the hospitals to be on the lookout for anyone with a serious arm wound.

I realized that the only possible candidate for the job of doctor was Alf Shaughnessy. I was reasonably certain he would help us if he had it in his power to do so, the only question being, did he possess the skill? It was a huge gamble but I couldn't think of any alternative. First we had to seek cover, as I saw it, and Belvedere's rooms offered our only hope. If I could find my way there before light, I might be able to smuggle both my charges up the stairs past Mrs. Flowers' and the neighbours' prying eyes. I debated jettisoning Madox into some bushes but dismissed this idea as I knew that Belvedere, should he survive, would be outraged at my lack of courage. Then for the second time that night I enjoyed a stroke of good fortune, as I spotted a lone gas lamp in the distance. I made directly for it and discovered a street sign indicating that we had reached the intersection of Huron and St. Patrick streets. I had only to remain southbound on Huron and I would shortly intersect Phoebe Street. Once Belvedere and Madox were safely installed in Belvedere's rooms, I would strike out for Alf Shaughnessy's.

When finally we made it to Phoebe Street, I dared not risk pulling up in front of Mrs. Flowers' house, so I urged the mare down the rear lane and reined in directly behind the house. The first problem confronting me was one of locked doors—both the front door to the house and Belvedere's door at the top of the stairs. I hated to lose the precious minutes but I had no option other than scaling the ladder to Belvedere's dressing-room window, and sneaking down the stairs to unlock the front door from within. I did so, and returned to the wagon in under five minutes.

Belvedere and I were still masked, so Madox had yet to see our faces, but if I wished to maintain our anonymity I had to prevent him from seeing Mrs. Flowers' house. To that end, I quickly tore a strip of cloth off the lapel of his brocade dressing-gown and blindfolded him with it. When I untied him and helped him down off the wagon, he was decidedly unsteady on his feet, and I realized for the first time that, in effect, he too had been under fire during our wild dash for freedom. I had to persuade him to move swiftly and silently. Recalling the persuasive effect of a blade to the eyeball, I withdrew my cigar-knife and pressed the blade flat against his blindfold.

"I am going to guide you quickly and quietly into a house and up a flight of stairs," I told him. "This knife at your eyes is not as refined a weapon as Dan the Dude Dougherty's eye gouger, but I think you will find it works very well just the same. I therefore suggest that, if you value your sight, you be absolutely silent and avoid provoking me in any manner whatsoever. Do you understand?"

Madox grunted in assent, but took care not to nod his head lest he cause me to pulp his eyeball.

"Let us hope that neither one of us trips," I added pitilessly.

Madox offered no resistance whatsoever as I marched him directly up the stairs into Belvedere's bedroom and forced him to lie down on the bed. I lashed his neck to the headboard and his feet to the end posts and thereby prevented him from stamping his feet on the floor and rousing Mrs. Flowers, as he might well have done had I merely lashed him into a chair. Then I slipped silently down the stairs and returned with Belvedere over my shoulder. I laid him down on his Turkish divan. His face was covered in a cold, clammy sweat and his monocle, still dangling from its black velvet ribbon, was encrusted with dried blood. On a positive note, however, it appeared that the tourniquet had finally stanched the crimson flow. As I drew back, he seemed a pathetic, desperate figure, with his large hookah pipe standing stone cold on the floor next to him and, beside that, his small, upturned Persian slippers awaiting his feet. I poured myself a stout brandy and gulped it down. Then I returned to the bedroom and the chairman of the Police Commission. He too presented quite a sight—bound, gagged, blindfolded, and lashed to the bed. His head turned as I entered the room, though of course he could see nothing.

"Listen to me, you fiend," I said. "I want you to know that I will be in the next room, tending to the wounds you inflicted upon my companion. I suggest you spend your time praying for his recovery, for should he die, you will be joining him in oblivion very shortly thereafter."

Whereupon I tiptoed down the stairs and struck out for Alf Shaughnessy's as fast as I could go.

CHAPTER XXII

CANCEROUS KISSES AND
UNUTTERABLE SLIMY THINGS

The sun was up by the time I reached Alf Shaughnessy's house. I
had to hammer on his door until my fist ached, but eventually
I heard a volley of Irish oaths and the door opened a crack.

"Who's there? What the shaggin' h-ll do ya want?" demanded
Alf.

"Good morning, Alf," I said. "I apologize for rousing you at
such an early hour. Do you remember me? I am Belvedere La Griffin's
friend—Reginald Ravencroft—we were here a few weeks back—I
was the one with the double shiners."

Alf squinted at me through bloodshot little eyes.

"Mr. La Griffin's chum?"

"Yes. You worked on my double shiners," I repeated.

"Well for heaven's sake, come you in, Mr. Ravencroft, sur.

Will ya take a wee drink? Sweet Jesus but yur a divil for the scrappin'. Yur covered in blood, man."

I entered Alf's and endured several highly frustrating minutes as I endeavoured to get it into his addled brain that Belvedere was injured and that, for reasons of discretion, he was unable to go to a hospital. Finally, however, the dawn of understanding broke through the fog of whisky fumes, and Alf put together a bag of potions and tools. To my credit, despite my extreme agitation and fatigue, I had the presence of mind to ask him if he happened to possess such a thing as knock-out drops. A wee twinkle appeared in his eyes.

"Well now, I'm tinkin' I just might," he said. And he stuffed a little blue bottle in his satchel.

I took the opportunity to wash the blood off my face and hands, and then together we headed for Belvedere's rooms. When we got as far as Beverley Street, I felt it was time to distance myself from Madox's wagon, so we abandoned it in a back lane and walked the rest of the way to our destination. I tried to hurry little Alf along but it was difficult—him being so old, and still half cut from the night before—and with each passing minute I grew more and more frightened that Belvedere's corpse awaited us. The ladder presented the next obstacle. I had a devil of a time getting Alf up it and in through the window but, after much slipping and Irish cursing, he finally landed with a thump on the dressing-room floor.

Belvedere was alive but he had definitely lost ground. Even Alf, who did not strike me as the sort of man who was easily alarmed, was clearly taken aback by his appearance.

"Sweet Jesus, he don't look good," he said. "He don't look good at all. He's lost a terrible lot a blood and that's a nasty ragged wound. Could be the bone's broke too."

We removed Belvedere's clothes and wrapped him in sheets and blankets that I pulled out from under Madox. His blood-soaked deer-skin glove was heart-breaking to behold, and I winced at the sight of the burn scars covering most of his body. Alf set to work immediately, and in very little time he had bathed Belvedere's wrist in some foul-smelling brown solution he had brought with him and was busy sewing the torn skin together. It was a huge relief to see the flow of blood right and truly stemmed, and Alf informed me that luckily no arteries had been severed. On the negative side, however, he also said that the wound was undoubtedly infected and that I should expect Belvedere to develop a very high and possibly deadly fever. To combat this fever, he made up a mustard poultice for Belvedere's chest, along with a bread poultice for his wrist. I took notes on the composition of these poultices and Alf set aside the ingredients for me to use. I offered him a brandy, which he accepted eagerly, and we sat beside Belvedere's prostrate form drinking in silence. It was Alf who had supplied the burgling tools, and I was wondering what I should tell him when he asked me the inevitable question concerning how Belvedere came to be in such a state. To his credit, however, he never raised the subject, and, since discretion was the rule of the day, I did not volunteer any information. After a time I summoned the courage to ask him what he thought Belvedere's chances were. Alf puffed on his stubby little pipe a moment before answering.

"I won't lie to ya, son, it's bad, real bad. He's terrible weak. All yi can do is keep him warm and keep them poultices fresh. I put that splint on just in case the wrist is broke but beyond that I'm afraid yi'll just have ta wait and see."

We both had another brandy and then Alf said he reckoned he'd best be on his way. He declined my offer of financial recompense for his trouble, but accepted my handshake and heartfelt thanks. When he had gone, I put several drops of his chloral hydrate knock-out drops in some brandy and took it in to Madox. He gulped it down without comment and was unconscious within minutes. I then returned to the Persian parlour and took up my vigil in the wicker chair beside the divan. The exotic room was wildly romantical and, just before I too slipped into unconsciousness, I remember thinking what an appropriate setting it was for a fallen warrior such as Belvedere.

I awoke to the sound of my friend's voice. The room was in complete darkness and he was saying something about being surrounded by brute skeletons and dead men's bones in smoke and mould. I was overjoyed that he had regained consciousness but my joy was short-lived, for the instant I struck a match, it was obvious that it was the delirium, not recovery, that had him talking. His face was as grey as a paving-stone, and glistening with perspiration. I didn't need a medical degree to know that the raging fever Alf had foretold was now upon him. He was muttering something indistinctly and I leaned in closer that I might make out the words.

"'The soft night is approaching. Death, old captain, it is time, let us raise anchor,'" Belvedere whispered.

I stifled a sob. My friend was dying and there was nothing more I could do for him. I thought of the advertisements in my magazines for Dr. Palmer's Pink Pills For Pale People, and fatuously thought to myself that even Dr. Palmer's pills could not put colour into Belvedere's leaden pallor. It all seemed so unreal to me that my reason refused to believe it. Mere hours ago, Belvedere had led me into battle and I had been his willing, if somewhat fearful, follower. He had seemed invincible, certainly his will had been indomitable, and yet now he lay like a crushed toy—slowly but inevitably slipping away. What was I to do if the unthinkable happened? All I could think of was to leave his corpse and anonymously alert the authorities to his and Madox's whereabouts. My eyes filled with stinging tears and I wept.

Sometime later, I got up to check on Madox's condition and found he was still dead to the world. It shocked me to see the chairman of the Police Commission drugged and trussed like a chicken. I wished to God we had simply left him behind, and it struck me that maybe the best thing I could do now was to smuggle him out of the house and leave him to be found unharmed a safe distance away. In that way I would no longer have to cope with him, and the police might relax their attempts to find us. But then I remembered my fallen companion's ravaged wrist and his tortured delirium and I thought, no, damn it, I'll hang on to you, Madox, and by God, if Belvedere La Griffin dies, I really will see you on your way to hell.

I made up fresh poultices for Belvedere and replaced the old ones, but beyond that, all I could do was bathe his fevered brow with a damp cloth. He grew restless as the cool cloth touched his forehead and resumed talking quite distinctly.

"Ring down the curtain for I must now depart," he said. "I have supped full of horrors this night. The farce is now over."

Once again I choked back a sob, for as I surveyed my fallen comrade he appeared, now more than ever, to be the living embodiment of Baudelaire's supreme Dandy—the last splendour of heroism in decadence, the setting sun—superb, without heat, and full of melancholy. His lips were now hideously parched and I remembered the decanter of Lafite '62 in the room down the hall, awaiting our triumphant return. I fetched it and began dabbing his cracked lips with the wine. He stirred the instant the glorious Lafite touched his mouth, and a moment later his eyes actually opened—

if only for a few seconds. Then, in a blinding flash of inspiration, I remembered La Divine Sarah's perfume-permeated hanky! What Belvedere needed most at this critical juncture was a magical elixir, and the aphrodisiacal power afforded by the ground lions' testes in her scent could well provide just such a life force. I fetched the hanky out of his jacket and laid it across his nose and mouth. I looked at La Divine's *Quand Même* stitched in blue thread in the upper left corner—and thought to myself that never had it been more important for her battle cry to prevail. I could only pray it was not too late.

Over the ensuing hours, Belvedere's fever rose to the point where he began thrashing around and I was forced to lash him down with a sash. I recognized snippets of Baudelaire's poetry on several occasions, while at another point he began issuing instructions to his tailor concerning the break of his trouser cuffs over his shoes and, later still, his father played a prominent role in his fevered imaginings. During one particularly violent episode he suddenly awoke and looked me full in the face.

"Reginald!" he cried. "I was kissed by cancerous kisses and confounded with unutterable slimy things amidst reeds and Nilotic mud!"

I could but stare at my friend in horror, and he fell back into unconsciousness. Then, just as my nerves were at the breaking point, I heard the unmistakable sound of a footfall on the stairs leading up to his rooms. Someone was coming! The blood drained from my head as if a plug had been removed. I had no idea whether I had locked the door behind me and, even if I had, it could only be the police, and they would have a key from Mrs. Flowers. Or—God help me—could it be Little Dave Goody and his Dead Dogs? I sat perfectly still and held my breath but I could hear nothing. Were they also listening intently, on the opposite side of the door, for tell-tale sounds? Or was it the sound of the door closing that I had heard and they were already in the suite? My hands began to tremble uncontrollably. Was a face about to peer around the open parlour door? I was so tired and worried and frightened—I simply was not prepared to deal with this fresh emergency. I listened with all my might but still I could hear nothing—not a whisper. Had I only imagined the sound in the first place? Finally I could stand the suspense no longer, and I crept out into the hall just in time to see a letter slide under the door. Then, mercifully, I heard the sound of a soft tread retreating back down the stairs. Apparently it was just

Mrs. Flowers delivering Belvedere's mail. I picked up the letter and was astonished to see that it was addressed to me. How on earth was that possible? Then I recognized my Uncle Jasper's handwriting, and remembered that I had instructed them to write me in care of Belvedere at that address. I returned to Belvedere's side and began reading the letter. It ran:

Dear Willoughby,
Thank you for your brief note explaining your prolonged and troubling silence. Your Uncle Harold and I were dreadfully sorry to learn of your being arrested as a white slaver. It must have been very unnerving to say the least. Still, we were pleased to hear that you have found a suite of clean and inexpensive rooms to share with your new chum, Mr. La Griffin. His is a most romantic-sounding name. Is he French, by any chance? How is your search for employment as a tailor's apprentice proceeding? Harold says you may well have to settle for something less desirable if you do not soon succeed in your quest. There is not a great deal of news from Balls Falls. The new foreman at the mill—Billy Brisbin—slipped and accidentally cut off his own leg last week. That was very sad but he is expected to live, although where a one-legged man is going to find employment in these parts I do not know. Harold says there is nothing for him at the mill but perhaps something will come up. Speaking of your Uncle Harold, he had a bad chest cold but he is all better now. And Lawyer Hog took a hard fall from his horse and broke his arm badly in two places. Things are going well here on the farm. The hay is in and I have spent the past week splitting winter wood. I got a dandy book from Eaton's by Thomas Chandler Haliburton called *Sam Slick the Clockmaker—His Sayings and Doings*. It is very amusing and I will be pleased to lend it to you when you return home for a visit. Or if you like, I will mail it to you. Let me know about that. Well, that is all my news for now. Do please write soon so we know you are safe.

Love,
Uncle Jasper
P.S. Your Uncle Harold says I should tell you to be careful.

Really, it was too dreadfully odd to be reading such a chatty, innocent letter in my perilous situation. I also felt extremely guilty for not writing my dear innocent uncles. I sank back in despair and closed my eyes. The conscious world was simply too horrific to be borne any longer, and I hurled myself down into a black void.

When I awoke I discovered that several candles had been lit, and when I turned I found Belvedere propped up on the divan cushions, staring at me. He held up his slashed wrist.

"Egad," he remarked softly, "very nearly success at last."

I need hardly say that I was overjoyed to see that my friend had returned to the land of the living—bloodied but unbowed. He was still very weak, of course, but his fever had broken. Clearly the rejuvenating power of ground lions' testes had been proven beyond doubt.

"So," he said. "What's the lay of the land? Apparently it's first blood to Madox."

I proceeded to recount the extraordinary events that had ensued after he lost consciousness—the wild chase, the efficacy of my Patented Dog Paralyser Pistol, Alf's healing powers, and of course Madox's presence in the room down the hall. Belvedere listened intently, his face a study in concentration. At the end of my narrative he looked me squarely in the eyes.

"Thank you for saving my life. You acted with courage and decisiveness, Reginald," he said quietly.

"Think nothing of it, old bean," I said, flushed with emotion. "It was my great pleasure."

"Yes, well, all I can say is 'He that fights and runs away lives to fight another day.'"

"Quite," I said. "It's a shame about our spiffing new bicycles, though. Obviously it would be suicide to go back for them now."

"And quite pointless. The grounds of Madox's estate will have been long since scoured by both his henchmen and the police, and our wheels discovered beside the chain stirrups we used to scale the fence. So it must be obvious to them that the bicycles were our method of transportation, and they will undoubtedly have taken them in as evidence. Fortunately there is no way they can be traced back to us, as there are thousands of bicycles like that in the city."

I was amazed by the suddenness of his return to consciousness, but he was still very weak and it was obvious that I had to start getting some nourishing food into him—as well as into myself and

Madox. There was not so much as a crumb of bread in his suite, for Belvedere ate all his meals in restaurants, and we decided that Mrs. Flowers would have to be taken into our confidence. She was quite taken aback when I presented myself at her door a short time later but, after I explained that Belvedere had been in yet another accident, she was most eager to see that we did not starve to death. From that moment onward she supplied all the nourishing soup and roast joints we could possibly consume. Belvedere built up his strength over the next few days and, with the aid of Alf's knock-out drops, I managed to keep Madox just conscious enough to eat and use the chamber pot. When he was not sound asleep he was in a kind of stupor, and really he caused me very little trouble at all. I had not seen a newspaper since abducting him, and when I announced my intention to purchase one Belvedere felt it was imperative that I return to my suite at the Queen's as well.

"I too am most eager to read the 'reviews' of our little caper," he said. "You can pick a newspaper up on your way back from the Queen's, for it is now of paramount importance that you return to your suite and collect all your things. I cannot think of any reason for you to be under suspicion, but we cannot afford to take any chances. Wear your false beard and enter the hotel by a rear door. Ditto for your exit, of course."

"So I am to join the fraternity of hotel deadbeats, am I?" I asked.

"You may of course wire money to cover your bill if that is a source of concern. While you are away, I will compose a ransom note, and when you return we will confront our guest and see how he feels about writing the note out in his own hand. With any luck he will refuse to do so, and I shall have the great pleasure of persuading him."

I checked on Madox to be sure he would cause no trouble while I was absent, and left via the dressing-room window.

CHAPTER XXIII

A MERCILESS STRUGGLE

Since Belvedere's clothes were all many sizes too small for me and Madox was still dressed in just his nightshirt and dressing gown, I was forced to continue wearing my blood-stained cycling suit, and it quickly became obvious that no cabby was going to respond favourably to my hail. Of course I continued wearing Oscar Wilde's dress pumps for luck, and I daresay they added to my rather disreputable appearance, so perhaps I cannot blame the drivers for spurning me. In any event, I was reduced to taking advantage of the streetcar along Queen Street. When I alighted, I spotted a newsboy in front of The Palmer House Hotel and purchased the morning edition of *The Globe* from him forthwith. Belvedere and I were front-page news.

FATE OF POLICE COMMISSION CHAIRMAN STILL UNKNOWN!
As yet no ransom note has been received in the daring
kidnapping of prominent financier Augustus Madox. Mr.
Madox was abducted at gun-point from his home on Queen's
Park Crescent in the early hours of Tuesday morning. When
interviewed, Detective Beavis of the Toronto Police said that
he is baffled and alarmed by the silence on the part of the
kidnappers. "In ninety-nine per cent of all kidnappings a
ransom note is received within twelve to twenty-four hours
after the abduction, for naturally the kidnappers are most
anxious to rid themselves of their charge and receive the
ransom money. You may rest assured however that no effort
is being spared to find Mr. Augustus Madox. We have several
leads and I want the kidnappers to know that if they harm
Mr. Madox in any way whatsoever they will most certainly
hang for it."

Shots were fired when the Madox's butler, John Roberts,
made an heroic attempt to save his master, and it is speculated
that one or more of the kidnappers was wounded. It is known
that one of the villains had already sustained a cut on his
wrist when he smashed a window. Mrs. Madox has issued a
plea to the kidnappers that they make their demands known.
She has vowed to co-operate in every way if only her husband
is returned safely to her.

The article offered no more details of the investigation but
went on to denounce "these tar-blooded parasites who feed day and
night on the city's quivering vitals", and to detail Madox's many fine
achievements and long years of service in the church and community.
Obviously either Madox's men had hidden the entire episode of the
animal trap in the safe from the police, or the police themselves were
suppressing that aspect of the story.

I cannot say that the newspaper account served to put my
mind at rest for, strange to say, up until that point I had not fully
appreciated the magnitude of the forces aligned against us. Belvedere
had proven himself to be fallible, very fallible. In fact, if it were not
for a certain hayseed named Willoughby Tweed, he would be dead.
There was a possibility, however slim, that the police and/or the
Dead Dogs had discovered my role in the abduction of Augustus
Madox and were in fact watching the hotel—lying in wait for me,

just ready to pounce. Belvedere obviously thought it a genuine possibility or he would not have cautioned me to wear my false beard and use a rear entrance. If they did catch me, they would undoubtedly think nothing of torturing me until I gave up Madox's whereabouts. I was frightened—very frightened—and I suddenly wanted more than anything to write my uncles a long, chatty letter telling them all about the wonderful theatres and restaurants I had visited, but of course that was out of the question. I noticed a street vendor selling postcards, however, and I quickly bought one depicting the towering Confederation Life Building on Yonge Street. I had but a moment to dash off a note. It ran:

Dear Uncle Harold and Uncle Jasper,
Thank you for your letter. I am having a wonderful time. I have yet to find employment as a tailor's apprentice but I am sure I will soon. Isn't the Confederation Life building a glorious Romanesque pile? It is so easy to imagine a damsel in distress leaning out of one of its soaring towers, don't you think? I will write a proper letter soon.

Love,
Willoughby

I affixed one of the penny stamps I habitually carried in my billfold, dropped the card in a mailbox, and struck out for the Queen's. I desperately wanted to first scout out the hotel lobby to see if the police or Madox's henchmen were lurking, for obviously, if there was someone watching for me in the lobby, then I would know that someone was waiting for me in my suite. But, as I was still dressed in my disreputable-looking cycling costume, I could hardly hope to blend in with the elegant guests in the Queen's lobby, so I had no choice but to sneak around to the rear door. Luckily it was unlocked, and I sprinted up the back stairs to the door opening onto my floor without encountering any guests or employees. I listened for a moment and then peered out into the hallway. The coast was clear and I quickly began searching for my suite. I was fairly sure I knew the way, but I could not rule out the catastrophic possibility that I was destined to wander the halls until inevitably encountering someone who would question my presence owing to my appearance. However, that did not prove to be the case. Shortly thereafter, I found myself outside the door of my suite. The moment of truth was upon me. I rapped on the door.

"Open up, it's me," I ordered. "There is no sign of Ravencroft."

I held my breath and listened, my ears straining to detect the slightest sound that could warn me of someone on the other side of the door. Nothing. I rapped again.

"Hurry up, open the door. I haven't got all day," I said.

Again I listened and detected nothing. Then I heard the swishing sound of someone coming down the hall and I knew action was imperative. I inserted my key, turned the lock, and peered inside. Nothing was disturbed. I slipped in, closed and locked the door behind me, and listened. The rich carpet in the hallways precluded the sound of footsteps, but again I heard the *swish swish* of someone approaching my door. I held my breath. The swishing sound continued on past the door without hesitation. I exhaled. Of course, my fears had been ridiculous. I was a wealthy American traveller living in the finest suite in the best hotel in Toronto. I had no criminal record. I had never met or been seen in the company of Augustus Madox. There was no possible way on earth of connecting me with his abduction.

I paused to survey my beautiful suite. It felt as though I had been away for months, and yet my Sherlock Holmes book was still on the settee before the fire and my brandy decanter and snifter sat awaiting my pleasure on the mahogany desk. Whatever happened, I would never regret my extravagance in taking the glorious Red Parlour Suite. But I did not have time to lose myself in reverie, and I decided to start by packing the clothes in my dressing room. I tiptoed over to the bedroom door and peered around the corner on the remote chance that someone was hiding in there, but I found it to be exactly as I had left it, and ditto for the dressing room. I chided myself once again for being so easily frightened and set to work neatly folding my clothes into my valise. This done, I turned my attention to the bedroom. I froze in my tracks. Dan the Dude Dougherty was standing in the bedroom doorway, blocking my path. I recognized the cruel smile on his face from when I had seen him standing just inside the door at Big Sue's, overseeing my beating at the hands of the evil Little Dave Goody. There was no escape. He had me trapped. I stood staring at his bloodless face for a moment before finding my voice.

"Who the devil are you, sir?" I demanded.

The Dude's piercing black eyes stared impassively at me. There was murder in those eyes. Then, without saying a word, he reached into his brocade waistcoat pocket and took out a coin which he flipped into the air with his thumb. I caught it and a horrible realization came over me. It was not a coin, it was a brass disk on which were stamped the words "Comet Cycle". I remembered admiring the shiny disks when the bicycles were first delivered to the suite. Belvedere was right—there were thousands of wheels like ours in the city, sold in dozens of shops—but it would not have taken long to go directly to Comet Cycle and ask who had recently bought two red Massey Deluxe bicycles and where they had been delivered. Roberts, Madox's butler, possessed the added information that one of the purchasers was very short. I tried my bluff once more.

"What the devil's this supposed to mean?" I demanded.

"Where is he?" he asked quietly.

"Where's who? What's the meaning of this?"

In answer to my question he reached into an inner pocket and withdrew a long, pearl-handled straight razor. He opened it slowly, never allowing his eyes to leave mine. Then he reached into another pocket and retrieved a copper spoon-like apparatus. It was his infamous eye-gouger!

"I am only going to ask you nicely one more time," he said. "Where is Augustus Madox?"

"He's safe."

"That's not what I asked you."

"I know that," I said. "But if you hurt me, my associate will kill him."

"No, he won't. You're going to tell me where that little sh-t is and I'll pay him a visit. Now where the h-ll is Madox?"

Dan the Dude Dougherty took a step towards me. I was so frightened I could not even remember if I was armed.

"The police will take a very dim view of you killing their prime suspect, you know," I said, playing for both time to think and the courage to act.

"Oh, you needn't concern yourself with the police. We've kept this a private affair, they know nothing about your bicycles or your identity." He held up his eye-gouger. "Do you know what this is?"

I edged my hand towards my waistcoat pocket.

"Yes I do," I said.

Then, as quick as thought, I whipped out my Defender and levelled it at him.

"Do you know what this is?" I asked.

Dan the Dude froze in his tracks for an instant. Then he relaxed, stepped back a pace, and smiled his hideous, icy smile.

"Well now, what's that supposed to be?" he asked.

"Take another step forward and find out."

"Drop the gun, sonny. I can cause you more pain than you'd believe possible," he threatened.

"You drop your weapons, Dude, or I'll embroider your chest with the contents of this revolver."

He took a step towards me.

"Let's talk about this, sonny boy," he said.

I took a step backwards.

"I mean it, Dude!" I shouted. "Drop your weapons or I'll blow your damn head off!"

He smiled and took a small step backwards.

"OK kid, relax," he said.

Then he charged at me. The gun exploded in my hands without my even willing it to do so, and Dan the Dude Dougherty crashed face downwards on the floor. I leapt back. Had I killed him? I couldn't see any blood or other signs of a wound, but he was lying on his belly. Was he faking? About to leap up at me? I stood back, my Defender trembling in my hands but still levelled on him. I waited. Nothing—no movement or sound.

"Get up, Dude!" I demanded. "I know you're faking."

He made no response. One of his arms lay extended on the floor and his eye-gouger lay beside it, but his other hand, the one holding the huge straight razor, lay concealed beneath him. Was he waiting for me to roll him over so he could lash out with the razor and slash my throat from ear to ear?

"Get up or I'll shoot you dead, so help me God!" I shouted at him.

Again no response. I stepped forward very slowly. I would prod him with my foot but be ready to spring back at the first hint of movement. I inched towards him and raised my foot. Suddenly his free hand snaked out, grabbed my ankle, and yanked it towards him. I felt myself falling backwards, my arms working wildly, and in the next instant I landed with full force square on my back. The force of the blow knocked the wind out of me and I was aware that my Defender was no longer in my hand. The Dude sprang at me with the fury of a madman and I saw him raise his vicious razor. He slashed in a downward arc but I rolled sideways just beyond its lethal edge. I bounded to my feet and frantically kicked out at him. My shoe connected with the razor and I saw it go flying across the room. Then he was on his feet and we were facing each other in a square-off. His normally bloodless face was now crimson with rage and his eyes blazed with fury. It was to be a terrible, merciless struggle to the death! I knew he would kill me in the next instant if I didn't somehow rise to the occasion, and I struck a pugilist's stance, with my fists upraised, hoping to fetch him a devastating example of Blow Number Two as detailed in Edmund E. Price's *The Science of Self Defence*— that is to say, a blow to the left side of the face with the right fist. I raised my right shoulder so as to draw my right hand on the same horizontal plane with it and at the same time I drew my left fist back so that, should I find it desirable, I might repeat the procedure a second time. I turned my body to face my adversary as per instructions. But at the last second I suddenly thought better of it and, lowering my head, rushed at him with all my might. I succeeded in butting him in the stomach but, regrettably, my spectacles were knocked from my face when I cannoned into him. He staggered back and before he had time to recover I sprang upon him and we fell on the floor together. The instant we hit the floor my fists became a blur as I began buffeting him about the head. In the wink of an eye I had been transformed from a civilized *homo sapiens* into a savage beast as I frantically fought for my very life! Somehow, despite my cruel pummelling, the Dude managed to lock his hands around my throat, and began choking the life's breath out of me. I rained blow after blow upon his face but seemingly the man could withstand any amount of punishment. My vision, already blurred due to the loss of my spectacles, was now beginning to grow dark. "Egad!" I thought to myself. "I'm blacking out!" I left off hitting him and rifled the pockets of my smart Norfolk jacket for some manner of weapon, but I could find nothing. Then I felt my arms slumping as I began to lose consciousness and, as I sank downwards, my hand came to rest on one of Oscar Wilde's dress pumps, which had been torn from my foot in the melee. With my last ounce of strength I raised the heavy pump high in the air and brought it down upon the Dude's head with all my might. No effect was apparent. I brained him again—nothing. The man's head was made of granite. I slugged him yet again and again and, mercifully, Dan the Dude Dougherty went limp and lay beneath me, senseless.

I fell to the side, my pounding heart threatening to explode within my heaving chest. But I could not rest yet, for the Dude could regain consciousness at any moment. I began crawling around the carpeted floor, blindly feeling for my spectacles, and eventually located them under a table. Fortunately they were not broken. I checked on the Dude's condition and discovered that his breathing was slow but steady. It was essential that I tie him up him before he awoke but I possessed neither rope nor twine. Then a solution occurred to me. I retrieved his pearl-handled straight razor and commenced cutting his finely tailored frock coat into long, thin strips. It was but the work of a moment before his arms and legs were securely bound and his mouth nicely gagged. I stepped back to savour the sight. The fiendish Dan the Dude Dougherty measured his length on the rug and I, Reginald Ravencroft, was the victor! I assumed my work to be done but then, looking down at him, I remembered his cruel smile and I thought to myself: hold on, Ravencroft, perhaps you are not finished with this evil fellow quite yet. "To repay them in their own coin with interest" was the way Belvedere had summed up our overall objective, and the Dude's henchmen had cost me my Imperial moustache. I held the razor over his face.

"And now I shall have yours—sonny boy!" I said.

In a trice I grabbed the Dude's sweeping black moustache in my left hand and cut it from his lip with his own razor. I held it in my fist in front of his face.

"I guess the Beau Brummel of Toronto gangland is not so beau now, is he!" I said aloud. "And now I will just help myself to the interest on your debt."

I stuffed his moustache in my pocket and turned my attention to the diamonds adorning his evil person. I stripped him clean— watch, rings, links, and all—and finally went for his pocket-book. My eyes swam in my head as I opened it to reveal a wad of banknotes fully half an inch thick. A fast estimate revealed over one thousand dollars. Reginald Ravencroft would not be leaving The Queen's Hotel via the back stairs after all, nor would he be joining the fraternity of hotel deadbeats! Of course, by going to the front desk I would run the risk of being spotted in the lobby, but the Dude had said the police were ignorant of my existence and I fancied he was the sort of man who would feel confident in taking on my capture single-handed. In any case I had no choice, for I was a gentleman first and last and I would leave the hotel as one—even at the risk of attack. However, I really had to get a move on, for someone might well have heard the discharge of my Defender. I quickly changed into one of my smart new day suits, and then flew through my suite flinging the remainder of my possessions into my valise. Finally, when I was all packed up, I found myself staring down at the prostrate Dude, wondering what I should do with him. He presented quite a ghastly sight—bound and gagged, thatches of black moustache sprouting from his upper lip, his coat in tatters, and his face covered with purple bruises. As I saw it, as long as he was not found in my suite, his condition would not be attributed to me in any way—and certainly the Dude would not involve the police, for he would be too keen to find me himself so as to rip out my heart with his bare hands. It was therefore a question of where I could stash him until he either woke up of his own accord or was discovered and revived. A linen closet would be just the place, and I knew one to be located a short distance along the hall from my suite. It took every ounce of strength in my possession to drag his dead weight down the hall to the closet, but I managed it without incident and swiftly returned to my rooms. I then took down La Divine's portrait from over the mantel and, after wrapping it carefully in brown paper, I returned Sir John A. Macdonald to his rightful place. I paused at the open door.

"Red Parlour Suite, I bid you adieu," I said with a doff of my bowler hat. "You have been a comfort and a delight to me. I will return to you one day—you may take it as fact."

And with that I tore off my false beard, picked up my belongings, and made my way down to the lobby to see what fate had in store for me next. As it happened, I saw no sign of anyone suspicious and the man at the reception counter, while surprised by my sudden decision to check out and nothing short of appalled that I had been forced to carry my own luggage, could not have been more pleasant. For my part, I thanked him for his courtesy and competence, and bade him good day.

The doorman summoned a hansom cab and I was soon on my way but, even though I had exited the hotel without molestation, I dared not let down my guard. There was always the possibility I was being shadowed—that is to say, that I had been granted temporary freedom in hopes that I would lead my pursuers back to Madox. I therefore instructed the cabby to drive past Eaton's and, once abreast of the front entrance, I suddenly ordered him to halt. I then leapt out of the cab and ran through the crowded store to a side exit—which was no easy feat given that I was carrying La Divine's portrait, my large valise, and my club bag. I continued my mad dash across the street and straight through Simpsons vast emporium, then hailed another cab, and eventually was deposited opposite the rear lane behind Belvedere's Phoebe Street rooms. I struggled to suppress my glee as I approached the house. Belvedere La Griffin was in for the shock of his life!

CHAPTER XXIV

TROPHIES OF REVENGE

T o my surprise, I found Belvedere not only bathed but dressed.
He was still recumbent on his Turkish divan but the sheets and
blankets were gone and, with his monocle screwed in his eye once
again, he looked quite the new man. He even had the curtains open
to admit the brilliant autumn sunshine.

"How did you fare? No trouble, I assume," he asked as I
entered the room.

"Well actually, yes, there was," I remarked casually. "That
tiresome Dan the Dude Dougherty made a bit of a nuisance of himself
but I dealt with him."

Belvedere started visibly but he suppressed the urge to rise to
my bait in an excited fashion. Instead he too adopted a languid,
casual air.

"Did he indeed? How so?" he asked.

"Oh, that's hardly worth discussing," I said with a dismissive wave of my hand. "However, I did bring back a few mementos of the occasion that might amuse you."

I produced my small satchel, and as I drew out each item of booty I named it and cast it down on the divan beside Belvedere. With each item his eyes grew ever wider.

"The moustache of Mr. Dan the Dude Dougherty."

"Good God!" Belvedere cried, almost against his will.

"His straight razor. His eye-gouger. His gold watch and chain—please note the diamond and emerald fob. His diamond studs and links. His diamond stick-pin. His diamond rings. His diamond-studded gold pocket toothpick. His gold pocket flask. His gold cigar case. His gold match safe. His billfold containing many hundreds of dollars. His walking stick with solid gold handle encrusted with diamonds. And, last but by no means least, my receipt from The Queen's Hotel for payment in full—compliments of Dan the Dude Dougherty—the *second* most dangerous man in all Toronto."

Belvedere's facial expression of shocked disbelief gradually changed to one of wonderment and admiration.

"Reginald," he said quietly. "You have behaved brilliantly. Brilliantly!"

I felt myself swell with pride, for I believe it was the first time I had really and truly impressed Belvedere La Griffin. Then suddenly he exploded into gales of uncontrolled giggles and pounded the divan with his uninjured hand.

"Tell me!" he demanded. "Tell me everything!"

I proceeded to explain about the brass disks and describe in minute detail how the Dude had come within an ace of killing me, and how I had eventually triumphed and stuffed him in the linen closet. When I had finished recounting the events Belvedere was, if anything, even more excited than I was by my tale.

"Now then," he said. "Can we be absolutely certain that we did not mention the existence of these rooms while within earshot of the Comet Cycle man?"

My memory of the event was vivid and I answered without hesitation.

"Absolutely certain, yes. You were standing at the back of the shop examining Eureka Cycle Lamps when I asked you where the bicycles should be delivered. I asked if they should be delivered to my rooms and you answered, yes of course, or words to that effect.

Having them delivered here was never directly debated."

"Excellent. That accords with my recollection as well. And what about the newspapers?"

I produced *The Globe* and Belvedere quickly read the article.

"Yes, you see the power over the police and the press these villains wield. No mention of the trap in the safe, and the officer in charge of the investigation is none other than Detective 'Basher' Beavis—the one we saw enjoying himself at the rat pit."

It was true—hideously shocking, but true.

"But, great God in heaven, you've done well, Reginald!" Belvedere continued. "Very, very well indeed. These sparkling battle trophies are stones of the first water and bound to bring in a small fortune. And not only have you done battle with the most vicious man in all Toronto and won the day—you even have the scalp to prove it! But by God, man, how did you resist the temptation to finish the brute off? I am not so sure I would have possessed your self-discipline. Oh, but of course I agree with your decision entirely—yes, very shrewd indeed. This way, as you said, the Dude will say nothing and the police will not be involved. Whereas if his corpse were found, a police investigation would be launched, and there are undoubtedly blood-stains on the carpet of your suite. Oh God, how I wish I had been in your place. To be denied such a thrill of victory is damnable!"

Suddenly I remembered an interesting list I had found folded up in the Dude's billfold.

"Look at this, Belvedere, as if we needed any more reasons to condemn these heinous criminals," I said as I handed the list to him.

Punching...................$ 1
Both eyes blacked.........$ 2
Nose and Jaw Broke........$ 4
Ear chawed off............$ 10
Leg or arm broke..........$ 12
Shot in leg...............$ 15
Stab......................$ 15
Doing the big job.........$ 45
Poisoning a team..........$ 8
Poisoning one horse.......$ 6
Stealing a horse and rig...$ 13

Belvedere shook his head slowly as he read it.

"And turn it over," I said. "On the back is a list of names and some of them have check marks beside them—presumably victims who have been dealt with."

"Yes, it's mighty cheap murder and mutilation," he said. "And you see how open he is about it—actually daring to carry a price list of abominable acts on his person. But then, why fear the police when the chairman of the police commission is your employer? And look here, all this poisoning of horses and stealing of rigs—I'll wager the Dude and his Dead Dogs are taking advantage of the rivalries between competing companies with delivery wagons. But by God, this makes me all the more eager for the fray! This drama is not over yet, Reginald—not by a long shot! I have drafted our ransom demand and, subject to your approval, we shall force Madox to copy it out immediately."

He handed me a sheet of paper which I eagerly read.

To my wife,

I have been abducted by a gang of ruthless villains. If you do not do exactly as I tell you to, they will surely kill me. This is what you must do: Open the safe in the bedroom and put the ENTIRE CONTENTS WITHOUT EXCEPTION into a satchel. Do not hold back anything for I have been forced to give my abductors a complete inventory of the safe's contents and they swear they will kill me if so much as one jewel or dollar is missing. You need not worry about the loss of your jewels for they are all fully insured and you can look forward to the pleasure of shopping for their replacements in Paris. You must also contact the manager of the Canadian Bank of Commerce on King Street and get twenty thousand dollars from him. This too must be placed in the satchel. Tell Roberts to get in touch with Mr. Dave Goody and give him the following instructions.

Mr. Goody is to collect the satchel from you at precisely ten o'clock this Thursday morning and drive alone IN AN OPEN GIG to the Sir John A. Macdonald monument at the southern entrance to Queen's Park. Under Sir John's right shoe he will find a folded-up map showing him where to go next for further instructions. When he has placed the ransom where the second map indicates, he is to drive straight back to our house and await further instructions as to where he is to pick me up. Armed men will be watching him from the moment he leaves the house with the satchel until he returns to the house. If he is followed, or diverges from his course in any way, he will be shot dead instantly—As WILL I! Once the satchel has been retrieved and the inventory found to be complete, I will be released unharmed.

Yours in captivity,
Augustus Madox

P.S. Show this letter to Roberts and only Roberts.

ROBERTS: See that these instructions are carried out to the letter. NO POLICE. NO INTERFERENCE FROM MY ASSOCIATES. NO TRICKS. TELL LITTLE DAVE. MY VERY LIFE DEPENDS ON IT!

I looked up from the letter.

"An additional twenty thousand dollars?" I asked. "Can she possibly raise that much money?"

"Of course, Reginald. To a man of Madox's immense wealth twenty thousand is nothing. Now to continue. The map awaiting Little Dave under Sir John's shoe will guide him down University Avenue to College, over to Simcoe, down Simcoe to Wellington, and along Wellington to The Shakespeare Hotel, which is on the north-west corner of York and Wellington streets. At the front desk of the Shakespeare, he will find an envelope awaiting him which you will have delivered to the hotel earlier. I have chosen the Shakespeare because it is now rather a seedy establishment and will not hesitate to hand over the envelope to such a rough-looking character as Little Dave. In this envelope he will find a second map which will lead him down York Street, east on Front to Lorne, and down to the foot of Lorne Street and the harbour clubhouse grounds of the Royal Canadian Yacht Club. It is one of several clubhouses lining the waterfront and behind them lie a series of storage sheds. I have chosen a particular shed where sails are stored behind the Royal Canadian Yacht Club as the drop-off point. You will have tied a red ribbon to the door handle so Little Dave will know which shed we mean. I have chosen this site because it is a fairly open area that we can easily keep under surveillance to see if Little Dave is being followed and, at the same time, it is in town and therefore we can melt into the surging population when the deed is done. It is virtually deserted at this time of year because all the waterfront clubs are closed for the season. You see of course why the two notes are essential—otherwise it might well be too tempting for them simply to await our arrival at the pick-up point and then torture us until we give them Madox."

"Yes of course, that much is self-evident," I said. "But one thing does confuse me. How are we going to shadow Little Dave from the Madox residence all the way to the storage shed without being spotted? Surely he will identify us right off and alert lurking confederates."

"Nothing easier. He won't see us because we won't be shadowing him. It is only a bluff on our part, for there is no need for us to do so. Little Dave will assume he is being watched at all times and, since he is completely exposed in the open gig, he will not risk being shot or causing Madox to be killed."

"I see, yes, but why involve such a dangerous brute as Little Dave in the first place? Why not get Roberts to be the delivery boy?"

"Very simply—this way we may have the opportunity to exact our revenge upon Little Dave as well as Dan the Dude. After all, it was Little Dave who coshed you and threw you in the harbour, and I should think you would savour revenging yourself upon him."

I felt my blood pressure rise at the thought of exacting a sweet revenge upon the little snake but I didn't see how this could be done, and I queried Belvedere on this point.

"I am not sure," he said. "I have a tentative plan but I would rather not voice it at this time. Unless of course you simply want to shoot him or beat the daylights out of him once he delivers the satchel—but I suspect you would enjoy something rather more subtle and sinister."

"Well yes, I would. But what about Madox? If we just leave him here, your identity will become known."

"Oh, we won't leave him here. No no, I have that all figured out as well. Once we have received the ransom and it's clear that no one is about to attack us, we will tie Madox up in the very same sail storage shed in which the satchel was left. We will then travel the short distance to the Toronto Club and you will dash in with an urgent letter for Mrs. Madox telling her where her husband can be found. I can assure you that there is no more reliable person than the head porter at the Toronto Club. Mrs. Madox will receive the letter within the hour, you may rely on it. Meanwhile, we will disappear into thin air. Now then, we need to get the instructions to Mrs. Madox as quickly as possible but with the minimum of risk to ourselves. The question is how best to achieve that aim. I thought of delivering the letter to Bullet Malloy at the Black Bull with instructions for him to deliver it to the Madox house, but he is too low down the pole to have even heard of Madox, much less know that he is Dan the Dude Dougherty's boss. I also considered having you hand it to a milk delivery man just before he enters Madox's house, or even wedging it in Madox's front door under cover of darkness, but the house is undoubtedly being watched and therefore these options are too risky. So, in the end, we have no alternative but to trust to the mails. If we post the letter today it should arrive tomorrow, but we will allow one extra day just to be sure. In fact you might drop it into the main post office on Adelaide Street to ensure speedy delivery. If we allow an additional day for Mrs. Madox to get the twenty thousand dollars, that means that in four days from now we will pick up the ransom, leave Madox to be found, and take the train to Montreal."

My ears pricked up.

"Montreal? Are we going to Montreal?" I asked.

"But of course, old lad. How else are we to board the *Campania* for our voyage to England? We sail two days after our arrival in Montreal."

I stared at Belvedere, for I had been hitherto unaware that I was about to set sail for England.

"Oh don't worry, I booked our passage weeks ago," he added.

"Weeks ago?"

"Oh yes, absolutely. I saw long ago that, come what might, it would be imperative that we leave the country. We must be quite clear about the risks involved in our little adventure, Reginald. Augustus Madox is the Professor Moriarty of Toronto gangland—a master-fiend, a butcher of men whose henchmen are numerous and whose tentacles are far-reaching. If his Dead Dogs catch us we will undoubtedly be tortured and eventually killed. If the police catch us we will wish for death, for the penalty for armed housebreaking and abduction is life imprisonment and at least fifty lashes. Personally I would kill myself before enduring such a fate."

"Death before dishonour?" I asked.

"Death before discomfort. No, we must be exceedingly careful. Nothing can be done without considerable forethought and assorted contingency plans. Our first step is to convince Mr. Augustus Madox to co-operate, and that is a job I reserve for myself. Come along, let us see if the chairman of the Police Commission is enjoying our hospitality."

We put on our false beards in anticipation of the fact that Madox's blindfold would have to be removed while he copied the letter, and we proceeded down the hallway to his room. He was in a state of semi-consciousness but with the ingestion of a quantity of strong black coffee he was soon sufficiently alert to do our bidding. Belvedere immediately assumed command.

"Now then, Madox," he said, "let me briefly explain the situation to you. We have composed a note demanding ransom for your safe return and we desire that you write it out in your own hand. If you comply, and your family and associates cause us no trouble, you will be returned none the worse for wear. If we are played false by you or anyone else, you will be the first to die. On that you have my most solemn word. This is the letter we wish you to copy out and here is pen and paper."

Madox looked Belvedere squarely in the eyes. A sneer crossed his face.

"If you two little sh-ts don't release me this instant I will personally see you gutted with broken bottles and your limbs ripped off your bodies like chicken legs!" he shouted.

Belvedere remained a study in composure.

"Copy it," he said softly, "or I will hurt you—with this."

Madox's eyes grew wide as Belvedere slowly withdrew Dan the Dude Dougherty's copper eye-gouger from an interior pocket.

"Great God," Madox said softly.

"Mr. Smith," said Belvedere as he turned to me, "won't you show our friend here the hirsute souvenir you acquired immediately after you had the pleasure of slitting Dan the Dude Dougherty's throat from ear to ear with his own pearl-handled razor."

I took his meaning and produced the Dude's silken moustache, bound by a ribbon, from my waistcoat pocket. Madox went ghostly pale.

"I assume it is this little rascal to which you refer, Mr. Jones," I said.

"Precisely right, Mr. Smith. Well, Madox, any questions before you begin?"

"No," said Madox, shaking his head. "Give me the pen and ink."

I wondered if Madox would balk afresh as he read the letter and discovered how much his freedom was going to cost him, but he might well have been copying out a dry-goods list for he uttered not one peep, nor did he hesitate even briefly. When he had concluded his task Belvedere fetched a beaker of brandy laced with knock-out drops and our illustrious guest was soon unconscious once again.

Shortly thereafter I set off to complete my various tasks. First I went to the main post office and mailed our all-important ransom demand to Mrs. Madox with the words "URGENT! OPEN IM-MEDIATELY!" scrawled across the envelope below the address. Secondly I went down to McLeod's Livery on Front Street and hired a brougham carriage. Thirdly I arranged for the packing, removal, and storage of the contents of Belvedere's rooms. Acting on Belvedere's precise instructions, I paid for one year's storage in advance and told them to remove the articles in five days' time—that is to say, the day after our departure. And lastly, I went to Eaton's and bought a ready-made suit of clothes for Madox to wear, as I was not about to sacrifice one of my own fine new suits simply to clothe the likes of him.

Over the ensuing three days, Belvedere packed his sea trunks, and under cover of darkness we loaded them into our hired carriage and I delivered them into the baggage handlers' hands at Union Station. Throughout this period I was torn between raging euphoria at the thought of being rich and going to glorious Europe with Belvedere, and stark terror at the risks we were running. I was also greatly troubled by the idea of leaving the country for an indefinite period of time without saying good-bye to my uncles. Indeed, the more I thought about it, the more I came to see that I simply could not do such a thing. I was tempted to raise the subject with Belvedere but he seemed to be in a distracted state of mind, and I decided to put it off to a more suitable moment.

CHAPTER XXV

ALL OR NOTHING

S leep was out of the question on the night before our ransom pickup, and Belvedere and I passed the time in front of the fire in his cosy Persian parlour reading—Belvedere being engrossed in J.K. Huysmans' *A Rebours* while I began Wilkie Collins' most excellent detective thriller *The Moonstone*. We did not indulge in conversation except when Belvedere suddenly looked up from his book around three in the morning.

"You do realize, Reginald, that it is an inner light that is guiding us to our rendezvous at the sail storage shed in a few hours—the same light that brought you to Toronto?"

"Well yes, quite," I answered.

"That is to say, regardless of how things turn out, I mean."

"Yes of course, Belvedere."

"Well, just so long as you know."

"Oh yes, I know," I said.

We resumed our reading until the clock chimed the hour of five and we both laid down our books.

"Well then," said Belvedere, "shall we make ready to depart?"

"Yes, I think we'd better. Dawn will be upon us shortly," I replied.

We were both wearing our travelling suits under our smoking robes so it was merely a matter of folding our robes and hats and Persian slippers into our valises and donning our false beards before waking Madox. We had taken care to reduce the strength of his sedative so it was not difficult to rouse him and we soon had him awake and dressed. For his part, I would describe Madox as being sullen but co-operative, resigned to the situation and eager to be free—if only to plot a hideous revenge upon us.

We crept downstairs and around to the carriage in the back lane just as the sky began to grow light, and a moment later we were on our way northwards towards Queen's Park—Belvedere and Madox safely ensconced in the carriage and myself at the reins. I confess that as we pushed on towards the park I grew increasingly apprehensive, for there was no doubt that the placing of the map under Sir John A. Macdonald's shoe represented the weakest link in our chain. That is to say, it offered the best opportunity for our enemies to attack us, for they had forewarning concerning this step in the proceedings and they could easily be lying in wait for my arrival, ready to pounce and force Madox's whereabouts out of me. I took care to park the carriage on a quiet street a good quarter-mile from the entrance to the park, and climbed down from my perch. Belvedere's side window slid down.

"You have checked that both your revolvers are fully loaded?" he demanded.

"Of course."

"If I hear gun-fire I will immediately shoot Madox dead and then come to your aid as quickly as possible. If I fail to find you, make your way directly to Union Station and we will rendezvous at the Lost Articles Counter."

"Agreed."

Belvedere nodded curtly and I headed up the deserted street towards the park. Whether he was sincere concerning his intention to kill Madox at the first sign of trouble I did not know. I hoped he had said it purely as a means of frightening Madox into continued co-operation.

I did not go directly to the statue but rather circled it at a distance, trying desperately to detect the slightest sound or movement in the trees and bushes, but, with the exception of an elderly grounds-keeper, I detected no one. I could not risk delaying my approach to the statue indefinitely, for soon the park would be alive with folk out for an early morning stroll and I would have no way of knowing who was an innocent stroller and who had designs on my life. I therefore stopped, drew in a breath, and, with my heart pounding, I walked smartly up to the statue, tucked the note in under Sir John's right shoe, and continued along the path without pause. With every passing second I fully expected to see a crowd of men emerging from the trees to ensnare me and, sure enough, I soon heard the unmistakable sound of heavy boots on gravel coming up fast behind me. Without thinking, I veered off the path and made a mad dash for the woods. I couldn't tell how many men were pursuing me so, just as I neared the trees, I risked a glance back over my shoulder— only to discover that a rag-and-bone man pushing his cart was the source of the commotion on the gravel path. Of course I couldn't rule out the possibility that he was a thug or policeman in disguise, so I continued my flight through the woods until eventually I stopped to catch my breath and listen for pursuers. I could hear nothing save the happy chirping of birds and my panting breath. Still, I dared not relax my guard just yet, so as I made my way back towards the carriage I took a highly circuitous route—several times suddenly darting through a stand of trees or behind thick bushes and then immediately taking cover to see if anyone came racing through the trees in pursuit.

The carriage window slid down the moment I appeared at the door.

"Well?" Belvedere demanded.

"All clear—as near as I could tell."

"Excellent. Onward to the Shakespeare," he said as he closed the window.

Happily my delivery of the note to The Shakespeare Hotel did not present a threat to my safety, for there was no way for our enemies to know in advance that the hotel was to be the next stop in Little Dave Goody's journey. I informed the clerk at the reception counter that a certain Mr. Goody would be checking into the hotel at approximately 11:30 p.m. and that he would be eager to receive the letter immediately upon arrival. Then, acting on an inspired impulse, I made a generous addition to the clerk's livelihood, and he promised me most faithfully that he would be on duty all day and would personally see to it that Mr. Goody received his letter promptly upon making his presence known.

Our next stop was the harbour grounds of the Royal Canadian Yacht Club. The clubhouse itself, with its tall white columns and verandahs on the first and second floors, reminded me of pictures I had seen of Southern plantation mansions in the United States. The ornate home of the Toronto Canoe Club lay to the east of the yacht club, and farther along the waterfront, the equally beautiful home of the Argonaut Rowing Club. They, like the yacht club, rose up out of the water on piers which extended out from the *terra firma* of the shoreline. Belvedere left Madox safely tied up in the carriage and we both went inside the sail storage shed to reconnoitre. The interior was just as you would expect it to be, with hundreds of heavy canvas sails stacked in rolls awaiting the following summer's breezes, and, once we had ascertained that the shed would suit our purposes, Belvedere secured a red ribbon to the outside door handle. I had assumed that we would wait in the carriage at a safe distance from the shed for Little Dave Goody to come and go but, to my surprise, Belvedere announced that I was to hide the carriage on the other side of the Toronto Canoe Club while he and Madox waited for me in the loft of the long boat-house that ran alongside the sail storage shed. To my mind this was ridiculous and I felt compelled to voice my objections immediately.

"Belvedere," I said. "Forgive me, but frankly your plan seems to me to be fraught with unnecessary risks. If Little Dave Goody arrives with friends in tow we will be not only surrounded by Dead Dogs, but cut off from our only means of rapid escape."

"True, but we will still have Madox and I daresay we can threaten *cum* barter our way out of the net should it close in upon us. I must ask for your blind trust in my judgement on this occasion, Reginald. I assure you there is method in my madness, for it may very well be essential that we be in immediate proximity to the storage shed when Little Dave Goody arrives."

His explanation made no sense to me—indeed it struck me as nothing short of lunacy to hide ourselves less than fifteen feet away from the shed door—but it seemed I could do nothing except follow orders. When I returned from hiding the carriage, I found Belvedere and Madox in the loft of the boat-house above dozens of rowing shells stored on the ground level. Belvedere was crouched beneath a window that looked directly down on the all-important door with the red ribbon attached to it. I took up a position on the floor beside him.

"And now," he said, "we wait."

The ensuing two hours proved to be the most torturous period of waiting I have ever been forced to endure, for every creak and groan in the old wooden boat-house signalled the arrival of brutal thugs bent on gutting us with broken bottles. Numerous times we started at the sound of footsteps on the gravel walks outside, and had our revolvers out and cocked in anticipation of an imminent assault, only to wait and wait until finally deciding it had been a workman or some such innocuous passer-by. We blindfolded Madox early on during this period for, with the tension and consequent perspiration, our false beards were itching us dreadfully. Then there were the questions concerning whether anything whatsoever was going to happen. Did the letter arrive at Madox's house? Did his wife have sufficient time to raise the money and get Little Dave Goody ready to fulfil his role? Did the note under Sir John's shoe blow away? Did someone else stumble upon it? If an innocent person did find it, he might well follow the instructions just for a lark. He might go to The Shakespeare Hotel, present himself as Mr. Goody, receive the final instructions, and arrive at the door opposite our vantage point. What then? Or, allowing that Mrs. Madox did get the letter in time and Little Dave Goody found the note under Sir John's shoe, what if the clerk at the Shakespeare was out for a walk when Little Dave arrived and the assistant clerk knew nothing about an envelope for a Mr. Goody? Or what if Little Dave came to the storage shed as per instructions but tried to be a hero and, having left the satchel, hid around the corner awaiting our arrival at the shed and then opened fire with us trapped inside? For that matter, what if an employee of the yacht club should suddenly stumble upon Belvedere, yours truly, and a bound and gagged man hiding in the loft—what could we say and, more important, what would Belvedere do? All of these questions and many more besides were stampeding around my brain when we heard the sound of an approaching carriage. We peered down over the sill of the multipaned window and a catch came in my breath as I saw Little Dave Goody driving a light gig down the lane towards the shed door below us.

"My God," said Belvedere, "there's Quasimodo now!"

It was the first time I had seen the malignant little rodent since my brief glimpse of him wielding his club in Pansy's boudoir, but I could never forget such a rare anthropological study as Little Dave Goody, with his straw-coloured hair sticking out from under his battered topper and his vacant protuberant eyes. This was a man with the viciousness of a wolverine and the tenacity of a bull-terrier. A man who would as easily plunge a knife into your throat as wipe his nose. He drew up directly beneath us and reined to a halt. A black satchel sat on the seat beside him and my heart leapt as I watched him climb down off the seat and slowly approach the shed door—satchel in hand—just as we had planned it. Suddenly Belvedere was up and running towards the stairs leading down to the ground floor.

"Wait here," he said as he disappeared down the steps.

I froze in my place, for I couldn't imagine what was wrong, unless of course he was going to confront Little Dave Goody—iron knucks and all! I looked back down on the scene below and an instant later I saw Belvedere climb up onto Little Dave's gig and remove a brown burlap sack from under the bench seat. It was the work of a moment and he disappeared just as Little Dave emerged from the shed *sans* satchel. I heard Belvedere sneaking back up the stairs and watched as Little Dave drove away. A moment later Belvedere was at my side.

"Hurry, put on your beard!" he ordered. "We've got to get Madox into that shed before Little Dave returns!"

I had no idea what was afoot so I obeyed his command without discussion, and after removing Madox's blindfold we marched him down the stairs and into the shed as quickly as possible.

"Tie him to that post as fast as you can!" Belvedere shouted. "And now, Madox, proof positive that there really is no honour among thieves. There sits the black satchel Little Dave Goody brought, and yet what do you suppose I have here in this sack that I retrieved from under the seat of Little Dave's gig?"

Madox and I both looked on in shock as Belvedere up-ended the dirty sack over a rough table and a fortune in jewels spilled out over the surface.

"Good lord!" I exclaimed. "That little rodent Goody tried to steal our ransom booty!"

"Quite so. Just as I hoped he would," said Belvedere. "But we haven't time to gloat. Madox, I must now bid you adieu. Assuming that Little Dave doesn't return to murder you once he sees that his booty is gone and therefore the jig is up, you may take it that someone will come for you later this afternoon. You should never have kicked me when you had me trapped on the floor of your study, Madox. Your fate was sealed the instant you struck me. Come along, Mr. Smith, we've little time to spare, and none to waste on this filthy blackguard."

Belvedere headed for the door leaving the black satchel behind, and it struck me that we should take it with us just in case Little Dave had left anything of value inside it—perhaps in an effort to convince us that Mrs. Madox had tried to pay a smaller amount for her husband's release. I therefore walked over to pick it up off the floor. I had my hand on the handle when Belvedere cried out.

"No, leave it!"

"But Bel—Mr. Jones," I began to remonstrate.

"I said leave it, you fool!" Belvedere shouted.

I could but stare at my friend, shocked by his vehemence and stung by his words.

"Please," he said more softly. "Come along now."

I followed him out without so much as a glance back at Madox and together we legged it at the top of our speed for the brougham on the other side of the canoe club.

"The Toronto Club, Reginald—quickly!" Belvedere cried as he leapt inside the carriage.

I turned the horse around and we struck out for the club as fast as I dared go without drawing attention to ourselves. It was but a short distance away and before long I reined in just past the front entrance. I then simply walked smartly into the foyer, handed the letter to the porter on duty, said the words "Right away please" to him, and walked directly back outside before he had a chance to say anything to me. The letter was addressed to Mrs. Madox, and beneath her name were written the words "To Be Delivered Immediately on Pain of Death!"

When I returned to the carriage Belvedere had yet another surprise for me.

"Small change in plan, old boy," he said. "We must drop by Alf Shaughnessy's before catching our train."

I nodded, and as I turned the carriage towards Alf's I could only suppose that Belvedere wished to thank Alf for saving his life, but of course I couldn't question him on that point or any other point since he remained comfortably seated in the plush interior of the brougham while I continued to play the role of coachman. Nor was I to gain enlightenment at Alf's for, when we arrived, Belvedere requested that I remain with the carriage while he alone went inside. Their conversation was a brief one and, upon emerging, Belvedere informed me that the time had come to return the carriage to McLeod's Livery Stable, which was located on Front Street no more than five minutes' walk from Union Station. During our journey my mind turned once again to the matter of leaving the country without saying good-bye to my uncles. Our ship was not due to leave for two days, which meant that, if I wished to, I could spend a night in Balls Falls before continuing on to Montreal and boarding the ship. In fact it occurred to me that perhaps Belvedere might even consent to accompany me to my uncles' farm. It would give us both a chance to rest up, and certainly Madox would never think of looking for us in Balls Falls. Really, nothing could be simpler—assuming, of course, that there were no police or Dead Dogs keeping watch on Union Station.

CHAPTER XXVI

DISTANT HORIZONS

In the end, Belvedere declined my invitation to visit my uncles, saying that his need was too urgent for the solitude and luxurious surroundings only Montreal's Windsor Hotel could offer him, and I proceeded on alone to Balls Falls. We parted with the understanding that we would rendezvous on board the *Campania* in two days' time. (It seemed prudent that we board separately for, although our appearance was greatly altered *sans* false beards, nonetheless there was a very real possibility that Madox would have men watching all the rail terminals and docks for a notably tall young man in the company of a notably short one.)

My uncles were surprised and highly delighted by my unexpected visit, and most impressed when I told them that, through a chance encounter, I had landed the position of valet to Lord Windermere of Berkshire, England, and would be travelling throughout Europe with his lordship indefinitely.

It was strange being in my old bedroom, surrounded once again by all my books and magazines. I had the sensation of great intimacy with every aspect of the room while, at the same time, feeling that I was trespassing, that it all belonged to someone else. My raven still sat atop the plant stand with his outstretched wings bearing him skyward and my calling card clutched triumphantly in his beak, but of course my Church of Self Creation no longer awaited my homage, and there was a blank space on the wall facing the head of my bed where La Divine Sarah's portrait had once hung. It scarcely seemed possible that it was leaning up against the wall in the Persian parlour of Belvedere La Griffin's Phoebe Street rooms, awaiting removal and storage along with Belvedere's wonderful possessions. As I lay in my bed, I looked out over the moonlit fields to the oak tree and my parents' grave beneath it, but this time I saw myself, not hanging dead from the stout tree limb, but rather kneeling in prayer before their gravestone. On the day I had left for Toronto, I had prayed to my mother and father to grant me the courage to plunge headlong into the glorious existence waiting to embrace me, and to give me the strength to quaff the purple cup of life to the very dregs. They had answered my prayer.

The time passed quickly, and no sooner had I arrived than it was time for Uncle Jasper to hitch up Cathy and Heathcliff and drive me to the train station. This time I was bound for my new life in Europe and, despite my misadventure at Big Sue's, I was still determined to become a lover of astounding accomplishments by dint of exhaustive tutelage in an academy of ecstasy. Now, however, I would receive my instruction in the embrace of a *fille de joie* in the finest *maison de plaisir* that Paris, France, could offer me, rather than in a mere Toronto brothel. As for finding a bride, my newly acquired wealth removed the immediate need for a rich father-in-law to take care of my financial needs and the fact was that, having tasted blood and the thrill of danger, I was loath to simply retire to a domestic life of ease. I had never felt so alive, and there was no question in my mind that risk and adventure were the two indispensable elements in every truly successful life. Indeed, it seemed to me that as long as Belvedere and I confined our depredations upon the cruel and vulgar of this world, there was no reason why we should not continue performing feats of outrageous derring-do whenever the mood came upon us to do so. Admittedly I was little more than Belvedere's assistant, but with him as my mentor I felt confident I could learn much and go far. Above all, I would continue to guard my life from monotony by the daring of my whims, and to burn always with a hard, gem-like flame.

Belvedere and I met on board ship as arranged and enjoyed an exquisite voyage—gorging ourselves on both the romance of the Atlantic and the astonishing luxury of the *Campania*. As it turned out, Mrs. Madox had indeed held nothing back from her husband's safe, for our booty was worth many times more than we had expected. When we reached London, we ensconced ourselves in The Savoy Hotel, and several weeks later we paid a visit to Canada House in Trafalgar Square, where we had the opportunity to catch up on the news from Toronto contained in past issues of *The Globe*. We learned that the body of one David Goody had been discovered floating in the Toronto harbour two days after our departure, and the coroner was quoted as saying that the body had been cruelly mutilated before death. Later that day, as we sauntered along Regent Street en route to a fitting at our new tailor's, Belvedere remarked upon the irony of Little Dave Goody's place of interment.

"Well, quite," I said. "The same watery grave to which he consigned me. Which reminds me, I remember asking you why we were involving Little Dave in the ransom delivery instead of a less violent person like Roberts the butler, and you said you had a tentative plan which you did not wish to discuss at that time. Am I to assume that the plan to which you alluded hinged on Little Dave's greed—that he would in fact try to steal the ransom booty?"

"Well . . . yes and no," Belvedere responded as he adjusted his monocle. "That is to say, I was in possession of a contingency plan as well."

"Really?"

"Oh yes. You see, I felt sure Little Dave could be trusted to steal the booty, and that is why I insisted upon our hiding in the loft within immediate striking range of the gig."

"But wait a minute, why didn't Little Dave just get the satchel from Mrs. Madox and run with it? Why did he bother coming to the drop-off point at all?" I asked.

"Because he believed he was being watched by us or even by someone else in Madox's employ. He thought that if we saw him diverge from the prescribed route we would shoot him—just as we promised to do in the ransom note. Furthermore, if Mrs. Madox or

Roberts had the brains not to trust him, and therefore had men on his tail, he had to make sure they saw him delivering the satchel as per instructions so he couldn't be blamed for Madox's fate. He assumed, of course, that we would kill Madox when we found the empty satchel. And if we didn't kill him, but rather renewed our demand, he would be long gone by the time Mrs. Madox divined his treachery. Of course, I also had to allow for the possibility that he was bringing the satchel because it contained a bomb rigged to blow up the instant someone opened it."

"My word," I exclaimed softly as I felt the blood drain from my face.

"Quite. And yet we now know that he did not rig the satchel for, had he done so, Madox would have been killed in the blast when he opened it, for you may be sure he did so the instant he was untied."

"Yes, I begin to see. But getting back to your alternative plan, if Little Dave had not attempted to steal the booty. . . . "

"I had to take into account the possibility that he lacked the courage to rob Madox, and I asked myself how else I could arrange things so that, in the end, Madox would take our revenge upon Little Dave for us."

Belvedere paused as he side-stepped a young street Arab selling newspapers.

"And?" I prompted.

"And? Oh yes, and my alternative plan was simply this. Some years ago, I came into possession of a large quantity of counterfeit money. It was of very poor quality and I certainly would never dream of trying to pass any off as the real McCoy, if only for that reason— its poor quality, I mean. But I hung onto it just on the off chance that some day I might find a use for it. Well, as we waited for Little Dave Goody's arrival, I had twenty thousand dollars' worth of this bogus currency concealed on my person, and had Little Dave failed to purloin the ransom, my alternate plan was to replace the genuine twenty thousand dollars in the satchel with my obviously fake twenty thousand before returning to the loft with the satchel. Then, under Madox's watchful gaze, I would open the satchel as if for the first time and immediately cry foul. Upon his release, Madox would question his wife, learn that she had put genuine bills in the satchel, and be forced to conclude that Little Dave substituted the counterfeit money and made off with the genuine. Judging by Little Dave's reputation and appearance, he was sufficiently stupid that Madox would easily believe him capable of attempting such a transparent deception. So you see, whether Little Dave attempted to steal our booty or not, his ultimate destination remained the same."

"The Toronto harbour," I said.

"Precisely. And incidentally, as it turned out, I was still able to put the counterfeit money to good use. You recall my last-minute visit to Alf Shaughnessy's?"

"Yes, I assumed you wished to thank him for saving your life."

"Quite right, old boy. I gave Alf the sum of one hundred dollars for his trouble, and he was most appreciative, I can tell you. But I also paid him an additional fifty dollars to perform a small service for me. I gave him Little Dave's burlap sack with the instructions that he was surreptitiously to conceal it high up in the rafters of Madox's coach-house."

"Go on," I said.

"Can you guess what I put in that sack?"

"The bogus twenty thousand dollars?"

"Yes indeed, the bogus twenty thousand dollars, but that is not all. Along with the bills, I included a unique pair of diamond earrings and a very fine string of pearls which I left in the sack when I transferred the booty to my own club bag on the way over to Alf's."

Belvedere paused and looked at me expectantly, but I was thoroughly confused and confessed as much.

"Alf will have hidden the sack in Madox's carriage house by now. In a few months' time, Madox will have settled his claim with the insurance company for the gems—in this case the British Mercantile Insurance Company, according to the report in *The Globe*. When he has done so, I will contact the insurance company anonymously and suggest that they search the rafters of Madox's carriage house."

"Where they will find the bogus money and some of the jewels for which they have compensated Madox," I interjected.

"Exactly."

"But what will they make of it all? I mean to say, obviously you hope to convince the authorities that either the entire kidnapping was a hoax in order to extort money from the insurance company or Madox never paid the ransom as he claims to have done, and that, either way, he has swindled the insurance company. But does the concealed sack constitute sufficient evidence?"

"Probably not—but! When the authorities also search his bedroom safe—as I will instruct them to do—then if Madox is half the greedy fool I take him to be, his goose is right and truly cooked!"

"Explain please," I said in exasperation.

"Cast your mind back to the night we shadowed Madox to the Toronto Club. Later that night—in my rooms—I showed you an article in a past issue of *Saturday Night* concerning a society charity ball that the Madoxes attended."

"I recall it. Go on."

"In that article, particular mention was made of the Star of Kambara—an exceptionally large and fine diamond set in a gold brooch belonging to Mrs. Madox."

"It wasn't in the satchel!" I cried.

"Actually, Reginald, yes, it was," Belvedere said patiently. "Mrs. Madox followed our instructions to the letter. She placed the entire contents of that safe into the satchel."

"But—"

"When I saw that Little Dave Goody was stealing the ransom just as I had hoped he would do, it suddenly occurred to me that there might be a way to orchestrate events so that, through his own avarice, Madox too would destroy himself. Later, in the sail storage shed, when I dumped some of the jewels out of the sack onto the table in order to prove Little Dave's treachery to Madox and thereby seal his doom, I saw the Star of Kambara among the other jewels and a plan hatched fully formed in my mind. As I put the jewels back into the sack, I 'accidentally' dropped the famous brooch on the floor and failed to notice my clumsiness. Madox saw me drop it and I am betting that he put in a huge insurance claim on the brooch even though it is still in his possession. The sack in the rafters of his carriage house is, by itself, perhaps ambiguous—questions concerning precisely what role twenty thousand dollars in counterfeit bills could play, etcetera. But it will be enough to encourage the authorities to search his bedroom safe, and I think there is a very strong chance they will find the Star of Kambara within."

"If they find that jewel, Madox will be ruined—at least socially—even if criminal charges are not laid," I said.

"Quite so. And the fact is that we could never have sold it, for it is far too well known, so we are none the worse off for my little game."

"And its unique qualities, its unsalability, is all the more reason why Madox will still have it in his possession."

"Quite."

I could only sit back in awe at Belvedere's devastating cunning.

"You, Reginald, were allowed the supreme satisfaction of literally beating Dan the Dude Dougherty senseless and taking his moustache as your scalp, whereas I was cruelly denied any similar joy due to my injuries. I can only take satisfaction in knowing that, while my wound will soon heal, the wound I have inflicted on Augustus Madox is sure to fester and ultimately destroy him. In the mean time, until we learn that Madox is a spent force, we remain technically 'on the lam', and it occurs to me that we should be travelling under new identities. For myself, I have been toying with the sobriquet 'Valentine Strange-Winter'."

"Valentine Strange-Winter? Yes," I said. "I think that a most excellent name. It suits you. As for me . . . I have always rather fancied the name 'Sebastian Manchester'."

"Excellent. Sebastian Manchester you shall be. Well, that's settled then. I shall have my new cards printed up when I reach Paris."

"Really? Are you thinking of going to Paris in the near future?"

"Yes, I rather thought I would pop over in a day or two. La Divine Sarah is staging a revival of *La Dame aux Camélias* at the Comédie Française, you know."

"No actually, I was not aware of that fact. Belvedere, I wonder, would you object to my tagging along?" I asked.

"But of course not, old lad. Only too pleased to have your company."

Suddenly my heart leapt into my mouth as I recognized the outline of a large man just up ahead of us. I grabbed Belvedere's arm.

"Great God," I said. "I just saw Oscar Wilde entering the Café Royal!"

"Never! Are you certain?"

"Absolutely positive. Could we join him, do you think? He might even agree to accompany us over to Paris for La Divine Sarah's performance!"

"I should think he would be only too charmed to join us," Belvedere replied.

"Egad," I said. "Wait until he hears how I wore his dancing

pumps on a daring moonlit robbery!"

I gave the points of my spiffing new Imperial moustache two quick twists, and into the Café Royal we sauntered.

THE END